THE BLOOD OF KINGS

KYLE ALEXANDER ROMINES

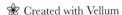

ALSO BY KYLE ALEXANDER ROMINES

To sign up to receive author updates—and receive a FREE electronic copy of Kyle's science fiction novella, The Chrononaut—go to http://eepurl.com/bsvhYP.

Five Kingdoms.
Five Kings and Queens.
One High Queen Sits Above All.
Her Wardens Keep the Peace.

Ard Ruide

Connacht, in the west, is the kingdom of learning and the seat of the greatest and wisest druids and magicians; the men of Connacht are famed for their eloquence, their intellect, and their ability to pronounce true judgment.

Ulster, in the north, is the seat of battle valor, haughtiness, strife, and boasting; the men of Ulster are the fiercest warriors of all Fál, and the queens and goddesses of Ulster are associated with battle and death.

Leinster, the eastern kingdom, is the seat of prosperity, hospitality, and the importing of rich foreign wares like silk or wine; the men of Leinster are noble in speech and their women are exceptionally beautiful.

Munster, in the south, is the kingdom of music and the arts, skilled ficheall players, and horsemen; the fairs of Munster are the greatest in all Fál.

The last kingdom, Meath, is the kingdom of Kingship, stewardship, and bounty in government; in Meath lies the Hill of Tara, the traditional seat of the High King or Queen of Fál.

—Adapted from Old Translation, Author Unknown

CHAPTER ONE

It was never a good idea to keep a king waiting—even for a warden.

Berengar ignored the hunger that had been gnawing at him for the better part of two days. He'd ridden practically nonstop since crossing the border into Munster. Were it not for the subtext of urgency contained within the king's summons, he would have stopped for food or rest along the way. Further complicating matters, King Mór had not disclosed the reason for the summons.

Unlike the High Queen's other wardens, Berengar rarely ventured so far south—another reason the king's cryptic message was so surprising. Nevertheless, he had little trouble finding his way on the road. He followed the course of the River Suir where it originated on the slopes of the Devil's Bit, certain of his destination.

The summer air was warm and pleasant. Munster was the southernmost kingdom on the island of Fál, and its temperate climate made for fair weather throughout the year, in contrast to the harsh winters to the north. Berengar hadn't seen so much as a cloud for miles.

He passed the first farm just after midday. More sprouted up along the road the farther he traveled. The castle was visible some distance away, looking over the land from atop a lush, green hill. The workers were already coming in from the fields as he approached the city, though sundown remained a healthy span away.

The Rock of Cashel—Munster's capital—was one of the most impressive cities in all Fál. Munster was the largest of the five kingdoms. In addition to the fair weather and an abundance of natural resources, the southern kingdom's easy access to the coasts ensured a lucrative maritime trade with Albion, Caledonia, and even Gaul. The music coming from the city reminded the warden that Munster was also the cultural center of the realm, fueled by commerce and monasteries of higher learning.

The city teemed with life, a sign of its booming population. Berengar regarded the masses with a wary eye. The warden greatly preferred the open road to the walls of any city, despite Cashel's beauty. He was skilled in the art of killing, not conversation. Berengar suspected his manners were as dull as his axe was sharp. All the same, he was looking forward to sleeping in a bed for the first time in recent memory.

As closing approached, the marketplace was seized by a flurry of activity. Blacksmiths and armorers plied their trade near the sculptors and jewelers, just a few of the tradesmen assembled around the city square. Berengar spotted the pointed ears of several half or quarter fairies among the crowd and even noticed a peaceful giant lumbering down the street. Historically, Munster was far more tolerant of magic and nonhuman creatures than the remainder of Fál. Berengar was of a similar disposition. Men were just as likely to try to kill him as monsters, though that didn't make the latter any less dangerous.

New sights, sounds, and smells awaited wherever he looked. Despite his hunger, Berengar forced himself to turn away from the aroma of freshly baked bread. There was no sense in stopping now that he was so close to his destination. He might as well wait to enjoy King Mór's hospitality.

The warden deftly guided his stallion away from the marketplace. As the crowd's ranks thinned, various onlookers began to take note of him. Some stopped what they were doing and stood in silence, watching as he rode by. Others murmured among themselves, likely unsettled by his appearance. Berengar wasn't surprised. In fact, he was rather used to the reception.

It was the same wherever he went, and not without reason. His appearance wasn't exactly normal by any definition of the word. The right side of the warden's face was marred by three deep, uneven scars that ran in parallel from his forehead down to his lip. A leather eye patch covered the place where his right eye once sat, partially obscuring the scars where the band wrapped around his head. Berengar's hair was a blazing red, brighter than the color of an open flame. The sides were flecked with gray, like his beard, which had grown considerably during his time in the wild. He only trimmed the beard before starting on a journey and had not had time to do so before setting off for Munster.

He steered the stallion onto the cobblestone road that led to the castle. A monstrous-looking hound, a wolfhound mix Berengar had raised from a pup, followed. Berengar appropriately named her Faolán, which meant *little wolf*—though there was nothing remotely little about her.

The castle stood in the heart of the city. The immense fortress was carved from the limestone rock jutting out from the earth beneath it. A wall surrounded the castle on all sides, barring entrance to the uninvited. Though originally constructed because of the site's defensive advantages, the castle had been improved over the centuries as Munster grew in wealth and power. There was nothing quite like it in all Fál.

"Halt!" a voice rang out as he neared the gate.

Berengar cast his gaze upon the place where two guards stood watch. Four more sentries looked on from the wall above. The warden's face took on an expression of annoyance but he brought his horse to a stop.

"You will go no farther."

"I'm expected." Berengar's voice was a low growl. He was hungry, tired, and not in the mood for games.

The guard's hand moved to his sheath. "Identify yourself." He was a young man, and Berengar doubted he had seen more than twenty summers.

When Berengar swung off his horse, the young man's companion grew pale. The warden was a great beast of a man, towering two heads over the tallest man among them. He wore leather armor and a flowing cloak made from the fur and skin of a bear. Both an axe and a bow were slung behind his back, and a short sword was sheathed at his side. The sight of the warden was enough to intimidate the guards, save for the overenthusiastic young man, and even he flinched when Faolán bared her fangs at the implied threat to her master.

Berengar lazily flashed his ring to the guard. The young man stared at it, puzzled. His defiant expression remained unchanged until the man beside him leaned closer and whispered something into his ear. The young man flushed a deep shade of red and bowed deeply. At the sight of deference, Faolán relaxed and let out a yawn.

"Apologies, Laird Berengar. We were not expecting you so soon."

"I'm not a lord. I'm a warden." His voice was deep and gravelly.

"Forgive me, Laird Warden."

Berengar sighed and shook his head in exasperation. "Take me to the king."

"Open the gate," the guard bellowed. "This way, sir."

Berengar led his horse by the reins and followed the guards beyond the wall.

The older guard addressed a messenger on the other side. "Warden Berengar has come to answer the king's summons." The messenger went sprinting uphill to deliver the news without hesitation.

The population inside the castle grounds was by no means modest, even in comparison to the city below. The group made their way across the busy courtyard, encountering nobles, priests, and soldiers engrossed in their own affairs. Their path again turned upward, where the castle waited, promising the end of one journey and the beginning of another. Golden banners waved proudly from a round tower, bearing the image of an eagle, the sigil of the king's house. Commanding statues of the great kings of old paid tribute to the realm's storied past.

The guards stopped just short of the castle entrance, and a young hostler came running to greet them.

"Take the warden's horse to the stables," the older guard instructed. "And find a place for his hound in the kennels."

At the mention of the word *kennel*, Faolán's ears perked up, and she flashed the guard a toothy warning.

Berengar relinquished the reins to the boy. "Leave her be. She won't attack unprovoked."

The guard looked hesitant but kept his doubts to himself.

Berengar ordered the wolfhound to sit. "Stay. Wait for my return."

Faolán snorted and trotted off the road, curling up under the shade of a birch tree.

A guard draped in a golden cloak and fine armor waited at the castle entrance, surrounded by a small number of subordinates. "I am Corrin, captain of the guard. Your weapons, please. None are admitted to his majesty's presence while armed."

Berengar glowered but did as requested, surrendering first his bow and then his short sword before entrusting the battleaxe to the young guard who had challenged him initially. "See that you handle these with care." He said nothing of the dagger concealed within the lining of his boot. Although he had not had dealings with Mór in years, they'd last parted on good terms, and Berengar did not expect treachery from him. Even so, experience dictated it was always better to be prepared.

Corrin nodded to the others, and the massive doors swung open, granting entrance to the castle. "This way, Laird Warden." He stepped under the detailed doorway arch and gestured for Berengar to follow.

"I'm not a..." Berengar trailed off. "Never mind."

They walked under a series of interior arcades, bathed in the sunlight that entered through magnificent stained-glass windows. Berengar's boots echoed on a well-swept floor. A tranquil quiet hung over the castle, where the thick walls provided a respite from the multitude of noises outside. The air was thick with the scent of lavender and chamomile. Rich tapestries and elegant silks adorned painted walls in the great hall, which currently lay abandoned.

The captain came to a stop outside what Berengar

assumed was the entrance to the throne room. The door opened, and the captain ushered him across the threshold.

Let's get this over with, Berengar thought, grouchy from a long ride and an empty stomach.

The throne room was larger and wider than the great hall—larger even than the High Queen's throne room at Tara. Aside from the throne itself, which lay at the opposite end, the chamber was largely empty. Below the barrel-vaulted roof, there was a single rose window behind the throne. Berengar guessed the chamber was designed with the intent of making most supplicants feel small in the king's presence.

Mór sat regally on the throne, watching him quietly with the cautious, appraising expression Berengar remembered so well. He looked every inch a king, in keeping with his notable ancestry. Mór's black curls were heavily streaked with gray, as was his well-trimmed beard. The king was dressed in gold and white, and a white cloak fell to his feet.

A silver crown rested atop the king's head. Each of the five kings and queens of Fál wore crowns of silver. They were the *Rí Ruirech*—the overkings. Beneath them were the *Rí Tuaithe*, the underkings or lords, who wore iron crowns. Only the High Queen wore a crown of gold.

King Mór's crown was adorned with precious jewels without price, a way of setting Munster apart from the other kingdoms. In the days of old, the line of High Kings came from Munster. When the kingdoms broke apart, the throne at Tara sat empty for centuries, until Nora of Connacht again united Fál under one ruler.

The chamber was suddenly filled with the voice of the herald who stood between Berengar and the throne.

"Welcome, Warden Berengar. You stand in the presence of Mór the Second of Munster, King from the Cliffs of Moher to the Celtic Sea, Lord of the Southern Islands, Master of the Golden Fleet, and servant of Nora, High Queen of Fál."

Berengar had other names too. Most were records of deeds, not titles of nobility. Many were not fit for polite company, and some, others dared not mention in his presence. He was known throughout various parts of the realm as the Bloody Red Bear, Berengar One-Eye, The High Queen's Monster, Berengar Trollslayer, Berengar Goblin-Bane, and Berengar the Unbroken, to name a small number. There were more than a few songs detailing his exploits.

Berengar did not kneel when the herald finished speaking, though he politely inclined his head in the king's direction. The gesture did not go unnoticed by Mór, who grimaced tersely in a sign of displeasure. It wasn't an unexpected response; most kings and queens were unused to anything other than complete and utter fealty. As a warden of Fál, Berengar stood apart. He was not subject to the king's laws and answered only to the High Queen. There were five wardens in all, tasked with keeping the peace across the land. Oftentimes this meant something as simple as settling disputes between local lords or hunting a particularly dangerous monster. Judging from Mór's troubled expression, this was not one of those instances.

The two men stared at each other across the throne room for a long interval before at last King Mór's lips pulled back into a genuine smile, and he rose from the throne. "It's been a long time."

"That it has, Your Grace." Out of respect, Berengar addressed the king in the manner the royals of Munster were styled.

Mór approached, and the two men clasped hands. "It is good to see you again, my friend."

"And you, Your Grace."

Though they had fought side by side in the Shadow Wars, in truth, they had never been entirely close. Then again, when one was royalty, everyone—and no one—was your friend.

Mór released his grasp. "You arrived sooner than we anticipated."

"I came at once after I received your letter." It wasn't technically true. He had stopped along the way to find a home for an orphaned goblin youngling and sent Mór's messengers ahead, but he had quickened his pace to make up for lost time.

"I thank you for your haste." Lines that were not there before appeared on the king's face. Despite his efforts at levity, something was clearly troubling him.

"What is this about? Your letter was rather cryptic, Your Grace."

Mór let out a dark laugh that betrayed an undercurrent of tension. "Straight to business. You haven't changed much, I see." His expression brightened considerably. "Let us not yet talk of such things. The hour grows late. It will be dark before long. You must be hungry and tired from the long journey. You shall dine with my family and me, and then we will discuss the reason for my summons."

Having ridden with such urgency, Berengar felt a tinge of irritation at the prospect of having to wait even longer to discover the reason for his presence in Munster. Still, he was sure Mór would get to the point before too long, and he could live with waiting until after his belly was full before he received what was increasingly likely to be bad news.

. . .

9

Night descended over the land as the last vestiges of sunlight were replaced by muted candlelight and the somber glow of torches. Berengar dined with Mór and his family at the king's table. Save for the servants and castle guards, the great hall lay empty. A band of court musicians played soft music. The musicians of Munster were widely recognized as the best in the land, and their presence at court was a testament to their talent. As Berengar recalled, the king himself was a musician of some fame in his younger days, though Berengar had heard it said Mór rarely played since the Shadow Wars.

A servant girl approached carrying a *mias*—the wooden board on which food was served. "For you, sir." She laid the board before him and bowed low. Her eyes lingered perhaps a moment longer than necessary on his scars. He saw a familiar expression like fear flicker over her face, and the young girl promptly retreated to the kitchens.

Berengar turned his attention to the meal prepared for him. Anywhere else, the vast assortment of richly prepared dishes would have constituted a lavish banquet or feast. Given Munster's considerable wealth and commercial prominence, the king's table boasted foods found nowhere else in Fál. There was wild boar; rashers, strips of salted bacon; salted butter; *mulchán*, a delicious milky cheese; plums; blackberries and sloes; hazelnuts; and many other foods. In addition, the dishes at the king's table had been prepared with herbs and spices including garlic, chives, and peppers. Most impressive was salted beef. In other parts of Fál, the number of cattle owned by a lord was a sign of social status. Only the exceedingly wealthy served beef, and rarely on an ordinary occasion.

The warden picked up the cutting knife with one hand

and a loaf of wheat bread in the other. He ate hungrily, though he remained mindful enough of his present company to display a modicum of manners. As warm food filled the space in his empty stomach, his spirits lifted considerably.

"How have you been these long years, my friend?" Mór asked. "There were rumors you had taken a wife."

"Just rumors, I'm afraid."

"But you were married once."

"That was a long time ago—before the Shadow Wars. At present, I've been rather busy about the High Queen's interests." The remark was a not-so-subtle hint to steer the conversation in another direction. Some things were too sacred to discuss lightly with anyone, even a king. The death of his wife was one of them.

"And how are affairs at Tara? I trust the High Queen is in good health."

Mór spoke of the Hill of Tara, the capital of Fál where Nora ruled as High Queen. The Hill lay within the borders of the Kingdom of Meath, though the territory was considered separate. Tara was also home to the wardens, but Berengar spent so much time on the road that, in truth, he no longer considered anywhere home.

The question was intended as small talk, to be sure. Berengar was certain the king's messengers kept him well informed of current events. He wouldn't have been surprised to learn the king of Munster had at least one spy among the High Queen's court.

The warden swallowed a portion of bacon. "From what I hear, she's close to reaching a peace accord with Caledonia. It's been some time since I was last at the Hill. I've only just come from an ogre hunting expedition in the Bog of Móin Alúin."

Mór's eyes danced in the candlelight. "Ogres? Fascinating."

Berengar held up a single finger. "One ogre, though the bastard was almost the size of a troll." His gaze fell on the others seated at the table, and he quickly cleared his throat. "Pardon, Your Graces."

The king's wife and daughter sat beside Mór on the other side of the table. Queen Alannah's hair had not yet begun to gray, though it was not as luminous as Berengar remembered. She wore a silver crown to match her husband's, adorned with a single, prominent sapphire. The queen's reserved expression did not so much as twitch at the coarse language.

On the opposite side to the queen sat the princess. Ravenna was her name, and Berengar thought it suited her well. He had heard the princess of Munster was a great beauty, and for once the stories were true. Her hair was black as the night sky, her complexion fair and milky smooth. She could hardly have been older than twenty, if that. Berengar saw little of her father in her appearance, except for the same appraising, calculated gaze. She said little, but he felt the weight of her attention on him throughout the meal.

When Berengar glanced in her direction, she held his gaze, which was unusual in its own right, regardless of sex or age. Her face was an expressionless mask, but there was something about her dark eyes that seemed older than the rest of her, almost weary. Ravenna wore a simple silver tiara with no stones, probably a statement of some kind, but he wasn't sure of what, or whose message it was.

"How did you get involved in something like that?" the king prompted.

"I was hunting a group of mercenaries known as the Black Hand. There was…an incident in a church. The local lord agreed to keep the matter quiet if I rescued his niece, who'd been taken by the ogre. There was a vengeful witch involved, and a curse, but I managed to recover her."

Berengar lifted his drinking horn to his lips and gulped down a mouthful of sweet honeyed mead. There was more to the story, but Mór clearly wasn't interested in the details, whatever he said to the contrary. It was common practice for royals to deal in subtexts and hidden meanings with their words, a game Berengar had little patience for. Since he was dealing with a king, he would have to take part in the dance regardless, until such time as Mór chose to reveal what was really on his mind.

The princess interrupted the lull in conversation. "What's she like? The High Queen, I mean. I've seen her thrice before but never spoken to her. If she's anything like the tales say, I daresay she's quite formidable."

Mór slammed his drinking horn against the table a bit harder than necessary. Irritation was evident in his expression. "You must forgive my daughter, Warden. She speaks her mind far too readily." His gaze fell upon his daughter. "You would do well to remember your place."

Ravenna shot her father a dark look but did not reply.

"She would have to be to bring an island of kings to heel. Not counting the Ice Queen, of course, who is formidable in her own right." Berengar casually raised the horn to his mouth. The mere hint of a smile on the princess' lips was reward enough to risk the king's displeasure.

"Will you be staying long, Warden Berengar?" Queen Alannah's hand fell gently on the king's shoulder, as if to defuse the tension between her husband and daughter.

Berengar shrugged. "That depends entirely on your husband, Your Grace." He hesitated for a moment before

13

addressing her again. "I was sorry to learn of the passing of your son."

Though the queen's expression did not change, it took a few moments for her to speak. "Thank you. You are very kind."

"I am young enough," Mór declared, as if the remark was addressed to him alone. "There is still time to produce another heir."

They ate the rest of their food in relative silence. The meal ended with a course of black pudding, made from blood, barley, and seasonings. Though served at breakfast in other parts of Fál, in the south the dish was considered a dessert. Once the table had been cleared, Mór waved a hand at the musicians, and the music promptly ceased. The others filed out of the chamber until at last Berengar was left alone with the king and his guards.

"Leave us," the king commanded Corrin, and the guards withdrew. Mór pushed away from the table and stole closer to the hearth's warmth. Berengar followed suit, ready to hear what the king had to say. "I need your help, old friend."

"I guessed as much, though I'm curious why I received your summons when you could have sent for Darragh, or Niall." The remarks were in reference to two wardens more closely associated with Munster. "You know I rarely travel south of the Silvermines, Your Grace."

Mór stared into the flames. "I would trust no one else with the task I set before you. It is true the others are all men of great renown, but you have no equal."

A gruff chuckle escaped Berengar's throat. "Darragh might argue with that, but I'll accept the compliment." He saw that Mór's expression remained serious, so he added a hasty addendum. "I mean no offense, Your Grace, but I'm still not entirely sure why I'm here."

Mór appeared to weigh his next words carefully before turning away from the fire. "You will have to forgive my secrecy, for reasons I will explain presently. There are two matters with which I require your assistance. The first and most pressing concerns Morwen, my court magician. A fortnight ago I received word that superstitious farmers have laid siege to the monastery at Cill Airne where she currently resides. She's been trapped inside since then."

"You want me to deliver her to you."

"She is...precious to me." Mór's expression was almost pained. "That is why it must be you. Of all the wardens, soldiers, and means at my disposal, there is no one alive I trust more than you to return her safely to the castle."

This is what comes of earning a reputation steeped in blood, Berengar thought. "And the second matter?"

The king began pacing the floor. He peered past Berengar into the shadows, as if to ascertain that they were still alone. "Now I must explain the reason my letter did not say more. A darkness has fallen over the kingdom, and I've begun to suspect powerful magic is involved."

Berengar kept his arms crossed. "Magic, Your Grace?"

The king came to a halt. Mór must have sensed his skepticism, for a flash of agitation came over the king's face, and he spoke through clenched teeth. "You think I don't know my own lands?" He lowered his voice, as if afraid of being overheard. "Famine has tainted our harvests. Our ships are sunk by strange storms that appear from nowhere. Bandits openly attack our merchants on the road."

"With respect, I fail to see what bandits have to do with magic, Your Grace."

Mór drew closer, until there was only a hair's breadth between them. Few dared such close proximity to the warden under most circumstances, but the king was blessed with that volatile mix of boldness and arrogance known only to those of royal stock. "Mark my words, there is a larger force at work here."

"Why not ask your advisers to root out the source of upheaval in your kingdom?"

"I am not sure whom I can trust. I sent Morwen to Cill Airne for this purpose. It was not an accident her location was betrayed. Perhaps she is close to the truth of the matter."

Mór led Berengar outside the room onto a balcony overlooking the surrounding lands. He gestured to the city at their feet, which slept quietly under the cover of night. "I dare not speak openly of these matters. There is peace between men and nonhumans, it is true, but it is tenuous at best. I fear that voicing my suspicions will stir long-simmering resentment between the races, and I will not suffer a repeat of the massacres that marked my grandfather's reign."

The king's concern was genuine. Berengar knew Mór cared for the Kingdom of Munster above all else. The king was stern and fair, and he took his responsibility seriously. He was far from perfect; in addition to a quick temper, it was rumored the king had a string of mistresses. Berengar had a number of vices himself and was not one to pass judgment. Whatever his faults, Mór was by all accounts a good ruler.

"I see." Berengar remained unconvinced by the prospect of a magical conspiracy. However, Munster's court magician was in danger, at the very least, and that was a matter he could do something about.

"Thus, these two tasks I lay at your feet: deliver Morwen here and assist me in unraveling the threat to my kingdom. Do this, and I will consider any debt you owe me repaid."

The request seemed simple enough. Rescue the king's court magician from a group of peasant farmers and return her to the castle.

He reached out and clasped hands with the king. "I will see it done, Your Grace."

CHAPTER TWO

HE WAS BEING WATCHED.

Two days had passed since Berengar forsook the safety of the Golden Vale for the wilds. The southern roads were more secure than those of the kingdoms to the north, but they were not without perils. Munster was a vast kingdom, and despite its wealth, the king's soldiers could not be everywhere. It was largely left to the *Rí Tuaithe* and the local lords to provide security to their territories, and their numbers were spread thin enough as it was.

The warden traveled alone on the road to Cill Airne. Berengar had departed the Rock of Cashel under the cover of night shortly after his conversation with the king. None might have known of the warden's presence in the capital at all but for those few with whom he had crossed paths upon his arrival. This was by Mór's design. The king's insistence on secrecy was the reason Berengar had not been formally presented at court, lest the circumstances of his task come to light and jeopardize the court magician's safety. It was why Berengar went alone, without a band of soldiers under his command. That suited him perfectly well, as he mostly preferred the open road to the company of others.

Dusk stretched across the sky. It would be dark soon. Berengar brought his horse to a halt and scanned the hilltops, searching for any hint of figures hiding in the shadows. The warden's vision was sharp—he could hit a deer with his bow at one hundred yards more often than not—but he saw no sign that someone was following his trail. He listened carefully and heard nothing—not even the wind, which had only moments ago caressed the back of his neck. Still, he couldn't shake the feeling that he was being watched, and Berengar had learned long ago to trust his instincts.

He glanced at Faolán, whose ears pricked forward alertly.

"That settles it." He would not be making camp that night, nor would he risk the attention a fire would surely draw. He would seek the company of men, if it was to be found, or else ride on. Perhaps the king's concerns were well founded after all.

Fortune proved doubly kind. When the sky grew dark, the waxing moon illuminated the road before him. Not long after that, the warden spotted the dim outline of a human settlement where smoke rose from the valley basin below. The settlement was rather humble in size; there were a few modest farms clustered around a smattering of buildings, without even a fence around them. Berengar half smiled in surprise at the welcome sight. If someone was following him, they would be forced to keep their distance or risk revealing themselves. Even if not, he could enjoy a night's rest free of the hard earth before setting out the next day.

Berengar entered the settlement and found his way to the local inn without attracting attention. There wasn't so much as a night watchman standing guard. Nor did he find anyone waiting at the stables, though given the late hour, that wasn't entirely unexpected. Berengar slid from the saddle and led his horse into an empty stall, guessing he could simply pay the innkeeper for the spot when he secured lodging at the inn. He removed his horse's saddle and saddlebags and rubbed the horse down before starting down the dusty trail that led to the inn.

A savory aroma emanated from within. *Roadside Inn,* read a sign hanging over the door. The unimaginative name and written sign seemed ill-suited for such a rural location, even if literacy rates were higher in Munster than in most of Fál's kingdoms.

A low whine sounded behind him. When he looked back, he saw Faolán sitting on her haunches, watching expectantly.

He bent down and patted her head. "I'm afraid you can't follow me inside."

The wolfhound wrinkled her face in a show of irritation. Berengar offered to bring her back some food, but Faolán rose and stalked off in the direction of the trees, likely intent on hunting her meal. The warden chuckled softly. Sometimes he wasn't entirely sure who owned whom.

He lifted the cloak's hood over his head to obscure his face and slid on a pair of gloves to conceal the ring he wore. Music spilled out as he pushed open the door, and Berengar ducked underneath the lintel to fit inside. Considering the time of night, coupled with the settlement's meager size, the hall was surprisingly crowded. Men of all stripes and sizes were spread across the room, though there were no womenfolk in sight. Patrons sang and danced to a lively tune played by a troubadour beside the raging fire. Others tossed back drinks and told stories at the bar.

The music died without warning, and a deathly silence fell over the hall. Everyone's attention was locked on the stranger who towered at the doorway, or else on the weapons he carried. No one moved an inch as he crossed the room, the wooden floorboards groaning in protest under his weight. Berengar stopped at the bar, where the innkeeper stared at him slack-jawed. Then the warden produced a pouch of coins and laid it on the counter, and the hall again filled with music and laughter.

"I'd like a room. I took the liberty of showing my horse to the stables."

"Certainly." The innkeeper was a rotund man with a ruddy face and thick, graying mustache. He reached under the counter and handed Berengar a key. "The room will be up the stairs at the end of the hallway." His gaze lingered on the short sword at Berengar's side a moment longer than necessary before looking the warden up and down. "From the look of things, I'd wager you've been on the road for some time."

"You wager correctly." Berengar didn't specify where he was coming from or where he was headed. As a rule, he usually didn't volunteer information unless it was necessary.

"A man of your size—you must be famished! I can serve you a bowl of stew if you'd like, sir. My lad caught the hares just this morning."

Berengar sniffed the air. "I'd like that very much." He pocketed the key and slid onto the barstool as the innkeeper retreated to a kettle steaming over the hearth.

The man returned moments later with a bowl of piping hot stew.

"Anything to drink, my friend? I'm not one to boast,

but our stores of wine and mead are some of the finest varieties around."

"Mead would do nicely." The people of Munster were excessively proud of their wine and mead. As a foreigner, it would have been considered rude not to order some.

A friendly smile spread across the innkeeper's face, as if he had quite forgotten his initial reaction to the warden's appearance. He set a four-handled *meadair* in front of the warden and watched expectantly for a brief moment before Berengar realized the man was waiting for him to drink. He lifted the wooden cup to his lips and drank the first mouthful. Although the meadair was a far cry from the ornate drinking horn at the king's table, the honeyed mead was just as good as far as Berengar was concerned.

"It's good." He wiped his mouth with his sleeve, reached into his bag, and handed the innkeeper another coin. "Join me, will you? I prefer not to drink alone. Especially not a fine brew like this."

The innkeeper beamed. "Thank you kindly." He took the coin and poured himself a cupful of mead. "There's lots to be done around these parts, if you're looking for honest work. You might even put that bow of yours to good use. We've had terrible trouble with predators of late."

"I'm just passing through, I'm afraid." Berengar set the mug down and studied the man with a cautious eye. "I was hoping you might point me in the direction of Cill Airne. Do you know the way?"

The innkeeper's smile faded. "Aye. Follow the road until it branches into three parts and take the trail leading west. You'd do well to be careful if that's your destination. There's a bit of trouble out that way, from what I hear."

"Is that so?" Berengar suppressed a smile as the innkeeper took another drink of mead. Though each of

Fál's five kingdoms was unique, some things were the same wherever he went. Lords and nobles kept their tongues closely guarded, trading in riddles and half-truths. Common folk, however—particularly merchants and innkeepers—were more liable to divulge their true thoughts freely, especially when alcohol was involved.

The innkeeper looked around to make sure no one else was listening. Then he leaned closer and lowered his voice. "Word is that Morwen, the king's court magician, is holed up at the monastery at Inis Faithlinn. The villagers want her head on a pike, but the monks refuse to hand her over. Laird Tierney is quite beside himself, from what I hear."

"What's their gripe with the magician? Surely they know the price for murdering a servant of the throne."

The innkeeper shrugged. "You know how people get about magic. Morwen showed up about the same time the planting season went to hell."

"So naturally they assumed she placed a curse on the land."

"Or some other devilry." The innkeeper shook his head sadly. "And we're supposed to be the civilized kingdom. Still, if you ask me, I think there's more to this matter than meets the eye."

Berengar casually raised an eyebrow, careful not to betray his keen interest in the subject. "Oh?"

"A group of *déisi* stopped in here a short time before this mess started. Like you, they were headed to Cill Airne. One made mention of Morwen's presence on the island." The innkeeper finished his drink and set it aside. "If you ask me, I'd say someone stirred the farmers up. I can't say why."

"Interesting." The déisi were cutthroats—professional mercenaries. Who hired them, and what was their interest in the king's magician?

He started to inquire further, but before he could pose the question, the inn door fell open and three men entered the hall.

"You'll have to excuse me, friend," the innkeeper said as the band of flashy-looking newcomers approached the bar. He took a moment to top off the warden's meadair before promptly departing to tend to the new customers.

Berengar rose from his place at the bar and carried his food and drink to a secluded table beside the warmth of the fireplace. The stew had cooled down enough to sample without singeing his tongue. He leaned back in his chair and lifted a spoonful to his lips. The flavor was gamey, but it remained the best meal he'd had since departing the castle.

In light of what he'd learned from the innkeeper, Berengar thought back on his dinner with the king. Mór said his court magician was precious to him, and Berengar wondered if they were engaged in an affair. As a young man, Mór was well known for his conquests of beautiful women. He was different in those days, before the death of his older brother elevated him to the rank of king. He was known across Fál as the Poet Prince, trained in the arts by great masters far and wide. The responsibilities of the throne had erased the easy smile from his face, if the Shadow Wars had not already done so.

One of the patrons at the bar slammed his meadair against the counter. "Another!" When the innkeeper hastily shuffled to refill the trio's drinks, the man muttered something under his breath, and the innkeeper flushed a deep shade of red. The patron's friends laughed loudly, stirring the warden from his thoughts.

Berengar glared at them from underneath his hood. All three were relatively well dressed, at least by local standards. He guessed they were minor nobility, or else from prosperous farming families.

The first man mockingly flicked a coin at the innkeeper's feet. "Go on." He spoke with an air of command. "Be on your way."

The innkeeper bowed low and picked up the coin before disappearing behind the bar without a word.

"Drink up, lads," the first man said as the troubadour began a new song. His clothes were finer than the others', and he wore a sword sheathed at his side. He drank a sip and made an unpleasant face. "These are dark times indeed if this is the best swill this establishment can furnish. Mark my words, the greedy bastard will be raising the prices again before too long to pay the High Queen's taxes." He spit on the floor as he finished speaking, and the others murmured in assent.

"You have that right, Brandon," said one of his companions, a thin man with a resentful expression. "Why should Munster pay tribute to a foreign queen while we have enough trouble here? You heard what that merchant from Limerick said last night. He barely escaped with his life from the brigands who robbed him. Then there are the Danes, who raid our coasts, burn our ships, and plunder our villages."

Berengar listened intently to the local gossip.

"It's worse than that," the other said in a hushed tone. "You've not yet mentioned all the strange talk about magic run amuck in our borders. I've heard more reports of monster sightings in the last year than in all the stories my mum told me when I was a boy. Why, just the other day, I heard a rumor that an oilliphéist had come down from Mount Cuilcagh and was killing passersby along the River Shannon."

Brandon wrinkled his nose in disgust. "The work of the

Witches of the Golden Vale, no doubt. What a sad state of affairs. Our once-great nation brought low. Still, if there's anyone who can restore the peace, it's good King Mór." He raised his meadair in a toast, and the trio drank deep. "Long may he reign. We don't want the Tainted Princess sitting on the throne."

There was a brief lull in the conversation until one of their number spoke up. "There's even talk the warden is about."

"Which warden?"

"Which do you think?" Brandon's voice was full of contempt. "*The* warden." His lips spread into a savage grin. "If you ask me, the Bloody Red Bear is more trouble than the rest of them combined."

Berengar merely listened, expressionless, as Brandon's face grew animated and he spoke with wide, sweeping gestures.

"You've all heard the stories. They say he's a bear wearing human skin, or that his mother was a giantess. Only one thing is for certain: the trail of blood he leaves wherever he goes. There's a reason they call him the Bloody Red Bear."

"I thought it was on account of his hair," said one of his companions.

Brandon shook his head somberly. "Not if you've heard the tales of the Shadow Wars."

None seemed to notice that the subject of their fascination was sitting in their midst. Berengar noted the irony with little satisfaction. He was loath to hear yet another account of his deeds. The tales always portrayed him as either a hero of great renown or else a bloodthirsty monster with no remorse. At best, most contained a mixture of half-truths and complete fabrications.

Brandon started to speak, but the music stopped, and

he peered past his friends in the direction of the troubadour as if suddenly struck by an idea. "You there! Play
the one about the warden."

The troubadour hesitated, uncertain, until Brandon
pointed to the pouch of coins he carried with him. Then
he lifted the flute to his lips and the room went quiet as he
began to play. Berengar held his teeth clenched tight.

Oh hear ye the tale of the Bloody Red Bear
With an axe swing that blots out the sky
And the burn of the glare from the eye of the Bear is the last thing
men see ere they die

The Bear was a cub only twelve years of age
When he trekked into desolate lands
To hunt down a beast so his village could feast on the blood laid bare
by his hands

The Cub tracked a beast to its shadowy cave
And the Cub died within that dark lair
Then into the light and roaring with might emerged the Bloody
Red Bear

Blood on his blade and flames in his hair
Scars down his arms,
And a cruel one-eyed stare
Mothers tell children
You better beware,

That you don't ever cross the Bloody Red Bear

As the Bear grew so too did his deeds
Saved his village from raids at fifteen
Whispers of his name gathered the fame that would draw the eyes of
the Queen

Goblins hewn down by the axe of the Bear
Cursed his name with every last breath
But only when his town burned did the Bear truly learn his calling
was death

A man meant to kill, he was a scourge
To the enemies of the new throne
He stopped those who opposed and as the Queen rose, the Bear got a
job of his own

A Warden of Fál, the Bear stands apart
From the polished four with the same ring
He travels the land as the Queen's trusted hand and now all of the
bards sing…

Blood on his blade and flames in his hair
Scars down his arms,

And a cruel one-eyed stare
Mothers tell children
You better beware,
That you don't ever cross the Bloody Red Bear

The troubadour finished playing and bowed his head. A dreary mood hung about the inn until Brandon and his companions broke the silence, clapping their hands together loudly.

"Good! Now play the other one. You know, the one about the Doom of Dún de Fulaingt."

At the mention of the name, Berengar felt a chill run down his spine.

The musician shook his head sadly. "I'm afraid I must decline."

Brandon was taken aback. "But you must know it. Every child in Fál's five kingdoms is familiar with the tale of the Fortress of Suffering."

The troubadour stood firm. "I would not pollute my trade with such a song, not for all the money you carry with you."

Brandon bared his teeth angrily. He pushed away from the table, sending the chair crashing to the floor behind him. "You dare insult me?" He glanced at his friends, who moved to join him. "Perhaps we should teach this one a lesson about respecting his betters."

Berengar was already on his feet. "That's enough. Leave him alone."

Brandon turned and took note of him for the first time. He whitened slightly at the initial sight of the warden, but wine or natural-born foolishness made him brave. "My God—take a gander at this one, lads. He looks as if his mother lay with a bear."

"That's a good one. I've certainly never heard it

29

before." Berengar's tone dripped with sarcasm.

Each man looked at the others, not knowing quite what to make of the remark.

Brandon sneered when his gaze swept over the fox sigil pinned to Berengar's cloak. "This isn't your concern, foreigner." He made a show of resting his hand on the hilt of the sword sheathed at his side. Berengar very much doubted the man knew how to use it.

"I wouldn't do that if I were you."

Brandon's companions looked at him warily, but the man himself remained undaunted. "We will not be intimidated so easily. There are three of us, and only one of you. We are men of Munster. We serve the one true king, not some foreign whore."

He was on the ground before the others could so much as move. Berengar held his boot pressed against the man's throat. "Now you've done it. You've gone and made me angry." It was one thing to insult him. Impugning the queen's honor was another matter entirely.

One of Brandon's friends started toward him but stopped when Berengar lowered his hood. "The Bloody Red Bear." He took a step back.

Berengar glanced down at the man under his heel, whose face had started to turn a shade of purple. There were tears in his eyes. The warden dug his boot deeper. "You will not insult the High Queen in my presence. You're not worthy to speak her name. But for the queen, these lands would all be enslaved under a dark sorcerer. Apologize—now."

"Forgive me, great Warden," Brandon coughed out when Berengar eased off his throat.

The warden withdrew his boot. "Get him out of here."

Brandon's friends helped him to his feet, and together the trio stumbled toward the door.

"And leave something for the innkeeper on account of the trouble you caused."

The group hesitated at the door before leaving a bag of coins on the counter.

Berengar turned to the troubadour. "Thank you for not playing the song."

Then he excused himself and made his way up the stairs to his room. Before he went to sleep, he peered out the window one last time to see if anyone had followed him to the inn. For a moment, he imagined he saw a shadow standing among the trees, but in the next instant it was gone. Berengar looked down and noticed Faolán curled up beneath his window as if keeping watch over him. He chuckled, grateful the wolfhound hadn't been there during the fight. She would have ripped out the man's throat merely for threatening him.

He arrived at Cill Airne late in the morning. His path led through the Gap of Dún Lóich, a narrow mountain pass between the Black Stacks to the west and the Purple Mountain to the east. Fál's topography consisted of a vast central plain surrounded by hills and coastal mountains. Berengar had come of age far to the icy north, and as such was well accustomed to navigating such terrain.

His stallion's hooves clattered over an old arched bridge that ran across a lake beneath red sandstone peaks, and Cill Airne came into view. Three lakes formed a sea of blue beyond the town's border. When he peered closely enough, Berengar saw several islands scattered across the lakes.

He was a stranger to Cill Airne but knew it well enough by reputation. Though modest compared to

Cashel, the bustling village that spanned the valley below was impressive in its own right. Cill Airne was known across Fál as a center of learning. Its monasteries boasted some of the most extensive libraries in the land, and craftsmen of all trades studied under the masters of its various academies and institutes. In the days of old, great mages and magicians had come from far and wide to learn the mystic arts, until the purges had forced the school to shut its doors.

Berengar guided his horse down the path that led from the gap. It was a steep descent of at least five hundred feet, if not more. He passed dozens of farms along the road, spread out across vivid green pastures. Cill Airne was home to a host of peasants and farmers in addition to varied classes of merchants, craftsmen, and winemakers. It was this diverse mix that yielded such a vibrant, thriving community. Nestled under the protection of the surrounding mountains, the town had a reputation for peace, current circumstances aside.

Berengar slowed his horse to a trot as he entered the village, Faolán trailing behind. It was still relatively early. With a little luck, there would be time enough to rescue Mór's magician and start on the return journey before the day's end.

Life in the village seemed nothing out of the ordinary. There was hardly any indication of an ongoing siege, other than a slight tension in the air. His appearance drew the typical number of intrigued stares, but for the most part the people paid him little attention, preoccupied with their affairs.

He stopped in the marketplace and bought an apple from a vendor, taking the opportunity to ask for directions. "Any idea where I can find Laird Tierney? I have an urgent matter to discuss with him."

The seller pointed north. "I'd suggest you start at the castle." He wore a bemused expression as if to say, *where else would he be?*

Berengar thanked the man and went on his way. The warden could have easily been forgiven for his failure to notice the distant structure among the tall buildings spread across the village. Unlike the Rock of Cashel, where the castle loomed above the heart of the city, Laird Tierney's stronghold was relatively secluded at the edge of the lake. The castle was a good deal smaller than the one at Cashel, consisting mostly of a keep and a tower house. Archers and sentries were perched atop each of four round corner towers along a protective *badhún* wall.

When he was within walking distance of the castle, Berengar descended from his horse and continued on foot. The guards looked at him warily at the entrance.

Berengar produced a letter marked with the king's seal. "I've come to see Laird Tierney. I carry a message from King Mór."

Judging from the brief look exchanged between the guards, they'd been expecting something like this to happen, perhaps for a while. They nodded and motioned for him to come with them. Berengar left his horse with a squire and motioned for Faolán to wait for him outside before following them beyond the gate.

"We knew the king would send someone before too long," one of the guards muttered. "Nasty business at Innisfallen, if you ask me. Never would have happened even a few years ago. Thought there'd be more than one of you, if you catch my meaning." He looked Berengar over. "I mean no offense. I'd wager you'd be right handy to have in a fight."

Berengar held back a grin.

They escorted him to the keep, where Laird Tierney

waited. Berengar slowly made his way across the noisy chamber, crowded by the members of Tierney's court. A guard stood on each side of the lord, who was dwarfed by an uncomfortable-looking stone chair. Tierney appeared impossibly old, with pale skin and shrunken, slow-moving eyes. What little remained of his hair was white, and a long, flowing beard swept down his face. If not for his splendid clothes, the warden might have mistaken him for a sage.

Berengar came to stand before the stone dais. "Laird Tierney." He spoke before realizing the old man's eyes were closed.

The lord did not stir until a younger man closer to Berengar's age approached the stone chair and bent low, whispering into Tierney's ear. He leaned forward and squinted in the warden's direction. "You'll have to speak up. I'm afraid my ears aren't what they once were."

"I am Berengar, Warden of Fál and Sworn Sword of High Queen Nora." Tierney made no response at this, though the younger man at his side appeared alarmed by his words. "I come at the behest of King Mór." Berengar reached into his cloak and withdrew the sealed letter. The younger man took it from his outstretched hand and offered it to Tierney.

The lord broke the seal and unfolded the letter but before he could read it, he erupted into a serious of violent coughs. He said something to the younger man too quietly for Berengar to hear, and the man took the letter and briefly glanced over its contents.

"I'm afraid Laird Tierney is feeling ill at the moment." He briefly laid a hand on the old man's shoulder, a gesture that was not lost on Berengar. "Perhaps we might continue this conversation elsewhere, away from prying eyes and ears."

Berengar glanced over at the lord, who had already fallen asleep again. "Lead the way."

The man led him from the chamber, and they walked together down a long corridor. "I am Desmond, Laird Tierney's eldest son and heir." He paused as two noble-women approached from the opposite direction and whitened at the sight of Berengar's scars. The warden nodded politely in their direction as he passed by, and Desmond promptly resumed speaking. "As my father has grown ill, I have taken over many of his responsibilities in his stead."

The pair passed under a white arch and emerged into the fresh air. They stood atop one of the wall's corner towers, awash in bright light, and stared across the serene waters of the lake below.

"I trust you understand why I'm here."

Desmond nodded. "I knew that before I saw you enter the keep. We are well aware of the high esteem in which our king holds his court magician, although I did not expect King Mór would send the High Queen's execu-tioner. Your reputation precedes you, Bear Warden." The contempt conveyed by his tone was clear.

"I take it you're not pleased by my presence here."

"Lady Morwen is well known to us. She is a kind and decent sort and has provided her assistance to us on more than one occasion. I would see her safely returned to the king. I had hoped it would not involve the spilling of blood, but given what I know of you, that seems unlikely."

Berengar chose to let the remark pass. He often received a similar reception from nobility. Some resented the authority he had been given. Others believed the stories they'd heard. Others still were worried he would discover their culpability. He wasn't certain what category Desmond fit into, but it didn't matter now, at least not for the moment. There were more important matters to tend to.

"Tell me what happened."

"The lady Morwen arrived in Cill Airne two moons ago and was received at court. I assume she was on the king's business, though she made no mention of her purpose. She then traveled to the monastery at Innisfallen, an island on Loch Léin, and dwelled among the monks."

Desmond pointed at a speck of land in the distance, surrounded on all sides by the lake's dark waters. Berengar could barely discern the outline of the monastery rising from the island like a tower.

"She was undisturbed for a time, until a crop of farmers got it into their heads she had placed a curse on the land." Desmond stopped for a moment, as if deliberating his next words. "You must understand, there was an unusually poor planting season this year, and many of the farmers have lost cattle to disease. The old superstitions run strong here."

Berengar turned away from the lake and cast a dark gaze over Desmond. "I understand superstition well enough. What I fail to understand is how Laird Tierney allowed this to occur when he has a sizable number of fighting men at his command."

To his credit, the lord's heir did not avert his eyes. He let out the protracted sigh of a man who had exhausted all options available to him and now found himself in an untenable situation. "The peasants took up arms and laid siege to the island, demanding the magician so she could be burned. The monks continue to refuse to hand her over. We've tried resolving matters peacefully, but the villagers won't listen to reason. One of our soldiers was killed attempting to restore order."

"You still haven't answered my question."

"There has already been one uprising in the last year. My father will not risk a massacre that could cause the peasants to revolt. We requested more men from the king, but you're the only one he sent."

The wind shifted, and a cool breeze came from the west, carrying the scent of the lake.

"By showing weakness, you've only made it more likely people will get hurt." The warden paused, studying Desmond carefully. "Unless you have another motive for allowing the siege to continue."

Desmond's brow furrowed. "What do you mean?"

"Word has it that a group of déisi was seen traveling toward Cill Airne before this began."

If Desmond was surprised by Berengar's knowledge of the mercenaries, he gave no sign of it. "You're correct. They stayed at the tavern for one night and day before moving on."

"Long enough to spread more than a few rumors among the villagers about the presence of a certain magician, I'd say. Maybe even pay off one or two farmers."

"What exactly are you implying?"

The warden leaned closer, and this time Desmond took a step back. "The déisi are hired killers—professionals. Their services don't come cheap. Perhaps whoever paid them also offered your father something out of the deal."

Anger flashed over Desmond's face. "My father would never betray King Mór. Not for all the wealth of Fál would he do such a thing."

If Desmond were involved in treachery, he would likely have used the opportunity to defend himself. Instead he had chosen to defend his father's honor. Coupled with the tender gesture Desmond displayed toward Laird Tierney in the keep, it was clear Desmond was devoted to his father. Still, people were capable of just about anything, in

Berengar's experience, and members of the nobility were especially susceptible to the lure of wealth and power.

The warden held up a hand in protest. "Calm down. My only concern at the moment is delivering the magician safely to King Mór. I'm more than happy to do it on my own."

In truth, Berengar didn't require Laird Tierney's blessing, or even his approval. As a warden, his authority came from the High Queen herself. He was empowered to mete out justice as he saw fit. Although he could not make laws —that power belonged to the ruler of each kingdom—he answered to Nora alone, though he did feel a sense of deference to the kings and queens of Fál.

"You won't be alone. They are my subjects too, and my responsibility. If you are on the king's business, then you will have my father's assistance. I will accompany you to the island."

Berengar felt a growing sense of respect for the lord's son. "Very well. But I warn you—if you get in my way, I will kill you."

"I would expect nothing less from you. I suppose warning you against the folly of threatening a lord's son would be pointless, so what now? I take it you've been involved in this sort of thing before."

"I sail for Innisfallen at once and give the villagers the chance to lay down their arms."

"And if they do not disperse?" Desmond asked warily.

"Then there will be blood."

CHAPTER THREE

AN UNDERCURRENT OF tension hung in the air.

The warden stared over the surface of Loch Léin—the Lake of Learning, named for the island monastery—from his perch at the head of the *curach*. The boat's narrow wooden frame creaked under the whisper of the steady breeze. The small vessel sailed alone across the lake's smooth waters, Cill Airne shrinking ever smaller behind them.

Berengar hated the water. He had almost drowned on three separate occasions. The first happened when he was a boy, in icy reaches far to the north. The last was during the Shadow Wars, when he fought on the banks of the River Shannon, weighed down by his armor and surrounded by stacks of muddy corpses. Even now water held a dark power over him, beautiful and treacherous at once.

A flag bearing Laird Tierney's sigil flapped wildly on the deck, though it was the axe Berengar wore that sent the clearer message. No one had uttered a word since they set sail. The pair of oarsmen rowed in silence, their paddles striking the water in near-perfect rhythm. Faolán watched the others from where she lay at the back of the boat.

Desmond had kept especially quiet since their departure, no doubt troubled by those who remained behind, watching from shore. Berengar guessed many in the crowd were family or friends of the villagers taking part in the siege. Some had even attempted to follow, but Laird Tierney's soldiers kept them from taking to their boats. Had Tierney not been so averse to a show of force in the first place, Berengar doubted his presence would have been necessary.

The island grew in size at their approach, a soaring colossus of volcanic rock and red sandstone emerging from the depths like a crown of stone. Near the center of the island, two peaks rose above the others, creating a steep ascent to a tower that loomed at the top of the lower peak.

"There it is. Innisfallen." Desmond whispered the name with reverence.

The monastery was far larger than Laird Tierney's castle, and much older too. With its lofty black walls, the monastery seemed more like a fortress built for war than a place for peaceful, learned monks. It was easy to see how a group of monks might endure a siege of armed men in such a structure, so long as their food stores endured. Its storied halls were where Brian Boru, first and greatest of Munster's line of High Kings, had learned as a boy. Within the monastery were kept the Annals of Innisfallen, a chronicle of the entire history of Fál. Berengar didn't want to know what the monks had written about him, though he was curious how they managed to separate fact from fiction.

Gulls circled the lower peak, perhaps interested in the

outcome of the spectacle below. As the boat drew nearer to the island, he noticed a number of curachs and fishing boats abandoned along the shore. They ran aground beside the other boats, and the warden disembarked to inspect the area with a closer eye, glad to be on dry land once more. Faolán leapt over the side of the boat to join him. There were more than a few footprints in the dirt, all leading up the steep path to the monastery. Most of the prints were faded, suggesting the villagers had been there for some time, which accorded with Desmond's account.

"They couldn't have brought many supplies, given the small size and number of boats." Berengar waited for Desmond to make his way ashore. "They obviously didn't anticipate a protracted struggle. I'm surprised they haven't given up yet. They either truly believe in what they're doing, or else external forces are involved."

Desmond followed his gaze to the two oarsmen who remained seated in the curach. "They're not coming with us."

"Smart of them." Berengar rose from where he had crouched beside the footprints. "If this goes south, you'd be wise to consider running yourself."

"I'm not going anywhere."

"At least you had the sense to bring a sword, even if you don't plan on using it." Berengar was pleasantly surprised that Tierney's son had proved true to his word, though he doubted Desmond would have any better luck convincing the villagers to set aside their arms this time around. "Let's go. We've a steep climb ahead."

The two men started up the winding road, an uneven stair that looped around the island as it led to the peak, and the sound of waves crashing against the shore below soon grew fainter. Faolán easily outpaced them, occasionally glancing back with an annoyed expression, as if to say, *what's taking you so long?* Patches of emerald grass and several varieties of wildflower sprouted from a thin layer of topsoil on either side of the stair and up the sides of the stone columns looking down on them.

Berengar heard raised voices calling out as they neared the peak. He held a finger to his lips. "Quiet." Faolán sank low to the ground in a stalking position.

A crowd of villagers had assembled outside the monastery. They faced the tower, their backs to the pair approaching from the road. The mob numbered no more than twenty men in all. Few possessed actual weapons. For the most part they carried pitchforks and torches, with a few bows tossed in for good measure. Berengar doubted the villagers had any real combat training. If it came to it, he could slaughter them with ease, regardless of their numbers.

"Give us the magician," their leader shouted up at the tower, where a man in brown robes watched them from the safety of a balcony. "Hand her over, and we'll be on our way."

"I'll tell you what I told you yesterday, and the day before that. She is our guest, and you will not harm her." He was a large man—though not nearly as large as Berengar—and bald, with a short white beard. Were he not a monk, Berengar might have taken him for a former brawler. Though since the man was of Fál, such a thing was still possible. "Besides, I rather like her. She makes this old man laugh."

The villagers murmured among themselves for a few moments before their leader spoke again. Berengar caught a glimpse of him between gaps in the crowd. The man was better dressed than the rest, and unlike the others, he carried a sword. If someone was in the employ of the déisi, he was the most likely candidate.

"The woman is a witch. She has cursed our lands and polluted our waters with her foul magic. Do you deny the poor planting season or the decline in fishing yields? Surely you can see that she must be burned, man of God. Are not the old ways of the devil?"

The monk laughed outright at that. "She is a servant of the throne. As for the other, how do you know her magic does not come from the Lord? I sense no darkness in her."

"Enough." Berengar stepped forward before the villagers could offer a response. He pushed his way to the front of the crowd with Desmond following reluctantly behind. "This siege ends now."

"And who are you, stranger?" the villagers' leader demanded.

Berengar's expression darkened, and the man retreated to the protection afforded by his ranks. "I come on the authority of King Mór. I swear to you that if one hair on the magician's head is harmed, I'll gut the lot of you."

For a moment, there was silence as the villagers stared at the warden's imposing figure. Like infants attracted to a shiny object, their eyes sought out his weapons. Then one voice sounded above the others.

"The Fortress of Suffering," the villager said. "The High Queen's Monster."

Berengar's first impulse was to frown at the mention of one of his less than savory monikers, but instead he put on a false smile. "So you've heard of me. Then you know I will kill every man here if it means getting what I want. And what I want is to return King Mór's magician safely into his hands." Berengar took out his battleaxe for good measure, positioning himself between the villagers and the tower.

Desmond held up a hand in protest. "It need not come to this. Laird Tierney will pardon any man here who lays down his arms. There is no need for bloodshed."

"He's lying." The villagers' leader faced his ranks. "We've come too far to turn back now. Unless we rid the land of the witch, we will never break her spell." He drew his sword, and several of the archers trained their bows on Berengar and Desmond. Faolán snapped her jaws angrily at the threat to her master, waiting to kill if Berengar but said the word.

"I've had just about enough of this." Berengar's gaze fell on one of the archers, a young man barely out of adolescence whose bow was pointed in his direction. "You ever fire that thing at a human before?" The bow wavered in the archer's hands.

Berengar broke the young man's nose with the flat of his axe. Before the others could react, he disarmed the archer with ease and grabbed him from behind as if to use him as a shield.

"What are you doing?" Desmond hissed.

"We tried things your way." Berengar pressed his axe against his captive's throat and raised his voice so the others could hear him. "Is this boy a friend of yours? Maybe you've traded goats with him. Perhaps he helped you with the harvest. Do you want to see him die?"

Terror was readily apparent across the sea of faces. Half the men lowered their weapons. Berengar had no intention of killing an unarmed prisoner, but they didn't know that. Sometimes there were advantages to having a dangerous reputation.

Their leader waved his sword about. "Don't listen to him. Whoever he claims to be, there's only one of him."

Faolán bristled, her fur standing on end, but did not yet attack.

"With only twenty men? I've killed more than that stinking drunk." Berengar stared down the crowd, prepared to act. "I'm really not looking forward to picking pieces of you out of my axe, but I will if need be. One way or another, I'm leaving here with the magician."

"My name is Morwen," a woman's voice declared, and every head—Berengar's included—turned in the direction of the tower's entrance, where the king's magician stood outside the door. A flock of nervous-looking monks stood behind her just inside the tower.

The moment Berengar saw her, he knew at once his assumption about Morwen and the king was wrong. Morwen was barely fifteen, if that, much too young for even Mór's liking. She had a round, earnest face framed by long, bushy brown hair. She wore elegant blue magician's robes lined with the gold and white colors of the king's house. There was something familiar about her appearance, although he wasn't entirely sure why.

The warden quickly recovered from his surprise. "Go back to the tower. It's too dangerous for you here."

Anger flashed through her eyes momentarily. "I'll decide what's too dangerous. I will not stand by as blood is shed on my account." She started forward before he could offer a word of protest. Morwen looked over the villagers, ignoring the warden. "I don't see enemies here. I see friends." She gestured to a middle-aged man with a pitchfork. "Finley, when your niece was ill, who treated her with potions and stayed by her side until she was well again?"

Finley bowed his head, unable to meet her gaze. "You did."

"And Lucas," she said to another. "When your wife

complained of nightmares, who showed you what herbs to burn so she might sleep peacefully once more?"

The man flushed, clearly embarrassed. "It was you, Lady Morwen."

She nodded. "I am a loyal servant of King Mór. I care deeply for Munster and its people. I know you've had a hard season, but I have placed no curse on your farms or waters."

Berengar saw the villagers' leader tense as she spoke, though the others seemed swayed by her words. Morwen's hand reached out and lightly touched the leader's arm. Berengar alone was close enough to hear her mutter a word under her breath, and the man lowered his sword and fell silent, as if in a trance.

Morwen continued. "Killing me would only taint these lands forever. If you'd like, I can request that the king send relief. We've enough stores of grain in the capital to last seven winters."

By the time she finished speaking, the remaining villagers had already lowered their weapons. Berengar released his hold on his captive and pushed the young man toward his companions. The crowd laid down their arms and dispersed, tracing the path that had brought them to the monastery. Only their leader remained, a vacant expression on his face.

"You should go with them," Morwen said, her hand still on his arm.

The sword toppled from his hands. "Yes," the man mumbled. "I should be getting home."

Berengar watched him go. "That's a nice trick."

Morwen let out a deep breath and wiped a trickle of blood away from her nose with her sleeve. Her skin was a good deal paler than it was only a few seconds before. "I'll be drinking elixirs for days because of that." She wobbled where she stood. Berengar reached out to steady her, but she waved him away. "I'll be fine. I don't suppose you might permit me a nap?"

Berengar had hunted his share of witches and knew a fair amount about magic and its practitioners. A sorcerer might have frozen the entire crowd in place without difficulty. For a magician, it was a considerably harder task. Although magicians were able to harness the magic in the world around them through spells, sorcerers were far more adept at it. Sorcerers also possessed far greater stores of magical stamina, in addition to inherent powers and abilities unique to each one.

Berengar shook his head. "It would be best to get you well outside the town limits before sundown, on the chance the others change their minds."

Morwen was about to respond when her gaze fell on Faolán. "And who might you be?" She grinned widely at the sight of the wolfhound and dropped to one knee, playfully scratching behind the dog's ears. For her part, Faolán lazily enjoyed the attention, her tail wagging with enthusiasm.

"I can't remember the last time Faolán took an instant liking to someone." Berengar laughed despite himself when the wolfhound licked Morwen's face. "I must say, you're not what I expected. My name is—"

"I know who you are. What were you expecting—a grizzled old man with a flowing white beard? We come in all kinds, you know." She said the words so cheerfully he couldn't tell if they were meant as a rebuke or merely an observation. "And I am Morwen, Court Magician of Munster, although I suspect you already know that." She offered a slight bow as she rose from the ground. "It is an honor to make your acquaintance, Warden Berengar."

"I am glad to see your safe return, my lady," Desmond

interrupted. "On behalf of my father, I apologize for your treatment here."

"Tell Laird Tierney to rest easy. I was fortunate to spend my time among friends."

The monks left the safety of the tower and approached.

"Your staff, Lady Morwen." The bald man who had appeared at the balcony handed her a satchel filled with books and a magician's staff made of ash wood. Symbols and charms were carved into the staff from top to bottom, and two runestones—one blue and one purple—were placed opposite each other near the staff's head.

Morwen accepted the staff reverently. "I'm afraid I must be leaving. The good warden here has come to spirit me back to the king." She wrapped each of the monks in a warm embrace. "I will miss your hospitality, my friends. I will always be grateful for the kindness you have shown me." She turned back to the warden. "Now then—I trust you brought transportation?"

Berengar merely shook his head and started walking, and Morwen and Desmond followed after him. It wasn't long before they were again on the waters of Loch Léin, Cill Airne growing at their approach. As they reached the dock, Berengar noticed a lone rider watching them disembark from one of the neighboring hills. The warrior was clad in armor, a cruel sword at his side. Berengar stared unwaveringly at the rider until the man galloped away. There was no doubt in Berengar's mind the rider was one of the déisi.

"Is something wrong?" Morwen followed his gaze to the place where the hill now stood empty.

The warden did not answer.

. . .

After a few farewells to Laird Tierney and the members of his court, a trip to the stables to secure a horse for the magician, and a brief stop at the market-place to restock provisions for the journey, Berengar and Morwen departed Cill Airne. They took the path that led through the Gap of Dún Lóich, a road both were familiar with. As planned, Berengar was in and out of the city in under a day, the magician successfully in tow. He hadn't even needed to use his axe, although truth be told, that was more Morwen's doing than his. All in all, things had gone even smoother than he'd hoped.

They rode side by side under the shade of the Black Stack Mountains, Faolán trailing a dutiful distance away. Berengar yawned and stretched comfortably astride the saddle. With the hard part behind him, there was nothing left to do but keep an eye on the magician and enjoy the weather. With any luck, they'd reach Cashel in two or three days' time, and then he'd be on his way back to Tara.

"It's going to rain," Morwen observed casually. It was the first time either had spoken since they set out, and the warden had grown accustomed to the silence. If it were up to him, they might have continued the whole way in such a fashion. It was difficult enough making small talk with most people. For all he knew about combat and killing, he didn't know the first thing about adolescent girls.

It was a bright, sunny day. There were no clouds anywhere in sight. Berengar raised an eyebrow at Morwen's pronouncement but offered no protest. When a magician said it was going to rain, it was probably going to rain.

"Anything you can do about that? I'd prefer clear skies on the way back."

Morwen looked at him with an expression of mock scorn. "I'm a magician, not a druid."

He wasn't certain, but it was almost as if the girl was teasing him. Berengar scowled at the idea and rode ahead of her.

Morwen pulled alongside him. "You're bigger than I thought you'd be. You know—from the stories."

He didn't reply, hoping she'd take the hint.

"Your cloak is true bearskin." She looked him up and down. "Did you really kill a bear with your hands at twelve?"

"Don't believe everything you hear in stories." He hesitated, noticing her disappointment. "I was fifteen, and I had a dagger."

Morwen's countenance brightened considerably. "I thought it might be true. It's the one story that's the same in all the songs about you."

"And what do the songs say about you, I wonder?" He found himself suddenly curious.

"There are no songs about me." Morwen glanced away with a slightly sullen expression. "King Mór rarely allows me to leave Cashel unescorted. I spend most of my days locked away among scrolls and potions, reading about others' adventures. It was my hope to use my time in Cill Airne to prove myself, until I nearly got myself killed." Berengar noticed her knuckles whiten as her grip on the reins tightened. "I can only imagine what the king will say upon our return."

"I thought you acquitted yourself well. It takes a great deal of resolve to retain your calm when men have weapons trained on you. Did you find what you were searching for at Cill Airne?"

"No, though I'm certain the king is right. Darkness spreads across the land. I've felt it for some time. Something is not right. If I'd had more time…" She trailed off.

"I can't speak to magic, but I'm certain the déisi were involved in the siege. They were seen in the village just before it began. I spotted one of them watching us when we arrived at the docks. I assume he left to join his brethren. If the déisi are involved, that means someone else is paying them—someone who wanted you dead."

Morwen stared at him, as if troubled by something. "The villagers—would you have killed them? If they hadn't laid down their arms, I mean."

He answered without hesitation. "I would have done what I had to." It clearly hadn't been the answer she was looking for, but it was the truth. For a moment, the warden caught a flicker of fear in her expression. "You're rather forthright and plainspoken for a magician. Aren't you supposed to speak in riddles?"

She laughed at that, and Berengar was struck by a warm feeling that reminded him of another time in his life, before the Shadow Wars. The memories left him uneasy, and he did not speak for a time.

"You carry great anger inside." Morwen's soft voice startled him from his thoughts. "You hide it well, but I've never sensed so much rage in another person before. Never."

Berengar shot her a withering gaze. "Stay out of my head," he warned, no longer amused. He dug his boots into the stallion's flanks and quickly outpaced her. This time she had the sense to remain behind.

They followed the path for several hours, until at last the sun hung low in the sky. True to Morwen's words, it began to rain. The sky, a deep blue only a short time ago, was now ominous and dark.

"There's a settlement a little ways down the road,"

Berengar yelled over the sweeping winds. "We'll seek refuge at the inn and wait out the storm. We can start again tomorrow."

A crack of thunder drowned out her response. Heaven's floodgates were thrown open, and what began as a light sprinkle soon evolved into a full-on deluge.

"Faster," the warden bellowed to his stallion, which kicked up mud at its back as it galloped along the trail.

Morwen's horse reared on its hind legs at the flash of lightning. For a moment Berengar worried she was going to fall from the saddle, but the magician reacted with a graceful speed that surprised even him. In one fluid motion, she held onto the saddle with one hand and touched the flat of her mount's muzzle with the other.

Her eyes closed, and her voice became a whisper. "*Síocháin*. Peace."

The horse instantly dropped down to all fours, as calm as if it were a sunny day once more. Morwen pulled her hood over her head to shield herself from the rains and spurred her horse forward. She took to the saddle so well it was clear she had the benefit of tutoring from Cashel's stable master. King Mór had evidently spared no expense with her education.

The pair rode neck and neck through the storm until they reached the settlement. Berengar slowed his horse's pace to a trot and Morwen did likewise. The warden dismounted in front of the stables and glanced behind, where Faolán had stopped at the outskirts of the settlement, her ears pricked alertly. He didn't need magic to know something was amiss. By the time their horses were safely squared away in warm, dry stalls, the wolfhound was waiting nearby. She gave him a knowing look, and he nodded to indicate he understood.

"Stay here. Keep watch."

Faolán stared unflinchingly in the direction of the forest.

"Come on." Berengar motioned for Morwen to accompany him. "A warm hearth sounds perfect right about now. Their soup's not half bad either."

They walked down the path to the inn. "I can't read minds." Morwen sidestepped a puddle, but Berengar splashed right on through it.

"What?"

"What you said back there, about me keeping out of your head—I can't read minds, you know. I can only sense the emotions and feelings of others. Most sorcerers can't even manage mind reading. And even if I were able, I wouldn't invade someone's privacy like that."

"Oh, that? I'd already forgotten about it."

Morwen regarded him doubtfully, but he gave her a look that indicated he had no wish to broach the matter again. The warden proceeded to push open the door to the inn for good measure, definitively ending the subject.

Berengar wiped the mud off his boots and swept the rain from his cloak before crossing the threshold. The room was quiet, save for the crackling of the fire and the storm raging outside the inn's walls. There was no music, suggesting the troubadour had moved on. The hall was relatively empty, at least by the prior night's standards. A young boy was sweeping the floor between rows of bare tables. The absence of patrons wasn't entirely surprising given the torrential downpour. Berengar made his way to the innkeeper, who looked as if he expected to see him.

"Greetings, Warden Berengar. It is an honor to have you with us again. I see you've brought a guest."

The warden grunted to acknowledge the greeting and laid a pair of coins before the innkeeper. "We'd like a room for the night, if it's not too much of a bother."

"Not at all." The innkeeper took the coins and handed him the key. "Oh, I almost forgot. A message came for you from the Rock of Cashel."

"Word travels fast around here. Are you sure it's from Cashel?"

"It's not every day we receive a messenger from the capital." The innkeeper let out a good-natured chuckle. "If he'd only stayed longer, the messenger might have been able to deliver this in person." He reached behind the counter and passed Berengar a sealed letter.

"That's the king's seal," Morwen said curiously. "What does it say?"

A chilling howl outside the inn interrupted him before he could break the seal. "Faolán." He knew that howl all too well. *That's not a good sign.*

Morwen closed her eyes, her hand on her staff. "There are men outside. They come with dark intent."

"Tell me something I didn't know." Berengar tucked the letter away. "It's the déisi, of course. They've followed us from Cill Airne. This is their last chance to finish the job."

"You were expecting them. You used me as bait to draw them out. You *wanted* them to find us."

"Not entirely, no, but it was always a possibility they'd track us down. If I take one alive, we can find out the name of their employer. If they all die, well, that also sends a message to whoever hired them. You're not in any danger, as long as you stay put." Berengar glanced over at the innkeeper and the boy sweeping the floor. "That goes for both of you as well. Get behind the counter. The déisi aren't known to leave loose ends."

The boy dropped his broom and did as he was told, leaving Morwen standing firmly with her arms crossed. "You're not going out there alone."

Berengar growled angrily, but she did not relent. "Fine. Just don't get in my way. And don't get yourself killed, either. I promised King Mór I would bring you back safe." He grabbed his battleaxe with a smirk. "It appears I'll get to use this after all." With that, the warden threw open the door to the inn and stepped into the pouring rain.

Lightning cast a pale glow over the darkening sky, revealing the menacing figures gathered outside the inn. All were clad in the same black and maroon dyed armor. Berengar counted seven déisi in all. Two were mounted on horseback. Of the five on the ground, two archers held their bows trained on him. The other three reached for their swords.

Berengar didn't flinch. He remained where he stood, sizing up his enemies. A savage growl sounded beside him, where Faolán crouched, ready to pounce. Berengar stared at their leader across the deluge, undaunted. He'd faced worse odds before.

The captain's gaze moved past Berengar to where Morwen lingered in the doorway just behind him. "Give her to us and we will spare the rest of the villagers." His voice was cold and cruel.

Berengar's grip tightened around the axe. "You wouldn't like her. She asks too many questions."

The captain frowned at his response. "Take her," he ordered his men. "Kill the warden."

Morwen was right about one thing. Berengar carried a white-hot fury within him. Most of the time he was careful to keep it restrained under a mask of civility. Only in battle could he truly release his hold on the anger that drove him.

Faolán moved first. The wolfhound leapt at the nearest archer before he could loose his arrow. The man was on the ground in an instant, and a scream died on his lips as she ripped out his throat.

Berengar fell on the swordsmen with a savage cry. He cut down the first to meet him, driving the great axe through the mercenary's armor. Blood spurted from the man's chest as Berengar ripped the axe free. He used the man as a shield as an arrow sailed through the rain, hitting the déisi in the back. Then Berengar spun around and disarmed the archer by literally removing the man's arm with his axe. The archer collapsed, bleeding to death.

The two remaining swordsmen rushed to attack him together. The warden fought like a berserker, gripped in the mad frenzy of bloodlust. Years ago, a sword master told him the lack of a calm, detached focus was the only thing that kept him from becoming a great swordsman. Berengar had still learned enough to handle a blade if need be, but he always led with the axe.

Faolán came sailing out of the darkness and onto the back of the man farthest from him. Berengar countered the other's sword with such force the man lost his grip on his blade. His next swing cut through muscle, bone, and sinew. The mercenary was dead before he hit the ground.

"Look out!" Morwen shouted.

When he looked up, Berengar saw one of the men on horseback riding toward him, wielding a spear. He braced himself for impact, holding his axe at the ready.

Morwen said something he couldn't hear and drove her staff into the earth. The ground shook and erupted around them in a deafening roar. The explosion knocked Berengar off his feet. The déisi was thrown from his horse, and they landed beside each other in the mud. The man pulled a dagger from his belt and lunged at Berengar, who caught his wrist and broke it. When he smashed his forehead into the mercenary's face, the man spit out a mouthful of teeth and crawled away as Berengar climbed to his feet and snatched his axe off the ground. Just as the déisi's hand closed around his spear, Berengar severed the man's head from his body.

He searched for the group's captain, but the man on horseback had disappeared.

"He's gone," Morwen said.

"What were you thinking, using a spell like that?" Berengar's heart still raced from the heat of battle. "You could have killed us both."

"I'm sorry." She spoke quietly and leaned on her staff for support. It was clear the attempt had taken its toll. "I thought I could make it work."

The sadness in her words caused his anger to abate, and for the first time he was reminded just how young she actually was. It occurred to him she'd been trying to protect him and her magic had failed. Berengar lowered his axe and glanced at the bodies littered across the mud, staining streams of rainwater with their blood. All lay dead.

He looked again at Morwen, who seemed as if she might topple over at any second. "Let's get you inside." She started to resist his assistance but stumbled and then allowed him to help her back inside the inn. "It's over. You can come out now." The innkeeper and his helper emerged from hiding. Berengar sat Morwen beside the fire. "Bring her some food, if you can spare it."

"Thank you," Morwen said to the innkeeper, who quickly arrived at their table with a loaf of warm bread and a bowl of soup.

Berengar watched her eat in silence. It wasn't until she finished her meal that he remembered the message from Cashel. The warden reached into his cloak and removed the letter he'd tucked away for safekeeping. "Now let's see what's so blasted important that it couldn't wait until our return." He broke the seal and unfurled the message, reading it under the light of the fire. He let the letter fall away after reading it, and it landed beside the flames.

"What is it?" Morwen no doubt sensed his unease. "What's wrong?"

"The letter is from Queen Alannah. She requests we return to the castle immediately."

Morwen tried to read his expression. "I don't understand."

A long moment passed before he answered.

"The king is dead."

CHAPTER FOUR

As THE TWO riders approached the Rock of Cashel, anguished cries greeted their return.

Weak sunlight poked through the remnants of storm clouds, which shrouded the land in a somber pallor. Puddles and mud were all that remained of the tempest that followed them all the way from the inn. The warden pushed toward the castle that lay beyond the city walls, and his horse's hooves kicked up mud as they galloped over the damp earth.

Berengar exchanged glances with Morwen when they passed through the gate. She had hardly spoken since he broke the news of the king's death. Initially he'd been concerned the girl would prove unable to keep up with the rigorous demands of such a swift journey, but she rode like one possessed, nearly outpacing him.

Bells tolled from the castle on the hill, one after another. The sound echoed loudly across Cashel. Berengar pulled back on the reins, slowing his horse to a trot to better navigate a course through the teeming crowds, and Morwen followed suit.

Apart from the High Queen's coronation and the great battles of the Shadow Wars, the warden had never seen so many gathered in one place. From the city gate to the castle stair, people of all walks of life lined the streets. They had come from far and wide in tribute to their fallen king.

There was a grim mood in the city, which had changed dramatically since his departure. All commerce and trade appeared to have ceased, and everywhere he looked businesses were shuttered. Many wept openly, including a significant portion of those meant to keep the peace. The guards' numbers had been bolstered. Berengar appreciated the show of force. Scanning the faces of those in the crowd, it was evident that many were on edge. Several jeered at Morwen as she passed by, and Berengar noticed more than a few nonhumans standing apart from the crowd, afraid.

"Mark my words, 'twas magic to blame," he heard someone say.

"The act of some foul sorcerer," another replied.

"There hasn't been a dark sorcerer in Fál since the High Queen began her reign," Morwen muttered under her breath.

Berengar understood her frustration. *There will be trouble now.* Unless the people were given answers soon, grief would quickly turn to anger. He'd seen it before. Human beings rarely needed an excuse to turn on each other, and for all its fabled civility, Munster was no exception. Berengar wanted answers too. Queen Alannah's letter made no mention of the circumstances surrounding her husband's death. He thought back to his last conversation with the king, when Mór spoke of an unspecified threat to the kingdom. That Mór should die while Berengar was away seemed too much of a coincidence for his liking.

Eventually the pair made their way through the crowd

and started up the castle stair. The guards stationed at the summit parted to allow them past the wall, where Berengar recognized Corrin, the captain of the guard. A number of helmeted subordinates with spears and shields on full display flanked the captain on either side, but it was to the man who stood with him that Berengar's attention was drawn. He was clean-shaven with noble-looking features, and Berengar put his age somewhere around forty, probably only a few years younger than himself. A yellow cloak fell from the pauldrons at the shoulders of his breastplate, which he wore over a long gambeson. A two-handed sword was sheathed in a scabbard that hung from his back.

Morwen dismounted at once and rushed to meet the others.

"Lady Morwen," said the stranger at Corrin's side. "I am glad to see that you are safe, though I am sorry you have returned under such circumstances."

Berengar climbed from the saddle and approached them, and the stranger took note of him. The man was tall —only a few inches shorter than Berengar, though Berengar was the larger of the two.

"You have our thanks, Warden. I regret that we did not have the chance to meet when you arrived earlier. I am Ronan, the king's thane."

Berengar had guessed as much from the insignia on Ronan's breastplate. A thane was someone who oversaw the daily affairs throughout their kingdom, second in command only to the king or queen. As such, they wielded a tremendous amount of power and influence.

"We received Queen Alannah's message."

Morwen interrupted before he could continue.

"Is it true, Ronan? Please, I need to know." Her voice broke with the final words, and despite himself, Berengar felt a stab of pity for her.

"I'm to escort you both to Queen Alannah at once. She will explain the rest."

Berengar and Morwen accompanied the cadre of guards inside the castle. This time there was no mention of surrendering his weapons. Nor did anyone remark on Faolán following at his side.

Morwen lowered her voice to a whisper. "Something is amiss. I can feel it."

Berengar agreed, though he made no reply. He expected Ronan and company to take them to the throne room. Instead, the men escorted them inside the great hall, where Queen Alannah was deep in conversation with a bearded old man who wore an elegant green tunic and multiple silver rings. When Alannah noticed Ronan and the others, she stopped speaking, and the hall fell still.

Alannah held up a hand to silence the herald before he could speak, and he bowed gracefully and quickly joined the ranks of guards along the chamber's walls. Corrin and the others remained behind as Berengar and Morwen approached with Ronan. When they drew nearer to the queen, Morwen bowed and sank to one knee in Alannah's presence.

"Arise, Lady Morwen." Alannah's gaze fixed on Berengar, who remained standing. The queen was adorned in mourning black, and a veil shrouded her face. In Munster, property was shared equally between men and women, which meant the throne had passed to Alannah, while Ravenna remained the heir. Berengar scanned the room, but the princess was nowhere in sight. He returned his attention to Alannah, whose expression was masked by her veil. "I see you fulfilled my husband's request. Thank you for answering my summons, Warden Berengar."

"King Mór was a man worthy of great respect, Your

Grace. I am sure his death will be mourned throughout the kingdom."

"My husband's death was no accident. He was murdered."

Berengar saw Morwen's lower lip tremble at the words.

"Murdered, Your Grace? Are you certain?" Although it was rare for a man of Mór's age and health to succumb to natural causes, there was no charge more serious than regicide. Few would be bold enough to make such an attempt, and the royal family was well protected.

"It happened within this very castle. One moment he was seated on his throne, and in the next he was on the ground, gasping for air as he tried to call for help. He died with your name on his lips."

"These are grave tidings. If King Mór was the victim of an assassin, you and your daughter could still be in danger."

The queen drew nearer until he could see her eyes peering back at him through the veil. "My husband had great faith in you, Warden Berengar. He trusted you with his life, in fact. That is why I have summoned you here. I want you to deliver the High Queen's justice. I wish to know who killed the king and why. I entrust this task to you and you alone, in my husband's name."

Berengar clenched his teeth. What began as a simple task to retrieve the king's magician had just become far more complicated than he ever could have guessed. "Very well. You have my word. I will find the truth of this."

"See that you do." The queen turned away, apparently satisfied by his answer. "Let it be known that I grant the warden full authority to investigate this matter." A scribe produced a piece of parchment, which Alannah marked with the royal seal and presented to Berengar. "This is Marcus O'Reilly, Chief Royal Adviser to the throne." She gestured to the man with the white beard and silver rings. "I can see you've met the other members of the court. They will assist you with anything you require, unless you have anything further to ask of me."

"I just have two questions at present, if you'll permit me, Your Grace. Would it be possible for me to examine your husband's corpse?"

"I thought you might make such a request. I ordered his body left undisturbed until your arrival. Be quick with it —we've delayed the funeral too long already. And your second question?"

"Were there any witnesses to the king's death?"

The queen's tone softened unexpectedly. "My daughter was in the room with him when it happened. She saw it all."

With that, Alannah motioned for her handmaidens to follow her and swept out of the room, accompanied by a host of guards.

A ny lingering doubts that the king had been murdered dissipated the moment Berengar saw his corpse.

The bells had ceased, leaving the vast throne room in silence. The doors were shut behind him. Morwen, Ronan, and the royal adviser were the sole other occupants of the room, save perhaps the corpse. The others said nothing as Berengar looked over the throne room. He was fortunate that there was both a witness and a body to examine, which was more than he usually had to go on.

Mór lay on his stomach, sprawled on the stone floor in a shallow layer of dried blood. His right hand seemed to be reaching out for the doors, as if seeking help that never came. It was an ignoble end for such a storied figure.

Berengar, who had always believed he would die with his axe in his hand, wondered briefly if a similar fate awaited him. Contrary to the queen's words, the body had not been undisturbed, strictly speaking. Someone had closed the king's eyes, an intimate, respectful gesture.

"The king was seated on his throne when it happened." Berengar spoke more for his benefit than for the others. Saying the words aloud helped him think better. "He toppled to the floor, spilling his goblet." The warden pointed to the spot where the goblet had rolled. Berengar's eye followed the trail of dried blood from the throne to the place where the corpse lay. "He managed to crawl several feet before he died." He glanced back at the others. "What time was it when he died?"

"The hour was late," Ronan said. "Most of the castle was asleep. Save for the guards stationed outside, King Mór and Princess Ravenna were alone."

"What were they discussing?"

Ronan shrugged. "A private matter, I'm sure." A reluctant shadow crossed the thane's face, and it was evident he continued against his wishes. "The guards reported raised voices coming from the chamber."

They were arguing about something, Berengar thought, taking note of the loyalty Ronan had demonstrated to the princess. "Did anyone hear what was said between them?"

Ronan shook his head. "No. I questioned the guards myself."

"Did anyone else enter the throne room during that time for any reason?"

Ronan seemed to consider the question carefully for a moment before his brow arched as if a thought had occurred to him. "The king's cupbearer, Matthias, entered briefly, though he was not present for King Mór's passing. The boy was in a state of shock when the guards questioned him, but I'm told he answered most of their questions satisfactorily."

"I would like to speak with him all the same."

"Very well." Ronan knocked on the door to the throne room. "The warden wishes to have a word with Matthias," he said to Corrin when the doors opened. "Find the boy and bring him here."

The captain of the guard bowed low. "It will be done, Thane Ronan."

Berengar waited until the doors were closed before touching the body. Footsteps sounded behind him as he crouched in front of the corpse, and when he looked up, Morwen was standing at his side. He recognized the look in her eyes all too well—it was the sting of loss.

He gently turned Mór onto his back and heard an audible gasp from the magician. "The queen was right. This was no accident."

From the bloodstains around Mór's mouth, it was clear the king had vomited a great deal of blood. Berengar inspected the body carefully and found no signs of other injuries, indicating all the blood on the floor had been regurgitated. The corpse was swollen and nearly translucent, a pale shade of the man Mór had been in life.

Morwen knelt beside him. "These are not normal signs of decomposition. Look at his skin."

The corpse's skin was a grotesque composite of sickly green and purple hues. Berengar followed Morwen's gaze to a multitude of black, threadlike cords that ran along Mór's veins and grunted in assent. "This was poison, and a nasty one, from the look of it. Whoever did this wanted him to suffer."

"They knew what they were doing. Only a very clever alchemist or herbalist could have concocted such a poison." Morwen's hand went to the king's black curls. "Look. Someone cut his hair recently."

"Why would someone do that?" Berengar felt fortunate to have a magician on hand, as he was far out of his depth when it came to the subject of alchemy.

Morwen shrugged. "Perhaps it was an ingredient in the poison. Certain spells or potions are more effective with something belonging to the victim, such as a lock of their hair."

So the murderer might have taken the trouble to get close to Mór beforehand, Berengar thought. "Can you tell me what poison was used?"

"Not without knowing more. There are too many possibilities. This was either the work of a particularly skilled assassin or…" She trailed off, as if struck by a horrifying thought.

"Go on," Berengar prodded.

Morwen shot a nervous glance back at the others and lowered her voice. "Or else magic was involved."

Berengar examined the goblet, which lay on its side. Most of the wine had spilled over the floor, but a portion had been left behind. "There's still wine inside. Could you identify the poison based on the contents?"

"Possibly. I can try separating the poison from the wine through distillation, though it will be a challenge with such a small amount of substrate. Afterward I would still have to break down the poison and analyze its components. It will take time."

As Berengar started to reply, he discovered a piece of parchment stuffed into the folds of the king's cloak. "It looks like the king left a message for us." He removed the parchment, which seemed to have been intentionally hidden away. The small scrap of paper was uneven at the edges, as if it had been torn from a book or scroll.

"Maybe it contains a clue to the killer's identity. What does it say?"

Berengar unfurled the parchment and saw letters written in blood. "It was meant for me." His gaze passed over the brief message. "King Mór reminds me of the debt I owe him and…" He paused.

"And what?"

"'Protect my daughter with your life,'" he read aloud.

Morwen's mouth hung open in shock at the words, and for only a moment, her cheeks flushed red.

The doors to the throne room opened again, and Corrin entered the chamber, accompanied by several guards. Berengar immediately noticed the cupbearer was not among their number.

"Apologies, Thane Ronan," Corrin said. "Matthias could not be found. No one has seen him inside the castle in days."

"People usually run when they're guilty of something." Berengar's rough voice betrayed his anger the thought hadn't occurred to the others until now. He rose from the king's side. "The cupbearer could be our only link to the poisoner. He must be found."

Ronan swore. "I want patrols on every street corner and at all the entrances to the city. No one leaves Cashel until he is located. Do you understand, Captain?"

"It will be done."

"I'm sorry, Warden Berengar," Ronan said. "I'm afraid you will have to excuse me while I tend to this situation. There are new security measures that must be implemented immediately."

"I was finished here anyway. There is nothing left to glean from the king's body."

"Very well. I will tell the holy men they can take King Mór for burial preparations. We will speak again shortly."

With that, Ronan departed the chamber together with Corrin, issuing orders to the guards.

Within moments after their departure, a small contingent of robed priests entered, chanting prayers and burning incense as they approached to carry the king's body away.

At the sight of them, Morwen gathered Mór's hands into her own and kissed them. "Farewell, my king," Berengar heard her whisper reverently as he started on his way. The magician caught up with him outside the throne room, where Faolán waited. "Where are we going next?"

"*We* aren't going anywhere. *I'm* going to speak with the princess—alone."

"You need me." Morwen raised her voice and jabbed her pointer finger at his chest to emphasize the point. "I can help. I know this city far better than you do, and it's clear you don't know the first thing about magic."

Berengar came to an abrupt stop just outside the throne room's entrance. "Bears don't hunt in packs. I promised Mór I would bring you back, but now that I've done that, I'm done babysitting you."

Her eyes flashed with annoyance. "I can look after myself. I spent a year in Gaul training with the Order of the Swordless Mage."

"That explains why you're such a pacifist." He chuckled, which only seemed to make her angrier. "If you want to help, identify the poison the assassin used. In the meantime, stay out of my way. The last thing I need is someone slowing me down while I do my job."

He shot her a menacing look intended to warn her away, but Morwen crossed her arms and stood her ground defiantly. "Is it because I'm a magician, or because I'm a woman? I thought you were different, but you're just like all the rest." With that, Morwen marched away, and

Berengar realized that she had taken the goblet from him without his noticing.

"Warden Berengar." The man Queen Alannah had introduced as Marcus O'Reilly followed him down the corridor. "I was hoping to share a brief word with you."

"I'm listening." Berengar was interested to hear what the king's chief adviser was so eager to discuss.

O'Reilly looked over his shoulder at the guards, as if afraid of being overheard. "Come with me to my chambers. We can converse there in privacy." Berengar followed the old man up a staircase to a wooden door in a secluded hallway. He soon found himself standing inside a spacious —if dusty—chamber furnished for a king. Rich tapestries hung from the walls, embroidered with O'Reilly's family arms. Shelves upon shelves were crammed with books and scrolls. Berengar noticed a large map of Munster spread across a table.

O'Reilly walked with a limp, though he made no use of a cane. His back was slightly hunched with age, and his hair and beard were wholly white. By all appearances, the man was impossibly old, and yet he showed no signs of weariness. O'Reilly seemed accustomed to the finer things in life, suggested both by the quality of his attire and the contents of the room.

"It will not be long before word of the king's death spreads across the land. Soon the rest of the *Rí Tuaithe* will come to swear fealty to Queen Alannah." O'Reilly approached an ornate *madia* against the wall and reached for a jug of wine. "Do you believe the king was poisoned?"

"Looks that way."

"Peace hangs on a thread as it is. When the people learn the truth…" He poured a cup for himself with a steady hand. "If the people suspect magic was involved, there will be massacres of the sort not seen since King Mór's grandfather's time."

It was an implicit warning. If justice wasn't delivered soon, the city would tear itself apart at the seams. It had happened before. After the Shadow Wars, most of the few magicians and mages were burned or else hunted to extinction. Munster was one of the only kingdoms of Fál to retain the position of court magician. Nonhumans fared even worse. There was a reason encounters with full-blooded fairies were now almost as rare as unicorn sightings.

O'Reilly turned his back. "Can I offer you some wine?" When Berengar didn't answer, he left the second cup empty. The bells again began to chime just before he lifted the cup to his lips, and both men stared off the balcony at the masses that watched the castle from below. The old man sighed and took a deep drink. "They mourn the loss of their king. Mór was greatly beloved by his people. Such a dreadful tragedy."

"It wasn't a tragedy. It was murder."

"Yes, of course," O'Reilly stammered. He spoke in a soft, soothing tone that nonetheless possessed a rushed quality. "And a terrible business it is. I knew Mór from the time he was a boy. I was already gray when he was but a lad. I served as Chief Royal Adviser to his brother, and his father before him."

The warden suppressed a chuckle. By reminding Berengar of his many years of loyal service, O'Reilly was subtly attempting to verbally affirm his loyalty. In fact, his comments suggested a greater loyalty to himself. "I can see the royal family has richly rewarded your years of service." Berengar spoke in reference to the chamber's splendor.

O'Reilly let the comment pass unanswered and turned to face him once more. "We are fortunate to have you with us. Your deeds are legendary. King Mór often spoke very highly of you."

He's a flatterer, Berengar decided. He used to think it was no small wonder that such men so often occupied positions of power, but after years of dealing with self-important nobles, it no longer surprised him. As a rule, Berengar had little use for men like O'Reilly, but that didn't mean he couldn't still prove useful.

"Tell me, Laird O'Reilly—what happened on the day of the king's death?"

"There was nothing particularly unusual about it, if that's what you're asking." O'Reilly's brow furrowed suddenly. "Except…a messenger arrived in the evening with a letter for the king. When King Mór read the letter, his face grew pale, and he cast it into the fire. As far as I know, he said nothing of its contents to me or anyone else."

Interesting, Berengar thought. "Any idea where the letter came from?"

O'Reilly shook his head.

"Had King Mór been acting strangely of late?"

"How do you mean?" O'Reilly seemed to regard him with a suspicious air.

He's trying to see how much I know. This meeting is as much for his benefit as it is mine. O'Reilly was a flatterer, but probably no fool. The warden couldn't imagine Mór bestowing such authority on anyone unless they brought considerable talents to the table, many years of service or otherwise.

"Differently, I mean. Did you notice anything odd in the days leading up to his death?"

"Now that I think about it, I suppose he was behaving a bit unlike himself. King Mór had withdrawn from court in recent weeks. In meetings with the royal council he was peculiarly reticent. One might have been forgiven for suspecting that he was keeping secrets."

"Perhaps he didn't know whom he could trust." Berengar's remark drew a knowing smile from the old man.

Mór had suggested as much before his death. Someone close to the king had betrayed Morwen to the déisi. *It's unlikely the poisoner acted alone. The assassin probably had help from inside the castle.* Tracking down the missing cupbearer might provide answers to that particular quandary.

Berengar decided he would have to be careful to trust no one, not that it would pose much of a problem. Apart from the High Queen and the other wardens, Berengar could count the number of people he trusted on one hand. Too many people had tried to kill him over the years for it to be otherwise, and he wasn't one to learn a lesson halfway.

In the end, the matter came down to a question of motive. Someone had assassinated the king, but why? Unraveling the answer to that question would shine a light on the rest of it. Whoever wanted Mór dead must have had a powerful reason to take such a risk. Usually in cases of regicide, there was a contested line of succession, or else a rival king in a warring kingdom. But Fál was at peace, and the line of succession was clear.

"Did the king have any enemies? Anyone who might have wished him harm?"

A cold breeze passed between them, and the old man turned away from the balcony. "No ruler is without enemies—even one as loved as good King Mór." O'Reilly approached the table with the map and set the cup aside before pointing out a spot on the coast. "From their stronghold to the east, the Danes raid our villages, led by Gorr Stormsson—a savage butcher through and through. Our armies have confined the territories he holds, but only at great cost. Stormsson has committed worse crimes than you could possibly imagine."

"I don't know. I can imagine quite a lot. What of magical threats?"

"Munster is not like the other kingdoms. We live in peace with nonhumans, for the most part. The giants are our friends. Even goblins live freely in our cities."

"And witches? Do you have any of those?"

"Four, to be exact." O'Reilly's finger moved to a spot on the map closer to the capital. "There is a coven of three less than a day's journey from Cashel. They are known as the Witches of the Golden Vale. King Mór left them largely to their own devices. He had an...*arrangement* of sorts with the coven's leader. Nobles and peasants alike come from all across the land seeking their aid. The witches peddle spells and useful enchantments—that sort of thing."

"Potions?" Berengar raised an eyebrow.

"With certainty, but you needn't concern yourself with them. They're harmless, really."

"No one who dabbles in the dark arts is harmless, Laird O'Reilly." Magic was a dangerous thing, which was one reason Berengar tried his best to keep his distance. None of his encounters with witches had ever ended well. Perhaps he shouldn't have been so quick to dismiss Morwen after all. "You mentioned a fourth witch. I take it she's not part of this coven."

"No, she is not." O'Reilly wrinkled his nose in disgust. "An old crone that dwells in the Devil's Bit. Many great warriors and heroes have attempted to slay her over the years at the king's behest. All perished."

"It sounds like King Mór made an enemy of her."

"Undoubtedly. It was said she placed a curse on the

king's family, which resulted in the death of his son and heir some years ago."

A curse. Could be a good place to start. Berengar made a mental note to check into the prince's death. Perhaps Mór was not the first victim.

The conversation was cut short by a loud knock at the door. A servant girl entered and offered an apologetic bow. "Forgive me, Laird O'Reilly, but the queen has requested your assistance with the funeral procession." Her eyes fixed on Berengar's scars.

"Yes, of course. I suppose we shall have to continue this conversation later," he muttered almost as an afterthought.

"Of that, I have no doubt." Whatever else he had learned from O'Reilly, Berengar knew one thing for certain: the old man was keeping something from him.

He found the princess in the chapel, where the king's body had already been prepared for burial. Ravenna stood over her father's corpse, which lay on a table in the center of the room. Two guards waited outside out of respect for her privacy. If the princess heard Berengar enter the chapel, she gave no sign of it. The mortician had done his work well; Mór looked almost the way he remembered. The king was dressed in splendid gold and purple burial clothes, and his hands were clasped around a sword that ran nearly the length of the table.

Candles burned softly, casting wavering shadows across the dimly lit room. The princess was also dressed in mourning black, though unlike her mother, Ravenna wore no veil. Her dark eyes shimmered like coals in the firelight. They were red, but he saw no tears.

"I remember that sword," Berengar said to break the silence. "It saved my life on at least one occasion."

"I can imagine. I grew up hearing the tales of the Poet Prince. I remember when they laid my brother to rest in the crypt. It felt at the time like the world had ended. That seems so long ago now." She glanced away from her father and held Berengar's gaze. "I gather you're here to discuss the night of his death."

Her words caught him off guard. With Mór not even cold in his grave, he had guessed she would want to wait until after the funeral. "There's no need—"

"Weep not for him who is dead, nor grieve for him. Instead, weep bitterly for him who goes away, for he shall return no more to see his native land." Ravenna's expression was hard, almost fierce. "Do you like those words? They're from a passage my father learned from the priests. He quoted it to me before my wedding day. At the time, I couldn't understand why they made me feel quite so sad. Now I think I do." She rarely blinked when she spoke. "Ask me your questions, Warden Berengar. I will do my best to answer, although I fear I will be of little help."

"You were the last person to see your father alive. What can you remember?"

"My father summoned me to see him. The hour was late, but there was nothing unusual about it. While we were speaking, he stopped suddenly and clutched his chest as if he couldn't breathe." Ravenna shuddered at the recollection. "It was terrible. I'll never forget the look in his eyes just before the goblet slipped from his hands. He fell from the throne, vomiting blood. By that time, I had shouted for the guards, but he was already dead." Her voice never wavered as she spoke.

"What did the two of you discuss? The guards reported they heard raised voices coming from inside, as if you were arguing about something."

She laughed—a dry, hollow sound that almost seemed

not to belong to the beautiful young woman across from him. "My father was a great man, Warden Berengar—a great king. He devoted his life to Munster. He placed his duty to the realm above all else. *Everything* else. He was a great king, but he was not a good father. Our relationship was contentious, to put it mildly. I trust you gleaned as much from our meal together."

"You don't mince words." With the exception of the High Queen, he had never met another royal who offered their true thoughts so freely.

"I've spent my whole life around people who've spent theirs playing games. I decided not to play games. That was what my father and I were discussing. I asked his permission to leave Munster."

"I take it he refused?"

"Curious. I thought you were going to ask why I wanted to leave in the first place."

"That's plain enough. It's clear to see that you're unhappy."

"I wasn't always." Her voice was wistful, and for a moment he caught a glimpse of the weariness that lay behind her fierce gaze. "You're very observant, Warden. Or perhaps you simply understand unhappiness better than most." She continued as if she already knew he would make no response. "Tell me, what's it like to be free? To go where you wish and do as you please? To chart your own course, free of whatever stories they tell about you?"

"They tell plenty of stories about me, Princess."

"Yes, I know." Ravenna smiled for the first time since the night he first encountered her, but it was a sad smile. "I've heard them all. I'm familiar with each of your titles. The people have names for me as well. Perhaps you've heard them. Do you know what they call me?"

She waited expectantly for a response, and this time he

felt compelled to answer. "Nothing that I would give any credence to."

Ravenna's smile vanished in an instant, and her eyes widened in a show of surprise. When she spoke again, her tone was so soft that it sent a shiver running the length of his spine. "I think you're rather kinder than you let on, Warden Berengar."

"You're wrong, you know. You're free to be anyone you choose."

"If only that were true." Her expression hardened once again. "How old were you when you were married?"

The question caught him off guard, so much so that he surprised himself by answering it. "Sixteen."

"I was younger than that when my father told me I was to be married off. I had never met the suitor. All that mattered was that the match would establish a valuable trading alliance for Munster. I did not want to go, but my father told me it was my duty to the realm. Munster's great king put me on a ship the next day. There was no choice."

"It must have been hard for you, leaving home so young." It was clear now why Ravenna spoke without trembling. The princess was someone who had endured life's cruelties and emerged stronger for them, like tempered steel. It was a trait they shared.

"I prayed every day and night to return. Eventually, my prayers were granted. My husband fell ill and died, and I was returned to Munster. Only the people believed he'd died because I was cursed, and that my brother's death was also my fault. They called me the 'Tainted Princess.' The rumors spread, as such tales are wont to do. No more suitors came for the cursed beauty of Munster. My father blamed me. He said it was because I was too independent, too headstrong."

Neither spoke for some time. They lingered in silence

on either side of the corpse, and he realized Ravenna was grieving in her own way. "Whatever his faults, your father loved you, Princess."

She regarded him with a puzzled expression.

"I found a piece of parchment hidden away in his cloak—something he didn't want his killer finding. He asked me to protect his daughter with my life, and that's exactly what I intend to do."

He expected the words to comfort her. Instead, Ravenna looked as if she'd been struck. Her face grew white and her bottom lip quivered ever so slightly. Berengar decided to leave the princess to her grief.

He stopped just short of the doorway. "One final question, if you'll permit me. Who was it who closed the king's eyes?"

Ravenna bowed her head and looked once more upon her father. "I did."

Berengar had a hard time believing most princesses would readily approach a fresh corpse. Then again, he was starting to suspect Ravenna was no ordinary princess.

"Warden Berengar," she called out to him before he left the room. "Whoever killed my father—if you catch them, what will you do?"

"Only what I must."

He left her as he found her.

They buried the king before the last light faded. Berengar watched the funeral procession from a secluded spot above the city, Faolán at his side. Crowds of onlookers packed the streets, undaunted by the icy northern winds in their hope of catching a glimpse of the king. The guards held the crowds back, away from the main road that ran from the city gate to the castle.

Berengar couldn't help wondering if the king's assassin was somewhere among the sea of faces.

Monks in simple brown robes carried the king's body, which was flanked on either side by brilliant golden banners bearing the sigil of his house. A priest in white walked ahead of the others, holding a processional cross. Two more priests followed at his heels, carrying lanterns meant to guide the king's spirit home—a tradition that endured from the old ways, before worship of the Lord of Hosts began to replace fealty to the elder gods.

Composed and resolute, Queen Alannah and Princess Ravenna walked behind the king's body. The king's thane and royal adviser followed a short distance away, alongside three men in iron crowns who were undoubtedly *Rí Tuaithe*. To Berengar's surprise, the king's court magician was not among their number.

The procession marched through the city, allowing the people a final farewell to their king before starting up the castle stair on the way to Mór's final resting place in the royal crypts. As the procession went by, Berengar looked on the king one last time, caught up in memories of days long past. Much had changed since then, but his debt remained.

I will find who did this to you, the warden promised Mór. *You will have justice.*

He would start by hunting down the king's cupbearer, but first he would have to send a message to the High Queen, letting her know all that had transpired. The death of a king was no small matter, especially if Mór's fears of a deeper conspiracy were true. News of the king's death would ignite a wave of chaos that if left unchecked could spread beyond Munster's borders and threaten the hard-won peace that had existed since the end of the Shadow Wars. That wasn't going to happen on his watch.

As Berengar turned away, he noticed someone else

standing apart from the crowd—a petite figure concealed by a gray cloak. Bushy brown curls poked out of a hood meant to hide her face, but despite the distance, he recognized her almost instantly.

Morwen didn't seem to notice him watching. She had eyes only for the king. Her shoulders heaved violently as the procession went by, and her whole body began to shake. When the king's body disappeared beyond the wall, she sank to her knees. Though it was too far away to see her tears, he knew she was crying.

Berengar forced himself to look away. "Come, Faolán."

Some things could not be fixed with an axe.

CHAPTER FIVE

HE STILL SAW the bear in his dreams. Its bloodstained maw opened to let out a ferocious roar, revealing a set of monstrous fangs inches from his face. Its black fur bristled at his touch, damp from the falling snowflakes. He caught a glimpse of its claws and the vision in his right eye went dark, accompanied by searing pain. They toppled backward together off the rock and landed in the snow. He felt its hot breath on his face just before he drove the dagger into its heart.

He skinned the bear, its corpse still warm, and wore its fur to keep from freezing as he wandered through the forest. Somehow he made it to the village before collapsing into the snow from exhaustion. He felt someone standing over him, and before his eye fluttered shut, he heard a voice.

"Esben?"

The warden woke and reached for his eye patch. The first morning light stole like a thief into his room. An actual thief would have had a far more difficult time of it, as Faolán lay guarding the door, already awake. Berengar sat up and looked around the unfamiliar room furnished for his time in Cashel. The well-appointed chamber was a far cry from the Spartan living conditions he was accustomed to. In truth, he would have preferred a room at an inn or tavern, but at least with a room in the castle he could keep a closer eye on the royal family and their court. He did, however, appreciate the bed, as it was hard to find a cot or bed on the road that could accommodate his size.

Berengar climbed out of bed and approached his belongings. He hadn't come to Munster to sleep—not that he ever slept all that well anyway. The dreams wouldn't allow it. Sometimes they were of the bear. Very rarely he saw his wife waiting for him on the other side, but more often than not, his dreams were haunted by the faces of the men he'd killed, a number that had grown beyond his reckoning. Even after so much time had passed, the memories weren't easy, but he supposed that was rather the point. That the deaths still weighed on his conscience at all was a sign that something of his soul remained, mangled though it was.

Berengar fastened his leather armor over the white undershirt he'd slept in and pulled on his boots. Then he reached for the weapons in the corner of the room and secured them one by one. Faolán growled and looked back at him with an annoyed expression, as if impatient to begin the day, and the warden swung the bear cloak over his shoulders and started toward the door.

"Time to get to work. We have much to do today."

Faolán wagged her tail enthusiastically at the prospect.

Though a significant number of leads had already presented themselves, Berengar knew exactly where to begin. It was no accident the king's cupbearer had disappeared not long after Mór was poisoned. If anyone had the answers he was looking for, it was Matthias. For the moment, everything else would have to wait.

Berengar wasted no time locating Corrin, whom he found outside the castle, listening to a report from two of his guards at the wall.

"Any luck locating the cupbearer?"

Corrin shook his head. "Not yet."

"He's probably lying low—waiting for things to calm down before he tries to secure passage out of the city."

"Rest assured, the guards will find him if he shows his face."

"I don't plan on waiting for the trail to grow cold, Corrin. What can you tell me about him?"

"Matthias is young—about seventeen, I'd wager. Quiet. Keeps to himself. From all accounts he's known to be a decent lad, which was why this business is so surprising. His father was a soldier who died in King Mór's service fighting the Danes, and I believe the king took Matthias on for that reason. The boy isn't particularly bright, if you catch my meaning. It's unlikely he would have secured the position based on merit alone."

Based on what he'd learned so far, Berengar already believed the king's assassin wasn't working alone, and Corrin's words only bolstered that suspicion. "Where does he live?"

"His home is in the Fisherman's District. We have guards watching it at all hours. I gather you want to take a look around for yourself?"

"Aye."

"I can send some guards to accompany you, if you'd like." Corrin motioned to a group of soldiers across the yard. He started to call to them, but Berengar held up a hand in protest.

"No. If he's in hiding, the sight of more guards would

only scare him away. I'll have better luck alone." Faolán's nose was easily worth a company of guards.

Berengar bid farewell to Corrin and made his way down the castle stair on foot. The morning sun glowed brightly overhead, warming the summer air. The city below was already brimming with life. People rushed about their business, filling the streets with a flurry of activity. Although there was still a somber mood in the city, the sight was a stark reminder that life went on, much as it always had, even in times of tragedy.

When he reached the bottom of the stair, Berengar put up his hood to conceal himself and stepped into the crowd. He stopped only once to ask for directions to the Fisherman's District from a vendor who didn't even bother glancing up at him. Few paid him any attention, including the guards. In a city the size of Cashel, it was impossible to notice everyone at once.

Faolán stopped suddenly, and Berengar followed her gaze to a place where someone in a gray cloak was watching him from among the crowd. Before he could get a better look, a farmer on the way to the market went by with his herd, obstructing the warden's view. By the time they passed, the figure was gone. Berengar lingered a moment longer and went on his way.

The Fisherman's District was in a poorer area of the city. Since Matthias came from the nobility of the sword, it came as a bit of a surprise that he would live in such a place unless his nobility was in name only. Berengar understood that all too well. He came from a family of lesser nobility that had lost all its wealth and resources by the time of his father. For a lesser noble, to lose one's land was to no longer be a noble, though the custom was different in the south.

He decided against starting at the cupbearer's home.

Matthias was unlikely to return there while it was being watched. Instead he set out to explore the neighborhood, asking locals what they knew of the young man. Most knew next to nothing, but a few said they had seen him in one of the local taverns on more than one occasion. The crowd thinned as he made his way to the tavern, which proved easy enough to find. Berengar entered with Faolán in tow, and the tavern's proprietor gave them an unpleasant look.

"I'll have to ask you to remove your animal," the man said from behind the counter. "We might not have all the amenities of those self-inflated braggarts up-city, but this is still a proper place of business."

Faolán snarled at the insult, causing the proprietor to whiten a shade, but Berengar calmly laid a pouch full of coins on the counter. "For your trouble. I promise we won't be long."

The man's gaze flickered over to the pouch, no doubt estimating the worth of its contents. "Very well. I suppose I could make an exception—just this once. Now what's this about? I'm guessing a man of your means didn't come here just for a drink."

Berengar fought back a grin. One of the advantages of being in the High Queen's service was that he was rarely short of funds. "I'm looking for Matthias. I understand he comes in here fairly regularly."

The proprietor looked troubled by the mention of Matthias. "He's not in trouble, is he? You aren't the first one to come looking for him. A band of guards was in here this morning."

"Relax. I just want to have a talk with him. He must be a good customer to warrant such concern."

At that, the man let out a hearty laugh. "Matthias isn't

a patron, sir. The lad works here, and a right good job he does too."

"He works here?" Berengar repeated, surprised. It was hard to imagine the cupbearer to the king scrubbing floors in such an establishment.

"Aye, whenever he can, usually in the evenings. His mother's been ill—very ill—for a while now, you see, and from what the lad tells me he's had a hard time of it trying to pay for medicine."

Interesting. Berengar wondered if anyone in the castle was aware Matthias had taken another job. "Had you noticed a difference in him recently? Maybe he'd been up to something unusual?"

The proprietor scratched his beard and seemed to think a moment before nodding. "There were a few times when he went out to meet with a strange man. Every time he came back, he was upset, but he never spoke about it."

"This man—can you describe him?"

"I'm afraid not. I never saw much of him, but I can tell you where they met. It wasn't far from here, just down the road across from the pavilion."

"Thanks." When Berengar looked away, he noticed Faolán staring at the door, her ears perked up. He turned back to the proprietor and lowered his voice. "Is there a back entrance?"

The proprietor looked at him quizzically but ushered them through the back door. Once outside, Berengar gripped the handle of his axe and quietly circled the tavern, where a familiar figure in a gray cloak was pressed up against the door, trying to listen in. Berengar grabbed the figure from behind and her hood slipped off, revealing the face of Munster's court magician.

"You." He released his hold on the girl. "What are you

doing here?" She must have followed him from the castle without being seen, an impressive accomplishment that only made him angrier. "I thought I told you to keep out of this."

Morwen didn't look intimidated in the least. "If you think I'm going to sit on my hands in the castle while you hunt for the king's killer alone, you've got another think coming. I—"

At that moment, Berengar glimpsed movement down the road, and he held up a finger to silence her. He nodded at the spot where an adolescent in nondescript clothes emerged from an alleyway and checked to make sure he was alone.

"That's Matthias," Morwen whispered. "What's he—"

"Look." A second man approached Matthias. Berengar recognized him immediately. It was the captain of the déisi —the same man who escaped after attempting to kill Morwen. What was he doing in Cashel? "Move, or they'll see us."

Morwen raised her staff and ran a hand over the purple runestone fixed near its head. The rune glowed as the magician's hand passed over it, and the letters of one of the charms etched into the staff glowed with purple light.

Matthias began to speak, but the déisi looked back suspiciously, and his gaze fell directly on them. Berengar flinched and started to move, but Morwen seized his arm and shook her head. The déisi stared right past them and returned his attention to Matthias.

"I've cast a spell of lesser concealment. They can't see us."

Berengar made no attempt at a response. He was too busy listening to the exchange.

"Where have you been?" he heard Matthias demand.

"I've been waiting for hours." The words were angry, but his tone was afraid.

The déisi ignored the question. "Are you certain you weren't followed?"

"Yes, but it's only a matter of time before the guards find me. The king is dead! You told me it was a potion of forgetfulness. You said no one would ever know."

A guard walked down the street, whistling a lively tune, and both men fell quiet until he was out of sight.

The déisi's voice was a low hiss. "You knew what this was when you accepted my offer. Or have you already forgotten about your poor mother?"

"I did what you asked. I want what was promised me."

"Don't worry. You will receive your reward." As the déisi handed Matthias a silver medallion, the warden saw his hand grasp the hilt of his blade. Matthias, his attention focused on the medallion, failed to notice.

He's going to kill him, Berengar realized. "Stop!" He threw himself forward, breaking the illusion, and the déisi met his gaze. There was no time to reach for his axe, so Berengar reached instead for the short sword sheathed at his side, but he was already too late. The déisi drew his blade and cut the cupbearer's throat in one clean sweep. Blood spurted everywhere, and Matthias crumpled to the ground, his fingers twitching as he held the medallion. He was dead before Berengar reached them.

The déisi captain raised his cruel-looking curved blade and swung it at Berengar. The pair exchanged precisely three blows. The déisi successfully parried his first two strikes, but on the third, Berengar felt his sword cut through skin. The déisi stumbled past him, his side dripping with blood. Hatred etched itself across his face, and he fled, still clutching his sword.

"After him!" Berengar tore down the street in pursuit with Faolán and Morwen close behind.

Berengar chased the killer from the Fisherman's District with neither showing any sign of slowing down. Despite his wound, the déisi ran like the wind was at his back, leaving a trail of blood in his wake. Bystanders grew more numerous as they crossed into a more affluent area of the city, and several people cried out when they saw the unsheathed swords. The déisi glanced over his shoulder and when he saw Berengar gaining on him, he shoved a spectator out of his way and joined the masses.

Berengar swore and slowed his pace, trying to spot his target among the crowd. Faolán came bounding up beside him, but Morwen seemed to have disappeared. *I should have known it would be too much for her to keep up.* "We can't lose him, Faolán."

The wolfhound sniffed the ground where a drop of the killer's blood had fallen, and her tail straightened instantly as she pointed in the direction of the trail. She ran following the scent, and Berengar went after her, pushing his way through the crowd.

There, he thought, spotting a figure ahead. The déisi darted into an alleyway, just out of reach. Seconds before the man would have reached the end of the alley, someone thrust a boot in his path. The killer tripped and crashed to the ground, losing his grip on his sword. Morwen stood over him triumphantly, a devious gleam in her eyes.

"I took a shortcut," she said to Berengar, who looked at her with astonishment. "I told you I knew this city better than you." Before the déisi could regain his footing, she tossed a blue powder in his face.

"What have you done, witch?" The man stumbled around blindly until Faolán jumped onto his back and pinned him to the ground.

"Firstly, I'm a magician, not a witch," Morwen explained. "Secondly, that particular mixture helps me hone my senses. On an ordinary human…well, I'd guess you're feeling more than a little disoriented right about now. Don't worry—the effects are temporary. But I'd say that's the least of your concerns at the moment."

"That's an understatement." Berengar grabbed the déisi and shoved him against the wall. The killer struggled to free himself to no avail. "Talk! Who gave the order to kill the cupbearer? Who wanted Morwen dead at Cill Airne?"

"I'm not telling you spit."

"I think you'll find I can be very persuasive when given cause." Berengar shattered his nose. "I'm going to enjoy smashing your face against this wall until you change your mind."

"You have no idea what forces you're meddling with, Warden. Munster will fall, and there's nothing you can—"

Berengar hit him again, and the man's knees went wobbly. "Don't go fainting on me." He held the man up. "We're just getting started."

Morwen cleared her throat. "Or we could take him back to my tower and I could administer a truth serum. He'll tell us everything he knows then, though I can't promise he won't lose his mind first…"

"Wait!" the déisi protested. "No more magic, please."

"Then tell us what we want to know," Berengar said.

The killer's expression wavered. "You don't understand. They'll kill me if—"

His words were cut short. An arrow struck him in the chest, and he slumped forward, dead, a trickle of blood running from his mouth. Berengar spun around, looking in the direction from which the arrow was fired. His gaze fell on the roof of a neighboring building, the only place from which an archer could have pulled off the shot.

The spot was empty.

That's impossible. No one could move that fast. He unleashed a profanity-laced tirade that caused Morwen to blush and examined the déisi's body, failing to find anything that might be of use.

"We *had* him. We were so close." Morwen's brow narrowed in anger, and when Berengar looked at her, he recognized something in her face and realized at once why she had seemed so familiar when they first met.

Suddenly, the cryptic nature of Morwen's relationship with the king made sense. So did the Mór's motivation for wanting her rescued from the monastery in the first place, and the reason why Morwen was so desperate to avenge the king's death. Berengar could have slapped himself for missing it before. The truth had been staring back at him from the beginning. It was even there in her name —*Morwen*.

"King Mór was your father, wasn't he?"

B erengar had little time to discuss matters further with Morwen before the castle guards appeared and found them with the killer's body, after which he was immediately summoned to the castle to report to the queen. A very different scene greeted him inside the throne room than the one he'd encountered when he first arrived at the Rock of Cashel. Queen Alannah was seated upon her husband's throne, wearing his crown. Although still adorned in mourning black, her face was no longer hidden behind a veil. There was no joy in her expression, not that he expected to find it.

Thane Ronan stood at her right hand, keeping a

watchful gaze over the chamber. From the way he wore his sword, Berengar guessed Ronan was a warrior. Thanes came from all walks of life—some were wizened old men or powerful nobles. It wasn't uncommon for thanes to be selected from the military ranks, especially for the purpose of maintaining order. Perhaps the most famous thane, Thane Ramsay of Connacht, was a great sorcerer known across Fál in the years before the fall of King Áed and the Shadow Wars.

The transformation in the throne room was startling. The blood that once stained the floor was gone, erased as if it had never existed—as were all signs of the king's death. With King Mór's corpse removed, the members of court once again occupied the room, and in great numbers. Judging from appearances, they were mostly nobles, although an impressive number of sentries were stationed inside, including two guards positioned between the crowd and the dais.

A hush spread across the throne room as the warden entered, and all eyes fell on him. Berengar suspected many had already heard the rumors of his presence at the capital, but this was the first occasion on which he had formally appeared in public since answering King Mór's summons. A series of shocked gasps and murmurs ran through the court, no doubt speculation as to why one of the High Queen's wardens had appeared so soon after the death of Munster's king.

The crowd shrank away from him, clearing a path forward as he approached the throne. Berengar stopped a respectful distance from the two guards and waited for the herald to announce him. Marcus O'Reilly, standing to the queen's left, leaned forward and whispered something into Alannah's ear.

"That will be all, Marcus." She waved the royal adviser

away, and her attention fell on Berengar. "From what I hear, it appears you've had an interesting morning." She held up a hand before he could respond. "Not here. Let us speak in private."

"As you wish." Berengar remained mindful of the interest of the members of court.

She led him into an adjoining room, a somber chamber carved entirely from limestone. Based on appearances, it was probably where the royal council met to discuss matters of importance to the realm. Large maps of Munster and the other kingdoms of Fál hung from the walls. Golden sunlight filtered in from a wide balcony that overlooked the city, shining on the smooth surface of a long alderwood table that was fixed in place, unlike the moveable trestle tables in the great hall.

Berengar waited for the queen to speak. He had been hoping for another chance to converse with Alannah, as their previous interaction in the great hall had been far too limited to ask her any meaningful questions.

The queen didn't waste another moment. "I apologize for leaving you so abruptly yesterday. Now that the burden of the crown has fallen to me, there are many demands on my time. It seems you've been equally busy. Laird O'Reilly tells me Matthias is dead. I take it he was the one who poisoned my husband?"

Berengar briefly recounted the bloody events that had transpired in the city. "Matthias might have added the poison to the king's goblet, but he was not acting alone. Someone else was pulling his strings—the same person who paid the déisi to attempt to murder Lady Morwen. We pursued Matthias' killer, but he fell victim to an assassin's arrow before he could tell us what he knew."

The queen's expression briefly betrayed her surprise, but she quickly recovered. "If the déisi were involved, this is the first I've heard of it." Her eyes narrowed at him suspiciously. "What exactly did my husband tell you before he sent you to Cill Airne?"

For the first time, it occurred to Berengar that King Mór might not have shared everything with his wife. Was it because he hadn't trusted her with the information? Perhaps Alannah was testing his loyalty. Berengar grimaced uncomfortably. These types of situations were exactly why he tried to avoid becoming entangled in royal affairs.

"King Mór believed the realm was threatened by unseen forces. He sent Morwen to the monastery at Innisfallen to see if magic was involved."

"I should have known. My husband had a preoccupation with magic, Warden Berengar. After the horrors he witnessed in the Shadow Wars, he was determined that Munster should never again come under magical threat. He spent a small fortune educating our court magician for that very reason, and he forged a peace with the Witches of the Golden Vale. It was never enough. Mór came to believe he was cursed…"

"Laird O'Reilly told me as much. He said there were rumors that a crone dwelling in the Devil's Bit had placed a curse on the king's family that resulted in the death of your son."

The queen paled, and her cheeks tightened with restrained anger. "I do not share my husband's fondness for magic. Let us leave it at that. My husband's murderers are flesh and blood, I assure you." She sighed, and her anger faded as quickly as it had appeared.

It must be tiring, Berengar thought, *having to project strength while in such pain.*

"I loved my husband. I grieve for him, but life

continues whether I will it or not. It is my responsibility to keep Munster safe—to keep my family safe."

"I didn't see Princess Ravenna in the throne room."

"My daughter has little use for life at court. Ravenna prefers to come and go as she pleases. She has her father's spirit, which caused Mór no little frustration."

"I gathered as much from the conversation I had with her. She suggested they had a troubled history."

"My daughter has had a difficult life." Alannah's voice was full of regret. "She was very different when she was younger. A happier child you've never seen. So full of life…" A wistful smile briefly graced the queen's face. "She and her brother were always going off on one grand adventure or another." Alannah looked away, as if overcome. "I don't think she ever forgave us for sending her away. Mór said it was a good match, and I supported the decision. I didn't believe the stories about her husband until…" She trailed off and fell silent for a time. "But I forget, you're a warden, not a priest."

"You were closer to King Mór than anyone. Is there anything he might have said that could point me in the direction of his killer?"

"My husband was a man who kept secrets. Sometimes I wonder if I ever really knew him at all. Follow the web of secrets, Warden Berengar. That will lead you to the truth. I'm sure of it. Now if you'll excuse me, I'd like to be alone for a moment before I return to court."

"Your Grace."

A messenger was waiting for him outside. "I've a letter for you, sir."

Find me in the tower, said the letter, which bore Morwen's name. *Come at once.*

. . .

It was a long climb to reach the magician's chambers. Berengar made his way up a winding stone staircase with only Faolán for company. Finally he came to a lonely door he assumed was near the tower's peak. Far above the rest of the castle, the spot was an ideal place for a practitioner of magic to study and work spells free of distraction or interference. Berengar raised his hand and rapped loudly on the door, which swung open of its own accord.

If Morwen was different in many respects from the typical magician, the room visible from the doorway appeared more in keeping with the traditional image he pictured in his mind. There were books, scrolls, and stacks of parchment everywhere—crammed on shelves, topping tables, and heaped in corners. Vials of powders and potions of all manner of colors were arranged in rows in cupboards full of herbs and various alchemical ingredients. Candles burned throughout the room, despite ample natural sunlight entering from the window.

Berengar sniffed the air when he crossed the threshold, and the scent of sulfur tickled his nostrils. Most of the space was devoted to the magician's laboratory. He glanced at an open spell book on a desk as he passed, before noticing the living quarters. A small bed stood in a cramped area of the room beside the window, where Morwen's staff rested beside a pile of runestones of different colors.

"Over here," a familiar voice said from the other side of the room, and Berengar noticed Morwen hunched over her alchemy workbench, her back to him. She was dressed once more in her blue magician's robes; the gray cloak and nondescript disguise she'd worn earlier hung on the wall.

Faolán dashed forward to meet her, and Morwen turned around and scratched the wolfhound behind her ears. "Hello again, little wolf." Faolán let out a contented yelp.

Morwen wore a strange lens over her right eye that seemed to magnify everything on the other side. Behind her, steam rose from the king's goblet, which sat over a fire on the workbench. The steam coursed through a peculiar set of glassware before distilling a dark substance into a flask.

"It is true." He looked her over. "You're the king's bastard daughter."

Morwen's mouth turned downward in a frown at the word *bastard*. Berengar was from the far reaches of the north, where illegitimacy carried far less weight. Things were different in Munster, even for a royal bastard.

"King Mór was my father, yes," she replied hesitantly, as if waiting for him to level an insult at her. When he did not, her face acquired a more quizzical expression. "How long have you known?"

"I've only just figured it out." The physical similarities she shared with Mór were unmistakable. "Does the queen know?"

Morwen shook her head. "I'm not sure, although I believe Princess Ravenna suspects the truth."

Ravenna. Berengar remembered her wounded reaction when he told her of the message Mór left, requesting that Berengar protect his daughter with his life. It suddenly struck him that Mór might have meant Morwen instead of his legitimate heir, and he felt a swell of pity for the princess.

"And your mother?"

Morwen shrugged. "He never told me her name, only that she'd died. I was brought to the castle to be raised from a very young age. King Mór introduced me to court after my magical abilities were discovered."

"You loved him. I can see it in you."

"He was a good father, even if he couldn't be so publically. I wanted for nothing. King Mór saw to it that I had the best tutors his gold could buy." She removed the lens and set it on the table before wiping her eyes. "Now do you see why I won't rest until I find the person who did this to him?"

"I do." Berengar understood the thirst for vengeance better than most.

Morwen started to speak but stopped short, as if overtaken by a new thought. "The message hidden in the king's cloak—it mentioned a debt you owed my father. What did he mean by that?"

"He saved my life once, during the war. When we were both much younger men." Even as he spoke, he saw the battle in his mind's eye. The horrific events of that day would never leave him. "The battle was lost. My forces were surrounded at the River Shannon. I was pushed back to the water's edge, two arrows in me, watching as my men fell one by one. Then the Poet Prince arrived. I saw his forces break through the enemy ranks just before the water took me. I would have drowned that day, but Mór cut a path to the river and pulled me from the water himself."

"Then let me help you," Morwen insisted. "We have a better chance at finding justice for my father if we work together."

Berengar weighed her request. "I can see you have your father's stubbornness. Very well, but remember—if we do this together, we do it my way. Understand?"

"Of course," Morwen answered with a grin.

"Good. It's just a shame we came up with nothing earlier. I would have liked to hear what that mercenary had to say under the influence of your truth serum."

Morwen laughed. "You don't actually think I have any

truth serum on hand, do you? It's a devil to make, and it costs a fortune. I was just trying to get him talking. People are more afraid of magic than you'd think." She reached into her robes. "Besides, I wouldn't exactly say we came up with nothing." Morwen produced the silver medallion given to Matthias by his killer. "Don't touch it. It was made to look like a healing medallion, but it's actually enchanted with a paralysis curse triggered by contact with the skin."

"The déisi was wearing gloves, so he wasn't affected," Berengar realized aloud.

"That's right, and there's only one place in Munster where he could have obtained something like this—from the Witches of the Golden Vale."

"It's time someone paid that coven a visit."

The fire under the king's goblet went out without warning, and the last of the distillate dripped from the glassware into the flask. "Not just yet." Morwen turned back to her project. "There's another reason I asked you here. I've almost identified the poison used to assassinate the king." She strained and filtered the distillate into several components in different bowls. "Hand me that book, will you?" She pointed out a book on one of the shelves without bothering to glance up from her work.

Berengar retrieved the book—a particularly heavy volume titled *A Treatise on Poisons*—and passed it to Morwen, who placed the book on her workbench and began flipping through the pages. Berengar, who loomed behind the magician, watching her work, observed several illustrations of nasty-looking poisons and their various effects.

"Here it is." Morwen showed him a particular entry with no small amount of pride. "The Demon's Whisper. As I suspected, the recipe calls for a lock of the victim's hair. The poison has no cure. The king was a dead man the moment he drank from the goblet. This is a very difficult poison to make—even I probably couldn't pull it off. A number of the ingredients, including the *Mitragyna* leaf and the *Amanitas* mushroom—more commonly called the Death Cap—are very rare in Fál."

"What does that tell us?" Berengar struggled to follow the alchemy jargon.

Morwen's smile widened. "There are only a few places these ingredients could be acquired, meaning whoever manufactured the poison has to have left a trail for us to follow." The magician slammed the book shut and crossed the room to retrieve her staff and gray cloak. Then she walked toward the door, stopping only to cast a glance back in his direction. "What are you waiting for? We have work to do."

Berengar shook his head and started after her.

CHAPTER SIX

THOUGH A LONER BY NATURE, the warden was accustomed to working with others when circumstances dictated he do so. Nevertheless, in all his years he had never been led around by a girl no older than fifteen—much less one who happened to be a magician. Life was not without a sense of humor, it seemed. Berengar wiped a bead of sweat away and followed Morwen into an upscale district, trying his best to avoid those in his path. It was a hot summer day, and the air had only grown warmer since he chased the déisi through the streets that morning.

According to Morwen, there were only three vendors in the city that sold both *Mitragyna* and *Amanitas*. A few sold one or the other. It was highly likely that whoever supplied the déisi with the poison had stopped in at one or more of these shops. Their first visit was to an herbalist, a kindly old woman with an obvious respect for Morwen. No one had purchased either ingredient recently, and there was no sign that either had been stolen. Next they stopped by a peddler of rare potions who had been sold out of both ingredients for months without replenishing his stocks.

With their first two visits largely dead ends, they were on their way to the final place on Morwen's list when Berengar heard a commotion coming from one of the nearby businesses, where a pair of men were harassing a goblin smith at his forge.

A hateful-looking man sneered as he turned over a hammer in his hands. "Look at this garbage. You call this decent craftsmanship?"

"Your kind don't belong in our city," said the man's companion, who was missing several teeth. He looked back to see the small crowd of observers that had formed. "We should have exterminated your filth after the war."

Several onlookers cheered as the first man turned over the smith's display rack while his companion held the goblin back. Others looked embarrassed, though none uttered a word of protest. Suddenly, the goblin let out a hiss and sank his file-point teeth into his oppressor's hand, but the first man knocked him to the ground.

The injured man swore and looked down at his bleeding hand. "Hold him." He unsheathed an iron dagger.

The goblin attempted to scurry away, but he wasn't fast enough, and the first man forcibly restrained him. He hissed as the man with the dagger approached.

"I wouldn't do that if I were you." Berengar stepped forward and drew their attention.

The man stopped dead in his tracks at the sight of the warden. "This doesn't concern you."

Berengar didn't bother reaching for a weapon. His hand shot out and snapped the man's wrist, and the dagger fell away. He punched the man in the jaw once for good measure, causing him to spit out even more teeth. "You have exactly three seconds to get out of here before I reach for my axe."

The first man released his hold on the goblin, who landed in the dirt as the pair sprinted away.

"That goes for the rest of you as well," Berengar said to the crowd, which quickly dispersed. He reached down and helped the goblin to his feet.

The goblin brushed himself off. "Thank you for your kindness. I am in your debt, human." When he started to reach for the overturned display rack, Berengar grabbed his arm.

"Those men would have killed you. You should keep your head down for a while. The city isn't safe." He walked away without another word.

Morwen was waiting nearby, wearing a bemused expression. "I knew it. I was right about you."

"Right about what?" Berengar was unsure if she was making fun of him. He hadn't liked the idea of being teased when they were on the road from Cill Airne, and he hadn't warmed to it since then.

"You could have gone about your business, but you chose to help that goblin—a nonhuman, I might add. I think you're more than you pretend to be, Warden Berengar."

"I don't like bullies, that's all. Besides, aren't you the one who told me I carry great anger inside?" he reminded her as they continued on their way.

"Aye, but now I wonder if perhaps you use your anger as something to hide behind."

He glared at her. "You don't know me. You've heard the stories and decided out of some misplaced romanticism to believe only the heroic ones. But I'm not the man from those stories. Don't believe something just because you want it to be true, magician. You'll only be disappointed."

Morwen acted as if she hadn't heard him. "Here we are. I have a feeling our luck is about to take a turn for the better." She pointed out a sign that hung in front of the alchemist's store. "Keep up." She headed for the door, and Berengar wondered if she was goading him for sport.

It was an impressive shop, especially compared to the two previous establishments they'd visited. There were even more shelves and cupboards than he remembered seeing in Morwen's laboratory, and all were stocked with expensive-looking potions, powders, and herbs. Berengar didn't know much about alchemy, but from the volume and quality of the selection he saw, he guessed the owner was able to charge a hefty fee for all transactions.

A bespectacled man in fine robes looked up at their approach. His brow furrowed when his gaze fell on Morwen.

"Greetings, Delvin," the magician said in a friendly tone. "You're just the man I was looking for."

"Lady Morwen?" He was clearly surprised to see her. "I almost didn't recognize you in those clothes. It's good to see you again. I hadn't heard that you'd returned to Cashel."

"That would be a surprise." She paused for what Berengar assumed was dramatic effect. "As my departure was a closely-held secret. Curious that you should be aware of it."

Delvin swallowed nervously. "I must have heard a rumor from one of my customers."

"It's funny you should say that, because I was hoping to speak with you about one of those customers. You wouldn't happen to have sold any *Mitragyna* or *Amanitas* recently, would you?"

Delvin backed away and nearly collided with the wall. "I don't know anything about that."

Morwen's customary smile faded, and she took a step forward. "In that case, I'm sure you won't mind if we take a look at your stock—seeing as how King Mór was poisoned with the Demon's Whisper."

At that, the alchemist attempted to flee, but Berengar grabbed him and held him in place.

"Please, Lady Morwen…"

"Don't worry, Delvin—I'm not going to hurt you. I'm not fond of violence. My friend the warden, on the other hand…"

Delvin's eyes darted over to Berengar, and he began to shake. "Which warden?"

Morwen laughed. "Which one do you think? I think the eye patch and the scars rather give it away."

"Who bought those ingredients?" Berengar demanded. "Tell us, or I'll use your face to sharpen my axe."

"A goblin merchant from Limerick. He's the one you're looking for. The scum probably crafted the poison."

Berengar started to relinquish his hold, but Morwen shook her head. "It's never wise to hide the truth from a magician, Delvin. We can always tell when you're lying."

Berengar didn't wait for a response before slamming Delvin into a row of shelves, causing numerous vials of ingredients to shatter as they spilled onto the floor. "Last chance. Or they'll be picking pieces of you off the floor."

"Fine. I'll tell you what you want to know. Just don't hurt me." Berengar released him, and the alchemist fell to the floor in a disheveled heap. "The *Mitragyna* and *Amanitas* were purchased through an intermediate by an anonymous third party. I had no idea what they were planning, you have to believe me!"

"This intermediate," Berengar said. "Who was he, and how can we find him?"

"I don't know his name. He's a man from Leinster. I suspected he was a member of the Brotherhood of Thieves. He has a shaved head and a well-groomed beard...and half his left ear is missing. I don't know where to find him. I was paid handsomely not to ask questions."

"That's not good enough." Berengar slowly reached for his axe.

Delvin held up a hand in desperation. "Wait! Ours wasn't the only transaction he was paid to arrange! There's an auction set to take place tonight in the underground market, and there's every reason to believe he'll be in attendance."

Morwen crouched beside Delvin, and her expression brightened once again. "See, Delvin? I knew you could be reasonable."

Berengar couldn't help being impressed. Despite her age, Morwen's methods had actually proven quite effective. "Any idea where we can find this underground market?" he asked as they left the alchemist's shop.

"Not the slightest, but I know someone who almost certainly does—Marcus O'Reilly."

"The royal adviser?"

"He's cleverer than he lets on. Laird O'Reilly has a network of spies that extends across Munster—perhaps even the whole of Fál. There isn't much that goes on in the city he isn't aware of."

When Berengar thought back to his initial meeting with O'Reilly, he remembered leaving with the distinct impression that although he had been doing the questioning, the old man was the one who was studying him. "The déisi didn't find you by accident. King Mór suspected someone close to him leaked word of your location at Innisfallen. We have to be careful. I've had dealings with the Brotherhood of Thieves before. If the intermediate gets word we're looking for him, he'll flee the city. Can we trust O'Reilly to keep our task a secret?"

Her expression told him the answer was no.

"We have no choice. It will be evening before long."

Together they walked along the road that led to the castle, once again on the assassin's trail.

M orwen's suspicions proved correct. Laird O'Reilly was able to tell them everything they wanted to know and more. The underground market was just that—a market for illicit goods and services hidden underground, somewhere in the maze of tunnels connecting the sewer system. Patrons wore masks so as not to compromise their identities, or else acted through intermediaries. There were said to be a number of entrances, though O'Reilly was only aware of three—one of which Morwen appeared to be familiar with. Although he didn't know the nature of the item to be auctioned off, it was rumored to be exceedingly rare and valuable.

Berengar noted that O'Reilly, who made no attempt to disguise his curiosity about the nature of their interest in the underground market, asked almost as many questions as he provided answers. If they had been conversing with anyone other than a member of the royal court, the warden wouldn't have hesitated to show his displeasure. Fortunately, Morwen proved adept at handling or deflecting each of O'Reilly's inquiries. She was careful not to mention the man from Leinster or why they were searching for him.

Could he have had a hand in King Mór's death? Berengar wondered. Someone so influential and well connected would have had little difficulty securing the poison used to murder the king. As one of the king's confidants, O'Reilly had probably known of Morwen's journey to the monastery, if not the reason why Mór sent her there. Despite it all, Berengar couldn't come up with a reason why O'Reilly might plot against the king. It seemed unlikely the old man would do anything to jeopardize his position when he already wielded more power and influence than almost anyone else in the kingdom. Still, Berengar made a note to look further into the royal adviser when the opportunity presented itself.

"Do you plan on bringing guards?" O'Reilly asked. "If you would allow me to speak with Corrin, I am sure we could arrange—"

Berengar cut him off. "No. It's important that no one learn of this. No one." He emphasized the words to convey he meant it.

Before they departed, O'Reilly added one extra wrinkle to their plan when he warned them that all weapons were barred from the underground market. They would be going alone into unknown circumstances without the company of guards or the protection afforded by the warden's axe. Berengar didn't like leaving his weapons behind, but he wasn't willing to risk their opportunity to find the man from Leinster.

He turned to Morwen when they were out of earshot. "Could you cast another vanishing spell? We could sneak into their gathering and grab the intermediate unseen."

"It's a spell of lesser concealment," she answered with a hint of irritation, "and it doesn't work like that. The rune casts an illusion. Whoever is looking at us sees something else, but only if we remain perfectly still. And before you go asking if I have a potion of invisibility, the answer is no."

Berengar had just removed his short sword when his attention fell on the magician's staff. "Your staff—you'll have to leave it behind. It would be too easy for someone to recognize you if they saw it."

Morwen hesitated, clearly reluctant to part with her staff.

"You can use magic without your staff, right?" He hadn't forgotten the spell she cast that had gone awry when they first encountered the déisi on the road from Cill Airne.

"Of course I can!" Color rose to her cheeks.

The crowds in the city had thinned, and a cool breeze blew gently at their backs. The sun had not yet set by the time they reached their destination, a large, two-story inn named The Troll's Landing. According to local legend, the inn was built over the spot where a troll had been slain during an assault on Cashel centuries ago. Although such stories were often exaggerations, the massive troll skull that hung above the door was real enough.

Inside, the lively inn was packed full of patrons. People shouted to be heard above the music, which coursed through the hall from a band that danced as they played. Several onlookers had gathered around a table near the roaring fireplace where two men were deep in a game of *ficheall*. A variety of banners, shields, and furs adorned the walls, and barrels and sacks were crammed into the corners of the room.

Berengar entered and deftly sidestepped a barmaid with a serving tray, Morwen following close behind. Unlike the tavern he'd visited earlier that day, no one seemed to bat an eye when Faolán entered. Judging by the somewhat seedy quality of the clientele, that didn't surprise him. His gaze swept the busy hall until at last he spotted an inconspicuous back room tucked away in a corner. Berengar drew nearer to get a better look, careful to avoid drawing unwanted attention. Though a parted curtain concealed most of the back room's interior, he caught a glimpse of a man keeping watch on the other side of the threshold.

After a moment, a patron approached from the crowd and stepped through the curtain.

"Password?" demanded the man posted on the other side.

The patron muttered a response, and Berengar heard something that sounded like the hinges of a door opening. He waited a few minutes longer, but the patron did not return.

"We have a problem. A password is required to gain admittance." Worse, he couldn't force his way inside without raising the alarm.

"The only way we're getting to the auction is through that door. To do that, we need a distraction. I'll keep everyone occupied while you deal with the guard."

"And just how do you plan on doing that?"

Without warning, the hall erupted in a wave of cheers where the game of ficheall had apparently just concluded. One of the players stormed away angrily while his competitor stood and took a bow, basking in the crowd's admiration. A hefty sum of winnings lay heaped on his side of the table.

"Is there truly no one else who wishes to challenge me?" the ficheall player asked with an arrogant smirk.

Morwen's eyes darted to the pouch of coins Berengar carried, and she lowered her voice to a whisper. "How much money did you bring with you?"

"What—" he started to ask before following her gaze to the table. "Have you lost your mind? That auction will be starting any minute and you want to play a game?"

"Trust me, and wait for my signal." With that, she walked off toward the fireplace.

Berengar glanced at the coin pouch again, but it was gone. He swore under his breath and retreated to the safety of the bar.

"I would like a game." Morwen meekly approached the ficheall player.

The man looked at her in surprise and let out a mocking laugh. "Run along, little girl. This is no place for someone like you."

Morwen flashed an innocent smile. "I can pay." She set the pouch of coins down on the table.

Berengar saw greed dance in the man's eyes, and the player's lips spread into a wide grin. "Very well! Never let it be said I refused a challenge." He motioned for her to take a seat. "Gather 'round," he said to the crowd. "Perhaps I'll take it easy on the lass, since she's so young."

I hope she knows what she's doing. Berengar started to order a drink before remembering she had taken his money.

Morwen and her opponent quickly gathered their pieces and organized them on a handsomely carved game board. The magician's pieces were a white bronze color, and those of her opponent were yellow gold. Berengar watched with interest from a distance. He was familiar with the rules of the game, even if he didn't play himself. There was an art to playing a game of ficheall, which required a strategic patience he didn't possess.

Ficheall was a strategy game played on a grid of seven squares by seven. One player's pieces were arranged around a king in the center of the board. These pieces were surrounded by an opponent's pieces, and in order to win the game, the player had to successfully clear the way for the king to reach one of the grid's edges. Their opponent's objective was to capture the enemy's king before this happened. A simple coin toss usually determined who played the role of the defender and who was the aggressor, and in sets of three, the players switched roles with each game.

Morwen's opponent started strong out of the gate,

providing a string of impressive moves for his enthusiastic fans in the crowd. Morwen seemed to struggle with each decision, although she managed a few successful moves that the spectators attributed to luck. For a moment, Berengar thought she was going to lose, but then she seemed to come out of nowhere to capture her opponent's king. The reigning champion was so stunned he couldn't speak.

"That was a good game," Morwen said. "I got lucky, I guess."

"Impossible! Everyone knows it's easier playing the aggressor. You must give me a chance to win back my money."

"Well…" Morwen trailed off and looked at the expectant faces in the crowd. "Double or nothing?"

Her opponent's eyes lit up at the prospect of winning back his money and then some, and they quickly reorganized their pieces.

When the next game started, Morwen dropped the façade of inexperience, and Berengar immediately realized the truth. The first game wasn't a fluke. Morwen wasn't a beginner—she was a master ficheall player. She winked at Berengar, and he rose and started toward the back room. He didn't need to wait to see how this would end.

"Not so fast." The voice belonged to a pot-bellied, middle-aged guard on other side of the curtain. "Do you have the password?"

"Aye. It's written down. I know I have it somewhere on me." As Berengar made a show of searching his pockets, the entire hall burst into thunderous applause. When the guard glanced curiously at the source of the commotion, Berengar knocked him out with a single blow and propped his body on a bench.

"A round of drinks on me," he heard Morwen's voice

ring through the bar, followed by another chorus of cheers. A few moments later, she stole inside the back room, her pockets overflowing with coins. "It looks like you did quite a number on *him*," she said, staring at the guard.

"Ready?" Berengar put on his mask, and Morwen did the same.

"Aye."

Berengar lifted a trapdoor in the floor, revealing a short set of steps leading down. Faolán leapt to the bottom, and Berengar followed after. "Remind me never to play you at ficheall."

"For heaven's sake, Berengar—I'm a magician." Morwen lowered the trapdoor. "If my mind isn't nimble enough to beat some regional champion in a game of ficheall, I don't deserve the title." It was nevertheless obvious from her tone she enjoyed the compliment.

Torchlight illuminated the way down the ladder, casting a soft glow on an abandoned chamber below. At the bottom, there was a man-sized gap between the wall and a rusted iron grate that led into the sewers. Voices echoed somewhere in the darkness beyond. Berengar took a torch from the wall to light their way through the tunnels and squeezed his large frame through the narrow passage. He was forced to duck to avoid hitting his head on the ceiling. Morwen slipped behind him without difficulty.

They followed the winding tunnels for several minutes without encountering a soul. The air was musty and cold. Rats scurried about at their feet. The sewer system was far more extensive than he ever would have guessed. Occasionally the torchlight revealed signs of prior occupation, including more than one wall drawing, and Morwen explained that in times past the tunnels were used to harbor the populace during dragon attacks.

Eventually the voices grew louder, and at last the

tunnel emptied into an enormous underground chamber at the center of the labyrinth. The tunnel they had taken was just one route into the chamber; other paths were faintly visible beside each of the four staircases in the corners of the room. Berengar peered over a rail and spied an impressive gathering of masked and hooded figures below. From the sound of things, an auction was already underway. He looked for any sign of the man from Leinster, without success.

"We need to get closer," he told Morwen.

With most of the room's occupants preoccupied with the auction, the pair descended the stairs without attracting attention. The bidding stopped as they reached the bottom, and a weathered piece of parchment— possibly a map of some kind—changed hands. Berengar lingered at the outskirts of the room, searching for a masked figure with half an ear missing.

A man in a wooden mask stepped forward, and the chamber fell deathly silent. "Our final auction of the evening comes courtesy of our friends in the Brotherhood of Thieves—an item so rare and valuable it had to be kept secret until now. Calum, if you will?" The man snapped his fingers, and a figure in a black cloak and matching mask produced a lidded crate and lifted the lid for all to see.

Berengar immediately noticed that half of Calum's ear was missing. *Now we just have to find a way to get him out of here without being seen.* He considered waiting until the auction had concluded and following Calum through the tunnels, but members of the Brotherhood of Thieves were notoriously difficult to trail. He was in the middle of cobbling together a plan when he felt Morwen tugging at his sleeve.

"If that is what I think it is, we have more pressing concerns."

The crate held a large egg unlike any he'd ever seen. Reptilian scales covered the egg's almost translucent surface, which pulsed with red light in a rhythm frighteningly similar to a heartbeat. "It's just an egg." He only half believed the words. A sinister aura seemed to emanate from the egg, spreading across the room.

"Not just any egg." Morwen remained unable to tear her gaze away from the open crate. "That's a coatl egg."

"Coatl?"

"A winged serpent twice the size of most dragons. They're so rare I've only heard about them in myths and legends. I didn't think they actually existed." Her eyes widened, and for the first time since he had known her, she looked afraid. "A single full-grown coatl could destroy the entire city. We can't let it fall into the wrong hands."

"What do you propose we do? We can't exactly walk up to him and take it."

Morwen flashed a mischievous grin that was becoming all too familiar. "That's exactly what I'm going to do. While everyone else is distracted by the auction, I'm going to steal the egg from right under his nose." She handed Berengar her winnings from the ficheall match. "Just keep bidding."

Berengar started to protest, but Morwen had already vanished into the throng of spectators. It wasn't an easy thing to steal from a member of the Brotherhood of Thieves. No matter how deft and nimble Morwen believed herself to be, the attempt was incredibly dangerous—especially when they had come unarmed. The warden clenched his teeth and stepped forward, feeling frustrated she had left him no choice but to play his part.

The first bid was a sum extravagant enough to outfit a private army. From the way the man who placed it carried himself, Berengar was certain he was a high-ranking noble.

He wondered what faces were hidden underneath those masks, and just how many supposedly model citizens showed their true selves underground where no one could see. Berengar pushed his way to the center of the room and noticed Morwen at the edge of the crowd, sneaking closer to Calum. As other bids came pouring in, he shouted a made-up number he assumed would be difficult to top, hoping the amount was believable given the size of the ficheall winnings. He was outbid before he had even finished speaking, just in time for Morwen—who had stealthily maneuvered her way behind Calum—to quietly reach out and grab the coatl egg.

Calum's hand shot down and grabbed Morwen's wrist in a flash, and she cried out in surprise. When the half-eared man jerked Morwen forward and ripped off her mask, everyone in the chamber went absolutely still.

"You think you can steal from me, girl?" Calum demanded with a cruel laugh.

Berengar inched closer to Morwen. *So much for doing things the easy way.* "Let her go." Every head turned in his direction at once.

Most enemies assumed he was strong—it was his speed that always surprised them. No one ever expected a man his size to move so fast. Calum scarcely had time to open his mouth before the warden's fist connected with his face, knocking the black mask away. In the next instant he drove his knee into Calum's groin as Faolán leapt in to join the fray.

"We're leaving," Berengar told the masked figures, holding Calum by his cloak. He stood back to back with Morwen, surrounded by the crowd.

"I don't think so," said the man in the wooden mask, and guards approached, brandishing swords.

Berengar swore. O'Reilly said there would be no

117

weapons. *If I find out the old man betrayed us, he'll wish he'd never been born.*

Morwen lowered her hood. "Stay back. I am Morwen, Court Magician to the Throne." She stretched her hands out as if to cast a spell, and the guards hesitated. "Gaoth soilse amach!" A gentle breeze rippled through the chamber, but nothing happened. Morwen bit her lip nervously and tried again with the same result. The guards exchanged glances and laughed, emboldened by her failure.

"Do something," Berengar said. When the closest guard attacked, he was forced to release his hold on Calum, who fled in the direction of the tunnels. Berengar caught the guard's sword arm and drove his head into the man's face, allowing him to pull the blade free. He held out the sword, daring the other guards to try him.

"I'm trying." Morwen attempted the same spell with different hand gestures while clutching the egg.

Just before the wave of guards hit, a strong wind rushed through the chamber and all the torches and candles in the room went out at once. Berengar felt Morwen grab his hand, and she guided him through the darkness, avoiding their attackers. Panicked cries sounded behind them as they sprinted toward the tunnels, where faint light glimmered in the distance, and Berengar caught a glimpse of the half-eared man's cloak vanishing around a corner.

"After him, Faolán! We can't let him escape."

The wolfhound took off in pursuit, hot on Calum's scent. She led them through the unfamiliar maze of tunnels, and they followed the sound of her howls. Berengar's boots splashed across the muddy ground, causing rats and other vermin to flee before him. He rounded a corner and emerged into a chamber not unlike the one underneath the inn, where a stair led aboveground. A boarded covering was halfway ajar at the secret entrance, allowing moonlight to steal in from above. Berengar heaved the cover aside and emerged from a stone well that had been boarded over.

Faolán barked loudly, and Berengar saw Calum throw a farmer from his wagon and take the reins. The horses charged down the paved road at Berengar, who stood calmly in the wagon's path. Just before it would have hit him, Faolán leapt onto the wagon and descended on Calum, who jerked the reins in surprise. The wagon overturned, skidding to a stop in the street. Calum crawled out from the wreckage, scraped and bleeding, and Berengar grabbed him by the hair and forced his head back. He trained the blade against the man's neck.

"You're done running," he said as Morwen caught up with them, panting for breath. "I want to know who hired you to arrange the king's assassination."

"Do you have any idea who I am?" Calum demanded. "When the Brotherhood learns of this, they will come for me, and you will—"

Berengar drove his knee into the man's face. He was starting to lose his patience. This was the second time that day he'd been forced to chase someone down on foot, and he was in no mood to play games. "Lie to me again, and I'll start taking pieces of you."

"I don't know anything." Calum spit at the warden's feet for good measure.

Berengar's sword flashed through the moonlight. Blood spurted into the air, followed by a terrible scream, and Calum's amputated hand landed on the ground. Morwen looked at him in horror, no doubt taken aback by the display of violence, but Berengar ignored her. A warden could dispense the queen's justice as he saw fit, and there was little anyone apart from a monarch could do to hold him accountable.

He tightened his grip on the whimpering man. "Start talking, or you won't like what I'll take next."

"The contract was paid in gold." Calum cradled the bloody stump. "I was to provide the ingredients and leave them at a prearranged location before returning to retrieve the finished product. I don't know who prepared the poison."

It must have been an outrageous sum, as the Brotherhood of Thieves rarely engaged in such activities. Assassinations were risky propositions at best, and often drew the sort of scrutiny the organization preferred to avoid. If Calum had possessed the foresight to turn down such a risky job, he might still have two hands.

"And the déisi? Did you hire them?"

Calum shook his head.

The individual behind the king's murder had been clever indeed to keep their pawns separate from each other, which limited the information each was able to provide.

"The cupbearer's killer was slain by an arrow before he could tell us what he knew," Berengar said. "Where did it come from?"

"I don't know," Calum answered, and Berengar found himself growing frustrated.

Morwen spoke for the first time, her voice quiet and thoughtful. "The egg—how did you acquire it?"

Calum hesitated, so Berengar applied pressure to his wound. "Gorr Stormsson."

Morwen knelt at the thief's side and began wrapping his wound. "He's weak from blood loss. He'll die if he doesn't receive treatment soon."

Berengar heard voices and looked up. A crowd had started to gather, attracted by the overturned wagon and

Calum's cries. His gaze swept the rooftops, which were cloaked in shadow. They were too exposed, out in the open. He didn't want a repeat of what happened that morning.

"Fine." He pulled the thief to his feet.

"Where are you taking me?"

"We'll see if a night in the dungeons will refresh your memory." Berengar started up the road to the castle, dragging the captured prisoner behind him.

"What are you doing?" Morwen whispered under her breath as Berengar approached the castle gate.

Berengar didn't answer.

When the guards noticed him, they regarded him curiously but parted to allow him entry. A group of onlookers watched as Berengar led Calum into the castle. Morwen continued to cast nervous, puzzled glances in his direction. The warden threw open the doors to the throne room and marched Calum toward the throne. All the members of the royal court immediately stopped what they were doing, and an eerie silence fell over the great hall.

Queen Alannah sat on the throne, looking particularly aghast at the scene. Ronan, beside the queen, put his hand on the pommel of his sword just in case. Laird O'Reilly went white at the sight of them. Princess Ravenna's eyes gleamed with interest—as if utterly delighted something had finally broken the monotony of court.

Berengar threw Calum to the floor. "I am Esben Berengar, warden of Fál." He spoke loud enough for everyone to hear him. "The man at my feet is responsible for poisoning King Mór, and I know someone in this room helped him do it."

CHAPTER SEVEN

IN THE WAKE of Berengar's dramatic entrance, the throne room quickly devolved into chaos, and it took some time to restore order. The commotion was by his design. By morning, half the city would have heard of what transpired in the throne room.

Once the prisoner was safely escorted to the dungeons, the queen summoned him to the limestone chamber where council meetings were held. Darkness seeped inside with night's descent, held at bay by flickering torchlight.

Queen Alannah paced the floor between pillars, her hands clasped behind her back. It was difficult to read the queen's expression in the dim light, but Berengar could tell she was angry nonetheless. "What were you thinking? You come barging into the throne room with a bleeding captive in tow—a man you claim arranged to have my husband killed—and have the temerity to accuse the members of my court of treachery?"

Alannah struck him as someone acutely mindful of the image she projected, a necessary trait for a woman who had spent much of her life at the king's side. Women in such positions were usually skilled at concealing their true feelings and opinions, often even more than the men. Now that the throne belonged to her, and she was free to do as she wished, he wondered what kind of monarch she would be.

No one spoke as the queen awaited his response. Morwen, Thane Ronan, and Laird O'Reilly had assembled around the alderwood table, forming an informal council of sorts. Only Princess Ravenna stood apart from the others, watching from the balcony with a somewhat bemused expression as the last members of court departed the castle.

"You were in no danger," Berengar said. "I made sure of that."

Alannah shook her head at the words, as if in disbelief, and her facial muscles tensed. "Do you have any idea what you've done? I've only just begun my reign. I need the support of the noble houses and the great lords of Munster to keep the peace. I would have thought you at least might have known better, Lady Morwen."

Morwen, still wearing the gray cloak and commoner's clothes that comprised her disguise, hung her head in shame.

"Worse still, you chose to hunt for this man alone, without consulting me first. What if he had eluded your grasp? Did the thought even occur to you?" Berengar held her gaze for a dangerously long moment. "With respect, Your Grace, I don't require your permission."

Coming from anyone other than a warden of Fál, such an impudent remark would have constituted just cause for flogging—if not worse.

It was a measure of the queen's restraint that she kept the anger from her voice. "Did anyone else know of this?" She cast a dark glance around the room.

Laird O'Reilly bowed low. "Warden Berengar and Lady Morwen came to see me earlier, making inquiries about the underground market. They made no mention of the reason for their interest. I offered to supply them with guards, but the warden insisted on keeping the matter a secret."

Like many royal advisers worth their salt, O'Reilly possessed an obvious talent for shifting blame. Berengar bit back the response already on the tip of his tongue. He and Morwen told no one else of their plan to enter the underground market—only O'Reilly, who had conveniently forgotten to inform them that a password was required to gain entrance. Had the man intentionally omitted the truth about the armed guards in the tunnels, or did he truly not know? Berengar decided to say nothing, at least for the time being.

Morwen glowered at O'Reilly, no doubt thinking along similar lines. "We almost lost our heads down there. You might have been more forthcoming with information."

"The underground market is steeped in secrecy, even to one such as me, who trades in secrets."

Ronan gave Berengar a look that reminded him of the way warriors sized each other up before a fight, as if seeking to determine whether the warden was a threat. "Which is why you should have requested aid. I would have gone with you myself, had you only told me."

"We only had one opportunity to apprehend the intermediate. The man is a member of the Brotherhood of Thieves. If he even suspected we were after him, he would have left Cashel, never to be seen again."

"It almost sounds," Princess Ravenna said softly, only half looking at him, "as if you don't trust the people in here either."

"My husband kept secrets enough. I will not have them

kept from me." With that, Alannah sat at the head of the table, and the others joined her—save for Berengar and Princess Ravenna.

"Whoever murdered King Mór doesn't like leaving loose ends," Berengar said. "They're too artful for that. The déisi we tracked down this morning was killed before he had the chance to tell us anything useful. If we're going to catch the king's killer, we're going to have to think like they do."

"Explain yourself." It was clear from Alannah's expression she remained unconvinced. Likewise, the others seated around the table seemed similarly perplexed—even Morwen.

Ravenna turned away from the balcony. "He's setting a trap. This was your plan all along, wasn't it? Word will spread that one of the conspirators has been captured alive. When they come for him…" She seemed to regard Berengar with something like admiration.

Berengar approached the table with a nod. "Aye. If the killer is afraid of being exposed, they're more likely to make a mistake. With Calum locked securely away in a cell right here under our feet, it's only a matter of time before an attempt is made to silence him. When that happens, I'll be waiting."

"And if the assassins don't take the bait? What then?" Ravenna approached, and as always, Berengar found himself drawn to her intelligent, somber eyes that seemed to burn with a hidden fire. If he had to guess, the princess was every bit as clever as her father—perhaps more so. Berengar wondered if that played a part in their troubled relationship.

"I think the prisoner knows more than he told me. Something has him too frightened to talk, even under the threat of losing his remaining hand."

Queen Alannah's lips formed a thin frown at that, hinting at her disapproval of such barbaric tactics, which were out of keeping with Munster's civic virtues. Berengar continued undaunted. "Perhaps he discovered something about his employer he wasn't supposed to. Even if he hasn't, the assassin doesn't strike me as the type to take that chance." The killer was patient, but Berengar could afford to wait for the right moment to spring his trap. There were more than enough leads to chase in the meantime.

Ronan at least seemed swayed by his explanation. "I'll tell Corrin to triple the guard. If anyone comes for the prisoner, we'll be ready." He rested his hand on the armrest of the queen's chair, which Berengar noticed with interest. Was it simply a familiar gesture between someone who had long served the throne and his queen, or was there something more there?

"These events have left me deeply uneasy," Alannah said. "First I learn Matthias and his killer were murdered, and then you appear with the man who arranged to have my husband poisoned. Warden Berengar, were you at least able to learn anything of use from him before you paraded him before the members of my court?"

"Calum mentioned dealings with Gorr Stormsson. That's how he obtained the coatl egg he was attempting to auction."

Queen Alannah pushed away from the table, and her counselors did likewise almost at once. She approached the map of Munster, where figures representing armies were scattered. "If the Dane is involved in this, the kingdom is in greater danger than I feared. Stormsson was a sworn enemy of my husband. Long has he sought dominion over Munster."

Ronan pointed out a mass of enemy figures in the east.

"He's also one of the few individuals with enough gold to pay off the Brotherhood."

"Send word to your spies, Laird O'Reilly," Alannah said. "Find out if Stormsson's soldiers are on the move. If he is preparing an attack, we must be prepared to meet him with force. As for you, Warden Berengar, I trust you will look deeper into this matter. If Stormsson had my husband killed, I wish to know."

"I'll do what I can. In the meantime, I suggest you and your daughter avoid leaving the castle for the time being. It's too dangerous for either of you to venture beyond these walls—not until we know more."

"I go where I please." The princess' demeanor changed to reflect the same defiance she had for Mór when they dined together. "I will not be caged. Not by you or any other man." The fierce reaction took him by surprise. It was plain from her resolute expression there was no changing her mind, and Berengar knew better than to try.

Alannah clearly agreed with her daughter. "The people just lost their king. We will not shrink from our duties and hide away from the world. I have absolute confidence in Captain Corrin and his men to protect us from harm."

Berengar respected the queen's resolve, if not her confidence in Corrin's men. The guards hadn't prevented her husband's murder—King Mór had died on his throne. Given the assassin's resources, any amount of public exposure was an unnecessary risk.

"What of this egg?" Ronan asked. "What should we do with it?"

A dark cloud seemed to fall over the room. No one seemed to want to go near the egg after Morwen had unveiled it at the center of the table. Even now it continued to pulse with a faint red light, matching the color of the flames.

Morwen perked up at the mention of the egg. It was obvious she had been waiting for this very moment to arrive. "We should destroy it at once. Were it to hatch, it would spell certain doom for the entire city, not to mention any so unfortunate as to be caught up in its path." Her passion was unsurprising; as court magician, it was her duty to safeguard the realm against magical threats.

Alannah looked to her thane for guidance. "What do you think, Ronan?"

"A creature of such power might be useful, if it could be used in defense of Munster, as a weapon against our enemies."

Morwen looked appalled by the very suggestion. "That would be a deadly gamble." She stared at the egg's scaled surface, which shimmered in the firelight. "Although a coatl will form a bond with whoever hatches it, they're said to be difficult for any ordinary human to control. It would be madness to attempt it." She seemed to plead with the queen with her eyes. "It must be destroyed, Your Grace."

Berengar was almost tempted to put his axe in the egg that very moment.

"We should not act with haste," Laird O'Reilly interjected, his voice a soothing whisper. "The egg's worth is more than that of a weapon. A treasure as rare as this has no price, my queen. One does not discard such a valuable asset lightly."

Why doesn't he want it destroyed? Berengar thought. Was it greed, or something more? He wondered if one of the masked spectators at the auction had been there at O'Reilly's behest. Perhaps the old man wanted the egg for himself all along.

"Lady Morwen, are we in any danger of its hatching, if left alone?" asked the queen.

Morwen shook her head slowly. "No, my queen. Only

the cry of another coatl or powerful magic can awaken what sleeps inside. But, Your Grace—"

"Very well. Let the egg be sealed away inside the royal vault. It will be kept safe there among our treasures, if ever we should have need of it."

Morwen kept her facial expression flat, but Berengar knew she was disappointed in the queen's decision.

"The hour is late. Unless there are any more pressing matters left to discuss, this meeting is at an end. As for you, Warden Berengar—I hope you know what you're doing." With that, Alannah swept out of the chamber alongside her daughter, trailed by a small contingent of guards. Berengar remained behind as the others followed after her. His gaze lingered a moment longer on the swath of enemy territory on the map of Munster before he turned away. Late or not, there was still work to be done.

When he looked up, he saw that only Morwen remained behind, leaning against one of the pillars. The pair had hardly exchanged a word since their arrival at the castle.

"You might have told me that was your plan. I wasn't sure what you were thinking, marching Calum into the castle like that." She ran a hand through her hair, which was still unkempt from their flight through the tunnels, before approaching with a half smile. "Still, I'd say we make a good team, all things considered—apart from that nasty business about the hand," she added with disapproval.

Berengar stared down at her with a dark expression. "I warned you to follow my lead. Instead, you ignored me and nearly got us both killed in the process."

Morwen's smile faltered, and she took a step back. "I was only trying to—"

"You told me you could manage magic without your

staff, but that was a lie, wasn't it? No wonder Mór never let you out of his sight. You run around like a little girl trying to prove herself, but we're not on an adventure, and I am not your friend." Her brow furrowed in surprise, and he saw tears glistening in the firelight. "Leave now. Before I lose my temper."

Morwen wiped her eyes before walking away. It was clear she was hurt. As Berengar watched her go, he remembered she was someone who had just lost her father. The thought filled him with regret. A part of himself that was usually quiet told him that he should apologize, but he couldn't quite bring himself to open his mouth, so instead he just stood there until she was gone.

When he was alone again, Berengar whistled for Faolán and made his way to the dungeon. No matter a castle's size, it was never particularly difficult to find the dungeon, even with no one to show him the way. As long as he kept heading down, he would eventually end up where he wanted to be. Berengar quickly located the entrance, and after a brief exchange with the sentries stationed outside, he started down a long, stone stairway that descended into the depths under the castle with a torch to guide his path. It was quiet, dark, and damp. There were no cries from below, unlike those that filled the dungeons in the Ice Queen's fortress far to the north. Munster did not condone torture, even before High Queen Nora outlawed its practice throughout Fál—a practice that had proven notoriously difficult to eradicate.

Finally he reached the bottom of the steps and set the torch in a bracket on the wall. The dungeon presented a stark difference from the splendor of the castle at the surface. There were no precious metals or statues in sight —only hard, cruel stone and cells behind iron bars. A chill hung in the corridor, permeating the ground. Mold grew freely along the walls, many of which were in varying states of disrepair. There was rot beneath the beauty, if one knew where to look. The parallel with the surface world was not lost on Berengar.

The jailers and guards ignored him, likely under orders from Corrin to accommodate him. He passed a row of empty cells until he came at last to the place where Calum sat behind unforgiving iron bars. There were a sizable number of guards stationed outside the cell. All remained quiet at the sight of Berengar and Faolán approaching, even Calum, whose remaining hand went to the base of his stump. Morwen had skillfully dressed the wound; the thief looked about as well as could be expected for a man who had lost a hand hours ago.

"I came to see how you were settling in," Berengar said. "I trust the cell is to your liking."

Calum opened his mouth angrily, as if to issue an insult, but stopped short when Faolán growled at him through the bars. "Have you forgotten that I make my living breaking into—and out of—places? This cell won't hold me for long."

"I doubt that. These cells were all enchanted by Munster's court magician. Unless you're carrying some magic in your pockets, you won't be able to pick the lock to escape. I wouldn't count on your friends in the Brotherhood showing up to free you, either—we both know you don't have that much time."

"What do you want from me?"

"Answers."

Calum laughed and shook his head. "Then you've come to the wrong place. I've already told you everything I know."

Berengar frowned. "Fine. I'm done wasting my time on you."

"Wait!" Calum shouted as the warden turned to go. Berengar looked back over his shoulder, where Calum had risen and stood clutching the iron bars. "It's not safe for me here. The guards want me dead for my role in the king's death."

Berengar faced him, their faces separated only by the bars. "It's not the guards you're worried about, thief. Tell me something useful, and I'll reconsider using you as bait."

Calum's eyes darted from the guards back to Berengar. "The gold that was used to pay for the contract—it came from Munster's royal treasury."

If there was ever any doubt that someone highly placed in the royal court had been involved in King Mór's assassination, there was none now. Only an individual with significant influence could have gained access to the royal treasury. Using Mór's own wealth to finance his death had a certain sense of poetry to it. Was that what the killer wanted—to send a message? Neither was the choice of poison accidental. The Demon's Whisper had clearly been selected to bring about a slow, painful death. What was the intended message in that? Whatever the answers, he wasn't going to find them standing in the dungeon. As clever as the killer was, if they had used gold from the treasury, there would likely be a record of it somewhere. That meant they'd left a trail for him to follow.

Berengar turned to go. "Thank you. You've been very helpful."

Calum banged on the bars. "You said you were going to reconsider using me as bait."

"I have reconsidered it." Berengar stalked away. "I think I like you right where you are."

The castle was deserted by the time he emerged from the dungeon. Berengar patrolled a castle parapet and looked for any vulnerable places along the wall. Save for the guards and sentries at their posts, there wasn't a soul in sight. The city of Cashel slept below in peace, but for how long? He was about to return inside when a soft sound echoed in the wind, and Faolán looked up alertly.

"I hear it too." The sound resembled a human voice. It was coming from the chapel, or somewhere nearby it. He followed the sound's source to the crypt, which lay shrouded in darkness. Something was singing. Berengar had hunted enough monsters to know few good things were ever found among the dead in the dark of night. He advanced slowly through the cemetery and reached for his axe, careful to keep to the shadows.

There was a figure in a long dress with her back to him standing over a tomb. She carried lilies in one of her hands. The woman was too far away for him to recognize the words of her song, but the pain and sadness were unmistakable. The clouds parted in the sky and moonlight illuminated the crypt, revealing the form of Princess Ravenna.

Berengar released his hold on the axe and took a step back, surprised, and a twig snapped under his boot. Ravenna glanced up suddenly, startled. She stared at the spot where Berengar stood for a moment longer before turning back to the grave, though she did not resume her song.

"Come, Faolán." He left her to grieve in privacy.

Only later did it occur to him the grave she'd visited wasn't her father's.

S omeone had been inside the king's rooms. Berengar made the discovery when he searched Mór's chamber the next morning. The room had been torn apart, a sign that someone was searching for something among King

Mór's possessions. According to the king's chamberlain, who let him inside, the room had been in pristine condition only one day ago. Whoever gained entry had done so while Berengar was busy on the hunt for Matthias and Calum. There was no sign of forced entry, but the chamberlain explained that many servants often came and went from the room, as well as—the man explained under his breath—the king's many mistresses.

If the intruder had left evidence of their identity behind, Berengar found no trace of it. Nor could he discern what the intruder was looking for. Although the intruder had been careful enough not to alert anyone to their presence during the search, there was a rushed quality evident from the scattered sheets and overturned furniture that seemed out of keeping with what Berengar knew of the king's assassin's cautious approach. But who, if not the assassin, would have risked ransacking the king's chambers—and for what purpose?

With these unanswered questions in mind, Berengar paid an unannounced visit to the royal treasury, a massive, open chamber in a remote location of the castle. The sound of Berengar's footsteps on the marble floor echoed across lofty domed ceilings. Despite its size, the quiet room was nearly empty. Two guards stood watch outside the entrance to the vault, behind which lay the wealth of Munster, which now included the coatl egg recovered from the auction. The chamber's sole remaining occupant was a middle-aged man at a large desk on the opposite side of the room, busy making notations on stacks of parchment with a quill pen.

The man at the desk appeared so absorbed in his work he hardly seemed to notice as Berengar approached. "Can I help you?" His stiff tone indicated he was little inclined to do so.

"I'm looking for the Exchequer."

"What is the nature of your request?" The man didn't bother glancing up from his work. "You'll have to obtain a writ of approval before you can make an official inquiry."

"I'm here to ask a few questions about the king's murder." Berengar slammed his hand down on the desk so the man would see his ring. "And this is all the approval I require."

At that, the man put down the quill and looked up at him with a shrewd expression. "I see. In that case, I am the Exchequer. You have my full cooperation."

"Good. I want to know who has access to gold from the royal treasury."

The Exchequer looked relieved. "That's an easy question to answer. Apart from members of the royal family, the vault remains sealed unless I give the order. I oversee all transactions, including matters of trade and taxation. Every piece is accounted for." He indicated a set of black books stacked on the desk. "I keep meticulous records of every transaction."

"And if gold were to go missing after it left the treasury, how would that happen?"

The Exchequer frowned. "It's odd you should say that. A shipment of gold was attacked in transit on the road just over a month ago. Rumor has it the Danes were involved, though none of our soldiers survived to confirm the accounts."

"Is that so unusual? I'm sure there are highway bandits even in Munster."

The Exchequer shook his head. "Our shipments are well protected and transported with the utmost secrecy. I plan and oversee each route myself. No one else should have known the details, and yet...the gold vanished into thin air, as if someone knew exactly where to strike."

This marked the second mention of the Danes in recent conversation—first the coatl egg, and now the mysterious disappearance of gold from the royal treasury. Berengar doubted it was a coincidence, even if there was no clear connection between the two. Was it possible someone inside the castle was working with Gorr Stormsson? He decided it was time to find out more about Stormsson and his plans for Munster.

"Let me take a look at those records," he said on the chance something in the books might explain how gold from the treasury ended up in the hands of King Mór's killers. He spent almost an hour combing through dusty pages full of numbers and transactions, until at last he noticed something off about the books. "These numbers don't add up." He pointed out a column of numbers to the Exchequer.

The Exchequer's eyes swept the page. "That's impossible. I total and record each sum myself." He suddenly stopped speaking, and his brow arched in surprise. "This isn't right."

Berengar noticed the content of a few entries had been erased and replaced by someone with handwriting distinct from the Exchequer's. "Someone changed the numbers. Why?"

"They were trying to cover something up." The Exchequer went back through the rest of the records, and after several minutes he laid another book out for Berengar to see. "These payments were authorized by King Mór himself."

The royal seal was unmistakable. Based on the records, Mór had been paying a substantial amount of gold to an unnamed individual over a period of years, and immediately after his death, someone had gone to great lengths to cover it up. That could only mean one thing.

"Someone was blackmailing the king."

The implications were grave. Who would risk such a bold gamble as to blackmail a sitting monarch, and—perhaps more importantly—what did they know that Mór had wanted kept secret? Suddenly the king's paranoia and desire for secrecy made sense. Was Mór's blackmailer also behind his death? The attempt to alter the books was rather careless compared to the resourcefulness the assassin had displayed so far, much like whoever searched the king's chambers.

Queen Alannah was right. Mór was a man of secrets. The responsibilities of the throne had changed him greatly from the lighthearted prince Berengar remembered from the war, perhaps to an extent greater than he had previously thought.

"Say nothing of this—to anyone," he told the Exchequer. "Do you understand?"

"You have my word." The Exchequer swallowed nervously and tugged at his collar before casting a glance across the room at the sentries guarding the vault, as if to make sure they hadn't been overheard. "Am I in danger?"

Berengar pictured the déisi's body slumped against the side of a building, an arrow protruding from his chest. "Until I find the person who did this, we're all in danger. I wouldn't be here if it were otherwise."

No sooner had he left the treasury than Corrin appeared, accompanied by a host of guards. "Warden Berengar, I'm to escort you into the city at Thane Ronan's behest. There has been some unrest in several districts this morning, and we would appreciate your assistance safeguarding the royal family during the Feast of Remembrance to mark the king's passing. Princess Ravenna specifically requested that you accompany her during the festivities."

Berengar didn't have to ask what kind of unrest, remembering the harassment of the goblin smith he'd witnessed in the market only one day prior. As rumors about the king's death began to spread, such acts would become commonplace until the culprit was brought to justice and peace was restored. That, along with the assassin's unknown motives and lingering presence, was why Berengar cautioned the royals to remain inside the castle for their own safety. Still, if they insisted on venturing into the city, he would be right there to watch over them.

The need for the show of force became readily apparent when he arrived at the feast. There were people everywhere, as far as he could see. The queen and her court occupied a place of honor in a pavilion near the base of the hill, looking over the rest of Cashel. The well-guarded area was mainly reserved for high-ranking nobles, including the *Rí Tuaithe*, who had arrived at the capital to pay tribute to Queen Alannah. Berengar recognized Desmond, son of Laird Tierney, among those who bowed and cast their iron crowns at the queen's feet to affirm their loyalty. Thane Ronan himself stood at Alannah's side, keeping a vigilant watch over the festivities. Just below, commoners and low-ranking nobles from all walks of life took part in various activities, including games, dancing, and eating. It was a lively gala, especially for one held in honor of a man so recently murdered by poisoning.

As Berengar searched for the princess, he passed a group of drunken nobles locked in a loud argument about the rights of nonhumans. Berengar saw Morwen nearby, trailed closely by a small group of children who pleaded with her to perform magic. Morwen ran her hand over one of the runestones at the head of her staff, and a swarm of butterflies composed of glowing purple light flew over the children. Morwen smiled as the children raced after the butterflies, laughing with delight, and Berengar felt guilty for the way he had treated her in their last encounter. Although Morwen was probably too headstrong for her own good, she had only been trying to help. Her heart was in the right place, even if she was naive about the world's harsher realities. He wondered if that was why she grated on him so. There was something wholesome about the girl —something good—that was at odds with the man he had become, reminding him of another time in his life.

He looked away from Morwen and noticed Princess Ravenna standing alone, observing the revelries below. Like him, the princess seemed to shun the company of others, and yet eyes followed her wherever she went. It wasn't hard to see why—although Berengar usually made it a practice not to notice such things, Ravenna was easily the most beautiful woman at the feast. The princess seemed to brighten when she saw him approach, although the change in her features was so imperceptible he might have been mistaken. He wondered if she had seen him in the crypt the night before. The princess was harder to read than her mother, who herself had no small skill at concealing her true feelings.

"You asked for me, Your Grace?"

"I'm glad you're here, Warden Berengar. These events are usually intolerably boring, and you're the first truly interesting person to come to this city in a long while." Ravenna showed no fear of Faolán, though she did not reach out to pet her as Morwen had. "Will you walk with me?"

Berengar nodded in assent, and they walked along the path together, taking in the sights and sounds of the feast. He waited for her to speak, but Ravenna seemed content to remain quiet. This suited Berengar perfectly well, as he preferred silence as a rule. He kept a cautious eye on the crowd, searching for any sign of danger. A group of onlookers shied away from Berengar's scars, murmuring in hushed tones as they passed.

"We must make quite a pair," Ravenna said. "The Tainted Princess and the Bloody Red Bear. Half these people think you're a monster, Warden Berengar, and the others believe you're a hero. I wonder which is closer to the truth."

I'm the monster they send to kill worse monsters. The sentiment didn't seem appropriate to share with the princess, so he said only, "I'm no hero."

"I believe there are no heroes. No monsters. Only people, capable of both good and evil."

"You see the world differently than most."

"A trait we share, I imagine. I sensed a kinship with you the moment we met. I could see it in you." She stopped and stood so near to him they almost touched, catching him by surprise, and her eyes moved over the ruined half of his face before meeting his gaze. "We both know what it is to be broken—to remake ourselves. Those who look only at the outside are fools. My husband had no scars, Warden Berengar, and he was as cruel a man as they come. But that is a story for another time. Tell me, are you closer to finding my father's killer?"

The pair neared the end of the path and turned back in the direction of the queen's pavilion.

"Perhaps. Your father had his fair share of enemies. I can see why he was short on trust." He glanced at the place where Alannah sat and saw the queen laughing at something Ronan had said. "Do you trust him?"

Ravenna appeared surprised he would ask such a question. "With my life. Thane Ronan grew up in my mother's household. No one in the kingdom is more loyal to the throne. He has always been very kind to me."

That explains the nature of his relationship with the queen, Berengar thought. If Ronan had a history with Alannah, did she also receive the greater extent of his loyalty? It was well-known Mór enjoyed a number of affairs, but perhaps there was something more between Ronan and the queen. That was the sort of secret one would kill for. Berengar's gaze wandered over to Laird O'Reilly, who was seated at one of the banquet tables, a goblet of wine in hand. "What about him?"

Ravenna regarded the royal adviser with thinly veiled contempt. "Be careful with him. Laird O'Reilly is more dangerous than he appears. There is little love between us. When I fled the castle after my father announced my engagement, it was Laird O'Reilly's spies that found me. I'll never forget the smug look on his face when the soldiers dragged me back screaming."

The warden was about to respond when shouts broke out nearby. He tensed instinctively and turned to face the commotion, where a growing multitude pursued a hooded woman down the street. When one of the woman's pursuers grabbed her cloak from behind, her hood slipped off, revealing a pair of faintly pointed ears.

"She's a half fairy," a voice cried out in alarm. "She'll steal our children and bewitch our households!"

"Get her!" another of the pursuers shouted.

They're out for blood, Berengar realized. It wasn't all that clear the woman in question had a drop of fairy blood running through her veins—not that it mattered to the bloodthirsty crowd determined to take justice into its own hands.

Chaos ensued as the woman fled blindly toward the pavilion. The mob followed, trampling and destroying everything in their path, while others ran in every direction, engulfed in panic. The guards stationed around the pavilion were caught by surprise and quickly overwhelmed by the angry horde, which pelted them with food from the feast.

"Stay back." Berengar pushed Ravenna behind him and reached for his battleaxe. He spotted Queen Alannah through the crowd, flanked by Corrin and his men.

"Get the queen to safety!" Ronan drew his longsword in defense of the queen as the guards surrounded her with their shields.

Berengar took Ravenna by the hand and led her toward the others. Just as she reached the queen's side, the ground shook as a giant came running to the accused woman's defense. The giant put himself between the woman and the mob, using his body to shield her from the stones and projectiles. Thrown off balance, the giant toppled over backward and crashed into the pavilion, cracking the stone as he fell.

"Monster!" someone shouted from the crowd. "Kill him!"

As the crowd advanced on the giant, who was sprawled helplessly on the ground, Berengar saw Morwen sprint to meet them without a moment's hesitation. The magician drove her staff into the ground and uttered an incantation, and an invisible barrier deflected the projectiles hurled at the giant, who struggled to regain his footing.

"Stay back!" She brandished her staff as a defensive weapon. "I won't let you hurt them." Morwen stood alone against the crowd, backed up against the giant.

What's she doing? Berengar thought. The mob showed no signs of slowing down. *She's going to get herself killed.* He left the ranks of the guards behind and charged to the magician's aid.

Just as the first attacker neared Morwen, Faolán leapt on him with a howl. Berengar cut a path toward the magician with his axe, watching as she attempted to fend off a man holding a knife. Blood trickled from her nose, and it was clear she was drained from the spell. Faolán bit the man's ankle, allowing Morwen to knock him flat on his back with her staff.

Berengar reached out to her. "Take my hand!"

"Berengar?" She stumbled, but he caught her before she could fall. The giant scooped up the accused woman into his arms and fled, easily outpacing the mob with each long stride.

"Don't worry. I've got you." Berengar pulled Morwen to safety, where the guards shielded Queen Alannah and Princess Ravenna.

"Get them to the castle!" Ronan ordered over the tumult. "Quickly!"

Faolán howled to warn him of danger, and Berengar spotted a bow trained on Princess Ravenna—a black arrow pointed directly at her heart. He didn't have time to think. He stepped in front of the princess and put himself in the arrow's path.

The warden felt a searing pain just below his shoulder, there was a terrible scream, and then his world went dark.

CHAPTER EIGHT

WHEN HE WOKE, there was a pair of amber eyes staring back at him.

Lying at his side, Faolán began licking his face affectionately the moment he stirred.

"Nice to see you too." Berengar ruffled the fur on the back of her neck.

Morwen stood over him. "The guards couldn't keep her away."

They were alone. Abundant sunlight entered through a window at the end of the hall, revealing the contours of an unfamiliar chamber. It was morning, which meant he'd slept through the night. Berengar glanced around the room and saw a row of cots lining the hall on either side. Judging from the view outside the window, he was inside the castle once more, though Berengar had no memory of how he'd ended up there.

"Where am I?" His throat was parched. The arrow was gone. In its place were fresh bandages. The wound would leave a scar—just one among many others he'd earned over the years. He sat up in sweat-drenched sheets, and Morwen put her hand over his chest to steady him.

"Take it easy. You're in the infirmary." She handed him a cup brimming with a mysterious elixir. "Here, drink this. It will make you feel better."

Berengar regarded the red liquid cautiously and took a small sip. The substance was surprisingly pleasant tasting, with a hint of cherries. As he messily gulped down the contents of the cup a light, tingling sensation spread through his body, and his mind began to clear.

"The arrow was poisoned," Morwen explained.

He followed her gaze to the bloody tip of the black arrow, which protruded from a bowl of water on a tray beside his cot.

That arrow was meant for the princess. If he hadn't acted when he did, another member of the royal family might have fallen victim to an assassin's poison.

"A cruder poison than the one used to kill the king, to be sure, but fatal nonetheless," Morwen finished. "Fortunately for us both, it was rather easier to cure than the Demon's Whisper." A makeshift alchemy workbench had been assembled nearby, littered with herbs and various ingredients, where Morwen had undoubtedly concocted a cure while the poison coursed through his veins.

"I am in your debt."

Morwen blushed and looked away sheepishly. "I might say the same. That's twice now you've saved my life. I haven't forgotten how you fought off the déisi on the road to Cashel. It seems you have a talent for keeping me out of harm's way."

"Maybe if you'd stop risking your neck so often, I wouldn't have to." From the look on Morwen's face she'd taken the remark as a rebuke, and Berengar struggled to choose the right words. Though well versed in coarse language, kind words came harder to him. "That was a noble thing you did—putting yourself in harm's way to protect that giant. Your father would have been proud." He hesitated. "I'm sorry for the words I said when we last spoke. I shouldn't have said them."

Morwen settled into the chair beside his cot and shook her head sadly. "You were right. I wanted so badly to prove myself to my father. It was never enough. I'm a good student, and rather talented at alchemy and potion-making, but I'm not much in the way of a powerful magician. I struggle to cast the simplest of spells without my staff, as you saw for yourself. It's why I was not allowed to continue my studies with the Order of the Swordless Mage." She said the last sentence in barely a whisper, her embarrassment plain.

"You think quickly on your feet, and you're a good deal braver than a girl your age has any right to be. That's more important than how long it takes you to cast some incantation."

She beamed at him. "Does that mean you've reconsidered letting me help you?"

"Aye." He suppressed a chuckle at her unbridled enthusiasm to resume the hunt.

The sound of footsteps approached, and Princess Ravenna appeared at the room's entrance. The two guards who accompanied the princess remained behind as she made her way to where he lay.

When Ravenna noticed Morwen there with him, her mood seemed to sour somewhat. "Lady Morwen." Her cold tone implied she was all too familiar with Morwen's true parentage.

Morwen bowed and stepped out of her way in deference to the princess, a sign of a dynamic that had probably played itself out many times before.

Ravenna's expression softened when she looked at the warden, and her eyes swept over his bandages. "You saved my life." Her voice was full of barely restrained emotion. Before he could reply, she slipped her hand into his and squeezed. Her hand was soft and warm. Berengar had not felt its like in many years. The princess quickly pulled back her hand, as if she had surprised even herself by the tender gesture. "You have my thanks, Lady Morwen, for treating the warden so diligently," she added with a brief glance in Morwen's direction, perhaps by way of apology.

"Of course, Your Grace."

"The guards have restored order in your absence," Ravenna declared. The flicker of vulnerability was gone, replaced once again by a mask of strength. "There were riots into the night, but the city is peaceful now. Most of the nonhumans have either left Cashel or gone into hiding. I can't say I blame them."

"What of the queen?" he asked.

"Safe, thanks in no small part to you. I'm not too proud to admit when I am wrong, Warden Berengar. We should never have gone into the city. I did not fully appreciate the extent of the danger until it was almost too late."

He remembered how fiercely the princess had argued for her independence after his attempt to convince them not to stray outside the castle walls. Ravenna was stubborn, which was at least one trait she shared with Mór. At least now she and her mother would be under constant protection, though they remained in considerable danger. The attack during the feast confirmed beyond any doubt that the assassin had also targeted Queen Alannah and Princess Ravenna, which meant the conspiracy extended beyond Mór.

Ravenna glanced over her shoulder at her guards, who waited for her at the entrance. "I shall leave you to your convalescence." She hesitated at his bedside a moment longer. "Perhaps when you are well, you might join me at our table in the great hall for my evening meal. I would be glad of the company."

Many strange happenings had occurred since Berengar first answered King Mór's summons, but none compared with his surprise at the princess' invitation to dinner. Members of polite society usually tolerated him at best, if only because of his position. With few exceptions, the warden was rarely greeted with open arms, which was probably on account of his rough appearance, reputation for killing, questionable manners, or some combination of all three. He was unsure what interest someone like Ravenna might have in him, but then again, the confident and outspoken princess was unusual in her own right.

"As you wish." He couldn't very well turn her down, even if he were so inclined. It was rarely wise to reject a request from royalty. Another conversation with Ravenna might shed more light on the castle's inner workings. Besides, there was an allure about the princess he found difficult to resist, something he couldn't quite put his finger on. There was a ring of truth in what she said to him during the feast—he did feel a kinship with her.

Satisfied with his answer, Ravenna left them without another word.

Berengar watched her go, his eyes lingering perhaps a moment too long. *Be careful,* he told himself. He couldn't afford to lose sight of the reason he had come to Munster, especially not with danger lurking in every corner.

He returned his attention to Morwen. "You were uncharacteristically quiet in the princess' presence."

"Princess Ravenna is not overly fond of me, though she has never treated me ill. The princess had a difficult relationship with her father, and my presence only made things worse. King Mór believed it was the duty of a princess to be seen and not heard, but Ravenna was far too independent for that. He visited upon me all the favor and attention he denied her, though she was his legitimate heir and I was not."

Her words were no surprise, given what Berengar already knew of Mór and Ravenna's relationship. The king valued Morwen for her magical abilities and spurned Ravenna for daring to exercise her nimble mind freely. The king's thoughtless partiality had done neither daughter any favors and probably deprived the two half-sisters of an otherwise meaningful relationship.

"Where are my things?" He looked around the room. His shirt had been removed, and he wore only his pants. Most of his belongings, including the bearskin cloak and his weapons, were suspiciously absent.

"Waiting in your room. I had your armor mended where the arrow pierced it."

"Good." Berengar cast the sheets away, put on his boots, and reached for the tunic laid out for him.

Morwen sat upright in her chair and sprang to her feet. "What are you doing? You need to rest."

"I've rested long enough." He pulled the white shirt over his head. Even with the shirt, he felt naked without his weapons. Thankfully, the hidden dagger remained in his boot, just in case the occasion demanded it. "Besides, that draught you gave me is working. I feel better already." It was true, though his wound ached more than a little. Berengar grimaced and willed away the pain. There was work to do.

Morwen frowned but offered no protest when he slid out of bed. She probably knew him well enough by now to know there was nothing she could say that would dissuade him. Faolán leapt off the bed and landed beside him deftly on all fours.

"Someone was blackmailing the king." Berengar started toward the doorway. "We need to find out who."

They were interrupted by the sound of a bell ringing loudly without warning from the watchtower, and Berengar stopped dead in his tracks. The last time the bells tolled across Cashel, they announced the king's death. He exchanged an apprehensive glance with Morwen, and the pair hurried to the window, where they could see a mass of people approaching the city from beyond the wall. Most were on foot, although a few appeared to be riding on horseback—probably soldiers, though given the distance, it was hard to tell. Even if their numbers were too few to belong to an attacking force, their sudden appearance was certainly cause for alarm.

"They carry the queen's colors," Morwen said of the golden banners flapping in the wind. "These are subjects of the crown."

"The guards wouldn't ring the bell unless there was something wrong. Come on."

There was no time to stop to retrieve his weapons. He quickly made his way outside the castle, Morwen at his side. As the bell continued ringing the alarm, scores of guards rushed to form ranks across the courtyard. Panicked cries broke out from below, where the approaching swarm had almost reached the city gate.

Berengar pushed his way through the fleeing spectators, but the line of guards marching down the road into Cashel was moving far too slowly, blocking his way forward.

"We'll never get there in time."

Morwen put two fingers to her mouth and whistled. A loud whinny from a horse over by the stables sounded above the ruckus. The horse reared up and tore free of the squire who held its lead rope before breaking into a run. It came to a stop just short of Berengar and Morwen, as if waiting for them to mount it.

"Nice trick," he muttered to Morwen as he stepped into the stirrup and took the reins. Animals were known to have an affinity for certain magical beings. The fact probably played a role in Faolán's favorable disposition toward Morwen, though he suspected Morwen's good nature also played no small part. Animals could sense good and evil as well as magic. Berengar trusted Faolán's instincts above anyone else's—even his own. He reached down and pulled the magician into the saddle. When Morwen put her arms around his waist, he kicked the horse and they started downhill.

Despite the alarm caused by the bells, Cashel had calmed somewhat since the upheaval at the feast, though the undercurrent of tension that remained was palpable. Berengar suspected it would be a long time before life in the city returned to normal. If Mór's killer wasn't brought to justice, the chaos threatened to spread across Munster. He'd seen it before, in the time of the Shadow Wars, when the five kingdoms of Fál were divided, even among themselves. The High Queen had appointed the wardens so that such times would never again return.

The wanderers had begun to trickle into the city when Berengar and Morwen arrived at the gate. The people were covered in mud and soot. Many wore torn and bloodied clothes. There were men, women, and children from all walks of life. United by common tragedy, all class distinctions were apparently forgotten in the wake of what they had endured. Berengar knew the hollow look in their eyes. These people had seen death.

"Make way," a familiar voice called above the clamor. "Grant these people passage into the city!"

Berengar spotted Ronan closer to the gate, issuing orders to the guards to allow for a greater influx inside the walls. He dismounted and approached on foot, brushing past the crowd. "What's going on?" he asked when he was near enough.

"These people are refugees." Ronan only half looked at him. "From the village of Ahenny."

"That's only a day's ride from here," Morwen exclaimed as wagons entered, carrying the wounded. Some, if not already dead, would soon be so. "What happened?"

"Ahenny was attacked," said a soldier at the head of the party. Like his companions, he was in rough shape. The man walked with a pronounced limp and had sustained a deep gash across his sword arm. "The raiders crossed the Ford of Eine and set fire to the village. We fought them off, but at great cost."

The soldier lost his footing, and Ronan grabbed him by the shoulders and held him upright. "Who did this?"

"We captured one. We tried to bring him back alive for questioning, but he succumbed to his wounds just before we arrived." The soldier nodded at a body slung across the back of a horse led by one of his companions. The corpse's skin was pale. Strands of wavy yellow hair spilled from a round-capped iron helmet that covered most of the face.

Berengar recognized the corpse's distinctive black lamellar armor at once. "Danes."

"Gorr Stormsson will pay dearly for this," Ronan promised the ashen-faced soldier. "The northman knows King Mór is dead, if he didn't have a hand in it himself. He's testing the queen, searching for weakness."

Berengar, who came from Ulster—the true north—was mildly annoyed at Ronan's use of the word *northman* to refer to Stormsson. The Danes were seafaring raiders from distant lands, invaders to be driven out of the kingdoms of Fál again and again. They worshipped war and sought only plunder and death. Warriors from Ulster were no less fierce, but they were men of Fál all the same.

"See that the wounded are tended to," Ronan directed his subordinates as the final refugees entered the city. "Bury the dead, and make sure the living have food and a place to sleep. Come," he said to Berengar and Morwen. "We must inform the queen at once."

Morwen removed two vials from her satchel and passed them to one of the guards. "Give a thimbleful of the red and purple elixirs to each of the wounded. Tell the healers to send word if they require my assistance."

The guard bowed. "It will be done, my lady."

Berengar and Morwen followed Ronan to his horse, where the guards quickly produced mounts for each of them. "Who is this Stormsson?" Berengar asked as he swung himself onto the saddle. Laird O'Reilly had called the man a butcher, and Queen Alannah identified Stormsson as the leader of the Danes, but apart from that, he knew little of the man.

"His brother Alfric was captain before him, until he was slain in battle when our forces pushed them out of Munster under King Mór. Stormsson swore revenge on the king and his line. He returned to our shores some years ago and began raiding villages. His numbers have grown in that time, though not enough to challenge our armies outright. We learned from Laird O'Reilly's spies that he has a stronghold in the east, but we have not yet been able to uncover its location."

The bells ceased, and they rode in silence, leaving

Berengar to contemplate Ronan's words. He was almost certain Stormsson was somehow involved in the events surrounding the king's death. His gift of the coatl egg to the Brotherhood of Thieves was not an accident, even if the reason for the exchange remained unknown. It came as no surprise that he could have obtained such a rare and valuable commodity—the Danes were well-known sailors and explorers.

Then there was the missing shipment from the royal treasury, which was also rumored to have been the work of the Danes. Had Stormsson used the stolen gold to finance the king's murder? He certainly had a motive to want Mór dead, but why would he bother attempting to cover his tracks, which the assassin had gone to great lengths to accomplish? The Exchequer had believed the theft of the gold was an inside job, and someone inside the castle revealed its location to the raiders. If that was true, Stormsson wasn't working alone. Perhaps that was what Calum had been keeping to himself—yet another reason for Berengar to pay the prisoner another visit when the opportunity presented itself.

They found Queen Alannah seated on her throne. She was already grim-faced when they entered. Laird O'Reilly stood at her side, holding a piece of parchment in his right hand. Berengar immediately took note of the increased number of guards.

The chamber was almost empty. Most of the royal court had been dismissed, leaving behind only the queen and the *Rí Tuaithe* to deal with the sudden turbulence.

"Thank heavens." Alannah was clearly relieved to see Ronan. "What's happened?"

Ronan briefly recounted what they'd learned from the attack's survivors.

"These are ill tidings. Laird O'Reilly just received word

from the coast, where the Danes have burned much of our navy in an ambush. Added to the ships we lost in the hurricane, our fleet is all but depleted. If he is not dealt with soon, Gorr Stormsson will be free to land more ships along the coast and amass his forces. It seems the kingdom is beset on all sides."

It was King Mór who first mentioned the loss of his ships under mysterious circumstances. Now, the king's suspicions seemed almost prophetic. Berengar recalled the conversation he'd overheard when he stayed at the inn on the road to Cill Airne. The patrons were concerned over reports of famine and increased monster sightings. Between the unrest in the city, the emboldened attacks from the Danes, and the strange happenings throughout the kingdom, there was a darker influence at work in Munster, but was it the result of magic, as Mór believed, or simply a byproduct of the fallout from his death?

Princess Ravenna held her hand on the seat of her mother's throne. "We cannot let this stand. These killers must be made to answer for what they've done."

Queen Alannah nodded deliberately. "Of the five kingdoms, ours alone has stood unconquered since the time of Brian Boru and the High Kings of old. Munster did not fall when the dragons came. We did not fall when the Lord of Shadows held all Fál under his sway. And we will not fall now." She rose from the throne, facing the ranks of *Rí Tuaithe*. "Lords of Munster, I call on you to uphold your oaths. Raise your armies. I want Gorr Stormsson brought to justice."

"I will oversee the effort myself, Your Grace," Ronan promised. As thane, he had command over the queen's armies.

Berengar frowned. Although Stormsson needed to answer for his crimes, armed conflict would only further destabilize the realm. Perhaps that was what the assassin had wanted all along.

Alannah beckoned her scribe. "Issue a royal proclamation. I want guards stationed in every city and town. Our roads and trade routes must be protected, by armed escorts if need be." The queen marked the proclamation with the royal seal and presented it to her thane.

Laird O'Reilly cleared his throat. "Your Grace, if I may—in light of these events, and the attempt on your lives, perhaps we should delay the coronation. Surely we cannot expect High Queen Nora to attend while the danger remains."

It was customary for the High Queen herself to place the silver crown atop the head of the *Rí Ruirech* when they ascended to the throne. Given the circumstances, Berengar would strongly advise Nora against making the journey to Cashel.

Princess Ravenna regarded Laird O'Reilly with an expression of pure loathing. "Would you have given my father the same advice, I wonder? The kingdom stands on the edge of a knife, and you would deny the people of Munster an opportunity to stand united? My mother is as strong as any man, Laird O'Reilly. As am I. You would do well to remember it."

O'Reilly, left flustered by the rebuke, muttered a hasty apology, but Queen Alannah held up a hand to quiet them both. "Ravenna is right. The people must see strength from their leader. The coronation will go on as planned. I believe the warden has the authority to act in the High Queen's stead." Her gaze fell on Berengar. "It is good to see you in good health, Warden Berengar. Words cannot express my gratitude for your actions during the feast. I have already buried a son, and a husband. I could not bear to lose my only daughter."

Berengar's frown deepened at the prospect of being caught up in the pomp and circumstance of the coronation. He'd have to put up with all those preening, self-important nobles for an entire day. Worse still, they'd probably even insist he dress formally for the occasion. "It would be my honor," he replied through clenched teeth. In truth he'd rather face down a tribe of bloodthirsty goblins.

Without warning, the doors to the throne room were thrown open, and the captain of the guard rushed into the chamber.

"Where have you been?" Ronan demanded as Corrin hurried to meet them. "We looked for you at the gate, but you were nowhere to be found."

Corrin was visibly shaken. "Forgive my intrusion. I bring urgent news."

Berengar knew at once something was very wrong. "What is it? What's happened?"

"The prisoner Calum was found dead inside his cell moments ago." Corrin's head hung low. "Murdered. I came as soon as I learned."

The entire chamber went deathly still.

"We were tricked." Berengar realized what had happened. "The attack on the feast was a distraction." While the guards were occupied with upheaval in the city, the killer was free to strike undetected. Berengar had used Calum as bait, hoping to draw out the thief's co-conspirators, but the assassin had outsmarted him. With Calum dead, any secrets he knew he took with him to his grave, and the king's murderer had again shown that no one in the castle was safe.

"Impossible," Ronan said. "The prisoner was under constant watch. How could this have happened?"

Berengar too looked to Corrin for answers, but the captain of the guard sounded equally perplexed. "The guards never witnessed anyone enter or leave the dungeon. They claim to have no memory of anything that happened since yesterday. When I spoke with them, it seemed they were coming out of a fog. It's as if they were under some kind of…" He hesitated, searching for the right word. "Enchantment."

Alannah's normally stoic expression gave way to shock. Ravenna seemed to take the news in stride, but the *Rí Tuaithe* murmured uncomfortably among themselves.

Morwen muttered something under her breath, and Berengar had a feeling he knew what she was thinking.

"I'd like to see the body," he said.

N o one spoke during the descent into the castle depths. Wavering torchlight reached into the darkness along the stair as Corrin led the way down. The guards at the rear exchanged nervous glances, as if half expecting the shadows to swallow them whole. Those who waited for them at the bottom seemed especially fearful. Berengar knew the word at the tip of their tongues, the one each feared to speak aloud. He needed more facts before he could be certain.

The dungeon air was colder than he remembered. Faolán's fur bristled as Berengar followed Corrin down the lonely corridor that led to the prisoner's cell. The wolfhound uttered a low growl when the torchlight revealed Calum's motionless body, left slumped against the wall, his head hung low. The door to the cell had been left ajar, probably by whichever guard discovered the prisoner's demise.

"The door was locked when he was found like this?"

"Aye," replied a stout, bearded guard who refused to

meet the warden's eye. "We had to send for the key so we could get inside."

Berengar reached for Corrin's torch and entered the cell with Morwen. He crouched beside the corpse. "There are no signs of trauma." He inspected the body. "No blood that I can see. He might have been poisoned—the assassin has a fondness for it. When was the last time he took a meal?"

"That's just it, sir," the guard replied. "The prisoner refused all food. Seemed he was afraid of poisoning."

"And none of you remember seeing anyone come or go?"

"No sir."

That doesn't mean magic was involved. Although Berengar was no expert on alchemy, there were other herbs, other powders an assassin might have employed that would temporarily stun the guards.

Morwen ran a finger over the stone floor and Berengar held the torch closer to her as she held the dust up to her eye for closer inspection. "No sign of residue." She sniffed the air. "There's no hint of chemical fumes in the air, either."

"Perhaps someone gained access to the cell in spite of your spell."

Morwen shook her head. "I would sense it if the charm was undone."

Berengar studied her face in the dim light, wondering what she was thinking.

She seemed to respond to his unspoken question. "Magic has left its mark on this place. I can feel it."

He heard once there was a small amount of magic in everything, at the heart of all life. Its presence was usually imperceptible to most humans, though when the magic was strong enough, even an ordinary human might experience a feeling of dread, or perhaps a cold chill. Some, like magicians, were far more sensitive to its presence.

As if struck by a new thought, Morwen rose from her spot and took his torch, pacing about the room.

"What are you looking for?"

She bent down and cast her light across the floor. "Signs of a circulum onerariis. It's a magic circle—a link between two places drawn in chalk or blood." She frowned. "I don't see one here."

He noted her concern. "Is that bad?"

"It could be. The use of a circulum onerariis requires a skilled magician, but it would take a very powerful magic to appear somewhere without one, or to kill someone sight unseen." Her voice was a mixture of fear and awe.

"Could this be the work of a monster? A banshee could have killed him without leaving a mark."

"I don't know. We're not dealing with any ordinary magic."

That was the last thing Berengar wanted to hear. The circumstances surrounding the king's murder were mysterious enough without throwing magic into the mix. "If the assassin can use magic to kill, why poison the king at all? Why not just stop his heart? Unless..." He lowered his voice so the others could not hear. "What if the killer *wanted* to draw attention to Mór's death?"

Morwen had no answer for him.

Perhaps Mór's killer had purposely left a trail to follow, while taking precautions to keep their identity concealed. Berengar felt a rush of anger at the prospect. He hated the idea of his actions being manipulated by anyone, let alone someone who murdered a man who was once a friend. The use of royal gold had led Berengar to the Exchequer, who in turn shed light on the blackmail of the king. The killer hadn't simply wanted Mór to suffer a painful death—

they wanted his secrets exposed. No matter which way he approached the murder, Berengar kept coming back to the selection of such a malevolent poison. His instincts told him there was something he was missing—something that was hiding in plain sight for him to see.

He lifted Calum's head and found two empty eye sockets looking back at him. "Look at this." There was no blood, no sign of stab wounds, and yet the thief's eyes were missing all the same. "Why would they take his eyes?"

"It might be a warning against looking too closely for the truth. Or perhaps whoever took them needed the eyes for a spell."

"What kind of spell?" Hunting a murderer was one thing, but this was far outside his realm of expertise.

"I'm not sure. Black magic isn't exactly my strong suit."

Berengar swore and released his hold on the corpse. "Then we've reached another dead end."

"Maybe not. There's one place we could go for answers, though it would not be without danger."

Berengar offered a rare smile. "Go on then. If magic is your domain, then danger is mine."

"Do you remember the silver medallion given to Matthias by the déisi?"

"Aye."

"Matthias was told it would heal his ailing mother, but in reality the medallion was enchanted with a paralysis curse. The déisi could only have obtained such an item from the Witches of the Golden Vale."

"Laird O'Reilly told me King Mór had a truce with the coven." Berengar looked over the corpse that lay against the wall. "You think they might have been the cause of Calum's death?"

Morwen shrugged. "Apart from the crone that dwells in the Devil's Bit, the witches are the only other practitioners of magic in Munster. Even if they aren't somehow caught up in all this, they're sure to know something."

Berengar nodded. "Very well. We set out at first light."

Ravenna found him in the stables, readying his horse for the road. The princess looked out of place amid the dirt and hay, but Berengar suspected she wasn't a woman who let appearances get in her way.

"I meant to join you at your table," he said by way of apology. "I was making preparations for the journey and lost track of time."

"Mother told me." Ravenna ran her hand along the horse's mane. "A pity."

Berengar had informed Queen Alannah and Thane Ronan of his discoveries soon after leaving the dungeon, as well as his intentions regarding the Witches of the Golden Vale.

He fastened a strap on the saddle and their hands nearly met. He took a step back and looked at her in the torchlight.

"I wanted to thank you again for what you did. I've not known much selflessness of the sort you showed."

"It was my duty. I would have done the same for your mother."

Her brows drew closer in displeasure, and he could tell he'd chosen the wrong words, though he wasn't entirely certain why. They stood in silence for several moments before Ravenna spoke again. "I would like to show you something."

She left the stall and emerged from the stables before he could reply, and Berengar headed after her into the moonlight. "Perhaps I should call for the guards." He glanced over his shoulder as they walked farther away from the castle.

"I am not afraid. Only a madman or a fool would try to attack me while you are by my side."

When they arrived at the crypt, Berengar realized she had seen him the night he'd heard her singing, and the princess' desire for privacy became clear. He followed her to the same grave she'd stood beside that night, which was still topped with the lilies she'd left behind.

"The grave is my brother's." She laid her hand on the stone with reverence. "Aiden was his name. When I had nightmares as a child, Aiden would sing to me. His voice was sweeter even than Father's, though he was too shy to share it with others. Now I sing for him."

"I had heard King Mór's son died."

"We were inseparable." She stared pensively into the darkness as if Berengar wasn't there. "My brother wanted to be a knight. He was always running off from his lessons to go on one adventure or another, usually pulling me along with him. It caused our father no small amount of frustration. He wanted a prince who would follow in his footsteps and a princess who would play the part and make a good wife when the time came."

"How did he die?"

"We went riding too close to the Devil's Bit. Aiden had it in his head that he would slay the crone who dwelled in the mountain. I knew when we drew near that something was wrong. An evil hung about the air. Our horses bolted. I held on, but Aiden was thrown to the ground, and he struck his head on a rock. I watched him bleed to death."

There were no tears in her eyes, but from the bitterness in her voice, Berengar knew that even now, the sting of her brother's loss had not diminished.

"I'm sorry. I know what it's like to lose someone you love."

"Your wife?"

He nodded.

"The stories about you make no mention of her."

"She came from my life before the stories. I was a different man then."

"You must have loved her very much. And after her? Was there no one else?"

"No," he answered. "There isn't room for anyone else."

Ravenna was quiet for a long while, and the wind began to stir at the graveside. "The pain changes us, doesn't it? Grief hollows us out and hardens what is left behind. I sometimes wonder if my brother would recognize me if he saw me today."

Berengar understood Ravenna's words all too well. He didn't want to dwell on what his wife might think of the man he became after her death.

"It is said that when my father returned from the Shadow Wars, he was determined to secure magical protection for the realm. Perhaps that is why he showed such favor to Lady Morwen. She was the daughter he wanted. Yes, I know the truth. I suppose I was always jealous of her for that, I'm ashamed to say."

"It only means you're human. There are worse crimes."

"Be careful with the Witches of the Golden Vale, Warden Berengar. Magic is dangerous, even for one such as you. I know firsthand of what I speak." She nodded at her brother's grave. "And your work is not yet finished."

CHAPTER NINE

THE GOLDEN VALE seemed an unlikely place to find a coven of witches. Berengar had encountered more than his fair share of witches over the years, an unfortunate byproduct of his line of work. They were nasty pieces of work. Almost without exception, they seemed to prefer to dwell in the darker places of the world—bogs, caves, and the like—where they were free to practice the black arts in seclusion. In contrast, the Golden Vale was a region of sprawling lowlands and fertile pastures, considered by many to have some of the best farmland in all Fál.

Berengar and Morwen departed the capital just before dawn. They went alone. Queen Alannah was reluctant to let them venture into the unknown unescorted, but Morwen insisted it was the only way to catch the coven unawares, as a larger number might draw their gaze. Alannah, who had a distaste for magic in general, expressed deep reservations about the existence of witches so close to her doorstep. The details of the arrangement between King Mór and the coven remained a mystery to her advisers. Now that a new queen sat on the throne, it was not entirely certain the accord would continue. Alannah asked Berengar to report on any findings that gave him cause for concern.

As Cashel itself lay within the Golden Vale, their destination was only a half-day's journey from the city. It was another peaceful summer day, and the pair rode with a gentle breeze at their backs. They passed a number of towns and farms interspersed with rolling green fields along the way. Faolán, who had grown restless after days cooped up inside the city walls, seemed to relish chasing the never-ending supply of long-eared hares into the neighboring forest.

Berengar used the time spent in the saddle to fill in Morwen on everything he'd learned from the Exchequer, as well as the potential burglary of the king's chambers, though he did not mention his conversation with Princess Ravenna. Morwen was at a loss as to what secret a blackmailer might have held over King Mór, but she acknowledged the king had been acting strangely in the days before he sent her away to Innisfallen.

"King Mór would sometimes to take me riding on days like this. We both wore disguises, of course. Those were the only times I saw the weight of his crown fall away." Morwen glanced over at Berengar. "What was he like, when you knew him?"

"I'm sure you've heard all the tales of the Poet Prince." He was afraid she was endeavoring to draw him into yet another protracted conversation.

She pulled her horse alongside his. "But you knew him. What was he like?"

Berengar chuckled softly to himself, though there was little humor to be found in his memories of the war. "Prince Mór was reckless—arrogant, even. He was overly fond of women and drink. He seemed a boy to me, while in truth he was my elder by several years. But Queen Nora always believed he would be a strong ruler. Even then she had a way of seeing something in people that others couldn't."

"What did the queen see in you?"

Berengar let out a frustrated sigh at the magician's seeming inability to temper her curiosity for even a moment.

Morwen, who had apparently accepted that he had no intention of answering, simply shook her head. "He was a good father—a good king. I still don't understand why anyone would want him dead."

There were many reasons someone might want a monarch dead, but Berengar could think of no good reason to share them with the man's grieving daughter. "We will find justice for King Mór."

Morwen's gaze lingered on him, and her brow furrowed. "What will you do when we find the killer?"

"You already know the answer to that."

"Cutting off limbs and killing whoever you deem fit isn't justice."

Berengar was used to being called a killer, but for some reason when Morwen did it, it made him angrier than usual. "You think your father didn't kill his share on the battlefield?"

"Yes, and it weighed on his conscience every day. The older he became, the more it burdened him. That's why he tried his best to teach me about honor and justice. Not everyone deserves to die. Even someone like my father's killer deserves a trial."

"Conscience is a luxury. The real world isn't like the one found in the books you read up in your tower. It's a violent, savage place that needs men like me to wade through the filth and blood for the rest of you."

"Sometimes I don't understand you at all." Morwen prodded her mare forward.

Berengar watched without a word as she rode ahead. Morwen soon began to hum a soothing tune to her horse, and the warden's ill temper quickly subsided. He found her stubbornness somewhat less grating than before, even if the girl was a misguided idealist. He wondered what would become of Morwen once the investigation was complete. Despite her disposition—which was sunny unless she happened to be arguing with him—surely Morwen was aware life at court would be very different now that her father was dead. She hadn't shown signs of having many friends, and life would always be more complicated for a magician, especially with all the unrest in the city. Should Queen Alannah discover Morwen's true parentage, she might even lose her position.

Their road led to the Glen of Aherlow, a narrow valley fed by a tributary of the River Suir. The Galtee Mountains were visible beyond a forest that shared its border with a peaceful-looking village. Berengar and Morwen arrived just after midday.

"What do you know about these witches?" Berengar asked Morwen as they dismounted and entered the village on foot.

"Many come to the capital seeking remedies for magical afflictions. Sometimes it's as simple as curing someone of their nightmares. Other times there might be a curse that needs lifting, or a spirit haunting a dwelling place. I turn away no one with an honest request. The witches, on the other hand, offer their services for a price. They're willing to do things I won't—things like love potions, curses, and"—her mouth curled into a frown as she chose her next words—"blood magic."

"Blood magic? Sounds serious."

"It is. It's evil, black magic of the highest order. But from what I hear, these witches are careful not to violate the terms of their agreement with the king. They're said not to harm anyone unless provoked, and most of their clients leave satisfied."

"You don't look convinced."

"There are rumors, but King Mór forbade me from pursuing the subject."

"Curious." From everything he had learned, Mór was fixated on protecting Munster from all magical threats. So why would he keep his court magician in the dark about the Witches of the Golden Vale? Was it out of a desire to protect his daughter, or was it yet another attempt to hide the truth? "Maybe the locals can tell us more."

By all appearances, it was an ordinary village. Fishermen fished salmon and trout from the river. Chickens, pigs, and even a few dairy cows were penned up outside the villagers' huts. Tradesmen plied their wares in a centrally located marketplace. Nevertheless, something about the village felt off. Berengar was well accustomed to receiving strange looks, but this was different. As he and Morwen approached, most of the villagers stopped what they were doing and watched with unmistakable suspicion.

"Hide your staff," he said to Morwen.

She quickly used a blanket to cover the staff, which was barely visible where it was fixed to her horse's saddle.

"Come on." He headed in the direction of the local tavern.

It was quiet inside, not that he expected to find it otherwise in the middle of the day. Berengar passed an adolescent girl cleaning tables as he approached the tavern's owner, who stood behind the bar.

"Can I help you, strangers?" the man asked without a hint of a smile.

"I'd like something to drink, to start with." Berengar slid payment across the counter.

The man behind the bar looked them over for an uncomfortable moment before filling a meadair and setting it before Berengar.

Berengar didn't touch the drink. "We're here to see——"

"I know why you're here." Like the other villagers, he was clearly not pleased to see them. "There's a path at the end of the village that leads through the forest. It will take you to what you seek."

Berengar put another coin on the counter. "I'd like to know more, if it's not too much trouble. Where did these witches come from? Have they caused you any trouble?"

The man looked him square in the eye. "Keep your money. I'll not answer any further questions, nor will anyone here."

Berengar took a step forward, towering over the man across from him. "I am a warden of Fál, here under the authority of Queen Alannah. You would be wise to remember that."

"It wouldn't matter if you were the High Queen herself. You had best be on your way, stranger. Either through the woods, or back the way you came—it's no concern of mine."

It wasn't that he didn't intimidate the man. As Berengar searched his face, it suddenly occurred to him that the man was afraid of something worse. He turned and left the tavern without another word, leaving the money on the counter.

"Well, *that* went well," Morwen said under her breath when they departed.

"These people are all terrified. It explains why they're so mistrustful of outsiders."

"Excuse me, sir." It was the girl who had been cleaning

the tables when they entered the tavern. "You said you were a warden. Are you the same warden who slew the Hag of Móin Alúin?"

Berengar looked down at her. "Why do you ask?"

The girl shot a nervous glance at the village and motioned for Berengar and Morwen to follow her behind the tavern, where they were out of sight of the others. "You can't tell anyone that I've told you this. You must give me your word."

"I swear it on the High Queen's name."

The girl lowered her voice. "They never come into the village. We aren't supposed to talk to anyone about them, not even to the people who come to see them. Sometimes…I can hear them in my head." Suddenly the words came pouring out of her in a rush. "They don't want us telling what we know. Old Tom wrote to the king once, pleading for help. He went mad after. The elders found him in the woods, living like an animal. Then there was Father Buchanan, who came from the abbey at Cashel itself. He went missing and was never seen again." Her whole body seemed to shudder, and Morwen used a comforting hand to steady her.

"I don't understand why the king didn't send anyone to look into these reports." Morwen was clearly upset. "What else can you tell us, my friend?"

"Men from the village are paid well to bring them whatever they require. They are very rich." The girl paused and stared in the direction of the forest. "Once a month, a delivery wagon arrives from the city with an armed escort."

"What makes you say it's from Cashel?" Morwen's tone conveyed she found the news particularly troubling.

"The guards. I overheard them once."

"What's in the wagon?" Berengar asked.

"I don't know—it's covered." She hesitated before continuing. "But just once, after the wagon vanished into the woods, I heard a terrible scream. When the guards returned, they were all ashen faced." She shivered at the memory and tugged on Berengar's sleeve. "Please, sir, you must help us."

"I will do what I can. You have my word."

The girl remained behind as Berengar and Morwen made their way on foot to the unmarked path where the trees had been cleared away. The villagers continued to watch them until they were out of sight.

"Wait." Morwen rifled through her satchel before they ventured farther along the path. "Let me see your axe, will you?"

Berengar regarded her with puzzlement, as the battleaxe was far too heavy for her to wield, but did as she asked.

The battleaxe didn't budge when she attempted to lift it from the spot where he placed it, and Morwen looked at him with an embarrassed grin before withdrawing a silver runestone from her satchel and fixing it to the axe. "Just in case."

Berengar lifted the axe and turned it over in his hands. It didn't feel any different. "What's it for?"

"The rune is infused with a charm of resistance—a ward of sorts."

"Mind explaining that again in words I can understand?"

"As formidable as you are, you're still vulnerable to magic. With the rune, your axe can block or even absorb lesser spells cast in your direction."

Berengar looked at the rune with new appreciation before returning the axe to its harness. "Thank you."

"Don't mention it. You're welcome to keep it. I'm sure

it will come in handy, given your vocation." She took out her staff and switched out the purple runestone fixed to the head of her staff, replacing it with a red one from her satchel. "The witches would be able to see through any illusion I cast," she said in reference to the purple rune, noticing his gaze. "As for this…" Her hand passed over the red rune, and another of the charms etched into her staff glowed with a fiery hue. "I hope I don't have to use it, but it's better to be prepared if I have to."

Berengar remembered watching Morwen's stand against the mob during the Feast of Remembrance. Pacifist or not, she was ready to put up a fight if the cause was just. Berengar wondered if she would be willing to take a life, if it came to it, and hoped she wouldn't have to. She deserved better than to have her inner light diminished by such an act.

When they resumed walking along the path, he expected to find the woods marred by the witches' presence, but he saw nothing out of the ordinary. Blackbirds sang cheerily from healthy broadleaf trees, which were nourished by the pleasant air. Neither Faolán nor either of the horses showed signs of alarm.

They didn't have to travel far. A clearing emerged farther down the trail, where a great hall loomed atop a sunlit hill. Morwen stopped at two misshapen stones on either side of the path.

"Look." She spoke with a quiet reverence. "Ogham stones—two of them, no less."

Both stones were vertical slabs, though one was a rusty iron color and the other was a dull gray. A series of strange-looking markings ran down each stone from top to bottom.

"What are they?"

"Relics from an age long past, when the world was

young and magic was new. Ancient spells are inscribed on the stones, and those who wield magic can gather magical energy from them. They're very rare. It's no surprise the coven would choose to dwell here when they have a constant supply of power available to them." The nearest stone seemed to reverberate with an inner energy as Morwen reached toward it. She promptly withdrew her hand just before it would have touched the stone surface. "These stones have been corrupted." She frowned and examined the markings more closely. "Someone has altered the spell with dark magic."

Berengar didn't answer. Something else had caught his attention. Music had begun to emanate from within the witches' abode. The soft, alluring tune spread to the forest's border, carried by the wind. Berengar followed the sound to the witches' doorstep as Morwen started after him. Proud and tall—almost the size of a manor house—it was an impressive structure, especially compared to the huts in the neighboring village. In a perverse way, it reminded him of an abbey or monastery.

When he reached for the door, it opened of its own accord, inviting them inside. He'd seen a similar spell at work in Morwen's tower, but this had a distinctly more sinister feel. Berengar and Morwen quietly entered, searching for any hint of the coven. The interior was illuminated by candlelight, and there were no windows that might permit natural light inside. The faint light revealed a spacious hall, as well furnished as any at the Rock of Cashel. The music came from the strings of a harp, which played on their own from some enchantment. Incense burned in ornate censers made of silver, casting an agreeable aroma across the room. Plates of grapes, cheeses, and other delicious-looking foods topped several tables. Jewelry, mounds of gold, and objects of other precious metals were on full display.

"There's no one here," Berengar muttered, though he knew appearances could be deceiving where witches were involved.

Morwen raised her hand slightly in the air, with only her first three fingers pointed up, and moved her arm from right to left. "A powerful spell of protection lies over this place—perhaps more than one. Touch nothing."

"Wasn't planning on it." He inspected the room. The number of scrolls and spell books exceeded even the contents of Morwen's library. His gaze came to rest on a black orb at a table surrounded by three chairs.

"We were right to travel alone. That's a seeing stone. It allows the wielder to observe faraway events, though it requires a tremendous amount of focus. They're very difficult to come by."

Faolán sniffed the floor, following a scent that led her to the back of the room. She stopped in front of a red curtain and let out a low growl. When Berengar walked toward the curtain to see what was on the other side, the front door swung closed. The hair on the back of his neck stood up, and he knew at once they were no longer alone.

"Welcome," a soothing voice declared, and he turned around to face its origin.

The Witches of the Golden Vale couldn't have looked more different from what he had imagined. The Hag of Móin Alúin was so monstrous she no longer resembled anything human. The three women before him were young and beautiful. Each wore a fine silk dress of a different color, and on their heads were wooden crowns.

Berengar's fingers inched toward his axe.

"There's no need for that, Berengar One-Eye," said the

woman in the middle. "I assure you we mean you no harm." Her long, brown curls showed a hint of gray, suggesting she was older than her companions. She wore a distinctive diamond-shaped ring that seemed to emit a faint glow. The woman flashed a haughty smile as Berengar released his grip on the axe's handle. "You need no introduction here—one benefit of having a telepath in our coven." Her eyes seemed to glow in the candlelight when they came to rest on Morwen. "As for you, Lady Morwen, I've waited a long time for you to walk through my door."

When Morwen shifted in place under the weight of her gaze, Berengar came to stand beside the magician in a show of support. "The last time a witch tried to sneak up on me, I cut off her head and put it on a spike."

At that, the other witches bared their teeth, but the woman in the middle remained undaunted. "You speak of Móin Alúin. It seems you're every inch the man the stories say you are. But where are our manners? I am Agatha, and this is Cora and Minerva," she said in reference to the fair-haired women at her right and left. "We are the Mistresses of the Vale."

"Then you must know why we're here," Berengar said.

"Naturally." Agatha pursed her lips. "The king's death. Such a tragedy. It must have hit you especially hard, Lady Morwen."

Morwen's eyes widened in surprise, but she said nothing.

Agatha lifted a goblet from one of the tables and raised it to her lips. "You've both traveled a long way. You must be thirsty. Can we offer you some wine?"

Berengar didn't need to see Morwen shake her head to know eating or drinking anything the witches offered was a bad idea.

Agatha only laughed. "Come, you two. Not all witches

eat children. Despite what you may have heard, we're good witches." Her eyes again lingered on Morwen. "Surely you know what it's like to be hated for what you are."

Her companions' expressions were decidedly less amiable. Both stared at Berengar with faces that might have been carved from stone.

"What was the nature of your agreement with the king?"

Agatha lowered the goblet, still smiling. "That's simple enough. We promised King Mór we would not cause trouble, and in return he allowed us to live here in peace. You can see the results for yourself," she added, gesturing to the splendor and finery found throughout the hall. "Why would we risk all this, Warden of Fál?"

"King Mór was poisoned with the Demon's Whisper." Morwen glared at Agatha. "I assume you're familiar with it."

"Of course. We're witches, after all. I can assure you the *Mitragyna* and *Amanitas* did not come from our stores."

"We already know who sold the ingredients, but did you make the poison?"

"Why would we do such a thing?" Agatha spoke in a way a teacher might labor to explain a lesson to an errant student. "There was no profit for us from the king's death."

Morwen delved into her satchel and retrieved the silver medallion the déisi had given to Matthias. "Mind telling us where this came from?" She tossed the medallion to Agatha.

Agatha took a moment to appraise the medallion before passing it along to the woman at her left. "This looks like your handiwork to me, Minerva."

Minerva ran her hand along the surface. "Yes. A paralysis curse. I remember it well. It was sold almost two years ago...to a grubby little dealer from Cork, as I recall. It could have changed hands a dozen times since then."

"Did the crone who dwells in the Devil's Bit place a curse on Princess Ravenna?" Berengar asked. "Did she cause the prince's death?"

Agatha's smile faltered at the mention of the crone. "Perhaps you're asking the wrong question. Haven't you asked yourself how the prince came by such an utterly foolish idea as to enter the crone's domain?"

"That's not an answer."

"You can always ask her yourself. The place isn't that far from here. I would caution you not to leave your axe behind, however. The crone isn't as fond of guests as we are."

"A prisoner in the dungeons was murdered in his cell," Morwen said. "I sensed magic at work."

"We had no hand in it."

"His eyes were taken. What would someone want with them?"

Agatha looked at her as if the answer were perfectly obvious. "To see through them, so they may know what the victim said and did before his death. It's a difficult incantation to manage, but not beyond the means of someone with enough skill."

Of course, Berengar thought. Calum was killed because of what the assassin was afraid he might know. Such a spell would have confirmed exactly what secrets Calum shared before his death.

"The prisoner was well guarded. This wasn't the work of some second-rate illusionist," Morwen said.

"You said it was a powerful magic." Berengar regarded the seeing stone. Even if Agatha and the others were telling the truth, there was something they were keeping from them. "You see much, witch, so tell me—if you didn't help kill the king, who did? The crone?"

Agatha's smile became a leering grin. She laughed again, but this time it was a cruel, harsh sound. The witch returned the goblet to the table and traced the surface of the seeing stone with a long fingernail. "What makes you think she is the only other practitioner of magic in the land?"

A chill ran down his spine. "What?"

"I have sensed a dark presence of late." Agatha's voice was no longer remotely soothing. "One strong enough to conceal itself from me, even with our seeing stone. Such power I've not felt since the days of the Lord of Shadows."

"There are no sorcerers left in Fál. The Lord of Shadows was driven out. He can never return."

She shrugged. "Perhaps. But I grow weary of answering your questions, especially since you've brought us what we want." Agatha and the other witches stared past Berengar, their gazes fixed on Morwen. "I always knew the day would come when the hand of fate would bring you back to me."

"Stay back," Morwen warned, training her staff on Agatha as she drew near.

Agatha ignored her threat and instead traced Morwen's staff with her fingers. "Ash—the wood of the scholar, perfect for balance of the mind. You're a clever one, aren't you?" She lowered her hand and stopped mere inches from Morwen's face. "What wasted potential. We could teach you to work such magics as would make the very foundations of the earth tremble. Here you would not be an outcast or a bastard."

Morwen shook her head defiantly. "You cannot tempt me, witch. I am the Court Magician of Munster, not some power-starved conjurer."

"Munster," Agatha scoffed, her voice rife with contempt. "Munster is a kingdom built on lies. And you, dear magician, are at the heart of those lies."

"What do you mean?"

Agatha turned away and glanced back over her shoulder. "You never thought it odd that King Mór just so happened to father a bastard who became the court magician, in a realm so bereft of them?"

"I—" Morwen hesitated, confusion on her face. "How do you know the king was my father?"

At that moment, Berengar realized what the witch meant when she said fate had brought Morwen back to her, and his skin crawled at the horrific nature of the agreement Mór had reached with the witches. Meanwhile, Faolán continued growling from the back of the room, and Berengar's attention fell again on the red curtain.

"Mór was so desperate to safeguard Munster against a magical threat," Agatha said. "He wanted a magic child he could call his own. He was willing to pay any price, no matter the cost. He came to me one night, and nine months later I gave him that child—*our* child."

"No." Morwen looked as if an arrow had struck her. "The king said my mother died years ago."

"Of course he did. The honorable King Mór couldn't very well have his adoring subjects learn that his prized court magician was the bastard spawn of his unholy union with a witch."

Morwen tried to form a response, but she fumbled for words, staggered under the weight of Agatha's revelation.

While the witches were occupied with Morwen, Berengar slowly began inching backward. Before the coven could react, he ripped the red curtain from the wall, revealing a sacrificial chamber on the other side. There was a large circle on the floor, encircling a second, smaller circle. Both circles were drawn in blood, as were the unfamiliar symbols between the two circles.

Though no expert, it seemed to Berengar this might be the *circulum onerariis* Morwen had described in the dungeon—the magic circle used for teleportation. If the witches had one, they could have easily used it to murder Calum, which meant they could have lied about everything else as well.

Last of all, he noticed the human remains at the center of the circle.

"The delivery wagons from Cashel—what did they carry?" Berengar asked.

Agatha fell away from Morwen. "Sacrifices. The king sent one every month."

Morwen's face was full of horror. "You're lying." The staff began shaking in her hands. "My father was a good man. He would never…" She trailed off, her head bowed.

"The king wanted to keep us quiet," Agatha continued. "I already told you he would pay any price." An evil gleam appeared in her eyes that had been absent only a moment ago. "It seems your father isn't the man you thought he was."

There it was at last: Mór's secret—the terrible truth someone would kill for. The revelation of Morwen's parentage alone would have crippled his reign, but the fact the king had been supplying human sacrifices to witches to keep the peace? The news would have destroyed everything.

The blackmailer must have discovered the truth, Berengar realized. Mór would have paid any price to prevent the facts from coming to light.

"This ends now. When the queen learns of this…"

"She'll do nothing—as will you. One word from us will bring this kingdom to its knees. Leave us the girl and be on your way, Berengar One-Eye. There is time yet for you to find the king's killer."

Berengar shook his head. "I'm not going anywhere."

The candles flickered across the room, and the light grew dimmer. The witches' shadows crept along the wall. Unlike the women who cast them, the shadows were twisted, bent, and deformed. When he started to reach for his axe, he heard a voice in the back of his mind and suddenly found himself unable to move. He struggled to speak, but an unseen force held him completely immobilized.

"Berengar!" Morwen exclaimed as the witches began to close in around her. "What have you done?" She held her staff out like a defensive weapon.

"I'm afraid your friend can't move," Agatha answered. "Cora is quite an adept telepath."

Even as she said the words, Berengar felt the fair-haired witch clawing her way into his mind, searching for a foothold.

Soon you will be mine, her voice whispered inside his head. *Give in.*

"Release him!" Morwen thrust her palm out toward Berengar. "Lig dó dul! I break the bonds that hold your mind."

When nothing happened, Morwen's brow arched upward in distress. Cruel, mocking laughter from the witches filled the chamber.

"It appears you're not as powerful as you think you are," Agatha said. "Cora, stop playing games and finish the warden."

Berengar stared hard at Cora, who shifted in place, wearing a pained expression.

"He's resisting." Her facial muscles twitched.

"Fool. He's only mortal," Agatha said.

"His will is iron," Cora replied through clenched teeth. Blood had begun to run from her nose.

"You won't touch him." Morwen took a step back, putting herself between Berengar and the witches. She ran a hand the length of her staff and held her palm over the red rune. Orange firelight from the rune leapt down one of the charms etched into the wood, and a small flame danced on the staff's head.

"A flame rune," Agatha said. "Mór must have paid a fortune it. I very much doubt you are powerful enough to control it."

Morwen flinched at that, and the flame at the staff's tip wavered as she lowered the staff.

"Forget the warden," Agatha said. "The king is dead. The life you knew before has ended. You know it in your heart. The human world will never accept you. Here, you will be young and beautiful forever. Reject my offer, and you will never be anything more than a weak magician."

"Maybe you're right." Morwen looked up at Agatha with a resoluteness that reminded Berengar of himself. "But I believe in good, and I choose the light all the same."

"In time, you will learn to love the dark. We'll just have to break you first."

As the witches advanced on Morwen, Berengar managed to unclench his fist.

Let me in, Cora shouted with all the force of her mind.

Fine, he replied. Berengar had spent a lifetime learning to hide his rage—to conceal the white-hot fury he carried behind a mask of steel—but it was always there beneath the surface, sharper than his axe and brighter than any flame. In that instant, he let his walls fall away and showed her what had happened at the Fortress of Suffering, subjecting her to full strength of his anger. The witch's mind recoiled from his in terror, enough for him to reach for his axe.

"Faolán," he called. "Maul."

Faolán lunged at Cora, savagely tearing at the witch with her claws. While Cora shrieked in pain, unable to fend off Faolán, Berengar broke through the lingering effects of her spell and charged at her. Minerva hurled a red powder in his direction, but Berengar deftly spun out of its path and brought his axe up in a clean sweep, cleaving half of Cora's face from her head. Writhing like an insect that had its legs plucked from its torso, the witch retreated across the room with a dissonant hiss.

"Kill him," Agatha said. "The girl is mine." The witches began chanting in unison, and the light dimmed as the room began to shake.

Morwen swung her staff around. "Dóiteán!" she shouted, and all the candles inside burst into flame as the rune ignited and a stream of fire shot out of the staff.

The flames began to spread, engulfing the walls.

Berengar started forward, but Agatha reached out at him with a claw-like hand, and a root shot out of the floor-boards and wrapped itself around his boot, anchoring him to the ground. With Berengar pinned, she hissed another spell, one likely meant to kill him. Just before the spell hit him, he held out his axe. The silver runestone Morwen had attached emitted a shrieking sound as it deflected the spell. The collision's force knocked him on his back, and the axe went sliding across the floor.

Morwen aimed a fireball from her staff at Agatha, but instead the flames shot through the roof, sending rubble crashing between them. "I can't control it," she screamed. Fire from the rune burned her hand, and the staff fell from her grip.

The witches spoke the words of a black tongue in unison, and the flames began to encircle her.

Berengar broke free of the root trapping his ankle, grabbed his axe, and threw himself at Minerva. She turned aside his axe with a spell, but it was too late for her to stop him. As she tried to cast another spell, Berengar tackled her to the ground. He drove the axe through her chest cavity and into the floor before ripping it free of her heart. The flames around Morwen dissipated instantly as the witch breathed her last.

Agatha screamed with unbridled fury, unleashing a terrible curse, and planks began tearing themselves from the building as a black maelstrom gripped the entire structure in its wake. Berengar tried to reach her but was knocked back, barely able to keep to his feet.

She's going to bring the building down on our heads, he realized.

Morwen stepped in front of him, staff in hand.

"You should have joined me," Agatha shouted above the sweeping winds as the building continued to burn. "Now you will die with him."

Morwen shook her head and pulled out a golden amulet that hung around her neck. "This amulet was enchanted by Thane Ramsay of Connacht, and you cannot match its power."

When Agatha reached forth her hand to crush them, the amulet began to glow, and Morwen's staff shone with white light. The magician's feet lifted off the ground, and a sphere of white light exploded outward, temporarily holding the witch's curse at bay. "Berengar, get to the circle. "Now!"

They ran together toward the circle, but Morwen's movements were slowed, a sign the casting had sapped her strength. The structure again began to shake, and planks began falling down around them, exposing the sky.

"Veterum," Morwen said as she stumbled after him into the circle. The circle's lines shimmered in the dim light.

Morwen held out her hand to him. When Berengar reached for her, she vanished just before their hands met.

CHAPTER TEN

THE WORLD SPUN AROUND HIM. There was a rush of wind, he felt a sensation of falling through the air, and suddenly everything stopped. Berengar landed on his back, staring up at the sky. He sat up and looked around. His axe lay beside him in the grass. Morwen's spell had dumped him in an open field, with no signs of human civilization within view. As far as he could tell, he was in the middle of nowhere.

"Magic," he muttered with considerable disdain. As far as he was concerned, the whole unpleasant business was further proof that no good ever came from mixing with witches, not that he needed the reminder. Mór should have known better.

He didn't see Morwen anywhere nearby. Faolán too was gone. Berengar called once for the magician, and again more loudly. There was no response. He wasn't sure if that meant she simply landed elsewhere, or if she hadn't made it out of the witches' abode. In either case, she was alone. He glanced up at the sun. There was still plenty of light, but sunset was only hours away. He needed to find her, and fast.

The warden climbed to his feet and dusted himself off. He stooped to retrieve his bow and a map of Munster, which had landed several feet away, before setting off in search of Morwen. The peaceful meadow seemed to go on for miles. There were no distant mountains looming overhead, which suggested he was far removed from the Glen of Aherlow, though still somewhere within the Golden Vale. He might reach the castle by heading east, but that wouldn't bring him any closer to finding Morwen. Instead he decided to search for higher ground.

After an hour or so, Berengar came across a stream and took the opportunity to fill the drinking horn he kept with him. When he knelt beside the running water and lifted a mouthful to his lips, he noticed movement at the edge of the forest. Just as he started to reach for his axe, Faolán came sprinting out of the trees. Despite her size, she crossed the space between them in moments. Berengar barely had time to return the lid to his horn before the wolfhound leapt to meet him, wagging her tail with unbridled affection. The blood on her muzzle from their battle with the witches disappeared as she dipped her face into the stream and lapped up water.

Berengar scratched her behind the ears and climbed to his feet. "Come along now, girl." He started up a hill to get a better sense of the lay of the land.

Faolán didn't budge. Berengar whistled, expecting her to follow, and still she remained where she was. He glanced over his shoulder with a perturbed expression, unaccustomed to having his commands disobeyed. The wolfhound barked and retreated to the border of the woods.

"Not that way."

Faolán would not be swayed. She barked again, signaling him to follow. Berengar stopped cold. Maybe she knew something he didn't. The warden left the grassy field behind and stalked after her.

It was dark inside the forest. Scores of ravens watched with shrewd eyes from their perches in the tall oaks and birches. The ravens deserted their branches and took to the sky when Berengar and Faolán passed underneath. He frowned. It was well known that witches, sorcerers, and the like used crows and ravens as spies. Minerva might have fallen to his axe, but either of the remaining witches could be out there somewhere, looking for them. He walked with his axe in hand, just in case.

Faolán led him deeper into the dense wood. She stayed a healthy distance ahead, forcing Berengar to hasten to keep up. The terrain sloped upward, and he had just grabbed hold of a tree trunk to steady himself when he noticed one of Morwen's runestones on the ground, shimmering in the dying sunlight. More were strewn across the hill's summit, all in close proximity to the magician's satchel, the contents of which had spilled out over the earth.

Faolán nudged the satchel with her snout.

"That's what you were trying to tell me. She's close, isn't she?" Berengar put the axe away and collected the scattered runestones, spell books, and potions that had fallen out, returning each to the satchel. Then he spotted her staff, which lay partially concealed by the bushes. *No magician worth their salt would leave their staff lying around—at least not willingly.* It was an unpleasant thought.

His gaze fell on the edge of a steep cliff, where the soil had recently been disturbed. *The spell brought her here.* Berengar stared down from the cliff. *She must have lost her balance and fallen.* Such a drop would not have been lethal, but it was a perilous descent nonetheless. He slung the satchel over his shoulder, grabbed the magician's staff—which to his surprise felt no different from an ordinary piece of wood in his hands—and carefully made his way to the bottom, where a clear impression had been left in the dirt.

His hand went to the grass. "This is where she landed." There were no footsteps leading from the place of impact. Instead, it appeared she had dragged herself away. *She's hurt.* "Come on. She can't have gone far."

The sunlight ebbed above. He followed the trail until at last he found her, curled up in the bushes underneath the shade of the trees, nursing a wounded leg.

"If you're going to tell me it was foolish to attempt that spell," she said weakly, "don't bother."

Berengar shook his head and crouched beside her. "I was going to say it was brave. Now let me take a look at that leg." Morwen winced at his touch, and he withdrew his hand.

"I broke it in the fall," she explained as the wolfhound licked her face as if to cheer her up. "My staff and potions were all out of reach. I tried sending Faolán to find you, but without my spell book I wasn't sure it would work. I thought—" Her voice wavered from the pain. "I thought I was done for."

"Not today." Berengar handed her the satchel. "You'll live, although the sooner we get that leg taken care of, the better. Wounds like that have a tendency to fester. I've seen it before."

"You don't have to tell me. I've been tending to the sick and injured since I was old enough to use a cauldron." Morwen glanced inside the satchel. "All my healing potions are broken." She withdrew a small vial with a murky maroon liquid in it. "This will help with the pain, but only a little, and there isn't much of it. I don't have the right ingredients to brew a healing draught."

"Then we'll just have to find a village somewhere and get you looked after properly. In the meantime, I can bandage the wound. I learned how during the war." He glanced at the sky, which had begun to dim. "Now if I were you, I'd drink that potion, because this is going to hurt."

After Morwen pried the lid off the vial and swallowed the contents in one gulp, Berengar bandaged her wound, gathered her into his arms, and carried her away.

"Where are we going?" She held on to him tightly. She seemed so small in his arms, much like the child she was.

"It's getting dark. We need to make camp for the night somewhere safe. In the morning, we'll find our way back to civilization. I'll carry you the whole way if I have to."

"You continue to astonish me, Warden Berengar." She yawned, apparently tired from the potion's dulling effects.

Berengar started to reply, but her eyes fluttered closed. He sang instead, a soft lullaby from a time long past, surprising even himself.

I t was dark before she woke again. Berengar was standing beside a roaring fire when he heard her stir.

"How's the pain?" he asked without looking away from the flames.

"I'll manage." She sniffed the air. "What's that smell?"

He carved a piece of meat off a stick with his dagger and brought it to her. "I went hunting while you were out. Thought you might be hungry, being out here so long on your own."

Morwen devoured her portion and licked her fingers. "It's delicious."

"Not the fare you're used to at the castle, I'm sure, but it'll do." He brought her more, which she consumed with no less fervor. "Here." He handed her his drinking horn. "You must be thirsty."

"Thank you." Morwen gulped down the water and messily wiped her face. "What about you?" she asked, as if it had just occurred to her there was not enough of either remaining for him.

Berengar shrugged. "I'll live. You're the one who needs to keep up her strength. We have a long journey ahead of us in the morning." He saw she was shivering so he helped her over to the fire, where Faolán curled up at her feet. Her shivering soon subsided, and Berengar plopped down beside her. Together they stared into the flames.

Both remained quiet for some time, until at last Morwen broke the silence. "How could he?" She wouldn't meet his gaze. "I thought my father was a good man. He sent all those people to their deaths. Everything he taught me about honor and decency…it was all a lie. He never cared about me. He just wanted a magician loyal to the throne."

"That's not true. Your father loved you, in his own way." He remembered how Mór had pleaded with him to retrieve Morwen from the monastery. Even dying, Mór's sole concern was for his daughter. In a sea of secrets and lies, the king's concern was the one truth—the concern of a father for his daughter.

"He took those people away from their families. They were sacrificed to invoke blood magic, all in the name of peace." The pain in her words was clear.

"I'll not pretend to understand the king's mind. The weight of the crown changed him from the man I once knew. Some men do evil in the service of what they think is good. I know of what I speak. Your father was human, Morwen—neither all good nor all bad."

"He lied to me. So many times I wondered who my mother was. He said she was dead when all along he knew the truth. He gave himself to her to make me. He was *with* her." Despite the warmth of the fire, Morwen shivered, as if repulsed by the very idea. "I'm the daughter of a witch." Her eyes red, she looked at him with a sad, questioning expression very different from the cheerful young woman he had come to know. "I came from evil. Do you think... does that make me evil?"

In that moment, Berengar couldn't help remembering the first time he met her at Innisfallen, and how he'd been willing to cut down all twenty men who stood in his way to fulfill his pledge to the king before Morwen had left the safety of the tower and put herself at risk to peacefully defuse the situation.

"In my travels, I have seen much darkness, but there is none in you. Your heart is true, Morwen of Cashel. The blood of kings flows through your veins."

"I miss him. I feel so lost without him—lost and alone."

"I know the pain. I had a wife once. She died in childbirth." He stared at her in the firelight. "If I had a daughter, I would want her to be like you."

Morwen started to reply, but her voice broke, and without warning she began to cry. Tears streamed down her face, and her entire body shuddered with each violent sob.

An instinct from another life took over, and Berengar reached out to her. His hand was more accustomed to killing than comforting, but when he laid it on her shoulder, Morwen threw herself against his chest and wept openly, holding him as if the rest of the world had fallen away and she was afraid he too might leave her. The warden hesitated before patting her on the back, as if to tell her everything would be okay, even if he wasn't certain he believed it.

Berengar held her until at last she cried herself to sleep. He eased Morwen down to the soft earth and covered her with his cloak for warmth as Faolán nestled beside her. Perhaps in sleep she would find some measure of peace, at least for a time. Wolves howled somewhere in the darkness as the sounds of night spread through the forest. Berengar turned away and gathered some firewood to feed the dying flames before settling in for the long night, his axe across his lap. There would be no sleep for him—not until they were out of harm's way.

In the morning, they started the trek back to the world of men. Berengar carried Morwen and her belongings in addition to his own, shouldering the additional burden without missing a step. He once had to haul a giant on foot across the frozen tundra to the north. In comparison, an adolescent girl weighed next to nothing.

Neither spoke of their conversation from the previous night. Despite her injuries, Morwen's spirits seemed improved, even if she remained somewhat subdued. She did not cry again. Her duel with the witches had left her drained, as had the extent of her fall. Berengar decided he wouldn't have minded if she teased or pestered him with questions if it meant she was on the mend.

More ravens flocked overhead, flying east. Berengar waited for them to pass before emerging from the forest. He hadn't forgotten what the witches had said about a darker presence that had taken root in Munster. Was it a veiled reference to the crone that dwelled in the Devil's Bit, or something else? Agatha denied any involvement in Mór's poisoning and Calum's death, but what if she was lying? The circulum onerariis would have allowed the witches to enter and depart the dungeons unseen, especially if Minerva erased the guards' memories. All the pieces seemed to fit, perhaps a little too perfectly, as if someone had intentionally left them for him to put together.

"You're troubled," Morwen muttered, her eyes closed. "I can sense it."

"I warned you to stay out of my head." This time he made the remark in good humor. "It's nothing."

"I saw your reaction when Agatha spoke of the Lord of Shadows. I don't think I've ever seen a look like that on your face before. Could he be active in Fál once again?"

"No. Magic prevents him from setting foot on the island. He was banished from Fál and can never return. The High Queen told me so herself."

Morwen yawned, and for a moment he thought she had again fallen asleep. "Tell me about the war. Father never spoke of it."

It wasn't a subject Berengar was particularly keen on delving into himself, but if it would keep her with him there in the present…

"Before you were born, these lands were full of terrible monsters and evil sorcerers, until Wise King Áed and Thane Ramsay of Connacht ushered in a time of peace between the five kingdoms. But no peace lasts forever, and when Áed fell, the whole of Fál descended into chaos and war. Out of that chaos rose Azeroth, the dark sorcerer who sought to bring the island under his rule. He might have succeeded had Áed's niece, Princess Nora, not stepped forward to unite the kings and queens of Fál under one banner." A snore pulled him from the past. Morwen had fallen asleep in his arms. Berengar stopped talking so as not to wake her and continued on his way.

They went the whole morning without encountering a soul. Sweat trickled from the warden's brow as the noon sun bore down from above. The sticky heat seemed to permeate every part of his being, and the fur cloak was like a furnace on his back. Morwen spoke less and less as the day went on. It wasn't long before she stopped responding to the sound of his voice altogether. Her skin grew pale and clammy, signs she was developing a fever.

Berengar kept on tirelessly, one step after another. Faolán barked loudly, and when Berengar glanced up, he saw smoke rising in the distance. The outline of a human settlement loomed ahead.

"Berengar?" Morwen's voice was no more than a whisper.

"Stay with me." She moaned as he jostled her about. The potion's effects were wearing off, if they hadn't already.

He carried her across acres of farmland, passing herds of grazing sheep and goats along the way. The shape of the town became clearer as they approached, a moderately sized farming community by the look of it. Berengar felt Morwen's hold on him weaken, and her breaths were labored and shallow.

He quickened his pace. "Hold on. We'll be there soon."

When he entered the settlement, the townspeople stopped what they were doing and gathered around him at the sight of the girl he held in his arms.

"She needs a healer. Now!"

"Take him to Iona, Thomas," a man from the crowd said to his son, a young boy of no more than eight or nine. "Go now."

"This way, sir." The boy hurried to a small hut at the edge of town. The door crashed open under Berengar's weight, revealing the interior of an herbalist's shop, where a woman at a desk was crushing dried leaves with a mortar and pestle. Berengar assumed this was the Iona the man spoke of.

The herbalist's eyes moved from Berengar to Morwen, lingering for a moment on the magician's staff. "Set her over there."

Berengar eased Morwen onto a small cot in a cramped corner.

Iona crossed the room and began rummaging through the contents of a set of cabinets. She returned with an armful of powders and ointments. "What happened to her?"

"She fell and broke her leg. A fever set in."

Iona grimaced as she removed Morwen's bandages. "It's broken in two places. Hold her down. I'll need your help for this." Her tone was sharp. She took a candle and began burning a mixture beside the cot. "It's for the pain." She stopped to wash her hands in a bowl of water at Morwen's bedside. "This will not be pleasant—for either of you."

Berengar forcibly restrained Morwen, who let out a terrible scream as Iona manually returned the bones to their natural alignment. When it was over, Morwen slumped on the cot, semiconscious. Berengar backed away to allow the herbalist to work unencumbered. He stood beside Faolán, watching as the woman applied a salve made of boiled elm and linseed before wrapping her in bandages soaked in oil and resin. Iona administered a milky white substance to Morwen by mouth. She looked her over for a long moment and turned away with a sigh.

"I've administered a decoction of yarrow and white willow for her fever," Iona explained. "She has an unusually strong constitution for a girl her age. She will live, but it will take time for her to fully recover. The bandages will need to be changed every few days."

Berengar stood at Morwen's bedside. The magician had fallen into a deep slumber and now lay perfectly still, lost to the world. "Thank you. I am in your debt."

Iona collapsed in the chair at her desk, seemingly exhausted from the sudden excitement. She glanced over at the boy who remained in the corner of the room, white as a sheet. "Be a dear and fetch your father, Thomas. I am sure he will wish to exchange words with our new guest."

The boy didn't need to be told a second time. He bolted from the herbalist's shop, running as fast as his legs could carry him.

"I can see you care dearly for her," Iona said. "She is lucky to have such a devoted father."

Berengar turned away from the cot. "She's not my daughter. I barely know her."

Though Iona appeared surprised, she did not comment further on the matter. When Berengar produced a pouch of coins and offered her payment, the herbalist shook her head and turned it away.

"I see you wear the High Queen's sigil. Many herbalists and alchemists perished in the purges that followed the Shadow Wars. Queen Nora put an end to them. I cannot accept payment from a servant of Tara."

After Azeroth fell, men saw magic and monsters lurking in every corner. Most alchemists and herbalists didn't have a drop of magical blood, but that didn't matter to the fanatics and a terrified populace. Even in a tolerant kingdom like Munster, there were still lingering resentments on both sides, years after the war.

Berengar took a look at the tight quarters of the shop, which paled in comparison with the establishments he'd visited in Cashel while searching for the source of the

Mitragyna and *Amanitas* used to produce the Demon's Whisper. Although the place seemed reasonably well stocked, the rural setting was far removed from the finery of city life.

"Are you sure? Must be hard for someone like you to make a living in a place like this."

Iona laughed. "I make do. The townspeople pay me in chickens and goats and the like." She smoothed the folds of her dress, which was soiled with blood and grime from the procedure. Iona was a few years younger than middle-aged. She was fetching, in her own way. Her hair was a dark chestnut, streaked with more than a little gray. "The people need me here. Besides, volunteering our services is one of the only ways we'll ever convince them we're not the monsters the stories claim we are." Her brow furrowed suddenly, and she studied him more closely. "Have we met before? I recognize your likeness."

"I doubt it. I am a stranger to these lands. The road is my home."

She shook her head, a hint of recognition in her eyes. "The riots at Dún Aulin. You were there, weren't you?"

"Aye. I was there."

He remembered it well. Five years into the High Queen's reign, a band of radicals stirred the populace of Dún Aulin into a full-on revolt in an attempt to cleanse the city of all undesirables. The warden was sent in to restore the peace, but by the time he arrived, the streets were already paved in blood. Even those who committed no crime other than expressing belief in the elder gods had fallen prey to the mobs. Berengar would never forget the image that greeted his arrival—that of an alchemist crucified outside the city gates.

"You're him, aren't you? The Bear Warden? I was a student at the Institute at the time. The school was under

199

siege for two weeks before you showed up. We would have died if not for you. You delivered almost everyone out of the city unharmed." She shuddered at the recollection. "After that, I traveled to Munster and completed my studies at Cill Airne. But I've never forgotten what you did that day."

Neither have the people of Leinster. When Berengar beheld the horrors at Dún Aulin, he was consumed by rage. He cut down all who played a part in the killings one by one, without mercy. Even those he saved were afraid of him after that. The Kingdom of Leinster was renowned above all else for its piety, and in the eyes of its people, he would forever be a monster for the sins he committed that day.

From her cot, Morwen gave a snort but did not stir. Suddenly there came a knock at the door.

"Come in," Iona called.

In stepped a man Berengar recognized as Thomas' father, a short but hefty man with a thick mustache. Though his attire was nothing out of the ordinary, he carried himself with an air of authority. The man nodded courteously at Iona, and then at Berengar, before looking over Morwen with a somber expression. "Thomas tells me she'll be all right."

"I think that's safe to say," Iona answered.

"Good," Thomas' father replied, turning to face Berengar. "You two caused quite a stir among folk in town, entering the way you did." He held out his hand by way of greeting, and the two men shook hands. "I am Nathan, the town elder."

"My name is Berengar. And what town would that be, exactly?"

"Knockaney, of course." Nathan regarded him with a curious expression. "I take it you lost your way."

"Aye. We made our way from the forest. Yours was the first settlement we came to."

"You carried her all that way on foot?" Nathan sounded both shocked and impressed. "I'd wager you could use a drink and something hot to eat. Why don't you come with me? I'll see about a meal, and finding you lodging while we're at it."

"That's the best offer I've had all day." Berengar lingered a moment longer beside Morwen before bidding Iona farewell.

Most of the townspeople seemed to regard him with unease as he emerged from the herbalist's shop.

Nathan noticed the source of Berengar's discomfort as they made their way across town. "You'll have to forgive their suspicions, I'm afraid. We've had word the village of Ahenny was set ablaze by Danes not far from here."

"I've heard."

"There've been sightings of strange riders about in at least two of the neighboring towns. Rumors, more likely than not, but between that and the king's death, I reckon everyone is on edge. Then you show up with that axe on your back…" Nathan stopped and looked him over carefully. "Well, you have the look of a Dane about you, if I'm being honest. You're not one of them, are you?"

"No." Berengar's tone implied he did not particularly care for the question.

"Bloody Vikings." Nathan spat on the ground in disgust. "Good for nothing but sailing and killing."

Berengar followed Nathan to the local inn, a respectable-looking establishment that nevertheless appeared to accommodate few guests. Consequently, unlike the other townspeople, the innkeeper seemed utterly delighted to have a new patron. Though Berengar paid the weekly rate, he was unsure how long they would remain in

Knockaney. Between the reports of Danes and the prospect of two vengeful witches lurking somewhere about, the town wasn't safe for them. Neither could he very well leave while Morwen was still recovering, and yet every hour he spent away from Cashel put the royal family at further risk.

With his business at the inn squared away, Berengar quickly consumed one helping of lunch, and then another. Nathan bought a round of drinks afterward in a show of hospitality, which they shared around a table with the innkeeper. The conversation quickly turned to the mystery of the king's death, a topic rife with rumor and specula-tion. No word had yet reached Knockaney of the Witches of the Golden Vale or their whereabouts, which wasn't entirely surprising, as the news was only a day old. Berengar mostly listened, grateful for the opportunity to quench his thirst.

Finally, Nathan pushed his chair away to return to his affairs, and Berengar thanked him for his generosity. He made arrangements with the innkeeper to have a letter delivered to the castle informing Queen Alannah of the circumstances of their arrival in Knockaney. He left out most of the details of their confrontation with the witches on the chance the letter was intercepted before it reached Alannah's hand. He then wrote a separate letter for the High Queen, detailing all the events that had occurred since he received King Mór's initial summons, and instructed that it be delivered to Tara. When he was finished, he emerged from the inn and set about purchasing supplies in the town for the return journey. Luck was on his side for a change, and he found a farmer willing to part with two reliable mares for a reasonable sum.

With his hunger satiated, Berengar finally began to feel

the effects of a night without rest and looked forward to taking advantage of the room he had purchased. The trek from the forest had taken more out of him than he thought. He was on his way to the herbalist's shop to check in on Morwen when a scream rose above the clamor of everyday life, and Berengar came to an abrupt halt.

The boy Thomas hurried through town, running in a blind panic until he nearly collapsed in his father's arms.

"What is it?" Nathan asked with concern, cupping his son's face.

"Riders!" someone else shouted.

The ground shook with the trampling of hooves, and a cloud of dust rose behind a company of horsemen quickly approaching from the outskirts of town. Berengar counted fifteen men in all, armed to the teeth. All wore a variation of the same black lamellar armor.

Danes. His gaze fell on Iona, who had abandoned her shop to see the source of the commotion for herself and now stood aghast as the riders drew nearer. "Get inside and bar the door. Hide her if you can."

"What about you?" the herbalist asked.

Berengar didn't answer. "Go." It wasn't a request.

He advanced stealthily and motioned for Faolán to keep low, careful to stay out of sight.

The townspeople clustered together in the center of town as the Danes surrounded them, preventing them from fleeing. The horsemen whistled and jeered, brandishing their weapons in a frightening display. Faolán growled restlessly, eager to attack, but Berengar shook his head. The warden was used to fighting against heavy odds. He had only recently dispatched six déisi with relative ease, after all—albeit with a little help from Morwen—but there was a big gap between six men and fifteen. While the déisi were mercenaries who killed for gold, the Danes killed as a way of life and were no less dangerous. If Berengar was going to make a stand, he needed to go about it smartly.

The horsemen parted and their captain emerged, a great beast of a man astride a black stallion. He wore a *byrnie*—a mail shirt composed of thousands of interlinked iron rings in a four-on-one pattern. Due to its expense and the level of craftsmanship necessary to hand-rivet the mail, such a shirt was a sign of the individual's status and power. The captain's horse trotted forward, and a pair of cruel-looking eyes stared at the townspeople from underneath a spiked helmet. He motioned to his men, and several dismounted and began to round up the remaining people.

"People of Knockaney." His voice echoed through town. "My name is Gorr Stormsson. I trust you've heard of me." At that, a round of whispers spread through the crowd of villagers, who fell silent when Stormsson spoke again. "We seek a man by the name of Berengar. A girl with a staff of ash wood accompanies him. They were last seen near the Glen of Aherlow."

Berengar gritted his teeth. How had they known to look for him in Knockaney? His letter to the castle hadn't even left town. More importantly, why was Stormsson looking for him in the first place? It seemed a turn of fate had provided him with an opportunity to find the answers he was seeking. The trouble was, he needed to get close enough to Stormsson without getting riddled with arrows in order to do so.

Nathan stepped forward, his hand on his son's shoulder. "There's no one here by that name. We are only humble servants of the crown."

"Loyalty." Stormsson rested his hands on his saddle horn. "I respect that. I hope you'll show me the same when I am your king. Now I'll ask you one more time: where is the warden? From what I hear, he's rather difficult to miss."

No one answered. The only sound was the wind whistling through the trees.

"Very well." Stormsson gestured to the soldiers on the ground. "Search the village. When you've finished, burn everything and take what women please you. That is, unless this lot has anything to say to make me change my mind."

The Danes fanned out across town in pairs. One soldier in each pair searched the huts and businesses while archers stood watch. The farther they spread, the more vulnerable they became.

Stormsson's attention moved from Nathan to the boy at his side. The Viking's lip curled upward in a malevolent sneer, and he swung his leg over the saddle and dismounted from his horse.

"Take the boy."

Nathan tried to resist, but one of the soldiers struck him with the flat of his blade, and he fell to his knees. Two men seized Thomas by the arms and dragged the struggling boy away while the rest held the townspeople at bay.

At the same time, one of the pairs of Danes neared Iona's shop. As the soldier started toward the door, torch in hand, Berengar pulled the dagger tucked inside his boot and nodded at Faolán. He slipped behind the soldier and clamped a hand over his mouth to prevent him from screaming before dragging the dagger across the Dane's neck. The archer spotted the attack too late, and Faolán leapt on him before he could fire. Berengar took the dagger and finished him off. He glanced at the center of town, where Stormsson held Thomas in front of the others. The boy shook from head to toe.

"Such a sweet lad." Stormsson pinched the boy's cheek

with a gauntleted hand and looked over at his father. "You southerners are so soft." He forced Thomas to his knees, and all the humor drained from his voice. "Tell me where Berengar and the girl have gone, or I'll start taking pieces for the hounds."

As Stormsson raised his sword, Berengar nocked an arrow in his bow and pulled back on the bowstring, aiming it at the Viking captain.

"There he is!" a soldier called from across town. "I see him!"

Stormsson looked up and locked eyes with Berengar, who released his hold on the string. The Viking threw himself forward as the arrow streaked through the air, instead finding the heart of the Dane at his side. Berengar quickly nocked another arrow and fired it at the closest warrior before casting the bow aside and seizing his axe. He stared down at Stormsson across the gap, and the warrior pushed Thomas aside and pointed his sword in Berengar's direction.

"The mighty warden, at last. I see the tales are true. You are a sight to behold."

"Gorr Stormsson." Berengar's voice rang across town. "It's time you answered for your crimes against the crown. In the name of High Queen Nora, I sentence you to die."

Stormsson laughed as his men moved to join him. "Your death will bring me much glory. I will enter Valhalla with your head in my hands."

Vastly outnumbered by his enemies, Berengar let out a fierce roar and charged forward to meet them, his axe held high. The archers trained their bows on him, but before any could fire, a mighty horn rippled through the air. Stormsson stared past Berengar, and his smile vanished. Berengar looked back and saw Ronan approaching the battle on horseback, his yellow cloak waving in the wind as he held his longsword high. No fewer than twenty members of the castle guard accompanied him, all charging into battle with the enemy force.

"Retreat!" Stormsson shouted when he saw them coming. He turned and threw himself onto his horse.

His dark gaze lingered on Berengar a moment longer, and then he seized the reins and fled.

CHAPTER ELEVEN

AN ARROW WHIZZED past his head as the people of Knock-aney ran, seeking cover. The cavalry had arrived, but the battle was not yet finished. Berengar diverted his attention from Gorr Stormsson to an enemy archer partially obscured by smoke from a burning wagon. Before he could close the distance between them, two swordsmen attacked, allowing the archer to nock another arrow and take aim. The pair of Danes struck in tandem, forcing him into a defensive position in order to avoid oncoming arrows. Faolán outpaced him and knocked the archer off his feet, causing him to misfire.

Berengar heard a horse neigh behind him as the cavalry approached. Moments later, one of his attackers was all but cleaved in two by Ronan's longsword. Berengar brought his axe around and beheaded the Viking's companion before the first man's corpse hit the ground. The queen's thane galloped in the direction Stormsson had fled until a spear came sailing out of the smoke and struck his horse, which crashed to the dirt and died with a whimper.

Ronan rose unharmed, his breastplate shining in the sunlight. His men moved to come to his aid, but he shook his head and gestured with his sword to the path the retreating Danes had taken. "After him! Stormsson cannot be allowed to escape!"

The horsemen thundered past them on their way out of town, leaving Ronan and a smaller contingent of castle guards to face the remaining Vikings. Berengar and Ronan fought side by side, cutting down all enemies until at last there were none left to stand against them.

"You fought well," Berengar said when it was over, impressed. Ronan used the two-handed sword to devastating effect, which was no small feat considering the demands of such a heavy blade.

"I was a soldier long before I was elevated to the rank of thane." Ronan's fine clothes and armor were stained with blood. "Fighting comes as easily to me as breathing."

Berengar understood that sentiment well enough.

Ronan issued orders to the guards. "Extinguish the fires and assist the townspeople. Pile the bodies of the dead. If there are any Danes left alive, we'll take them as prisoners. If not, search the corpses for any information that may be of use."

"It will be done, Thane Ronan," a guard replied with a bow.

Berengar accompanied Ronan as he supervised the battle's aftermath. "I don't know that I could have taken them all on my own."

"It's fortunate we came across you when we did."

"How *did* you find us?"

Ronan laughed for the first time since Berengar had known him, the only hint he'd shown of something underneath his reserved persona. "You have the princess to thank for that. She ordered a search party sent out when you did not return from the Glen of Aherlow. Given all that has happened, Queen Alannah was hesitant to allow my departure, but her daughter refused to entrust the mission to anyone else. Princess Ravenna can be quite…insistent."

"So I've noticed." Berengar found his already considerable admiration for the princess growing.

He noticed Thomas sprinting across town to the spot where his father waited. The boy leapt into Nathan's arms, father and son safely reunited.

The sound of hooves echoed nearby, where some of the riders Ronan sent in pursuit of Gorr Stormsson were returning. The riders slowed their approach as they neared Ronan and Berengar. "Forgive me, my thane. The Danes eluded us. We dispatched two scouts to continue the hunt."

Ronan flashed his teeth in annoyance. "There is work enough for you here." He turned to the crowd that had assembled in the marketplace. "People of Knockaney! This settlement is under the crown's protection. Good Queen Alannah will not permit her subjects to suffer at the hands of Danes. Mark my words—Gorr Stormsson will be brought to justice. Until that time, I will leave a number of guards here to bolster your defenses." With that, he issued commands to his men before pulling Berengar aside. "I take it your visit to the witches didn't go as planned."

"Not exactly."

"Were they behind the king's death?"

"Not here," Berengar said as townspeople and guards passed by. "We have much to discuss upon our return to the castle."

"Very well. What of Lady Morwen? I don't see her about."

"Come with me." He led Ronan to the herbalist's shop and rapped loudly on the door until Iona inched it open.

"Is it safe?"

He nodded. "How is she?"

Iona motioned for them to come inside. "See for yourself."

To Berengar's surprise, Morwen was awake and alert.

"I've never seen anyone begin the recovery process so quickly. Then again, you might have told me she was a magician."

"I imagined the staff gave it away." Berengar aimed a wink at Morwen, who laughed before breaking into a fit of coughing.

Iona propped Morwen up and passed her a cup of water. "Here. Drink this."

"Thank you." Morwen glanced around the herbalist's shop, clearly puzzled by the unfamiliar surroundings. "We aren't back at Cashel, are we?"

Berengar shook his head. "We're at Knockaney. You fell ill, so I carried you to the nearest town."

Morwen graced him with the easy smile that seemed second nature to her, though she remained noticeably pale. "Thank you."

"Now we're even."

Morwen glanced away, as if embarrassed. "I spent so much time wishing the king would let me go off in search of adventure. It seems the world was more dangerous than I realized." She shook her head. "I thought I could beat them, but I couldn't." She bowed her head. "I would have had to kill them, and I couldn't do it. Maybe if I were more like you…"

"Don't say that." The warmth was gone from his voice. "It's much easier to take a life than it is to show mercy. There are plenty of men like me. Perhaps this world needs more like you." He wasn't sure he believed the words, but they seemed to do the trick. Morwen perked up immediately.

"It is good to see you are well, Lady Morwen," Ronan said. "Life at court is diminished without your presence, even during a short absence."

"You're very kind, Thane Ronan."

Despite their age difference, in many ways they were counterparts of each other. A thane and a court magician were two sides of the same coin. Both were servants of the throne, and each protected the realm in his or her way. Thanes defended the realm from political and armed conflict, while court magicians were the safeguard against monsters and magical threats. According to custom, thanes stood at the right hand of the throne while court magicians were at the left.

Morwen grimaced as she shifted her weight and swung her feet over the side of the bed. "The queen must know what we have learned."

"Wait." Iona laid a hand on the young magician to restrain her. "You're in no condition to be walking around on your own."

"Nonsense. I'll be fine after a few days of healing elixirs from my stores. Not that I'm not grateful for your... remedies," she added hastily, glancing around the room.

Iona put her hands on her hips. "My remedies saved that leg of yours."

"She doesn't mean anything by it," Berengar interrupted. "We need to take her back to the castle. It's not safe for her here. Can we move her without risking further injury?"

Iona glared at him. "This morning the girl was at death's door, in case you've forgotten." She let out a frustrated sigh and began gathering balms and bandages. "Fine. Do as you will, but remember to change her bandages, and don't let her attempt to walk on that leg until it's healed—for any reason."

He nodded politely in her direction. "Thank you. I am in your debt."

"No, Warden Berengar." Iona's tone implied she had not forgotten the horrors of Dún Aulin. "I remain in yours."

With that, they parted ways. While Ronan oversaw preparations for their return to the castle, Berengar took the opportunity to catch up on some well-deserved sleep. In the morning, they bade the town farewell. Five guards remained behind to ensure the town's defense against further attacks. Thanks to Ronan's intervention, Knockaney had sustained only minimal damage and no loss of life. The Danes were not so lucky. All who attempted to stand their ground against the queen's forces had perished in the skirmish, which meant there were no prisoners who might reveal the location of Gorr Stormsson's hidden stronghold. Though the townspeople considered the Danes heathens who worshiped foreign gods, Ronan insisted they be given a proper burial, a sign he was a true man of Munster. In the far reaches of the north, the bodies might have been burned.

Morwen continued to show remarkable improvement overnight. Apart from her injury, she seemed to have returned to her usual good spirits. Much of the color had returned to her face, and her energy was good. She rode in the back of a transport wagon, grimacing only occasionally when the road turned bumpy. Faolán lay beside her in the wagon to keep her company while Berengar and Ronan rode ahead. Ronan remarked they were leaving empty-handed, though Berengar privately disagreed. He considered it fortunate they were leaving Knockaney with their lives intact.

Berengar attempted to draw Ronan into conversation. "You said you were a soldier before the peace. How did you come to enter the king's service?" Despite the position Ronan held, Berengar knew little of the thane's personal history.

"In the time of Azeroth, goblins spilled freely across our borders, their ranks growing by the day. The lowlands became unsafe, and many of the lords of Munster and their people sought safety in the fortress of Tuathal's Keep in the Black Stacks to the west. Laird Tierney of Cill Airne was one such lord, as was Queen Alannah's father, Laird McAllister, to whom I had sworn my sword."

The warden had seen the Black Stacks for himself when passing through the Gap of Dún Lóich on the road to Cill Airne. The mountain range contained Géarán Tuathal, the highest summit in all Fál—taller even than Ulster's icy peaks—where an ancient stone fortress served to protect Munster's people in times of war.

"I heard of Tuathal's Keep during the war," Berengar said. "The goblin army massed in the mountains and laid siege to the fortress." With the goblins fixed on the mountain, Azeroth's armies in Munster were divided, allowing Mór's brother to send aid to Nora.

"When my commander was slain by a poisoned arrow, I took command of Tuathal's Keep. For two long years our men held the besieging forces at bay, though our numbers and supplies were few and the goblins were many. After the war, when Mór and Alannah were wed, the queen insisted that I be chosen as thane. It was not my choice. I would have preferred the life of a soldier, but honor demanded I do what Munster required of me. I'm more comfortable in the thick of battle, sword in hand, than in some dusty council chamber or surrounded by those at court."

"In that, you and I agree." Berengar wondered if

Alannah had been there with her father at the keep. Ravenna told him Ronan grew up in the queen's household. Already he'd seen hints the two were close, but the exact nature of their relationship remained a mystery.

At first it had surprised Berengar that Mór had chosen him for the job when there were other wardens who possessed more knowledge of the inner workings of Munster's royal court. Then again, perhaps the king had requested him precisely for that reason, as he had no long-lasting relationships with those in the castle that might compromise his investigation.

Ronan glanced over his shoulder as if to make certain they weren't overheard. "The princess must be fond of you to have sent me to retrieve you. Tread carefully with her, Warden Berengar." The veiled comment almost sounded like a challenge.

"What makes you say that?" Berengar held his gaze.

"I have devoted my life to the crown. I have no family of my own, and Ravenna is the closest thing to a daughter I will ever have."

"She has not had an easy life, from what I've heard."

Ronan sighed. "You should have known her when she was young. She was kind and gentle—always ready with a smile. There was such a spark in her, not unlike Lady Morwen in that regard. The death of her brother changed her. I do not like to speak unkindly of the dead, but King Mór treated her ill by sending her away. She was never the same after that."

"I asked the witches about the prince's death, but they spoke in riddles on the subject."

"I knew the lad well. Prince Aiden was not overly studious, and he could be reckless, but he had the courage of a lion, and a heart to match. Had he lived, he would have made a good king one day."

"The circumstances of his death seem shrouded in mystery," Berengar said.

"Mark my words, it was the crone's doing. King Mór ordered a full inquest into the death of his son, but the results were never revealed. I believe the king had them sealed away."

The castle appeared ahead, towering atop the Rock of Cashel. Gathering winds howled from the north, and the company's golden banners rippled in the breeze. As they approached the city, a horn emanated from the other side of the wall, and the gate opened to grant them entry.

The mood in the city seemed more or less the same as it had when Berengar and Morwen set out two days earlier for their dealings with the Witches of the Golden Vale. There was perhaps an added element of friction, possibly from news of the Viking attacks across the kingdom, but life continued on uninterrupted in all its districts, much as it always had and always would as long as Cashel remained standing.

Ronan conferred with the sentries at the gate. "The scouts we sent after Gorr Stormsson have not returned. Still, it's early yet. They may be gathering intelligence and lying low until the time is right."

It was a clear attempt on Ronan's part to sound optimistic, but the warden had his doubts. While it was always possible the scouts were still on Stormsson's trail, it was far more likely they were dead, or else soon would be.

The castle walls were well manned. Anyone wrongly attempting to gain entrance would have a tough go of it, though the assassin had already demonstrated himself cleverer than most. When the horses reached the path's summit and made their way through the courtyard, Berengar noticed a place was already being made for a statue of Mór to join those of his ancestors. As the warden dismounted his horse, he caught Morwen trying to climb out of the wagon.

"Blast it," she muttered after falling on her back. "Lend me a hand, will you?"

Berengar shook his head. "Iona said you're to rest."

"I'll be fine. I think I know rather more about the art of healing than some country herbalist. Besides, the queen will want to hear our report."

She tried again to rise, but Berengar held her in place, drawing her ire.

"You're not going anywhere. I'll tell the queen what we learned from the witches. You'll wait here until you're escorted to the infirmary. It's not up for discussion."

Morwen shot him a dark look. "I could cast a spell on you. Maybe turn you into a toad."

"You wouldn't dare." Based on the admittedly little he knew of magic, he doubted very much she could accomplish such a task, even if she wanted to. By now, he had begun to understand when she was teasing him. He crossed his arms and tried not to show his amusement. "I'll come by and visit you later. Once you've had some time for one of those healing elixirs of yours to take effect, we'll talk. Faolán will keep you company until then."

"Wait," she called after him as he turned to go. "Can you at least leave me your axe?"

"My axe? What do you want that for?"

"So that I can enchant it, of course. I'm certainly not planning on swinging it around. There are a few improvements I'd like to make, and it should help me pass the time without dying of boredom. You didn't complain when I outfitted it with that rune of resistance, as I recall."

"No." He remembered how the rune had allowed his axe to deflect one of Agatha's spells. "It probably saved our lives." He laid the axe beside her on the wagon and left the magician sitting there, her feet dangling in the air.

Berengar steeled himself the moment he set foot inside the castle. Since their confrontation with the witches, an unpleasant question had slowly taken shape in his mind, and no matter the consequences, he intended to see it answered. A messenger informed them that Alannah was not holding court at the moment, and Berengar and Ronan found the queen in her council chambers, discussing matters of importance to the realm with her counselors.

"I want all those who have suffered from Viking attacks taken care of," Alannah said from the head of the table. "Make sure grain shipments are delivered to any towns or villages without enough food." Having failed to notice their entrance, she marked a proclamation with her seal and set it aside before turning to the next stack of documents. "It says here an oilliphéist is killing travelers along the River Shannon. Are there any other reports of monster attacks?"

Laird O'Reilly stood as a servant passed him documents of his own. "There have been several kelpie sightings near Lake Allua, my queen. And a woman from Helvick swears her children have been replaced by changelings."

"Lady Morwen assures me the fairies have forsaken these lands. Nevertheless, send someone to Helvick to be sure—and contract mercenaries to deal with any confirmed monster sightings." When Alannah looked up, her gaze fell on Berengar and Ronan. "I see you have returned from your encounter with the Witches of the Golden Vale, Warden Berengar, but where is Lady Morwen? Her counsel is surely needed for this of all matters."

Ronan approached the table. "Lady Morwen sustained

injuries during a duel with the witches. Though she looks to be on the mend."

Shock appeared on the queen's face, and the parchment fell away from her hands. "What happened?"

Berengar remained where he stood and ignored her question. "Did you know?"

"I don't understand your meaning." Alannah's expression suggested she resented his tone.

"King Mór's agreement with the witches." His eyes never left her face. "Each month he sent them another victim to be sacrificed. So I'll ask you again—did you know about it?" Though Mór had been a man of secrets, Alannah was a shrewd woman, and Berengar had a hard time imagining that she didn't at least suspect what was going on.

The room grew so quiet he could almost hear the sound of her breath as it caught in her chest. "I want everyone out—with the exception of my thane, Laird O'Reilly, and the warden."

As the last of the room's occupants filed outside the chamber, Ronan put himself between Berengar and the queen, anger evident at the apparent affront to his queen's dignity. "How dare you impugn the queen's—"

Alannah held up a hand. "Ronan, enough."

"Your Grace?" Ronan's eyes widened in astonishment, and he took a step away from her, looking horrified. "Alannah?"

"It's true. It was years before I learned of my husband's accord with the witches. Not that it mattered. I told my husband it was misguided and wrong, but he would not be swayed. If anyone dared expose the truth, it would bring my husband's reign—perhaps even the kingdom itself—to ruin. So I kept silent. Tell me, Warden, how could I have done otherwise?"

"Tell that to the families of those the witches butchered."

It was Alannah's turn to show anger. The queen snatched a scroll from the table and passed it to her chief adviser. "Laird O'Reilly, give the warden the edict I issued the day he rode from Cashel."

O'Reilly, already privy to the scroll's contents, crossed the room and handed it to Berengar.

This is an official proclamation outlawing the practice of witch-craft in Munster, he realized as he scanned the contents of the scroll. *It bears the queen's signature, but that means she had already prepared it before our return.*

"It was my husband's agreement, not mine. As far as I'm concerned, it ended the moment of his death. Mór was obsessed with magic. He traced his lineage back to High King Brian Boru himself and believed there was magic in his bloodline. He was disappointed that his children—the children I gave him—were born without magical ability." She looked disgusted at the idea. "I, on the other hand, was relieved. As you might suspect, I have contempt for magic, Warden Berengar."

"Your Grace—"

Alannah turned away and approached the balcony, where she gazed across the city. "When I was a child, my mother took ill. Through one of our servants, word reached my father of a traveling magician. Doubtless enamored by the prospect of the reward my father offered, the magician treated her with various potions and decoctions." She shook her head and glanced back at them, resolute once more. "She died in agony. Her screams carried to every room in the estate. The fool of a magician had made her worse, you see. He had the good sense to flee before justice could be done to him."

For the first time, Berengar understood the reason

behind the queen's distaste for magic. She not only lost her mother to a magician's incompetence, but quite possibly suffered the death of her son as the result of a crone's curse. Now that Alannah held the throne instead of her husband, the warden wondered if more changes were in the works regarding Munster's policy toward magic and magical creatures. There was a fine line between hiring a mercenary to slay a murderous kelpie and sanctioning the death of harmless magical creatures —a line other kingdoms had tried and failed to walk. It was still too early into Alannah's reign to know what kind of queen she would be.

"If it were up to me," she finished, "magic would be stamped out altogether—starting with the Witches of the Golden Vale."

"In that case, you'll be glad to hear I killed at least one of their coven. I put my axe through her black heart."

"That is excellent news. And the others?"

"Can't say for certain. Their lair went up in flames."

"We've sent messengers to the Glen of Aherlow to find out more," Ronan added. "Though if any witches survived, I doubt they would remain there."

"Then their power is broken," Alannah mused. "The realm owes you a debt of gratitude, Warden Berengar."

Laird O'Reilly cleared his throat. "Lest we forget the reason for your departure from Cashel in the first place, were you able to learn anything useful during your time with them? Did the witches arrange the king's murder?"

Berengar hesitated. While the queen might have been aware her husband was supplying the witches with sacrifices, he doubted she knew the full extent of Mór's accord with Agatha—the truth of Morwen's birth in particular. After witnessing the queen's disposition toward magic, Berengar had no plans to enlighten her on that subject.

Morwen had been through enough. If he could spare her further suffering by keeping her secret, he would.

He chose his words carefully. "The witches traded in riddles and lies. The cursed medallion the déisi used to kill Matthias came from them, but the coven denied having a hand in your husband's death."

"And did you believe them?"

"It's hard to think they would risk the peace accorded to them by King Mór, but the motives of witches are always difficult to unravel. I believe someone else discovered that King Mór was supplying the witches with sacrifices and used the information to blackmail him."

Laird O'Reilly practically coughed at the news. "What's this? Blackmail, you say?"

Berengar was left with no choice but to briefly recount what he had learned from the Exchequer. "The witches did mention something else that should merit concern, Your Grace. The coven's leader alluded to a darker power at work in Munster, perhaps even more powerful than the crone that dwells in the Devil's Bit."

"What sort of power?"

"I don't know. A dark mage, perhaps, or even a sorcerer." He went on to detail all that happened during and after their encounter with the witches, including Gorr Stormsson's attack on Knockaney. Neither Ronan nor the queen could account for how easily the Danes had been able to find Berengar when so few knew the reason for his departure from Cashel.

The queen considered his words for a long moment. "These are troubling tidings you bring me. I trust you and Lady Morwen will find the truth in all this. Ronan, see to it that a sizable bounty is placed on the heads of any surviving witches. I want them driven out of Munster. And bid my counselors and guards to return."

"It will be done, Your Grace." Ronan bowed and swept out of the room, still looking startled by the queen's revelation.

Berengar started to go, but the queen surprised him by grabbing his hand. "I have a request." She lowered her voice so that O'Reilly could not hear, and her expression softened. "Please don't mention what you learned from the witches to my daughter. I fear Ravenna never forgave her father for sending her away, or me for agreeing to it. This news would only further tarnish Mór's memory in her eyes, and perhaps destroy what little affection she retains for me."

"Very well." The prospect of keeping secrets from the princess was not particularly appealing. He and Alannah exchanged a final glance, and he left without another word.

Berengar searched for Ronan when he emerged from the council chambers, but the queen's thane was already gone.

"A moment, Warden Berengar." The voice belonged to Laird O'Reilly, who had followed him into the throne room. The chamber lay empty but for the two of them. "I would like a word in private."

That seems to be the way with you. O'Reilly was always off to the side, whispering in someone's ear, trading in secrets and court gossip. Such behavior would have appealed to Mór, who had always possessed an ear for flattery, but Berengar suspected it was all an act.

"Go on."

O'Reilly remained on the dais, hovering uncomfortably close to the throne.

"There were new developments in the investigation while you were away. You remember the king received a letter the day of his death, which he read and promptly cast into the flames?"

Berengar nodded.

"Though the letter's contents remain a mystery, we identified the messenger. He was a rider from Cill Airne."

Berengar scowled. That told him almost nothing. "Anything else?"

O'Reilly descended the steps from the dais one at a time. "It was rather convenient Thane Ronan happened to arrive just in time to lend you his aid against Gorr Stormsson. How unfortunate Stormsson managed to escape before he could be captured."

Berengar folded his arms across his chest. "What are you saying?"

"Only this: be careful whom you trust. Only someone in a position of power could have blackmailed the king. Few were closer to Mór than Ronan." O'Reilly made a show of looking around the empty chamber to make sure they were alone and lowered his voice to a conspiratorial tone. "There is a woman you should meet—one of the queen's former ladies in waiting. I think you will find what she has to say quite illuminating. Will you speak to her?"

So this is what he was after all along. O'Reilly used the information about the messenger from Cill Airne as a pretext to sway him against Ronan, but why? With Ronan out of the way, the royal adviser would become the second most powerful individual in the kingdom, but was there more to it than a petty rivalry?

"Fine. But this had better not be a waste of my time." Berengar didn't like the idea that O'Reilly might be trying to play him.

The old man rubbed his hands together with enthusiasm. "Excellent. I will make the arrangements. She'll be expecting you tomorrow afternoon."

"Wait," Berengar said when O'Reilly turned to leave. "There's something I'd like you to do for me. I want the results of the inquiry into Prince Aiden's death."

"Those records were sealed under order of the king."

"Then unseal them." Berengar took a step forward and stared down at O'Reilly. "Do we understand each other?"

To his credit, O'Reilly didn't flinch. "I believe we do."

"Good." His footsteps echoed as he departed the chamber, leaving O'Reilly standing before the throne.

CHAPTER TWELVE

WORD FROM CORRIN reached him the next morning that a peddler had arrived in Cashel with three corpses in tow —corpses she claimed were the remains of the Witches of the Golden Vale. The guards described the peddler as an old woman dressed in rags. Suspecting she was only after the reward, they dismissed the peddler's claims, and she abandoned the bodies on the back of a wagon and went on her way.

After voicing his displeasure at not being informed sooner so that he might question the peddler himself, Berengar left the castle and made his way down to the city at once. Though Cashel already showed signs of stirring, the hour was early, and the warden encountered a relative few along the road. He found the three bodies in a remote spot at the outskirts of the city near the cemetery, where they had been unceremoniously dumped under an elm tree.

Morwen was already there when he arrived. Evidently her healing potions had done the trick, though he noticed she continued to lean on her staff for support. She stood with her back to him, staring at the charred remains in the shade.

Berengar crouched beside the corpses. Scant remnants of dresses clung to each of the deceased, eaten away by the fire. They were women's bodies. He was certain of that much, at least. All three had long hair. Each corpse's skin was dry like parchment, cracked and blackened from the flames.

"Is it them?"

"I think so. Even with my abilities dulled, I sense magic about them."

It was the first time they had spoken since parting ways upon their return to the castle. When he attempted to visit her following his audience with the queen, he found her asleep, recovering from her ordeal.

The warden turned over a facedown corpse and saw that a large portion of her lower face had been cut away. Berengar knew the work of his axe when he saw it. The body belonged to Cora, the witch who tried to force her way inside his mind.

"Their crowns and jewelry are gone. The peddler must have taken them." He withdrew his hand and rose to a standing position. "Not one escaped the flames. We were lucky. This could have been our fate."

"The bodies mustn't be buried here. Lest their spirits linger in this place. They should be burned outside the city, their ashes consecrated by the priests and spread to the winds." She hobbled closer to him. "Will you help me?"

They've already been burned, he wanted to say, but when he saw her somber expression, he simply nodded and began stacking the bodies.

In the time it took him to load the witches' remains

onto a wagon and secure horses for the task, Cashel had fully awoken. Crowds impeded the wagon's progress as it rolled down the street. It was half an hour before they reached the gate. The clamor of city life slowly faded the farther they traveled from the city. Cashel was barely visible when Morwen pointed out a remote area off the road.

"This is the place."

Berengar guided the horses to the spot and brought the wagon to a halt. Morwen knelt beside the bodies and muttered a long chant over each one, waving her staff around in the air as if to ward away evil. When she finished, she leaned against Berengar for support, much to his surprise. She was either still too weak to light the fire with magic, or else considered it inappropriate to do so, so Berengar started one for her.

Together they watched as the roaring flames consumed the bodies, sending black smoke lofting into the sky. Even from a distance, the stifling heat from the fire joined with the considerable summer warmth, and sweat poured in torrents from the warden's brow.

"I used to wonder who my mother was," Morwen said after a time, when the witches' corpses were little more than soot and ash. "What she was like." The rest she left unspoken, but he knew all too well the sentiment behind her words. Neither of her parents were what she imagined them to be.

"My mother died when I was younger than you are now."

"Thank you for staying with me for this. I'm glad I didn't have to do it alone."

The last of the flames left only smoldering embers as they died away. Berengar led Morwen to the wagon and helped her up before taking the reins.

"What's next?" she asked when they started on the path back to Cashel.

"You're going back to the castle to continue your recovery. You can hardly stand."

"But I want to help!"

"I know. That's why I've arranged for Laird O'Reilly to have the records from the inquest into Prince Aiden's death delivered to the tower. I think there's more to his death than we realize, and you're better fit to determine if magic was involved than I."

Morwen rested her arms on the staff in her lap and leaned back her seat, appearing at least somewhat satisfied he'd given her something to do. "What about you?"

"Once I see you to the castle, I'll inform the queen that the witches have been dealt with. There's also a woman in the city Laird O'Reilly claims has important information for me."

"You should tell Corrin to keep a lookout for the peddler. We don't want any of the witches' belongings ending up for sale in the market. Their possessions might be cursed."

Berengar nodded. "When I'm finished, I'll come by and see what you've learned, provided you haven't dozed off again."

A wry smile crept over Morwen's face. "Did you actually just make a joke?"

Berengar merely grunted in response as the wagon rolled through the open gates.

Once inside the castle, he bade farewell to Morwen. When Corrin greeted him in the throne room, Berengar informed him of the witches' deaths. He made sure to pass along Morwen's instructions regarding the peddler. Several members of Alannah's court exchanged whispers and furtive glances as he went by. They no doubt remembered the disruption he'd caused when he'd marched Calum into their midst and declared one of their number a traitor. If they were expecting a similar commotion to ensue at present, they would be sorely disappointed.

As he approached the throne, Berengar spotted Ravenna standing off to one side. The princess wore a decidedly displeased expression. It wasn't hard to see why. Ravenna was surrounded by a flock of well-dressed nobles, many of whom wore iron crowns. All were men, and Berengar guessed they were suitors. He even spotted Laird Tierney's son Desmond among their number.

Without warning, Ravenna broke free of their ranks and stormed to the dais, interrupting the performance of a bard with a distinctly Caledonian accent. Although their voices were drowned out by the noise in the background, it was clear Ravenna and Alannah were locked in an argument of sorts. Ravenna put her hands on her hips and leaned toward her mother, who frowned, while Ronan and Laird O'Reilly appeared none too eager to get involved in the dispute. Finally, Ravenna shook her head and stormed off.

Berengar turned away and pursued the princess, who slowed at his approach. He felt the weight of Alannah's gaze following them from the throne, where the bard had resumed his song, accompanied by a fiddler who wore the queen's colors.

"Mother is encouraging me to marry one of the *Rí Tuaithe* or their sons." Ravenna nodded at the group of suitors from whom she had taken leave. "She says such a union would help stabilize the realm during these precarious times. She's even taken to bribing those frightened by rumors of a curse on our family. It's exactly what Father would have done."

"The lords of Munster are honorable men."

"Aye. They are worthy suitors all, but I do not want them."

"What do you want?"

"To be free." At that her anger seemed to abate, as if no one had thought before to ask her such a simple question. "I am glad to see you have returned safely, Warden Berengar. I was worried when you did not appear after your visit to the witches."

He found her words strangely touching. It had been some time since anyone voiced concern for his safety. "I owe you my thanks, Princess. Ronan told me you sent him to retrieve us over your mother's objections. Were it not for his arrival, I might have fallen prisoner to the Danes, or worse."

"Consider us even for saving my life."

Corrin interjected before either could say another word. "Forgive me, Your Grace, but the queen wishes to speak with you."

"I would have thought I made my position rather clear." Ravenna sighed. "No need to look so uncomfortable, Captain. Father taught me better than to cause a scene in public. I'm afraid I must excuse myself, Warden Berengar."

With that, she walked away, leaving Berengar to admire her.

"She's quite something, isn't she?"

The voice belonged to Desmond, who stood nearby.

"That she is."

"It is good to see you again, Warden Berengar, even under such circumstances." Desmond extended his hand, a sign that his attitude toward the warden had warmed since they last met. "I was wrong about you. Cill Airne owes you a debt of gratitude for resolving the situation at Innisfallen without bloodshed."

"That was more Lady Morwen's doing than my own, to tell you the truth. I gather you're here in your father's stead."

"You have the truth of it. As his eldest son, it is my responsibility to represent him in Cashel."

"And how is Laird Tierney?" Berengar remembered the image of the frail old man sitting in a stone chair, barely able to support the weight of the iron crown on his head.

"Not well, I'm afraid. His illness has only worsened. His physician does not know if he will survive. After the coronation, I intend to return to Cill Airne at once, if the queen permits."

Berengar followed his gaze to the throne, where Ravenna and her mother appeared to have made amends.

"She seems fond of you," Desmond mused. "If I might be so bold, what is the nature of your interest in the princess?"

"I'm here to protect the royal family until King Mór's killer is captured. That's all."

Desmond seemed to regard him with skepticism but had the decency to keep any doubts to himself.

"Do you know her well?" Berengar's gaze lingered on the princess a few moments longer than necessary.

"We were childhood friends." Desmond grew suddenly pensive. "The princess and her brother spent a summer in my father's castle when we were younger. It was King Mór's intention that Prince Aiden should study under the masters at the Institute." He chuckled. "The prince was more interested in seeking adventure, as I recall."

The description sounded in keeping with what Berengar knew of Aiden from Ravenna and others. He was reminded of his own adventure near Cill Airne, and the lingering questions that remained from his time there.

"When we set out from your city, Morwen and I were attacked on the road by the déisi—the same lot who passed through your city. Were you ever able to find out who hired them?"

"I'm afraid not, though not for lack of trying. The déisi aren't the sort to leave a trail."

"What about Gorr Stormsson? The Danes have been spreading across Munster of late. Have you had any trouble with them in your lands?"

"None. The Danes land their ships along the coast to the east and have little influence in the west. My father's soldiers stand ready to keep our lands clear of their threat."

Somehow there was a connection between the Danes, the déisi, and the Brotherhood of Thieves, but Berengar had not found it yet. He thought again of the assassin's cleverness and recalled Agatha's shrouded hints about a darker power exerting influence over Munster. What was he missing?

At that moment, a hush fell across the hall as a man in lamellar armor and a black cloak entered the throne room. His skin was pale, as if the season were winter, not summer. The yellow hair on his head and beard were braided. Berengar's gaze fell on the dagger he carried at his side.

A Dane, he realized.

The nobles drew back, clearing out of the man's way. Almost at once, Corrin shouted an order, and the guards surrounded the newcomer in a circle, pointing rows of sharp spears at him.

Ronan put himself in front of Queen Alannah, his

hand resting on the hilt of his blade. "You dare enter the queen's presence while armed? Who are you?"

The Dane leered at the guards with a pair of malicious blue eyes. "I come in peace." He raised his hands. "I am only a messenger—from Gorr Stormsson."

Ronan's voice carried across the chamber, full of loathing. "Your master is the enemy of peace. You will be lucky to leave this place with your head still attached."

The messenger only smiled. "You would be wise to hear my master's proposition. Much bloodshed might be avoided."

Alannah stood but remained behind Ronan's protection. "Let him speak."

At Corrin's command, the circle of guards broke, forming two rows that ran the length of the room. They continued to hold their spears out; if the messenger made an attempt on the queen, he would be cut down before he ever reached the throne.

"My master will have peace, if you meet his terms."

"And what are his terms?" Alannah's gaze was unwavering.

"First, your armies must disband and return to their lands of origin. Second, Gorr Stormsson is to be made a lord of Munster and raised to the rank of thane."

"Is that all?"

Berengar watched as the messenger's eyes fell on the princess. "He requests the hand of the Princess Ravenna in marriage. You will remain on the throne until the time of your death, at which time Gorr Stormsson will become king. In return, he pledges never again to wage war against Munster. The pillage and plunder of your kingdom will cease. My master will bring these lands under his watch and protect them as the High Queen and her wardens have failed to do."

Berengar's blood boiled at the man's audacity. He had half a mind to charge the messenger with his axe right then and there, without regard for the consequences, and not just for the insult to the High Queen. Forced marriage was once a fairly common practice throughout Fál. Nora herself had been abducted by a murderous lord who wished to make her his bride when she was the heir to the throne of Connacht, though she escaped his grasp. For Ravenna, who had already endured one marriage that had been imposed upon her, it would be an unimaginable fate.

"If you refuse my master's generous offer, know that ships carrying two thousand fighting men are on their way to Munster as we speak. With your fleet in ruins, you have no way to prevent them from landing on your shores."

"You dare threaten—" Ronan started to say.

Ravenna held up her hand to silence him. "I can answer for myself."

Before anyone could stop her, the princess descended from the dais and walked calmly toward the Dane. Berengar stood frozen in place, and his heart—usually steady no matter the danger—skipped a beat as she drew nearer to the messenger. He was too far away to reach her in time if she needed help.

Ravenna stopped mere inches away from the Dane, who averted his eyes under the force of her penetrating gaze. "Here is my answer. Never again will any man possess me. I do not fear your master, who was not even man enough to come here himself. I name Gorr Stormsson a coward, in sight of everyone here. He will fall like his brother before him, and the dogs will eat at his corpse."

As anger showed on the messenger's face, the princess deftly reached down to his waist and in one clean sweep drew his dagger and pointed the blade at his throat. The messenger's eyes widened in disbelief.

"If I were queen, I would have your head. How fortunate for you that I am not." Ravenna held the dagger point under his chin. "Now you will send a message for me. Tell your master the people of Munster do not frighten so easily. It's only a matter of time before our soldiers smoke him out of hiding like the rat he is." The dagger clattered to the floor, and Ravenna turned her back on him. "Escort this worm from the castle at once. And Captain? There's no need to be overly gentle about it."

Corrin laid a gauntleted hand on the messenger's shoulder. "As you wish, Your Grace."

As Ravenna returned to the throne, the cadre of suitors seemed to shrink back from her, as if startled by the princess' display of ferocity. Berengar only smiled, unable to help himself. *The king's killer should hope Mór's daughter doesn't find him before I do.*

T he woman Laird O'Reilly wanted him to meet resided in a merchant class neighborhood, home to neither the poorest nor the wealthiest of Cashel's citizenry. Berengar arrived at a modest one-story home with a thatched roof, one of many clumped together. At first no one answered when he knocked on the door. For a moment he thought perhaps he had come to the wrong address, but after a few moments he heard footsteps inside, and a young woman opened the door. Her fine clothes and expensive jewelry seemed out of place compared to the humble dwelling.

"My name is Berengar. Laird O'Reilly said you'd be expecting me."

"Yes, I know. My servant should have let you in. I don't know where the old fool has gotten off to now. She's deaf in one ear and nearly lame. I've told Father she's impossible to manage, but he refuses to listen to me." She waved him inside. "Do come in."

After telling Faolán to wait outside, Berengar ducked under the doorway and stepped over the threshold. The home's interior was even less impressive than the outside. Though the hall was spacious enough, there were only two additional rooms, a bedroom and a kitchen. Although her surroundings were commonplace, the woman herself was striking. Berengar noticed a select number of more valuable items in the room, including an ornate chest at one end and a shield bearing a family coat of arms adorning the wall.

"I am Lady Elaine of Clan McClellan. Laird McClellan is my father. I assume you've heard of him?"

Berengar grunted a noncommittal response.

Lady Elaine took a seat in front of the hearth and gestured for him to sit across from her. Her eyes gleamed when she noticed his ring. "You're one of the wardens, aren't you? I used to dream of being presented at Tara's court. Tell me, are all its halls as wondrous as the legends say?"

Berengar shrugged. "It's been a while since I was at court. I spend most of my time on the road. In truth, the castle here is probably more impressive."

Elaine seemed disappointed by the answer.

"I'm looking into the king's murder." Berengar noted that at the mention of Mór, Elaine's bottom lip seemed to quiver. "Laird O'Reilly said you might have some useful information for me. He mentioned you were one of Queen Alannah's ladies in waiting."

"I was more than that." Her voice betrayed obvious bitterness. "Once."

Berengar wasn't sure he understood her meaning. "In

your time at court, did you notice anything that troubled you?"

Elaine nodded. "Despite appearances to the contrary, the royal marriage was not a happy one. The king and queen were fighting more and more as time went on. Then there was the gossip about Alannah and Ronan. I even heard a rumor that Alannah left her chambers the night of Mór's death, though by then I had been banished from court."

Berengar frowned, already uneasy about the nature of the relationship between Alannah and her thane. "You were close to the queen. Was there any truth to the rumors?"

"Ronan loves her, that much was clear. A woman always knows these things," she added before he could interject. "A fleeting glance here, a light touch there…"

"And did the queen reciprocate his feelings?"

"I'm afraid I don't know the answer to that. If she did, she would have been careful to conceal the truth from Mór. A secret like that could have cost her dearly."

"You mentioned you were banished from court. Why?"

She sighed wistfully. "Alannah was too old to produce more children, and the king desired another male heir. Mór was going to set his wife aside and take a new queen."

Berengar realized the truth had been staring him in the face all along. Elaine was one of Mór's mistresses. "And he told you it was going to be you."

"We were in love. When she discovered us, Queen Alannah exposed the affair, and I was asked to leave court. She ruined my life. Because of the scandal, I was disowned and disinherited by my family. My father permits me to retain one of the household servants and provides me with a meager allowance each month, but there is no chance any man of worth will have me for his wife. I might still become some wealthy merchant's mistress, but no more than that."

Elaine's words cast everything he knew about Alannah and Ronan in a new light. There was a history between them; he had learned that much from Ronan himself. Berengar wondered what it must have been like for Alannah—or for Ronan, who loved her—to suffer the indignity of Mór's endless parade of mistresses. He doubted Mór ever really intended to make Elaine queen, but if the king was planning to put Alannah aside, she would have had motivation to kill him.

These are dangerous accusations. I must tread carefully. Even if he discovered that the queen arranged her husband's murder, he could not act without the High Queen's permission. It was unlikely Alannah would allow him to leave Cashel with his life if he learned a truth that could end her reign. Then there was Ronan. Were the two working together, or had the thane acted alone to avenge his queen's honor and create a place for him at her side? None of those possibilities explained Gorr Stormsson's part in the events surrounding the king's assassination, or the veiled magical threat Agatha spoke of.

Everything assumed he could trust Elaine, who clearly harbored a grudge against Alannah, not to mention Laird O'Reilly, who seemed to have an agenda all his own. It was O'Reilly who had spoken against Ronan, though it was notable he did so only in private. Looking around the room, Berengar questioned what Elaine might have been willing to say in return for compensation, as she was well accustomed to the trappings of finery.

Before going on his way, he thanked Elaine and requested that she keep what she told him to herself. She had given him much to ponder. Berengar had agreed to Laird O'Reilly's request with the hope of finding answers.

Instead, he was left with more questions than before. *I hope Morwen has had better luck.*

Upon his return to the castle, he made the climb up the tower's winding stair until at last he reached the magician's quarters. Again the door opened of its own accord when he knocked on it, and Berengar briefly wondered if the charm she'd placed on it had a way of distinguishing friendly visitors from unwelcome guests. The scent of musty parchment had replaced the smell of sulfur from Morwen's distillation apparatus, which had been removed from her alchemy workbench. On the whole, the chamber was even more of a mess than he recalled, with vials, spell books, and strange contraptions scattered about the room in no discernable pattern.

"Keep away from that," he muttered when Faolán sniffed a blue powder in an open container. Morwen might not have the ill intent of the witches they'd encountered, but that didn't make her possessions any less dangerous. The last thing he needed was Faolán turning into a mouse or sprouting antlers.

His battleaxe lay beside a stack of spell books atop an enchanter's table. Berengar stared down at a page of an open book. Though unreadable to him, the text appeared to be a set of incantations. There were also accompanying illustrations of several weapons, including a sword, a dagger, and an axe. He returned his focus to the axe and noticed that the silver runestone she'd given him had been set permanently in place. When he gripped the weapon, a series of blue, green, and yellow symbols appeared, running the length of the haft. The charms quickly faded, leaving the axe looking exactly as it had before he left it in Morwen's custody. He shifted the axe from hand to hand to get a feel for it and realized the magician was watching him.

She used her staff to move about the room. "Do you like it?" Morwen popped the lid from a bottle and choked down the clear liquid within before making a sour face. "Dreadful stuff, although at least I won't have to walk with this awful limp the rest of my life." She placed the empty bottle beside others of its kind in a cupboard and crossed the room to join him. "Anyway, what do you think of the axe? There was only room for three enchantments. I used a charm of endurance, which will keep your axe from breaking, and a charm of resilience, which will keep it sharp so that you won't need to get it repaired or replaced."

"You mentioned a third charm."

"The last enchantment was the most difficult to manage." She spoke with considerable pride. "It's a spell of sanctity. Your axe will repel creatures of evil. It can even draw on the magical energy the rune absorbs to do increased damage to your foes."

Berengar stared at the axe in awe.

"Well, don't just stand there. What do you think? I could alter the enchantments if you like."

Berengar shook his head and returned the axe to its harness. "It's perfect." The axe was his weapon of choice and had seen him through many battles. Now it was even more formidable than ever, and its legend would continue to grow. "How can I repay you for such a gift?"

Morwen grinned. "Wait until you try it out first. Casting enchantments is more difficult than alchemy, but I think I managed well enough." She hobbled across the laboratory and settled at her desk, surrounded by a sea of papers and scrolls. "I heard there was some excitement in the throne room earlier."

He briefly recounted all that took place after the messenger's appearance, along with how Ronan had flown into a fury when it was discovered the Dane had disguised himself in order to slip past the guards. Berengar felt it was unlikely the messenger managed such a feat on his own and wondered if Gorr Stormsson's accomplice at court had assisted with the task. In the aftermath, Corrin promised to tighten security even further—there was even talk of restricting access to court to all but the most powerful and wealthy lords—but the risk remained all too real. If Stormsson could smuggle a man into Cashel, what else might he be capable of?

Morwen appeared particularly uncomfortable when he told her what he had learned from Lady Elaine. He could tell she didn't want to believe the worst of either Queen Alannah or Ronan. She also implied Elaine wasn't particularly trustworthy, recalling the disgraced noblewoman as a silly girl from her days as a lady in waiting. Berengar wasn't convinced. He still needed to know more.

"Were you able to learn anything of use from the inquest records?" he asked once he'd told her all he knew.

"I think so." She shifted through a heap of papers. "Most of the information comes from Ravenna's account. There is little information about the crone herself—mostly stories and conjecture. No one in the kingdom knows where she came from, or even her name."

"I'm aware of the rumors that the crone placed a curse on the king's house. Some even believe the curse has been responsible for all the hardships suffered by the royal family over the years." He thought again of Ravenna and all she'd endured.

Morwen shook her head. "According to these records, most of the heroes and mercenaries who fell to the crone were sent by the crown *after* Aiden's death. I found nothing to suggest a reason for animosity between the crone and any member of the royal house before that. If there was a cause, it's been stricken from all records." She showed him another set of reports. "King Mór even consulted with a seer from Albion who told him though it was possible such a curse existed, she did not sense it."

"Why didn't you tell me that earlier?"

"The king never informed me he'd consulted a seer. It was done in secret."

Berengar recounted the story as told by Ravenna, which was confirmed by the reports. Prince Aiden had ridden in secret from Cashel with the intention of slaying the crone, his sister in tow. When his horse became frightened, it threw him, and he died after striking his head on a rock.

"It still doesn't make sense," Morwen said. "It's always bothered me that the prince just decided one day he was going to slay the crone, all by his lonesome. Even Prince Aiden wasn't foolhardy enough to take such a risk or bring his sister into harm's way."

"Perhaps the crone drew them to her with a spell. In one stroke she could have eliminated both the king's heirs."

"Perhaps." Morwen appeared unconvinced.

"Did you find anything that might link the crone to Gorr Stormsson or the déisi?"

"I'm afraid not. The crone shuns all others. She's not like the coven we countered. It's a shame Agatha was less than forthcoming with us. The witches might have been able to provide more information, but they took their secrets to the grave."

"Even so, the threat of magic remains." If Agatha was to be believed, there was another magic user in Munster. With the Witches of the Golden Vale unable to help, there was only one place he could go for answers.

"You've got that look in your eye." Morwen frowned.

"The one you get when you're about to do something dangerous."

He nodded. What were the wardens for, if not to do what others could not, to venture where they would not?

"I'm going to the Devil's Bit to find the crone. I'll get the truth from her, one way or another."

CHAPTER THIRTEEN

THERE WAS another attack in the night. A group of hooded assailants in masks seized a widow from her home after dark and burned her at the stake. The murdered woman was a reclusive seamstress from an impoverished district. During a dispute earlier that day, one of her neighbors had accused her of being a shape shifter, though Berengar thought it unlikely—rather than suffering the flames, an actual shape shifter would have taken another form to escape. The confederates fled before the guards on patrol arrived to find the poor woman's remains.

The crime was simply the latest example of the widespread anti-nonhuman sentiment that had gripped Cashel since the king's death. In the aftermath, the queen and her counselors—including Morwen—gathered in the throne room to discuss what to do. No sooner had Berengar arrived than the guards dragged a man into the chamber, along with evidence he had participated in the attack. Instead of denying his crime, the man actually seemed proud of it, believing he was acting to defend Munster's people from the monsters at their door.

"What should be done with him, Your Grace?" Corrin asked when the man refused to name his confederates.

Berengar only watched. If it were up to him, they'd take the man's head then and there and be done with it.

One of the *Rí Tuaithe* suggested the queen show leniency, which drew a sharp rebuke from Ravenna.

"He killed a defenseless woman for no other crime than he thought she was different. I believe the penalty for murder is clear. He should pay for the crime with his life. Or do you believe the lives of peasants and nonhumans are worth less than your own?"

"I would counsel restraint, Your Grace," Laird O'Reilly told the queen. "Public sentiment is on this man's side. If the crown orders his execution, it could provoke more uprisings in the future."

Ravenna appeared to find it incredible that the queen would even entertain such a proposal. "We cannot stand by and watch as magical blood is shed." She looked to Morwen for support. "As court magician, surely you agree with me, Lady Morwen. He must be punished."

Morwen averted her gaze uncomfortably and did not answer. Berengar suspected she could not bring herself to condemn anyone to death, no matter what they had done.

Alannah kept her gaze on the prisoner. "And he shall be. Henceforth you are banished from the realm of Munster under penalty of death. Your assets are forfeit and are now property of the crown. Now remove this man from my sight." She sank back on her throne when he was gone. "Marcus is right. We can't risk turning the people against us, not with Gorr Stormsson in open rebellion."

"A wise decision, Your Grace," O'Reilly said. "Though I fear there will be more of these unfortunate incidents in the days to come. The king's assassination has thrown the people into a panic. Even the church has decried these atrocities to no effect. Half the city believes magic and monsters lurk around every corner. Just this morning one of my servants encountered a man who claimed a strange woman attempted to drink his blood after nightfall."

Berengar stepped forward. "I've heard enough. It's clear this isn't going to end as long as there's suspicion that magic was involved in the king's death."

The warden announced his intention to seek out the crone that dwelled in the Devil's Bit, followed by an audible gasp from several of the lords of Munster. Even the normally stoic Alannah appeared shaken, the memory of her dead son likely weighing on her mind.

"This is madness," O'Reilly said. "No one has ever survived an encounter with the crone."

"Then I'll be the first."

"Take me with you," Morwen said. "You'll need my help."

"No," he replied firmly, as he had when she brought up the subject when he first shared his plans with her. "You're still on the mend. You'd only put yourself in danger, and me in the process."

She folded her arms across her chest, and her eyes narrowed at him in irritation. "You saw how you fared against those witches on your own. What makes you think this time will be any different?" She knelt before the throne. "Send me to accompany the warden, Your Grace."

"She's right," Ravenna agreed. "Warden Berengar should not go alone."

"Then I will go," Ronan volunteered. "The warden and I are more than capable of leading the hunt for the crone. You are needed here, Lady Morwen. If there is treachery afoot, you will sense it."

"I agree." Berengar was secretly pleased. This was exactly the reaction he'd been hoping for. Hunting for the crone together would give him the chance to get to know the kind of man Ronan really was. They'd be on the road for hours, an ideal situation for questioning an unwitting suspect. Moreover, outside the castle walls, they would be beyond Alannah's reach.

"It's settled, then. I'll assemble a force of my best soldiers and we will set off at once—that is, with your leave, Your Grace."

Alannah nodded somewhat reluctantly, giving her assent. "Very well, my thane. I trust you know what you're doing."

Ronan bowed. "Together we will avenge Prince Aiden's death and bring justice to the crone. I will make preparations for the journey."

Morwen rose, clearly unhappy with the queen's decision. "You might have told me this was your plan from the start."

She has courage. I'll give her that, Berengar thought as she stalked away, still leaning against her staff for support. Morwen had only barely survived their encounter with the witches, and now she appeared ready to throw herself into harm's way again. Still, there was a fine line between bravery and recklessness—a path Berengar had walked for a long time.

Ravenna caught up with him just outside the throne room. "You've only just returned, and now you're leaving us again?"

"You're not going to ask me to stay, are you?"

"From what I know of you, there's probably nothing anyone can do or say to dissuade you when your mind is made up. I suspect we're alike in that. No, I came to tell you to be cautious. I have not forgotten what I witnessed at the Devil's Bit."

"I'm a warden. Danger goes with the job. I'm used to it by now."

She stared at him hard. "Doesn't it ever trouble you that you're always on the road with nowhere to call home? Throwing yourself into fight after fight, facing death— perhaps even welcoming it?"

Berengar frowned. He could handle being treated with contempt, or even revulsion. They were familiar reactions —comfortable in the way one grew accustomed to an old scar—but this... More so even than Morwen, the princess seemed to see into his very soul. He knew what he was, deep down, and he didn't like being reminded of it.

"This is who I am," he said, as much to himself as to her. "It's the life I chose."

"You don't think you deserve happiness." It wasn't a question. "You're wrong."

Berengar turned to go. "Farewell, Princess."

"Farewell, Warden Berengar."

She left him there, the scent of her perfume lingering in the air.

They rode north with haste. With the date of the queen's coronation fast approaching, his chance to catch the killer before the ceremony was slipping away. Whatever the assassin's true motives, the king's murder was clearly meant to send a message. Berengar suspected another attempt on a member of the royal family would be made at the coronation, if not sooner. He needed answers before it was too late.

The sky took on a sickly gray pallor the farther they traveled. It wasn't long before the sun was lost behind ominous storm clouds. Thunder sounded above, though no rains came. The air grew cold enough that one might have been forgiven for forgetting it was summer. A hush fell over the company as the mountain came into view.

"There it is," Ronan said. "The Devil's Bit."

Berengar was familiar with the mountain, having passed it when he first crossed the border from Leinster. A large gap was visible between the rocks near the mountain's peak, giving it the appearance of missing a piece. The mountain had been the source of many stories and myths long before the crone took up residence there. Berengar heard several such stories as a child. It was said the devil himself took a bite from the mountain—forming the gap—only to spit it out when he broke a tooth. According to legend, the place where the stone landed became the Rock of Cashel.

"I'm surprised Darragh hasn't dealt with the crone already." Berengar searched for the entrance to the cave among the stones, but the mountain remained too distant.

"Munster is too vast a kingdom for one man to rid it of all its evils, even a man of renown such as Warden Darragh. It was Darragh who broke three of the four Viking captains at Cill Chainnigh. Only Gorr Stormsson escaped him. He also slew a Fear Liath at Cnoc Buí and defeated the Conjurer of the Copper Coast, all in the last year."

"No need to recount all his deeds." Berengar was certain such a list would take all day to recite. "I'm sure the whole of Fál will hear of them soon enough, if the bards have their say."

The remark drew a chuckle from Ronan. "Warden Darragh is well loved by the people of Munster."

"I don't doubt it. He's loved by all, it seems." While Berengar was looked down upon or despised in many quarters, Darragh was almost universally revered as a great hero. In truth, Berengar actually respected and admired him, though he would never admit it to his face. "Do you know him well?"

"Well enough to know him to be the man the legends claim. King Mór often invited him to court."

Darragh possessed a fondness for Munster and its people, though his duties as captain of the wardens took him across Fál. Most of the time, Warden Niall of neighboring Leinster stepped in for him in Munster when Darragh was about the High Queen's business elsewhere. Niall probably would have done the same had Mór not specifically requested Berengar for the job of retrieving Morwen from Innisfallen.

"We must be careful." Ronan trained his gaze on the Devil's Bit. "I do not know what awaits us at the mountain. None of the heroes King Mór sent to slay the crone ever returned. Many times, I asked the king leave to hunt the witch myself, but Queen Alannah persuaded him against it."

"You're close with her. I've seen the two of you together."

Ronan nodded. "I've known her all my life. We grew up together. Munster could not ask for a better queen."

"You love her, don't you?"

To his credit, Ronan didn't feign shock. He merely bowed his head in acknowledgment. "Aye. Since Tuathal. I've never told her. Not long after the war, Mór proposed, and who was I compared to the Poet Prince? Seeing them together…it's why I never wanted the rank of thane."

Berengar could only imagine what it must have been like for Ronan to be so close to the object of his affections, who would forever remain out of reach. "Yet you've stayed by her side all these years."

"I served the king, but my loyalty was always to Alannah. There's nothing I would not do for her."

The two men exchanged a knowing look, and Berengar couldn't help feeling a kinship with Ronan. He knew what it was like to possess such unwavering loyalty to his queen, though his love for Nora was of a platonic sort. In many ways, a thane was like a warden. Both held positions of great responsibility, even if Berengar's authority extended to each of the five kingdoms. Like Ronan, he was a warrior who was more comfortable on the battlefield with a weapon in his hands than at court with a wine goblet.

"It must have been difficult for you, watching as she endured the king's multiple affairs." Berengar thought again of Lady Elaine.

"Mór was unworthy of her. He treated Alannah poorly, and their children as well."

"There are rumors there's something more to your relationship with the queen—that you had cause to want Mór dead."

Ronan shook his head in disgust. "Lies, probably from the mouth of that snake, Marcus O'Reilly."

"He warned me you were not to be trusted," Berengar admitted.

Ronan didn't seem surprised. "O'Reilly has always resented that I was made thane and he was not. He knows nothing of loyalty or honor. Power and gold are all that hold sway over him."

"Even so, you have to admit the circumstances are suspicious. You've told me openly of your feelings for the queen."

"That's all they are. Feelings. Alannah is an honorable woman. Even if I had wanted something more, she would never have reciprocated. For all his faults, she loved her husband."

Ronan spoke plainly, without regard for how his words might be perceived. Most of the potential suspects

Berengar questioned proved evasive or untrustworthy, and he found it a nice change of pace to converse with someone who was forthright. Ronan seemed honest enough, but Berengar had met some very talented liars in his time.

"We're here," Ronan said before he could ask another question.

They had arrived at the mountain. It was as if a pestilence had fallen over the land. Unlike the green fields of the Golden Vale, the area surrounding the Devil's Bit was barren and covered in rocks, with only sparse vegetation. Even the trees were leafless husks, which bent under the weight of the fierce winds moaning from the mountain.

"Dismount," Ronan told his men. "We go on foot from here."

Apart from a few crows that watched from their perches as the company passed by, there were no animals anywhere in sight. The mountain was lifeless and deserted. Even the horses were spooked, as Prince Aiden's mount must have been when he bashed his head on one of the very stones underfoot. Berengar tightened his grip on the lead rope and led the reluctant animal into a gathering fog, which hung around the mountain like a veil. A skull leapt out at him as he peered through the mist, and he saw a human skeleton lying slumped against the base of a tree.

Murmurs came from the others as more remains came into view. Bones belonging to hundreds of corpses were scattered everywhere, as well as the remains of horses and other animals. Based on the way many of the bones were strewn, it almost looked as if they'd been ripped to shreds by scavengers, not murdered at the hands of a witch. Berengar used his axe to prod a dust-covered shield that bore the coat of arms of one of the many unfortunate souls who sought to hunt the crone. Swords, spears, and even wagons were visible in the fog, abandoned and forgotten by time.

"Stay alert," Ronan said. "Keep your eyes open for the entrance to the crone's lair."

The soldiers drew their swords and advanced farther into the mist, careful to keep close to one another. The crows' black shapes soon disappeared. The fog grew denser with each step Berengar took until the soldiers' outlines were barely discernable. Sensing trouble, Faolán began to growl, and her ears perked up.

The winds. They've stopped. He held his axe close.

Berengar imagined he heard the sound of high-pitched laughter. An unearthly howl echoed from the mountain, and a shape darted past him through the fog, followed by a scream from one of the soldiers. Berengar raced toward the sound of the cry, Faolán close behind, just in time to see the soldier's sword clatter to the hard, lifeless earth. Moments later, another scream rang out. Somewhere nearby, Ronan attempted to shout a warning to his men, but his voice was drowned out by another hair-raising howl.

The form sailed past him again, and Berengar swung his axe, connecting only with empty air. One by one the soldiers cried out and were silenced. For a brief moment, Berengar glimpsed part of the mountain through the fog. He started upward in search of higher ground and nearly collided with Ronan, their weapons inches from meeting. The queen's thane appeared unharmed. Faolán barked, warning of impending danger, and Berengar spun around as a shape broke through the fog.

Instead of the crone, he found himself face to face with a monstrous beast at least twice his size. It looked almost like a werewolf, though larger and less human in shape. Its hair was shaggy and white, apart from its maw, which was stained crimson with blood that matched the color of the beast's eyes. It had a mane of fur like a lion and a long tail like a serpent. Berengar recognized it instantly. The creature was a Cù Sith, more commonly known as a grim—a monster known to dwell in places of death. He had never encountered one before, though he knew them well enough by reputation.

Faolán bared her fangs and leapt at the grim, which batted her away with its black claws. The thing moved like the wind. When Ronan rushed forward with his longsword, the blade didn't even graze it. The grim disappeared into the fog again, followed by another ear-splitting howl. Berengar spotted its red eyes glowing in the mist and stood his ground, waiting for the right moment to strike. His axe made contact, but just barely. The monster roared and lifted him into the air. Berengar's back struck a large rock, and he fell. Just before the creature could strike while he was defenseless, Faolán jumped on its back long enough for Ronan to slice it across the flank.

With a violent shudder, the monster heaved Faolán to the ground. This time, its howl was one of pain. Ronan stood between Berengar and the grim, holding out his sword, now stained in silver blood. The creature regarded the three of them, unsure whether to strike, and the fog lifted enough for Berengar to catch a glimpse of a stone ladder carved into the mountainside. His eyes followed its course to a cave's entrance.

"It's there," he said to Ronan, who traced his gaze. "The crone's lair."

With a savage roar, the grim sailed over Ronan's outstretched sword and landed atop the rock before crouching, intending to pounce. Ronan grabbed Berengar's arm and pulled him to his feet, and the pair sprinted away with the grim in pursuit.

We're not going to make it, Berengar thought as the steps of the ladder drew nearer. *That monster's too blasted fast.* He could feel it closing in on them. At the last moment, he pivoted and put himself in the creature's path, swinging the axe with everything he had. It felt as if he had rushed headfirst into the mountain itself. The axe seemed to burn the creature when Berengar ripped it free, which he was sure was the work of Morwen's enchantment. He swung again, severing one of its limbs as he toppled backward and crashed to the earth. The grim held him pinned to the ground, its fangs inches away from his face. Berengar struggled under its weight until Faolán came sailing through the fog and ripped out a chunk of flesh from its throat as Ronan smote the creature's face with his longsword.

The grim collapsed in a great heap and reached out for him with its claw. Berengar was already on his feet, the ladder within reach. He began the climb, Ronan beneath him. The mist receded near the ledge at the top, and Berengar heaved his axe over the side. They had almost reached the top of the ladder when Ronan lost his footing on the damp stone and nearly fell. Berengar reached out and caught him at the last moment, though the longsword slipped from Ronan's grip. Before he could pull his companion over the edge, the grim leapt from below. The monster seized Ronan with its dying breath, and the red glow faded from its eyes as they fell together, vanishing into the mist. Berengar looked at his empty hand and shook his head before pulling himself over the ledge.

The cave was cold and quiet. A narrow path led deeper into the darkness. There was no telling how far it went. Berengar crept forward with the axe, the pale light fading behind him. He glanced from one side to the other, searching for the crone, and his gaze passed over a vaguely human shape waiting in the shadows. When he returned his attention to the place where it had stood, the form was gone.

The warden frowned. *I'm not alone.*

He felt something move behind him, but when he looked back, there was nothing there.

The crone's voice reverberated across the cavern to produce a harsh and high-pitched sound. "You shouldn't be here."

"Show yourself." Berengar held his axe at the ready.

The figure moved again, this time ahead of him. The crone scaled the wall and crawled along the ceiling like a spider until she again slipped beyond his sight. She moved too fast for him to catch much detail, apart from the rags she wore.

"Turn back."

This time her voice was louder—more distinct. He was getting closer.

A repugnant odor filled his nostrils, reminding him of an ogre's den. Firelight danced farther down the path, which ended in a wide chamber framed by stone columns. The unpleasant smell came from a cauldron over the fire that bubbled with what appeared to be a broth of some kind. The flames revealed heaps of fish bones, probably taken from the River Suir, which had its source at the mountain.

I guess she doesn't eat humans after all.

Berengar heard the sound of breathing behind him and turned around just as the crone threw herself at him from the ceiling, her long fingernails outstretched liked claws. He grabbed her and flung her across the room. The crone crashed against the wall and landed in a mess on the floor.

There was a clear contrast between the crone and the beautiful Witches of the Golden Vale. She was impossibly

257

old, her wrinkled face heavy with age. The strands of her sparse, wispy hair were matted and dirty. Her nose was hooked and crooked, and her back was hunched. She was thin and small, so pathetic-looking he would probably be doing her a favor by putting her out of her misery.

When he trained his axe on her neck, the crone's large eyes widened and welled up with tears. "It's not fair." She buried her face in her hands. "Why can't you just leave poor Lissa alone?"

Berengar had spent enough time in the company of evil to recognize its presence. The crone looked just like he imagined a witch should, and yet something felt wrong. He again looked at the pile of fish bones. "You didn't kill those people?"

The crone looked up at him again and shook her head with vigor. "Never! Lissa never hurts people, even when the king sends his knights to kill her."

Those soldiers were torn apart before they ever reached the cave, he realized. *It was the grim that killed them.*

"The grim." He watched her carefully. "Did you summon it here?"

Again she shook her head. "The grim scares the bad men away, but it is not Lissa's friend."

"Lissa? Is that you?" Berengar lowered his axe.

Now that he wasn't a threat, the crone seemed to look at him with a new expression. She smiled and nodded in the way a child might. There was an innocence about her that seemed impossible to reconcile with her appearance. This was not the monster the stories told of.

"It was, it was, it was." She seemed to sing. "So very long ago. Before the bad witch came."

"Bad witch? Do you mean Agatha?"

The crone held her finger over her mouth and looked around, as if to make sure they weren't overheard. "She came to Lissa's village. Told Lissa she could help her use magic. Said she would be beautiful and young forever."

Berengar suspected Agatha had attempted to recruit Lissa to her coven—much as she had with Morwen. "What happened?"

"Lissa's magic turned wrong. Bad things started happening to her family. Lissa told the bad witch she didn't want to hurt people, but the bad witch got angry."

"She cast a curse on you, didn't she? She turned you into this."

Her expression told him he was right. Agatha probably corrupted Lissa's magic so that she would harm those she cared about, causing her to flee to the Devil's Bit. There she lived in isolation for decades, all the while people thought she was a monster who needed to be slain. In truth, Agatha was the monster.

"Warden nice to Lissa? Warden kind?"

"Afraid not. Wait. You know I'm a warden? So you can use magic."

The crone didn't answer. Instead she scurried over to the cauldron and dipped a ladle into the boiling mixture. "Would warden like soup?" She offered him a ladleful of the foul-smelling substance, which Berengar politely declined.

"Maybe you can still help me. Do you know who murdered the king?"

She looked at him long and hard, and for a moment he thought she might be able to do just that. "Powerful magic. Shadow magic."

"Shadow magic? Is it Azeroth? Has he found a way to return to Fál?"

"Lissa does not know." She took a sip from the ladle before returning it to the brew. "The Lord of Shadows seeks to take back what was stolen from him, but there are others as well."

"What others?"

She merely shrugged.

Berengar looked her over carefully. While he was the farthest thing from an expert on magic as there was, he knew that Agatha's death didn't necessarily mean the crone's spell had been lifted, but it was still possible. He would have to ask Morwen about it when he returned. Perhaps she could lift the crone's affliction, though he doubted even Morwen could foresee the lingering effects such a curse might have over time.

"I think I know someone who can help you. If you come with me to the castle, she might be able to undo what Agatha did to you."

"And bad men not hurt Lissa?" She seemed skeptical.

"Not unless they want to pick a fight with me."

At that, the crone's pale lips pulled into a toothy grin. She lunged forward as if to hug him, but Berengar held her back. "Just one more thing. Did you put a curse on the king's family?"

"Lissa would never do that!" she protested emphatically.

"What about the prince? How did he die?"

"Lissa remembers. The prince and his sister were good and kind. Lissa sorry she could not help them."

Berengar frowned. "Help them? What do you mean by that?"

The crone opened her mouth to speak, but a sword burst through her chest.

Ronan loomed behind her, his blade covered with her blood.

CHAPTER FOURTEEN

THE CRONE'S KNEES BUCKLED, and she toppled to the ground. Berengar rushed forward to help her, but it was too late. She was already dead, sprawled in a pool of her own blood. Almost at once, the crone's appearance began to change. The crooked nose and hunched back melted away, and her body became rather ordinary looking. Berengar's gaze moved to Ronan, who stood with a vacant expression over the body.

He didn't know. After surviving his fall, Ronan must have retrieved his sword and returned to help. It was likely he saw only the crone's monstrous features and assumed she meant them harm. Or did he? The crone was on the brink of a revelation when Ronan's blade cut her down. Perhaps she was about to share information he wanted kept secret. Then again, if the queen's thane wanted to thwart the investigation, why defend him from the grim? Ronan seemed an honorable man, but he had also admitted he would do anything for Alannah. If the queen asked him to do something wrong, like murdering her husband and helping to cover it up, would he consent?

Berengar closed the crone's eyes. There was nothing more he could do to help her, but he could at least do that. "I didn't hear you enter the cave. How long were you standing there?"

The words seemed to shake Ronan from his trance-like state. He looked from his sword to the crone's corpse, and his brow furrowed, as if he was unable to reconcile the two images. "Berengar?" His voice sounded unsure. From the way he glanced around the cave, it almost seemed like he was acclimating himself to new surroundings.

"Are you all right?" Berengar studied his reaction carefully.

Ronan winced and rubbed the back of his neck. "I think so. For a moment, I thought I heard…"

"What?"

"It's nothing. I suppose I hit my head harder than I thought, but I feel better now. It must be the cool air." Ronan sheathed his sword. "It appears I arrived at the right moment to help."

Berengar remained unconvinced. Was there something Ronan wasn't saying, or did he really not remember?

Ronan knelt down to inspect the corpse, and his nose wrinkled in disgust. "What a mess. She doesn't look at all like the stories claim."

Berengar hesitated. If Ronan had killed the crone in ignorance, telling him the truth would only be cruel. On the other hand, if Ronan did so to keep the secret she carried hidden, Berengar would be better served to let him believe he had accomplished his purpose. It was best to keep the tragic truth of the crone's origin to himself for the time being. In the meantime, perhaps Morwen would know what to make of the crone's cryptic final words. Like Agatha, Lissa too had referenced the work of a magical presence in Munster, though he was no closer to unraveling its nature.

"You did well. I am sure you will be richly rewarded for your service to the throne."

"Avenging Prince Aiden's death is the only reward I require. Here, help me with the body. We have to cut off her head and burn the remains."

It was a gruesome fate. The crone deserved better—a proper burial, to start with—though Berengar couldn't very well tell that to Ronan. The kingdom would continue to believe Lissa died a monster, and her family and friends would probably never know what happened to her.

The fog had all but lifted by the time they made their way down from the cave's entrance. Whether it was the crone's death or the grim's that did the trick, Berengar wasn't sure. The monster's body rested where it had fallen on its back. Its body was broken, and there was silver blood smeared across its white fur. The full extent of its savagery was revealed in the fog's absence. The mountain was a graveyard. There were more skeletal remains strung over the Devil's Bit than he could hope to count.

A few members of their company survived the grim's attack. Most were injured, some grievously so. Two men found an abandoned wagon that remained in good enough condition to use. It was a fortunate discovery, as their mounts proved more difficult to find. Most of the horses fled in terror when the grim appeared, while others were eviscerated by it. Still, they managed to round up enough horses to pull the wagon. The living worked together to help bury those whose remains they were able to recover. When they were finished, Ronan severed the crone's head with his longsword and set her corpse ablaze. Berengar pointed out that some creatures associated with death could return from beyond the grave, and with no magician to provide guidance, they burned the grim's corpse too, just for good measure.

They waited until the two were reduced to ash before making the descent from the mountain. The Devil's Bit loomed behind them, still ominous and dark. Even with the grim gone, the mountain remained a place of death. Berengar suspected it would be many years before the living no longer feared to tread there. As the peak slowly shrank into the distance, the clouds lifted, and the sky returned to its natural blue color.

He watched Ronan carefully on the road home, searching for a hint of the strangeness that came over him in the cave, but the queen's thane appeared quite himself. Despite the sun's renewed warmth, the survivors' spirits were low. More than one of the injured soldiers died of their injuries within the first hours. Most were shaken by the events that had transpired. It wasn't every day the men of Munster encountered a monster.

It had taken them a little over half a day to reach the Devil's Bit. The return journey was much longer. The terrain, coupled with the loss of their horses, slowed their progress considerably. Night descended over the land, and the company stopped to make camp off the road. After digging fresh graves for those who succumbed to their injuries, they settled in for the night. Berengar and Ronan alternated taking watch until sunrise.

It was just before noon when the wagon rolled into the city. Of those who set out from Cashel, only five men remained. The sentries at the gate greeted their return and furnished fresh horses for the journey to the castle. The city streets were full of life in a way Berengar hadn't seen since he first arrived in Munster. The whole of Cashel buzzed with excitement on the eve of the queen's coronation. He wondered if the killer lurked somewhere among them, hiding in plain sight.

There was considerable disorder inside the castle at their return.

"What's going on?" Ronan demanded of a guard when no one appeared to meet them outside the castle.

The guard quickly stopped what he was doing and stood at attention. Berengar recognized him as the young man who attempted to deny him entrance to the castle when he first answered Mór's summons.

"Apologies, my thane. It seems Captain Corrin has gone missing. His lieutenant has had to assume responsibility for preparations for the queen's coronation until such time as he is found."

"Missing?" Berengar scowled. The timing was suspect —the captain of the guard having vanished just before the ceremony.

"Aye, Warden Berengar. No one has seen him since yesterday."

"This is troubling news." Ronan took note of the disarray. "I must have words with Corrin's replacement."

The somber mood that hung over the castle since Mór's death seemed to have abated somewhat at the prospect of Alannah's ascension, as if the kingdom was finally ready to turn the page from the unpleasant chapter. The various members of court all appeared in good spirits when Berengar entered the throne room with Ronan. He noticed Ravenna and Desmond standing apart from the others, conversing and smiling. He heard a rare laugh from the princess as he passed, stirring up unexpected and unpleasant feelings in him.

"You mentioned that Laird Tierney was present at Tuathal's Keep during the war. What of his son?" He indicated Desmond, who was probably closer to Berengar's age than Ravenna's.

"I remember him well. He was little more than a boy at the time. His father kept him out of the fighting. It was too dangerous to risk losing a potential heir to the throne, had the king fallen to Azeroth's armies."

Ronan's words took him by surprise. "Desmond is in line to the throne?"

"Aye. Laird Tierney also shares the bloodline of Brian Boru and Munster's High Kings of old. After Alannah and Ravenna, the crown would pass first to Laird Tierney, and then to his eldest son." He watched Ravenna and Desmond with fondness. "They would make a good match, would they not?"

Berengar didn't answer. Ronan's words instantly changed his perception of events surrounding Mór's initial summons. The attempt on Morwen's life came at Innisfallen, on Laird Tierney's lands. The déisi passed through Cill Airne. Then there was the mysterious letter King Mór received on the day of his death, also sent from Cill Airne. With Laird Tierney at death's door, it wouldn't be long before Desmond inherited his father's lands and title. If the assassin's plot succeeded and Alannah and Ravenna were killed, Desmond would become king of Munster. Given his wealth and influence, Desmond certainly possessed the means to arrange the assassination, and with his presence in the capital for the coronation, he was perfectly poised to see it carried out. Then again, that still wouldn't explain Gorr Stormsson's role, or his conspirator inside the castle.

The warden reluctantly tore his gaze away from Desmond and Ravenna and approached the throne with Ronan. The chattering died away as they neared the dais. He expected the nobles and counselors were eager to hear what occurred at the Devil's Bit. A few remarked on

Ronan's torn and bloodstained clothes, out of keeping with the thane's usually well-kept appearance.

Berengar scanned the room but failed to see Morwen among the room's occupants. *I told her to stay close to the queen,* he thought, irritated. *Where's she gotten off to now?*

"My queen." Ronan knelt before Alannah and bowed low, his hand to his chest in a sign of deference.

Berengar, who remained standing beside him, noted Alannah's relief at Ronan's arrival.

"Rise, my friend. It is good to see you have returned to us. Was your mission successful?"

"It was. With the help of the warden, we slew the crone and her pet and avenged the prince's death."

Alannah addressed them both. "Thank you. I shall see to it you both receive the rewards merited by such heroism."

"Munster owes you a debt of gratitude," Laird O'Reilly said. "You have done the realm a great service this day."

Though O'Reilly praised Ronan to his face, Berengar hadn't forgotten the inferences and accusations he alleged in private. In sowing doubts about Ronan, he had done the same about the queen herself, or was that his intention?

Alannah bade them come closer to recount the details, and the background noise resumed as the pair joined her on the dais. "Did you find the answers you sought, Warden Berengar?"

"I don't believe the crone was behind the king's murder. Nor do I think she placed a curse on your family, though Morwen assures me such a curse would be broken upon her death, in any event."

Alannah appeared satisfied by his response. When they were finished speaking, Berengar asked for leave to find Morwen. Laird O'Reilly stopped him before he could get far. Berengar expected him to launch into another veiled accusation against a member of the royal court, but the old man managed to surprise him.

"I thought you should know I've informed the queen I intend to step aside after the coronation, though she has convinced me to remain in my position until the matter of her husband's death is settled."

With the murder still unsolved, coupled with all the challenges faced by the realm, it seemed a peculiar time for the royal adviser to announce his retirement. O'Reilly was by all accounts a man fond of power and influence, so why would he choose to give it up?

It sounds a lot like he's running from something. "Why now?"

"I have served the crown since I can remember," O'Reilly said. "I have not been a young man for a long time now. I wish to live out my remaining years in peace at my estate in Cóbh. I've even thought of writing an account of my life. I daresay it would be worthy of a place in the annals of Innisfallen."

"But you're staying until after the king's assassin has been apprehended?"

O'Reilly offered a rare smile. "We both know it is unlikely King Mór's killer will ever be brought to justice." The implication was plain: Berengar had failed thus far to catch the culprit, and with every passing day it grew less likely the killer would ever be found.

He bristled at the remark. "I know nothing of the sort. In fact, I think we're closer than ever to the truth."

"I suppose we shall have to see." O'Reilly's expression was doubtful. "Now if you'll excuse me, I must attend to preparations for the coronation."

. . .

He found Morwen coming out of a tavern in one of the city's less reputable districts. The magician's blue robes had been set aside in favor of the hooded disguise she used to avoid drawing unwanted attention when among the public.

Berengar folded his arms across his chest. "I'm not one to judge, but isn't it a little early in the day?"

"Another joke? Were I not a magician, I might begin to worry you'd been replaced by a changeling."

"Don't changelings only take the place of children?" He tried to remember the stories he'd heard as a child.

"Not always. Dark fairies most often used changelings to appear in place of the children they abducted, but in truth, the creatures can take almost any form they desire."

Berengar almost regretted his choice to leave her behind on the hunt for the crone, injuries or not. Her knowledge of magic and magical creatures vastly exceeded his, which was based mostly on lore or experience and often proved unreliable at best. The loss of lives to the grim could have been avoided, and if Morwen proved able to lift the crone's curse, he might have learned the secret she was about to reveal before her death.

"What are you doing out here? I thought I told you to keep close to the queen while I was gone." He loomed over her and added a hard edge to his voice for good measure.

Despite his best efforts, Morwen didn't appear intimidated in the least. "I wasn't going to sit on my hands inside the castle while you took all the risks. I did what I thought you would do and started looking into Corrin's disappearance."

"What have you discovered?"

Morwen glanced back at the tavern, where a drunken patron had just emerged, and waited until he passed before replying. "Corrin went into the city to search for the peddler who found the witches' bodies and never returned."

"Did he ever find the peddler?"

"I don't know. No one seems to have seen her since she set foot in Cashel." She looked up at him like she was prepared for an argument. "I suppose you're going to tell me I've been wasting my time."

Berengar shook his head. "I know you're only trying to help, but the safety of the queen and her daughter comes before everything else. I went to the Devil's Bit because if I fell there, you remained to protect Queen Alannah. Yours was the greater responsibility. I'm expendable. You're not."

Her defiant expression faltered. "I…didn't think about it that way."

"For what it's worth, I think you're on the right track with Corrin. This close to the coronation, there's probably something sinister behind his disappearance. Now unless there's anything else, I suggest we return to the castle."

Morwen bit her lip. "Well, there was one other small matter I wanted to see to while we're here. It won't take long, I promise."

Faolán sniffed curiously at the walking stick she carried. Morwen caught Berengar's gaze and tapped the stick against the ground twice. There was a gleam of purple light, and he found himself looking at the magician's staff, the illusory rune once more fixed in place. Morwen tapped the staff against the ground again, and the image of an ordinary walking stick took its place.

"Nice trick."

She smiled. "I picked it up during my convalescence. Now, shall we be off?"

Berengar sighed. "Very well. Lead the way."

"By the way," Morwen said as they started down the path, "I didn't realize you cared so much about me."

The warden narrowed his eyes in her direction. "What? I never said that."

"You might as well have. You said I was indispensable. Just admit it—we're friends now."

Berengar clenched his teeth. She was teasing him again. "I take it you're feeling better." He noted she now walked without a limp.

"I probably won't be running for a while, but at least I won't have to take any more of that awful potion. So, how did the axe handle?"

As they walked together through the city, Berengar filled her in on the details of his journey to the Devil's Bit. Morwen was visibly upset to learn the truth about the crone and of her death at Ronan's hands. She listened with rapt attention when he revealed the crone confirmed Agatha's claims of an unseen magical presence at work in Munster.

"Whatever it is, it must be powerful indeed to keep its true nature hidden not just from my sight, but that of Agatha and the crone as well." She looked over at him suddenly, as if drawn out of her inner thoughts. "There's something else that troubles you, isn't there? I sense there's something more you're not telling me."

He lowered his voice, careful not to be overheard. "The crone suggested shadow magic is involved."

Shock registered on her face. "You don't mean—"

Berengar nodded. "There's a chance the Lord of Shadows is active in Fál once again. I will write to the High Queen at once asking if she has heard anything of Azeroth from her spies and scouts. In the meantime, I would advise you to say nothing of this to Queen Alannah until we know more." Any mention of Azeroth would undoubtedly cause a panic.

"Azeroth." Alarm was written across her face. "But I don't understand. What would he want with King Mór?"

Berengar shrugged. "Who can fathom the motives of a dark sorcerer? Make no mistake, if Azeroth is involved, it's power he's after."

There was good reason for Morwen's concern. Even a powerful, well-trained magician was no match for a sorcerer, and the Lord of Shadows—as skilled with a blade as he was with magic—was no ordinary sorcerer. Whatever it was they were up against, it would probably take the both of them to confront.

Berengar came to a sudden stop. "Wait. We've been here before." There was something familiar about the neighborhood Morwen led him through. They were back in the Fisherman's District, where he chased the déisi captain through the streets.

Morwen nodded. "If you remember, Matthias made a deal to add the poison to the king's goblet in return for an enchanted medallion he thought would help his mother's illness. With Matthias dead, the poor woman has no one left, so I made inquiries to see if there was something I could do to help."

Few would have thought to help the family of someone who abetted the king's murder, Berengar observed. It certainly wouldn't have occurred to him. Then again, Morwen was kinder than most.

"I expected to learn she had been reduced to begging, but instead I discovered someone has been paying for all her needs."

Berengar frowned. Had the conspirators actually honored their promise to Matthias, even after silencing him? "Who would offer such help?"

"That's just it. The healer I spoke with doesn't seem to know. They say she's not long for this world, so I came to see if there was anything I could do for her."

They soon arrived outside the house where Matthias had lived with his mother. There was not a soul in sight, as the guards once stationed outside were removed after the cupbearer's death. No one answered when Morwen knocked on the door. After a few moments, Berengar tired of waiting and forced his way inside.

Matthias' mother lay in bed, her eyes closed. Berengar could see why the cupbearer was so desperate to get help for her. The woman was in bad shape. Her complexion was waxy, and her breaths were labored and shallow. She had been propped up in bed, as if unable to sleep lying flat on her back. Morwen tried rousing her, but the woman let out a painful moan and refused to stir.

After placing her satchel on the bed and sitting at the woman's side, Morwen gripped her hand and listened intently.

"It's her heart. There's nothing I can do for her. She's beyond my skills as a healer or the use of potions."

The admission served as a reminder there were some things even magicians couldn't accomplish, even with all their arts. Morwen withdrew a bottle that contained the same maroon substance she took to dull the pain of her broken leg and left it at the woman's bedside. Berengar turned and started toward the door, but Morwen stopped behind him, wearing a peculiar expression.

"What is it?"

"I sense something. It almost feels like my father's pres-ence...but it can't be." Morwen shut her eyes at once and raised her hand to the level of her face, extending her first three fingers as she had in the witches' abode. Berengar followed her as she walked into the pantry, a small space crammed with stores of food. Morwen opened her eyes again and stared down at the floor, which was partially covered with a worn and faded rug.

"I don't understand," Berengar said. "There's nothing here."

Morwen knelt on the floor and moved the rug aside, revealing the wooden floorboards underneath. Her hand sought out one floorboard in particular, and the loose floorboard came away in her grip, exposing a small hideaway spot. Inside was a small book.

Morwen took the book and opened it to the first page. "It's written in the king's hand." She looked up at him in amazement. "This was his journal."

"Matthias must have stolen it and hidden it away here as insurance. It must contain something his conspirators didn't want coming to light." He paused. "Whoever ransacked King Mór's chambers must have been after this book."

Morwen started to reply, but her eyes widened, and she spun around, glancing at the window.

"What is it?"

"We're not alone. There's someone outside."

Berengar cleared the room in an instant and burst out the door, his hand on his sword, but there was no one there.

Morwen stood behind him. "They've gone."

Berengar's gaze wandered to the journal in her hands. "We need to know what it says. We should leave for the castle at once."

"I agree." Morwen hastily stuffed the book into her satchel, and they hurried down the street.

The city was on high alert in preparation for the impending ceremony. There were guards posted on every corner, and for good reason—the crowds continued to swell as the day marched on, both from those coming and going in the marketplace and the newcomers arriving for the queen's coronation. The flurry of activity slowed their pace considerably. While making his way through the market, Berengar quickly found himself wishing he'd brought a horse. When Morwen stopped to purchase a morsel from a vendor, the warden noticed a man in a hood staring at them through the masses.

To avoid alerting the man, he turned his back and whispered into Morwen's ear. "There's someone following us. Perhaps he's the person you sensed earlier."

"What should we do?" she asked in a hushed tone, clearly fighting the impulse to look back.

"Nothing. Let him come to us."

She nodded to show she understood.

They resumed the walk through the market as the hot sun bore down overhead. Berengar pretended to peruse the wares of various craftsmen along the way, occasionally catching a glimpse of their pursuer's brown cloak out of the corner of his eye. Each time the man appeared closer than before, until at last he was right behind them. Berengar exchanged a glance with Morwen, who walked with the hint of a smile. He waited for the hooded figure to silently reach his hand into Morwen's satchel before seizing him. The man thrashed against his grip until Berengar slammed him against a vegetable stand, causing fresh carrots and lettuce to fall to the ground. When the angry vendor stepped forward to give him a piece of his mind, he took one look at Berengar and apparently thought better of it.

"Looking for this?" Morwen held the journal just out of reach.

When the man tried stretching out his hand to grab it, Berengar hurled him onto the road. He tried to escape, but

Faolán leapt on his stomach and pinned him to the ground.

Berengar knelt beside the man and held him by the throat. "I'm only going to ask this one time. Who are you?"

"I'd answer him if I were you." Morwen returned the journal to her bag. "He means it."

"Have mercy," the man coughed out when Berengar released his hold. "I was only following orders."

"Whose orders?"

"Laird O'Reilly's. He sent me to follow you. He thought you might lead him to the book."

"Why?"

"He didn't say—I swear it. He was convinced the king's cupbearer hid something away inside the house. I searched but found nothing."

Berengar glanced over at Morwen. "I'd wager all the coins on me that O'Reilly was paying for that woman's care. He didn't want anyone else poking around inside, at least not until he found what he was looking for." He turned his attention back to the man quivering below him. "Did O'Reilly have a hand in the king's death?"

"I don't know. Please, I'm only a servant."

"I believe you." Berengar held out his axe inches from the man's face. "Do you see this axe? My friend, the magician, has enchanted it to withstand almost anything. I could cut into the street and the axe wouldn't break. Imagine what it could do to your bones." He gripped the spy by the shirt and held him up. "If you mention any of this to your master, I'll show you myself. That's a promise." With that, he released the man, who scrambled to his feet and ran away as fast as his legs could carry him. "If Laird O'Reilly went through all that trouble to get to the journal, there must be something in its contents he doesn't want anyone to see. Or perhaps he's just afraid of what it might contain. Either way, it doesn't speak well of his motives."

"I agree. He could have had his spies trailing us for days, possibly since you arrived."

Berengar still hadn't forgotten how O'Reilly nearly sent them both to their deaths in the underground market. "What do you know about him?"

"Beyond his position?" Morwen shrugged. "Very little. Only that he's been at the castle for many years, long before I was born. I believe he comes from privilege. In his youth, he received a prestigious education at Cill Airne. Apart from that, I cannot say. He's always been difficult for me to read, but it's hard to think of him as a murderer. Do you really think he might have been involved in the plot against the king?"

"There's something he's hiding. I know that much. Just earlier he told me he was planning to retire. It's hard to see why he would run if he was innocent. Let's go through the contents of that journal first. Then we'll decide what needs to be done about Laird O'Reilly."

On the eve of what should have been a joyous occasion, the mood in the queen's hall was strangely somber. Berengar observed the chamber's occupants from where he sat at the end of the banquet table. Alannah herself was quiet, as was her way. Ronan sat at her right hand, once again dressed in fine clothes. He did not appear shaken in the slightest by their journey to the Devil's Bit. Berengar noticed Princess Ravenna again deep in conversation with Desmond, though her gaze occasionally drifted in his direction. The warden turned his attention to Marcus O'Reilly, who, if he had learned of what transpired in the market, was careful not to show it.

He again considered everything he'd experienced since his arrival at Cashel. For each secret he uncovered, two more rose in its place. There were still many unanswered questions concerning the attempt on Morwen's life, the plot to blackmail the king, Mór's deal with the Witches of the Golden Vale, and the mystery of the magical threat to the realm, to name but a few. Then there was Corrin's disappearance and the threat of Gorr Stormsson, which hung over the room, unspoken. Despite all he had learned, he seemed no closer to identifying Mór's killer than before. Many had cause to want the king's death. Unless the king's journal contained some clue, the trail had run cold, and with the queen's coronation looming, his time to act before the ceremony was running out.

Morwen, seated far to the queen's left, hardly touched her food, and Berengar caught her stealing furtive glances in his direction throughout dinner. When the meal was over, Berengar fed his scraps to Faolán and excused himself. There were still questions that needed answers.

Desmond and Ravenna left the table early, and he found them in the courtyard, strolling through the garden as the princess' guards trailed a respectable distance behind. When they saw him approaching, the pair stopped and waited for him.

"Forgive me, Your Grace," Berengar said. "I was hoping I might have a quick word."

"Of course." Ravenna turned to her companion. "Will you excuse us, Desmond?"

"Actually, it was Desmond I was hoping to speak to."

"How may I be of service?" Desmond asked when they were out of earshot.

"It's come to my attention that Laird O'Reilly spent some time in Cill Airne as a young man. As Laird Tierney's son, I thought perhaps you might be familiar with his background."

"Laird O'Reilly is well known to us. He was a friend of my father in their youth. He's widely considered one of the cleverest students to come through the Institute, though he was forced to leave for a time before he completed his studies."

"Why did he leave?"

"It was on account of his father, as I recall—a lesser noble who became entangled in a dispute with Munster's thane during the reign of King Mór's grandfather. The king stripped O'Reilly's father of his title and holdings, leaving him penniless."

"But he later completed his education?" Berengar asked.

"Yes. He sided with the king over his family and in so doing earned his favor. The crown even paid for his education. When his schooling was finished, he took a position in Cashel and has been here ever since."

"Thank you. You've been very helpful." Berengar didn't have to try hard to imagine what it would have been like for someone of O'Reilly's ambition to lose his fortune and position at a young age. If anything, such a blow probably made his inclination to hold onto power and wealth that much stronger.

A messenger appeared, dressed in Laird Tierney's colors. "There is urgent news from Cill Airne. Your presence is required."

"It appears I must leave you. Give my regards to the princess." Desmond paused, as if dancing around a delicate subject. "There's nothing between the two of you, is there?"

"No." Berengar's voice was almost a growl. He was growing tired of being asked that question.

Desmond nodded, as if expecting this answer. "There's one other thing. I hesitate even to bring it up, but it was rumored Laird O'Reilly lost a great deal of his wealth some years ago due to an ill-timed trading investment. I trust you will be discreet with this information?"

"Of course."

Desmond smiled. "Farewell, Warden Berengar."

Ravenna, who had lingered in the background during their conversation, again drew near at Desmond's departure. "It seems I am in your debt again, Warden Berengar."

"How so?"

"The timing of your arrival was perfect, as I had just rejected Desmond's proposal. We are old friends, and I had no wish to cause him pain. Like me, he is no stranger to life's cruelties."

"Really?" Berengar offered her his arm, and they walked together.

"We both had miserable fathers, for one. Desmond wanted to be a scholar when he was younger, until Laird Tierney forced him to abandon his studies in the wake of the war. He feared his subjects would not want an alchemist for their future ruler."

He was probably right. Berengar remembered the ease with which the people of Cill Airne accepted the lies of the déisi, eager to blame magic for all their problems. He had no doubt those in the siege party would have burned Morwen at the stake without a second thought.

"Then some years ago, Desmond's escort was attacked on the road by Danes. He was taken prisoner. Laird Tierney refused to pay the ransom, and Desmond was held hostage for months."

"I didn't know that."

"He rarely speaks of it. I'm sure it's not a happy

memory. But we should not dwell on these things tonight of all nights. Come—allow me to show you the rest of the garden. It's always been Mother's great passion."

Though such an indulgence kept him from his other responsibilities, Berengar found himself unable to refuse the princess. He stayed with her until the sun's dying light retreated from the courtyard. There was one more stop to make before he made his way the tower, where Morwen awaited.

Alannah remained in the great hall. With her lords and servants dismissed, she was alone but for the guards. She stood with her back to him, drinking from a goblet. It was not lost on Berengar that she was facing the crypt.

"The warden is here to see you, Your Grace," a guard said with a bow, and the queen turned to face him. Despite the occasion, she looked unhappier than anyone.

"Forgive me for the intrusion, Your Grace. There's something I need to ask you, but I wanted to wait until we could speak in private."

"You're going to ask if I'm in love with Ronan." Alannah was characteristically inscrutable. "You want to know if I had my husband killed. Tell me, what would you do if I said yes?"

Berengar eyed the queen's guards. Alannah had to but give a command and they would attack without hesitation. Strong as he was, he couldn't fight them all. He returned his attention to her gaze and held it, unwavering. "I must follow the truth, wherever it leads."

"You are as bold as they say you are. I must disappoint you, however. I'm aware of Ronan's feelings. I care for him, yes, but as queen there are more important matters than my own personal wishes."

"In all these years, you have never acted on them—not even once?" He looked for a crack in the stone of her face.

"This is Munster, after all, not Leinster. You might be forgiven an indiscretion."

"You think us soft, don't you? That is why you hold our kingdom in such contempt, is it not? You see only our love of culture—of music, wine, and dancing—and think we do not understand hardship. You think I do not know suffering—I, who loved a man who cared only for himself? My daughter is all I have left in the world, and yet she keeps me at a distance. I long for the days when she would laugh as I put flowers in her hair, but they are lost forever. Sometimes I think she died with her brother. No, you have not known pain until you have lost a child."

Berengar said nothing, but his facial muscles tightened.

When the queen studied him, her brow furrowed as if comprehending something she had not thought of before, and her mouth opened in surprise. "I see. You hide your pain well, Warden Berengar."

Berengar excused himself and left at once. He did not want her to see his fists shaking at his sides.

W hen he reached the tower, Morwen was already reading King Mór's journal under the candlelight. "Have you found anything of note?"

She didn't bother to look up. "Not yet. The journal contains a detailed account of the king's daily life." When she flipped to the next page, her brow arched suddenly, as if she had read something that troubled her.

Berengar started to speak, but she held up her hand to silence him and turned to the next entry, and the one after it.

"No." She repeated the word several times in rapid succession. "It can't be." Morwen practically leapt from her seat and hurried across the room, hastily removing a collection of books and scrolls from their shelves. When she returned, she swept everything apart from the king's journal aside and dumped the contents onto the desk.

"What is it?"

"See for yourself." She slid the journal toward him.

Berengar took the book into his hands and began to read.

The dreams are getting worse. I'm losing track of time. Sometimes I wake in the strangest places, with no memory of anything that came before. My head is in a fog. I'm sleeping more and more, and yet I'm as tired as I've ever been. Is it the weight of my years, or is it something more? There are moments when it feels as if there's something stirring in the back of my mind, something else staring out of my eyes...

Berengar frowned. Mór's writings sounded like the ravings of a madman. He continued reading.

I dare not voice these concerns openly. A shadow has fallen over Munster, and I no longer know whom to trust. I am certain I did not issue that proclamation, and yet my seal is unmistakable. I have begun to suspect that my mind is not always my own. Something else has its claws in me...something evil and familiar. I have dispatched Morwen to Innisfallen to look into these matters, though I have not told her the true reason behind my request. I think I am cursed. Perhaps I have brought this evil upon myself. My sins weigh on me like a stone around my neck. I fear it is far too late to make amends. There is one I could turn to, but would he heed my call? The war was so long ago...

Berengar didn't have to read any more. He knew what had happened after that.

"I took these tomes with me when we left the

monastery," Morwen said, racing through the pages of a large volume in black binding that appeared to be a book of curses. "I didn't know what I was looking for at the time. Now I do."

She pointed out an illustration of a man with a vacant expression and empty, blank eyes. Another pair of eyes stared back at the viewer, just above the man's head. Berengar found the drawing oddly familiar, and he remembered where he'd seen a similar expression not long ago.

"Ronan," he muttered. "When he killed the crone, he had the same look on his face. Afterward, he couldn't seem to remember doing it, as if—"

"As if someone else made him do it," Morwen finished for him.

"Was he possessed?" Berengar was familiar enough with entities that attempted to take possession of their hosts, including ghosts and evil spirits.

She shook her head. "I don't think so. I think someone used magic to take over his mind, and they did the same thing to the king."

"How is such a thing possible?"

Morwen shrugged. "Even those with lesser magical abilities can often sense or even manipulate the feelings of others. Remember when you came to retrieve me from the monastery, and I put the siege's leader into a trance with a simple touch? Then there are those like Cora, who can enter the minds of others to read their thoughts, or even bend their will. To fully take control of another person's body for any length of time would require a tremendously powerful individual."

"I don't understand. If this individual had Mór under their control, why kill him at all?"

She just looked at him. "I would have thought the answer to that was obvious—it was your arrival that changed everything. When King Mór sent for you, the conspirators must have been afraid you would discover them. They killed the king to cover it up, perhaps hoping to seize control of the throne using other means. Or maybe they planned to kill him all along."

She pointed out one of the spell's requirements, and Berengar felt his blood turn to ice.

A lock of the victim's hair.

"The same as in the Demon's Whisper."

"Did your father's journal make mention of Laird O'Reilly?" He was still unsure why the old man was so concerned with the journal's contents.

"Only in the earlier entries, when he wrote of day-to-day affairs."

"You mentioned earlier he was educated in Cill Airne. That would have been well before the purges, before the school of magic was shuttered. He might have crossed paths with a mage or magician. Maybe even picked up some of their tricks."

Was there another magician in Cashel under his very nose? If O'Reilly was secretly allied with such an individual, he could have elevated them to a high rank in his capacity as royal adviser, with none the wiser. Then there was Desmond, who was also from Cill Airne and might have access to former students from the school of magic.

"Morwen, if this person can truly control the mind of another, then…"

"It could be anyone," she finished for him. "Anyone at all."

CHAPTER FIFTEEN

AT LAST THE day of the queen's coronation arrived, and even with what they learned from Mór's journal, Berengar was no closer to uncovering the identity of the king's assassin. He had faced down the déisi, infiltrated an underground market of criminals and thieves, taken a poisoned arrow for the princess, and clashed with a coven of witches, yet the danger seemed greater than ever before. He returned again to his final conversation with the king, whose only real concern had been Morwen's safety. Though Mór had fallen a long way from the man Berengar once knew, in the end he expressed remorse for his actions. Berengar hoped that was enough for him to find peace in the afterlife. Now it fell to the warden to honor his friend's last request and keep his kingdom safe. Berengar planned to do just that, no matter the cost.

Blasted ceremony. The whole thing seemed pointless to him. He didn't care for public events as a rule, but what was the point in holding another coronation when Alannah was already queen of Munster? Though the purpose was to mark her full acquisition of Mór's powers and responsibilities, in reality she was simply swapping out her existing crown for her husband's. It was the kind of pageantry typical of Munster. Such a thing would certainly never be done in Ulster. As far as Berengar was concerned, it was foolish to hold such an event with the king's killer still at large. The last time Alannah and Ravenna ignored his advice it hadn't gone so well, but the queen seemed determined to proceed as planned. He supposed he could understand her desire to start anew, but that didn't mean he had to like it.

As he readied himself for the day, there came a knock at the door. "Stay put," he said to Faolán, who let out a low growl. If anyone was foolish enough to attack him in close quarters, his axe was within reach. "You may enter."

The door opened, revealing a young woman. Berengar recognized her as one of Ravenna's attendants. In her arms she carried a set of dress clothes. "Apologies, my lord. Princess Ravenna wanted you to have these for the coronation. She picked them out herself."

The woman left the clothes behind and departed with a bow, leaving him to inspect them. He liked dressing up in fancy garments about as much as he enjoyed formal events, but it was clear the princess had put much thought into her selections, and he had no intention of disappointing her. Berengar removed his cloak and put on the elegant high-collared doublet over the simple white tunic Ravenna had chosen, coupled with a matching *trias*—wool pants that fit tightly around his calves. It was nearly impossible to find formal attire in his size, but the clothes Ravenna selected fit him perfectly. Although he left his cloak behind, he took all his weapons with him, save for his bow. He was still a warden, after all.

Berengar left the castle and made the walk to the wall, where he stared down across the city. An audible roar came from those gathered below in anticipation of the coronation. The staggering numbers stretched all the way from the foot of the hill back to the city gate. None would catch more than a glimpse of the ceremony itself, which was to take place behind closed doors. Only those who were invited were permitted entrance past the sentries at the gate, mostly Munster's nobles and representatives from each of the neighboring kingdoms, along with foreign dignitaries from Albion and Caledonia.

Berengar made inquiries of the guards and discovered there was still no word of Corrin. Given the extent of Corrin's devotion, the warden thought it highly unlikely he would miss Alannah's coronation of his own accord. Had he uncovered something that put him in the assassin's path? If the goal was to throw the ceremony into disarray, it seemed to have failed. Upon Berengar's inspection, Corrin's replacement appeared to have done an admirable job of arranging the defenses.

Before returning to the castle, he sought out the guard who had informed him of Corrin's disappearance. The young man took a step back at his approach and swallowed uncomfortably, likely remembering the warden's displeasure when he failed to recognize him on their first meeting.

"You," Berengar said. "What's your name?"

"Seamus, sir." The young man's gaze lingered on Faolán, who'd nearly attacked him when he had threatened her master with expulsion from the castle grounds.

Although the guard's behavior had caused him some annoyance—Berengar hadn't forgotten how hungry he was after the journey from Leinster—it was born out of the young man's sense of duty, and perhaps a desire to prove himself.

"There's something I want you to do for me."

Seamus bowed. "Of course, Laird Warden—whatever you ask."

Berengar flashed his teeth to express his irritation at being called a lord for the second time that day before explaining the task he needed Seamus to perform. "Choose three men you trust to accompany you. You must leave with haste if you are to return in time. Do you understand what I ask of you?"

When Seamus nodded, Berengar slipped off his ring and put it in the young man's palm. "Take care not to lose this. It is precious to me. You now go with the authority of the High Queen."

After the guard departed to carry out the task entrusted to him, Berengar cast one final look over the city before following the road that led from the castle gate. Music played in the background as the arriving guests admired Cashel's splendor under the watchful presence of the guards. The warden wandered the grounds, observing the festivities. The people of Munster were certainly fond of their parties—overly fond, in his opinion. Examples of Munster's culture and arts were on full display for all to see. There was even a ficheall tournament for renowned players from all five kingdoms. Watching them play, Berengar suspected Morwen was more than a match for any of the participants. More than one of the bards and troubadours in attendance did a double take when he went by, recognizing his description from their songs and stories even in the absence of his bearskin cloak.

Berengar tugged uncomfortably at his collar. He was so accustomed to his armor it felt as if a part of him were missing without it. There were more than a few faces he recognized in the crowd, especially members of the official delegation from Tara. Several lords—mostly those from Leinster—turned up their noses as he passed. Others still, including one of the Ice Queen's many sons, regarded him with cold indifference. No matter how much he dressed the part, he would never be one of them. The scars were a reminder of that.

The warden was on the verge of inquiring if any among the messengers from Tara brought word for him from the High Queen when he crossed paths with Morwen. The magician's gaze swept over him, and she held her hand over her mouth to stifle a laugh, unable to hide her amusement.

"I'm sorry." Morwen noted his sour expression. "I wasn't expecting to see you dressed in such a fashion, that's all."

"Careful," he warned. "I might say the same of you."

Morwen grimaced in displeasure. A simple blue dress had replaced her robes. Her brown curls, worn loosely instead of in a braid, appeared difficult to manage. The whole getup had the pronounced effect of making her appear even younger than her years.

A dark expression crossed her face. "I hate wearing dresses. I hope you've had a productive day. I spent most of the night reading up on various spirits and monsters before I fell asleep. Nightmarish creatures. I wanted to rule out possession, so I paid a visit to Prince Aiden's grave to confirm he hadn't become a vengeful spirit after his death."

"What did you discover?"

"Nothing. I believe his spirit has passed on."

At that moment, a trumpet sounded, and the ornate chapel doors opened. Berengar recognized the priest inside as the same man who led Mór's funeral procession. He wore white and green vestments, which set him apart from the priests in black at his side or the monks in their plain brown robes. Berengar and Morwen entered along with the others. The vaulted ceilings were higher even than those in the throne room, as if reaching out to heaven. Even Berengar felt small in comparison as he passed under a series of wide, rounded arches. Each boasted a carving bearing the likeness of one of Munster's kings. Elaborate frescos ran along the sandstone walls all the way to the ceiling, each depicting a different scene from Munster's storied past. A sarcophagus said to contain the remains of High King Brian Boru stood along the western wall. Entwined serpents were carved into its stone surface, a symbol of eternal life from the time of the elder gods that predated worship of the Lord of Hosts.

Ronan was dressed in his finest clothes. "You look lovely, Lady Morwen. Warden Berengar, the queen would like a word before the ceremony."

Alannah waited in the narrow chamber where Mór had been prepared for burial. He wouldn't have picked the place for a private audience, but southerners weren't as superstitious about such things. When he entered the room, Berengar's eye fell on the table where the king's body had lain when he first spoke with Ravenna about her father's death.

"Leave us," Alannah instructed her attendants.

"I wish to apologize for my words when we last spoke."

"There is no need." Her voice was softer than usual, perhaps in the face of the responsibility she was about to assume. "It is almost time. I am ready to do my duty." She drew nearer, and he could see her features clearly in the candlelight. "The hour grows late, Warden Berengar."

Berengar lowered his head. "I'm sorry, Your Grace. I swore to find your husband's killer and bring them to justice. I failed."

She nodded as if she had known that would be his answer all along. "Do not despair. You have not failed. I've watched you from the moment you set foot in Cashel. You saved my daughter's life, defeated the Witches of the Golden Vale, and avenged my son's death at the hands of the crone. You have proven yourself a true friend to Munster. I do not know what happened between you and Mór, but when this is finished, you will always have a place in this kingdom."

"You honor me, Your Grace."

"My husband was more than a great king when we married—he was a good man. He lost that somewhere along the way. I hope to be the ruler he should have been." Alannah looked up at him, and for the first time a true, genuine smile formed on her face. In that moment, he knew the kind of queen she would make.

The bell tolled, announcing to the city that the moment of the coronation had come. The queen's escort arrived, and Berengar was about to leave when Alannah spoke to him again.

"One more thing. With the witches and the crone gone, it seems Munster is no longer in need of magical protection. After speaking with my counselors and advisers, I have decided to follow the example of Leinster and eliminate the position of court magician once your investigation is complete. The time of magic and monsters is coming to an end, Warden Berengar. We must look to mankind to chart a new future."

Berengar tried not to show his surprise. He understood the way Alannah felt about magic better than most, but despite what she wished to believe, there was no shortage of magical threats. Based on the contents of her husband's journal, some were perhaps closer than she even suspected. Moreover, Berengar knew the news would crush Morwen. She had been preparing for her service to the throne her whole life, and it meant everything to her.

He returned to the chapel and took his place beside the priest at the head of the room. With Nora at Tara, he would act in the High Queen's stead in his capacity as a warden of Fál, one who stood apart. Princess Ravenna was closest to the throne, ahead of Thane Ronan, Marcus O'Reilly, and the *Rí Tuaithe*, though he noticed Desmond was absent from their number. He had difficulty taking his eyes off Ravenna, who was easily the most beautiful woman in the room. It occurred to him that he had rarely seen the princess when she wasn't wearing mourning black, but the color seemed to suit her well.

The musicians struck up their instruments and the choir began to sing. All heads turned toward the entrance, where Alannah appeared. She walked down the center aisle and stopped before the throne as those gathered in her presence stood out of respect.

The priest draped her in a cloak of gold and bestowed upon her a golden scepter, as the church had since Father Pádraig carried the word of the Lord of Hosts to the island centuries ago. The priest uttered a simple prayer for the queen and her reign before he anointed her with holy oil and made the sign of the cross on her head.

Berengar took the silver crown that once belonged to his friend and held it above Alannah's head. "In the name of Nora, High Queen of Fál, I name you Queen Alannah of Munster, from the Cliffs of Moher to the Celtic Sea, Lady of the Southern Islands, and Mistress of the Golden Fleet." He scanned the chapel a final time to make sure there was no danger before setting the crown upon Alannah's head. "Long live the queen."

"Long live the queen," came the response from those in attendance.

When Alannah sat on the throne, all but Berengar knelt in her presence. She bade them rise, and the festivities commenced anew. Berengar stepped away from the throne, hoping to steal away to a remote corner of the room to observe in silence.

"You clean up rather nicely, Warden Berengar," Princess Ravenna said. "All the same, I'm glad you didn't shave your beard—I might not have recognized you."

"You have my thanks for the clothes, Your Grace. By the way, there's something I've been meaning to ask you."

"Oh?" She looked intrigued.

"It's about the crone."

The princess laughed.

"What?"

"I thought you were going to say something else, that's all."

Unsure how best to respond, he chose to continue. "When I questioned the crone, she mentioned something about not being able to help you or your brother. Do you know what she meant by that?"

Ravenna appeared confused. "I'm afraid not. Aiden's accident occurred before we ever reached the crone's lair."

Another dead end. "There's something else the crone told me. There's no curse on you or your family. Never was. I thought you'd want to know."

He wasn't certain how she would react to the truth. All the rumors that were spread about her over the years were all based on a lie, and yet it did not change that the people believed it, or the things she had endured.

Ravenna squeezed his hand. "Thank you."

When he started to remove his hand, she held onto it a moment longer. A look passed between them, and for a moment, it was as if they were the sole occupants of the room. As he looked into her dark eyes, Berengar felt something stir he hadn't felt in many years.

He pulled away abruptly, still able to feel her touch on

the hand she'd held. He'd almost forgotten it was the hand of a murderer.

"I'm sorry. I can't be what you want me to be."

"You don't have to hide yourself from me. I accept you for who you are. Can you do the same?"

He looked away. Why didn't she know to run, like the others? She knew the stories as well as anyone. She understood what he was capable of, the things he'd done.

"So that's your answer." She turned away with a look of disappointment.

Berengar watched her leave, conflicted.

A guard interrupted before he could decide whether or not to pursue her. "Pardon me, Warden Berengar. We've had word of a man asking for you in the city."

Berengar's gaze remained on the princess. "It can wait."

"I've been told he's rather insistent. He claims to carry a message from the High Queen, and that it's for your eyes alone."

Berengar frowned. If Nora had gone to the trouble of sending him a secret message, why hadn't she entrusted it to a member of the delegation from Tara? "Very well. Where can I find him?"

The guard gave him the name of the inn where the messenger waited, and Berengar made his way through the crowded room. He stopped at the chapel's entrance and glanced back at the throne, where Alannah was surrounded by admirers. She would be safe in her thane's capable hands, at least long enough for Berengar to learn what Nora wished to tell him. It was a short walk, one that shouldn't take much time. Besides, the journey from the castle into the city would give him an excuse to get away from the packed gathering. He needed the chance to clear his head.

Morwen caught his gaze from across the room and shot him a questioning look. She started to follow him, but Berengar shook his head and crossed the threshold. When he whistled, Faolán came running from where she waited under the trees. Together they followed the road that led down into Cashel beneath the darkening sky. The crowds below had already begun to disperse, breaking up into smaller parties to celebrate the occasion or else returning to their homes.

Again his thoughts returned to the princess. He hadn't cared about anyone or anything in so long he doubted he was even capable of such a thing. Whatever it was she thought she might find in him, he would bring her only pain. She'd suffered enough already. A long time ago he made the choice to harden his heart, to be strong where others were weak. He had to be, to do the things he did. It was too late for him to change, and he refused to drag her into the darkness with him.

When he arrived at the inn, he found no sign of the man who asked for him. The innkeeper proved of little use even in describing the individual, as his attention was occupied by the influx of guests who had traveled to the city to observe the coronation. He mentioned only that the man wore a hooded cloak. Berengar surveyed the busy hall a few moments longer before departing. He was about to return to the castle when he noticed a hooded figure watching him from the shadows. Berengar stepped closer and caught a glimpse of the lower half of the man's face.

It was Corrin.

Berengar called to him, but the captain of the guard seemed not to hear him. He wore a vacant expression reminiscent of how Ronan had appeared in the crone's lair, but there was something different about it.

Something's not right.

"Follow me." Corrin's voice was flat.

Berengar glanced at Faolán, who regarded him warily.

We're walking into a trap. If he wanted to know who was behind it, there was nothing to do but to allow Corrin to lead him to whatever destination awaited them.

He trailed Corrin to an abandoned warehouse in a quiet part of the city. The empty building was stocked with barrels and bottles full of wine.

"This way," Corrin said.

Berengar passed through a hidden doorway into a back room, and followed Corrin down a narrow corridor. The path ended in a flight of stairs that led to the cellar. As they descended, Berengar felt a chill in the air he hadn't noticed before. The weathered wooden door at the bottom creaked on its hinges when Corrin pushed it open, revealing a dimly lit underground chamber where another figure waited at a round table. Corrin came to an abrupt halt and stood motionless.

Berengar glimpsed the face of a kindly old woman in the candlelight. He hesitated in the doorway. Despite her nonthreatening posture, something about the woman's appearance seemed wrong. Faolán sensed it too; the wolfhound bared her fangs and barked loudly.

The woman gestured to a chair on the opposite side of the small table. "Please. Have a seat."

Were he a lesser man, the sound of her voice might have sent a shiver running the length of his spine. Berengar's gaze lingered on the familiar diamond-shaped ring the woman wore on her left hand. He peered through the darkness and stared hard at her face, feeling as if his eye was playing tricks on him. It seemed another face was hidden underneath the pale skin and wrinkles, and in an instant he knew to whom the ring belonged.

"We both know if I sit down, only one of us will leave the table alive, witch."

The spell that concealed the woman's true face vanished the moment Berengar saw through it. Just like that, Agatha was looking back at him, young and attractive once more. The warden had no doubt of her intentions. She used Corrin to lure him down to the cellar, away from others, for one reason alone.

Agatha made no attempt to move. "Very perceptive. It seems Cora was right. Your will is strong."

"You survived."

Her lips pulled back into a haughty sneer. "I can disguise my appearance easily enough if I choose. Once I made it appear I perished in the flames along with my sisters, it was child's play to gain entrance into the city. From there, it was just a matter of finding the right soul to bring you to me."

"Why risk coming to the city at all? Why not flee?"

"My plans for Munster are not yet complete." She motioned to the seat across from her again, and this time her voice was firmer. "Now sit. Don't bother calling for help, either. I've enchanted the room so no sound can escape."

"That's a shame. No one will be able to hear you screaming."

Rather than reach for his axe, Berengar ordered Faolán to remain at a distance and approached. He pulled back the chair and took a seat without breaking eye contact for even a second. A deck of cards lay face down in front of Agatha. The witch's black seeing stone sat inert at the center of the table, surrounded by four candles.

"I'm not in the mood for games, witch."

"If you want answers, you'll play mine. Each member of our coven possessed certain gifts. Cora could enter minds freely. Minerva was a talented alchemist. For my part, I have the sight. I can glimpse fragments of what was, what is, and what is to come." With that, she began shuffling the deck with dexterous hands.

"You speak in riddles and lies. There's no answer you can give that I can believe."

"Yet here you sit." Slowly, she spread the cards face down. When she finished, her hands disappeared underneath the table. "Pick three cards."

This is dangerous magic, Berengar thought. Agatha was tempting him with the answers he sought, but meddling with the strands of fate was an unnerving proposition, even for a man like him. Knowledge was power. It was possible that by manipulating his perception of the future, Agatha could actually influence the way events unfolded. He would have to tread carefully, especially without Morwen to guide him.

"First I want the truth. Did you plot the king's death?"

Her eyes seemed to glimmer in the candlelight, and at last she shook her head. "No, though I was more than happy to provide my assistance. Thanks to them, all that I've worked for is finally within my grasp. Bastard though she is, my daughter is a potential heir to the throne."

"Morwen will never serve you."

Cackling laughter sounded through the chamber. "We will see how strong her resolve remains when you are no longer there to hold her back. Mór was never a threat to me. It was only his wife and heirs who stood in my way."

"The crone didn't cause the prince's horse to go mad. It was you."

"I waited years for the opportunity. I never imagined Prince Aiden would be foolish enough to ride alone with his sister to the Devil's Bit. A pity the Tainted Princess wasn't killed as well, though that mistake will soon be rectified."

The corners of his mouth twitched in anger. "Call her that again, and I will take your tongue before I kill you."

Agatha started to reply, but when she saw his seriousness, her brow furrowed and she stopped. "You're in no position to make threats." Her voice wavered, if only a little.

"Are you in league with Gorr Stormsson or the déisi?"

Agatha waved a finger at him. "That's not how this works. First you must choose a card. Then I will answer a question."

"As you wish." Berengar reached out and slid a card in front of her.

Agatha held her hand over the seeing stone before turning the card over, revealing the image of a heart with a sword through it. "The heart of a hero."

"You must not have been paying attention," he said, his voice a harsh growl. "I'm no hero."

Agatha chuckled softly. "You cannot hide the truth from me, Warden. The world may know you as a monster —you might even believe it yourself—but I see what you really are, underneath it all. Already the wall of stone you've tried so desperately to build around your heart is beginning to crack. The card represents love, and it does not lie. You lost your wife, but you're not truly afraid that you won't find love again. You're afraid that you *will*. Despite your better judgment, you find yourself caring about the magician, even as she softens you around the edges. And no matter how you try to ignore it, you can't deny the feelings that have developed for the princess, though you know she can never be yours."

Berengar showed no emotion. "If you're done talking, I'd like an answer to my question."

Agatha appeared slightly irritated by his lack of reaction. "You're asking the wrong question. Who financed the déisi in the first place? Where did the gold come from?" She leaned forward and leered at him. "You can sense it, can't you? The truth is right in front of you, and yet you cannot see it."

He folded his arms across his chest. "That's not an answer."

"Some time ago, Gorr Stormsson came to me in secret. I assumed he wanted his future read, but his intentions were far more sinister. He would procure the necessary ingredients for the Demon's Whisper, using various agents from the Brotherhood of Thieves. Yes, Warden—it was my coven who prepared the poison that killed King Mór."

One by one, the pieces started to fall into place. The use of the Brotherhood of Thieves ensured the poison's origin would remain hidden, while the déisi eliminated or attempted to eliminate loose ends, like Matthias, the king's cupbearer. With Mór out of the way, Stormsson would be free to take the throne in the ensuing chaos. There was just one thing that didn't fit. Why would Stormsson, already an openly declared enemy of the king, bother to conceal his involvement in the plot? Based on the stolen shipments of gold, Berengar already suspected the Dane wasn't working alone, but if that was true, who was his co-conspirator—and who was the true mastermind behind the king's murder? There also remained the mystery of Calum's death, and the magical threat Agatha spoke of during their initial confrontation. Or had that been a lie as well?

When Berengar opened his mouth to speak, the witch shook her head. "It's time for you to choose another card."

"Fine," he said through clenched teeth. He grabbed a card near the end of the row and turned it over himself.

An image of the moon stared back at them from the other side.

"The moon. Deception and betrayal." Again she held her hand over the seeing stone. "Yes," she whispered almost reverently, and her eyes widened with glee. "How do you know that everyone around you is truly who they say they are? What if someone you believe to be an ally is actually a foe?"

For the first time, Berengar felt a flicker of doubt. *She's lying. Trying to get into your head.* But what if she wasn't? He had enough trouble trusting others to begin with. If he learned anything from Mór, it was that everyone had secrets. His thoughts turned again to Morwen, who seemed so innocent, so good. As the king's court magician, she would have been perfectly placed to commit the murder. What if she had been helping her mother from the start, her eyes on the throne the whole time? It would have explained why she was so eager to help him in the investigation.

"You've played perfectly into our hands," Agatha said. "Even now, those you have sworn to protect are in mortal peril, and you sit here, unable to defend them."

Berengar's eyes widened. It was a trap from the start, one meant to lure him away from the castle long enough for the assassin to strike.

"It was you, wasn't it?" He thought of Corrin. "You used magic to control the king. You seized control of Ronan to murder the crone."

Though she recovered quickly, Agatha's face betrayed her surprise. "There is much you fail to see, Warden of Fál. But it matters not, for your time is short. Soon you will be dead, along with the queen and princess. Now, I believe you've one card left."

Berengar reached across the table and began to go for

a card, when suddenly he stopped and flipped over another, as if pulled by an unseen force. He didn't need Agatha to tell him what the skeletal image of the reaper meant. Agatha's expression faltered, and it was Berengar's turn to smile. Death had surrounded him his whole life. The halls of hell were full of those he sent there with his axe. To him, death was nothing more than an old friend.

His hand shot across the table and seized her by the throat before she could say a word. The chair fell away as he stood and tightened his grip. "You can't cast a spell if you can't get out the words."

Berengar felt a sudden stab of pain in his forearm where she raked one of her long nails across his skin. His hold on her slipped, and he staggered back.

A characteristic arrogance had returned to Agatha's face. "The poison will not kill you, at least not right away. You will not suffer as Mór did, but still the great Bear Warden will die here, alone in the dark, like the feral beast you are."

"Not yet." He reached for his axe as Faolán leapt to his aid.

The witch's brow arched in disbelief, and she took a step back. "How can this be? You should hardly be able to stand!"

He stared her down, drawing strength from the feel of the battleaxe in his hand. It wasn't the first time he'd been poisoned, even during his time in Cashel. Agatha failed to take his size into account and had overestimated the speed of the poison's effect. For that, she would pay with her life.

"I'll simply kill you another way. We will see how you fare against me without a magician to aid you."

"I've killed witches before." He raised his axe.

Agatha formed her left hand into a claw and shouted the words of a spell at him, but Berengar absorbed it with the silver rune on his axe. When the witch poured more of her energy into the spell, pushing him back, Berengar powered through until he was close enough to shift his axe to one hand and swing at her. When Agatha ducked underneath the axe, he slid his sword free with his remaining hand and slashed her across the right side.

They stood there locked together for a moment, looking back at each other. The streaks of gray in Agatha's hair spread, and new signs of aging appeared along the lines of her face. She fell away, blood dripping to the floor, regarding him with an expression of pure loathing. The wound closed, and her hair became a vibrant brown once more, though some of the lines of aging remained behind.

Agatha opened her mouth to cast a curse, but before she could get the words out, the room began shaking violently. A black fire burst to life from the seeing stone as shadows moved along the walls. One by one, the candles went out.

"What is this?" Berengar yelled above a booming, dissonant voice that reverberated across the chamber in a black tongue.

Agatha didn't answer. For the first time, she looked afraid.

The ground trembled, causing the seeing stone to roll from the table to the floor, where it shattered into a thousand shards. Cracks appeared as the floor shifted under their feet. Suddenly the earth opened up at the center of the room, and a hole formed in the ground, leading to a pit of darkness. Agatha lost her footing and slipped. At the last second, she grabbed hold of the stone floor, her feet dangling over the edge of the deepening pit.

Berengar thought the crumbling floor would devour him too, but the cellar door swung open, as if granting him passage.

Corrin stirred, suddenly freed from Agatha's influence. "Berengar? What's going on?"

"There's no time." Berengar helped Corrin to his feet as the chamber threatened to come down over their heads.

A terrible cry came from the center of the room, where Agatha's hold seemed about to give way. "Help me!"

Despite the fierce urgency of the moment, the warden's lips curled into a cold sneer. "No."

With Faolán at his side, he raced up the staircase and along the corridor. The ceiling came crashing down behind him, and the cellar collapsed in on itself. Berengar threw himself and Corrin from the entrance to the warehouse, landing on the ground outside. A cloud of dust rose where they had stood an instant earlier.

Alannah and Ravenna are in danger, he thought, recalling the witch's ominous warning.

The warden grabbed his axe and struggled to his feet, leaving Corrin's unconscious form behind.

CHAPTER SIXTEEN

BELLS TOLLED across the city as Berengar raced toward the castle. People everywhere fled, seeking refuge from the chaos. Fires raged atop the Rock of Cashel, and the sounds of battle were audible behind the walls. Fighting had broken out at the gate, and Berengar reached the summit just as the last of the guards were overwhelmed. The first attacker failed to see him in time. Berengar ripped his axe free of the man's spine and charged at his companions. Moonlight broke through the stacks of smoke, revealing their distinctive armor.

Danes. It was a raiding party. Somehow Gorr Stormsson managed to slip his men inside the city, using the distraction of the queen's coronation to launch an attack. The Vikings were well known to use smaller forces to move unnoticed and disappear before an enemy's superior numbers regrouped. If Stormsson was willing to take such a risk, it could only mean he planned to murder the queen.

An archer took aim at Berengar as he beheaded the last fighter at the gate, but Faolán savaged the Dane before he could get off a shot. A horn bellowed across the court-yard, coming from the chapel, where a band of castle guards were doing their best to hold off a larger attacking force. Time seemed to slow as Berengar rushed to help, though it might have been an effect of the poison still flowing through his veins. The earth was littered with bodies of Munster's defenders and of Vikings among fallen arrows and blood, along with those civilians unfortu-nate enough to find themselves caught in the crossfire. It was as if the world around him had descended into hell. Nobles and servants alike hid behind what cover they could find, frozen in horror. Berengar felt the searing heat from the fire as one man ran past him consumed by flames. He coughed down a lungful of smoke and was nearly bowled over by a panicked horse. Again the horn blew. One by one, the queen's defenders were pushed back to the chapel steps.

"Fall back!" the guard with the horn shouted to his companions. "Fall back to the queen!" An arrow struck him in the throat, and the horn rolled away when he fell.

One of the advancing Danes loomed over the dying guard and raised his spear to finish him, but Berengar threw himself into the enemy ranks and severed the Dane's hand at the wrist. Side by side with Faolán, he struck down one Viking after another while fighting his way closer to the chapel. When the last of the attackers thrust a spear at him, Berengar moved too slowly to evade the strike, and the spear's tip grazed his doublet, tearing it free of the white tunic underneath.

It was a reminder that without his armor he was vulnerable, even while the poison spread, slowing his reactions.

Fight it, he ordered himself, pivoting in time to avoid a second thrust of the spear. He stunned the Dane with the flat of his axe, wrenched the spear free, and impaled the man with his own weapon.

The bell continued to toll from the watchtower. More were coming, though he wasn't certain if they were Danes or the queen's reinforcements. He cast the body aside and stumbled inside the chapel, which was already overrun. Alannah was huddled behind the throne, defended by Ronan and a final remnant of guards. Morwen was deep in the thick of the fighting, casting protective wards and enchantments to hold the enemy at bay. One of her spell books lay at her feet, its pages torn and trodden upon. The magician deflected a torrent of arrows away from the throne, blood running from her nose, and the enchantments began to fail, allowing the enemy soldiers past her.

"Kill the magician!" ordered a Dane in a horned helmet.

Morwen delved into her satchel and hurled a vial of black powder at her nearest attacker, causing the man to drop his sword with a scream. Before she could reach for another, the Dane in the horned helmet brought his war hammer down on her, and she barely had time to bring her staff up to protect herself. The blow sent the staff sliding across the room, and Morwen fell on her back, defenseless.

The Dane raised his war hammer to finish Morwen, but Berengar let out a roar and thundered down the hall, propelling himself forward with all the strength he could muster. He put his axe through the man's skull, and the corpse tumbled to its knees and slumped to the ground.

When Berengar reached out to help Morwen to her feet, he heard a terrible cry from the throne, where three attackers had overwhelmed Ronan. One of the Vikings slipped past him, and Berengar's eye met Alannah's just before the soldier put his sword through her belly. Ronan struck down his foes and beheaded the Dane in the next instant, but it was too late. The queen's gaze wandered down her dress, freshly stained with crimson. Ronan took Alannah into his arms and cradled her body.

With her dying breath, the queen reached out to Berengar. "Ravenna…protect Ravenna."

A shriek sounded across the room, where a group of Danes had seized Ravenna and were dragging her from the chapel.

They're taking her to Stormsson. With Alannah dead, the princess was next in line to the throne. If Stormsson abducted her and forced her to marry him, he could legitimize his claim over Munster. Berengar didn't intend to let that happen. He ran forward, swatting aside arrows and spears on his way from the chapel. Outside, the princess' captors had already bound her hands.

"Ravenna!" he shouted, and she noticed him just as they forced her onto a horse.

"Hurry," one said. "The queen's forces are coming."

As the horsemen bolted, Berengar unsheathed his sword and hurled it through the air. The weapon impaled the rider at the rear, and as he toppled from his mount, Berengar swung himself onto the horse and took off with Faolán in pursuit. The horse jumped over a flaming wagon, and Berengar ducked under an arrow, clutching the reins in one hand and his axe in the other. He tore down the hill after the princess' kidnappers. Most of the Danes had fallen in the initial skirmish. Munster's reinforcements marched toward the castle, unaware that their sole remaining monarch was being spirited away from Cashel. There was no time for Berengar to stop to send word to Ronan or get help. He couldn't allow Ravenna out of his sight.

The abductors took advantage of the confusion to pass

through the city gate unimpeded. Berengar chased them from the city in the moonlight until at last Cashel vanished behind him. There would be no second chance. If Stormsson's emissary had told the truth that day in the throne room, two thousand Danes were on their way to Munster's shores. If they landed before the princess was recovered, it would be too late.

Hold on, Ravenna. I'm coming. He was alone and poisoned, without his armor, sword, or bow, but he still had his axe, and he had Faolán. That would have to be enough.

Berengar rode like a man possessed. He did not stop to eat or even to sleep in his pursuit of the Danes, who had a head start on him. The princess' captors led him east, into the wild. Though they knew the country better than he, Berengar had been a hunter long before he was a warden. Even when they were out of his sight, he was never far behind. If he could track a single goblin on foot through a forest, he could follow the trail left by a band of fleeing horsemen, especially with Faolán hot on their scent.

The first day, the Danes dispatched riders to meet him in battle. When the third rider did not return, they stopped trying. Though they outnumbered him, the horsemen didn't dare confront him, on the chance that Munster's soldiers were at his back. No, they planned to take the princess to Stormsson's hidden fortress, where they would be safe.

For three days he hunted them. The Danes' path turned south, following the course of the River Suir. The trail led him through dense green woods and rocky plateaus. The witch's poison wore on him even more than the lack of food or sleep. He felt its full effect weighing him down, sapping him of strength and energy. It was all he could do to remain upright in the saddle. His white tunic was stained with sweat from the overbearing sun. Still, he couldn't give up, not with Princess Ravenna counting on him.

At last he came to a place where a skeletal structure loomed not far from where the river emptied into the Celtic Sea. Vines crawled over half-finished ramparts that rose above the trees that concealed the hidden fortress. Berengar slowed his pace and dismounted to continue on foot before his horse collapsed from exhaustion. The battleaxe weighed heavy in his hands, and each footstep felt weaker than the last. Sounds of metalworking carried through the woods, suggesting swords and spears sharpened for war.

As he drew nearer, he could see the stronghold was only partially complete. Stormsson's men had made camp in tents at the center of the basic fortifications. It appeared construction would not be finished until after the Vikings' reinforcements arrived. Berengar crept along the camp's perimeter, careful to stay out of sight. The fortress boasted an impressive number of warriors, and he was hardly at his best.

A cheer rang out as Ravenna's captors rode into camp. Berengar watched from a safe distance as they hauled the princess into a large tent, which he was sure belonged to Gorr Stormsson. The warden crept forward, quietly making his way closer to their camp. When Faolán attempted to follow, Berengar shook his head.

"There are too many to fight our way in. You need to turn back."

She wouldn't budge, refusing to leave his side.

"Now's not the time for stubbornness. I need you to trust me. Turn back and find the others. Bring help."

Faolán looked at him for a long moment before at last retreating into the brush. When she was gone, Berengar waited for the sentry stationed outside the western wall to pass by on his patrol and stole into the camp. He found the entrance to the tent where they had taken the princess surprisingly unguarded. Once Ravenna was free, they would steal a horse from the stables and, with any luck, they'd be gone before the Danes were even aware she was missing. It was quiet inside the tent. Berengar looked around, searching for the princess, but Ravenna was nowhere in sight.

"Warden Berengar, look out!" he heard her shout. "It's a trap!"

Footsteps sounded behind him. Before he could turn around, something hit him in the back of his head, and everything faded away.

T he sun had already begun to set when Berengar woke, a sign he'd been out for a long time. Though he'd been left alive, the Danes had gone to great lengths to ensure he did not escape. He was trapped inside a net that hung above the earth, suspended from a rope tied to one of the trees. Ropes bound his hands and feet. Even tied, his first instinct was to reach for his axe, and yet he knew at once it was gone.

A cool breeze caressed his face, causing the net to sway back and forth. Berengar shifted uncomfortably within the confines of the net, unable to fully extend himself. His head still ached from the blow that rendered him unconscious, but at least he felt more rested. The effects of the witch's poison seemed to have abated somewhat, though they'd left him weaker than he would otherwise have been.

"You're awake."

The voice came from Ravenna, who was strung up in a separate net nearby. She'd been stripped of her silver tiara, and her dress was dirty and disheveled, but she appeared unharmed.

Berengar craned his neck in order to better see her. "Why didn't they kill me?"

"Once the rest of the ships arrive, Gorr Stormsson plans to march his army to Cashel and behead you outside the gates. Then he'll threaten to do the same to me unless Ronan surrenders the city to him. I'll die before I let that happen."

The last of the light faded, replaced by the glow of the flames below. The Vikings celebrated their victory around the campfire, drinking and feasting while Stormsson looked on like a conquering king. Berengar's battleaxe lay at his feet like a prize. The men shouted and jeered, some even fighting among themselves. A few had already managed to consume more mead than they could hold and were passed out at tables or engaged in drunken brawls with their companions.

"You shouldn't have come after me on your own. Why did you do it? Now we'll both die."

"You know why."

The trees moaned in the wind, and as the nets swung past each other, Ravenna reached her fingers through the gaps in the net and grazed his fingers. Berengar closed his fingers around hers, holding her hand as they swayed in the breeze.

"I won't let this happen to you. I'll find a way to get you out of here, no matter what it takes."

Even if the queen's forces had followed his trail—and by some miracle Faolán found them—there was no way they'd reach the Viking stronghold in time to rescue them. If they were going to escape, it had to be now. The sentries had left their posts to join the revelries below. Night crept over the sky, ushering in darkness across the fortress. With the whole camp distracted by the festivities, he might stand a chance of surprising them if he could just get free. Berengar tried pulling at his ropes with all his strength, but it was no use. Without a weapon, there was nothing he could do.

That was when it hit him. His captors had taken his axe, and his sword and bow were back in Cashel, but there was one weapon that might have escaped their notice.

"Ravenna, do you think you can reach inside my boot?"

"I think so. But why?"

"I keep a dagger inside it for occasions just like this. Our hosts might have missed it. If you can get your hands on it, you might be able to cut through our bonds."

"I understand."

The princess leaned forward and reached through the gaps in the nets for his boot. She struggled to slip her hand inside his boot, and for a moment he thought she would fail, but her fist came free with the dagger. Ravenna quickly cut through her own restraints, stopping to conceal the knife only momentarily when a Dane wandered past them on his way to the bushes below. Then she went to work on Berengar's ropes. When his hands were liberated, Ravenna passed him the dagger, and in an instant his feet were also free. He stared down at the drop before returning his gaze to the princess.

"What now? Are we going to escape?"

"This ends tonight, one way or another." If they fled, Stormsson's men would only hunt them down. Even if they managed to escape, once the Viking ships arrived, Munster would face the threat of war. This was his only chance to break the Danes once and for all. He started to cut the net. "You're not going to want to see what comes next."

She shook her head. "I won't look away."

The bottom of the net opened up, and Berengar tossed her the knife. "Find a place to hide. Get a horse. If I fall, leave me."

He let himself go and landed hard on the ground. He kept to the shadows, moving unseen, and slipped behind a man at the periphery of camp. Before the man could react, Berengar clamped his arm around his mouth to prevent him from crying out. He dragged the struggling Dane into the bushes and crushed his windpipe before tearing the dead man's sword from its sheath.

Then he came for the others. He started slowly, picking off stragglers at the outskirts or those who had wandered away from their companions. He fell on them one by one. With each man he killed, his rage burned even hotter. He slashed, hacked, and ripped them apart with his sword, leaving a trail of blood in his wake. Any lingering weakness from the witch's poison was burned away by the unbridled fury that gripped him.

It wasn't long before someone cried out a warning, and a bell began to toll to alert the camp. Those who had fallen asleep started awake in confusion. Some ran to find weapons while others fled in terror at the sight of the bodies, unaware their doom was at hand.

"There he is," one shouted as Berengar strode confidently into the heart of the encampment. A host of warriors ran to meet him and he stood his ground against the onslaught of swords and spears. A lucky few got close enough to cut him before he put them down. The pain only made him angrier.

Berengar spotted his axe and cut his way toward it. Just before he reached the axe, a Viking came rushing toward him, swinging his hammer. He caught the man's forearm in one hand and pitched him into the campfire in time to

315

defend himself against the man's companions. One dealt him a wound across his torso before the warden gutted him. Blood soaked through his tunic from the injury. He growled from the pain like a wounded animal assailed on all sides.

"Esben Berengar!" Gorr Stormsson blocked his path to the axe. The Viking's eyes seemed to glow in the firelight within the spiked helmet he wore. Stormsson raised his double-edged blade and pointed it at the warden across the flames to challenge him. "You die tonight, Warden of Fál."

Berengar approached, and the two men faced each other. The muscles in his face tensed with loathing, and he raised his sword and charged with a savage cry. Stormsson ran to meet him, and the battle began with a clash of swords. Though Berengar held a slight advantage in size, it was his only such edge in the fight. Already he was weary from the effort he'd expended killing dozens of men, unlike his enemy, who was well rested. Berengar was without armor, whereas Stormsson wore mail over his leather armor, coupled with the added protection of his iron helmet. Even more frustrating, Stormsson wielded a murderous greatsword while Berengar possessed only a single-handed blade. Nevertheless, with each exchange his foe gave ground. Their blades met again, and Berengar struck his opponent in the face and sent him stumbling back in the dirt.

Before he could advance, two more warriors came running toward him, each equipped with a shield in one hand and a sword in the other. Berengar took them on at once, battering their shields aside and forcing them to the ground. Stormsson leapt at him while he was distracted, and Berengar met him in a forceful collision that sent the Viking's helmet flying. Stormsson attacked in a frenzy, raining down a flurry of attacks. Berengar countered his last attack and knocked his foe off his feet. The Dane's sword landed beside him.

Stormsson reached for the weapon only to find Berengar's blade at his throat.

"You're beaten. Yield." Berengar seized Stormsson and forced him to his knees. "Now tell me—who's been helping you inside the castle? Who helped you arrange the king's murder?"

Before Stormsson could open his mouth to speak, a dagger exploded out of the front of his mouth, and he pitched forward, bleeding.

"That was for my mother," Ravenna whispered to him, holding Berengar's dagger.

Stormsson gasped and reached out for his blade. "Please," he managed to say as blood spurted from his mouth. He wanted his sword, so that he might take his place in the afterlife.

Berengar kicked the sword away. "Your gods are false, Dane. You will never enter Valhalla. Your home will be the halls of Hell, where your brother awaits." He cast his blade aside and picked up the axe, turning to the princess. "Now we must leave. You won't be safe until we reach the castle."

They started toward the stables, but he staggered and fell, feeling the full effect of his injuries.

"Berengar!" Ravenna ran to his side.

"It's all right. You're safe. That's all that matters. Leave me behind. I'll only slow you down."

Ravenna's expression hardened. "Never." She helped him to his feet and managed to support his weight with her slender frame. Together the pair made their way to the stables, where they took one of the horses and fled into the moonlight.

. . .

The warden drifted in and out of consciousness. On more than one occasion he woke with a start, jostled by the horse underneath them as it galloped across the plains. He found himself held tightly in the arms of Ravenna, who gripped the reins while at the same time guiding the horse through the darkness. The people of Munster were renowned for their horsemanship, and their princess was no exception. He closed his eyes and took solace in the warmth of her body against his amid the winds.

Ravenna followed the river north. Eventually they came to the place where the Suir joined the Rivers Nore and Barrow.

"Hold on." The mare's hooves rattled over a bridge that spanned the rushing waters. "There's a town ahead." The princess brought the horse to a halt in front of the Inn of the Three Sisters—named after the confluence of the three rivers—and helped Berengar off the horse. Together they stumbled into the inn, which was all but deserted at the late hour.

The innkeeper quickly emerged, drawn by the loudness of their sudden appearance and perhaps expecting trouble. He stared at the two newcomers, bewildered.

"Good heavens," he stammered. "Is that blood on your shirt?"

"He's been hurt." Ravenna helped Berengar to a table near the fireplace. "Send for a healer and bring this man something to eat. We'll need lodging at least for the night, if not longer."

The innkeeper bit his lip and looked over the two travelers with considerable skepticism. "I don't want any trouble. This is a respectable establishment."

The princess' expression flashed with anger. She

slipped a golden ring from her finger and thrust it into the man's hand. "I believe that should cover our costs. Keep it."

The innkeeper stared at the ring in wonder, as its worth was more than anything inside the inn. He bowed low. "Of course, my lady. I will get help at once."

"See that you do." Ravenna settled into a chair next to Berengar as the innkeeper scurried away.

"You shouldn't have done that," Berengar said. "We can't risk anyone learning who you are. The Danes may have spies in town, and we're still too far from Cashel."

"Gorr Stormsson is dead. The Danes are broken. And if you think I will allow you to bleed to death after what you've done for me, you're gravely mistaken."

"Most people would have left me there to die."

They gazed at each other for a long time, with only the crackling of the burning logs for noise.

"I was wrong before," Ravenna said. "When I told you I didn't believe in heroes. I do now." When Berengar looked away, she laid her hand on the ruined half of his face and turned it back toward her. "I don't care about the scars. I have them too."

She showed him her back, lowering her dress to reveal dozens of lash marks marring her otherwise perfect skin. Berengar traced the edge of one such scar with his fingers, causing her to shiver before she returned her dress to its proper place.

"My brother was hardly cold in the ground before my father announced my engagement." Her eyes were distant at the memory. "I was little more than a girl. When I tried to flee, Laird O'Reilly's spies discovered me and dragged me back to the castle. I pleaded with my mother to change my father's mind, but in the end she stood behind his decision, as she always did. Munster was the only

319

home I had ever known, and they sent me away, overseas."

The tension in the air was thick. Though Berengar had heard this part of the story before, it was clear the princess was on the cusp of a new revelation.

"For my husband, inflicting pain was an art. An old injury had left him half a man, and he took joy only from causing misery. His cruelty wasn't limited to beatings. He killed the handmaidens I brought with me from Cashel and made me watch. He wanted to break me." Her voice grew cold. "But I refused to break."

"I'm sorry." The words felt hollow, but they were the best he could offer.

"Since then I've let myself care for no one and nothing. Until you."

Berengar shook his head. "You don't know the things I've done."

"Then tell me. Tell me your story."

The warden averted his gaze and stared into the fire. He rarely spoke of his past to anyone. "The songs remember it as the Doom of Dún de Fulaingt." The story he was about to tell was one no living soul had heard, at least as it actually happened.

"The Fortress of Suffering."

He nodded. "In the time of the Shadow Wars, darkness reigned across the land. Each of the five kingdoms teetered on the brink, divided against themselves in civil war. Rebellious lords raised armies to seize large swaths of territory for themselves. Bandits and cutthroats ambushed those travelers on the road fortunate enough to avoid the monsters. Famine and disease spread like wildfire.

"For my part, I wanted nothing to do with the war. My wife died in childbirth some years earlier, and I sought only to be left alone. The war came to my door anyway. There was a village within a half-day's walk from my farm. The people there were kind. In my youth they gave me a home and nursed me back to health when the bear nearly killed me. One day soldiers came to the village. The people offered no resistance, and still they tore the village apart, burning and looting and killing." He expected the old anger to stir at the words, but he just felt empty and tired.

"What did you do?"

"The soldiers had taken refuge in a fortress said to be unassailable. Forces loyal to the Ice Queen tried and failed to recapture it. I let myself be captured. That day the soldiers tortured me, having killed their other prisoners already. When night came, I broke free of my restraints and..." He trailed off, lost in a fog of memory. "It was a slaughter. I killed them all, down to the last man. But I didn't just kill them. Something broke inside me. I took them apart, like a mad beast gripped by rage. Some attempted to surrender. Others fled. None were spared from my wrath. They showed no mercy, and they received none.

"When the gates were opened to them the next morning, the Ice Queen's forces were terrified. They'd heard the sound of screams all night. Some thought a monster had been unleashed inside the fortress, and in a way, they were right. The scene they encountered was a nightmare. Body parts were strewn across the camp. Corpses were impaled, strung up, or nailed to walls. And there I was, covered in blood from head to toe.

"When I spotted the battleaxe among the remains, it was as if it called to me. Others joined me, and together we patrolled the countryside, defending the forgotten people. We served no ruler and carried no banners. I lived only for vengeance, until..."

"Until what?" Ravenna asked.

He turned back to her at last. "Until I met *her*. Nora. Without her, I would be lost. She saved me from myself—showed me a better way. When the war ended, she made me a warden and gave me something to fight for. Since that day, I've tried my best to be the man she would want me to be, but always the rage is there, just beneath the surface. There's a reason I didn't want you to see what I did to those men tonight. Now do you understand, Princess?"

A lone tear ran down her face. "I don't care about the past. Run away with me. We can make a fresh start, together. The throne, your oaths—let's leave it all behind."

She leaned closer to him, searching for something with her eyes, and the warden found himself inescapably drawn to her. Their lips brushed, and Berengar held her close. They kissed again, a long, deep kiss. Ravenna closed her eyes tightly and pressed her forehead into him, as if afraid of being pulled away from his embrace.

"I didn't know it would be like this."

Berengar looked back at her, at a loss for words. Before he could give her an answer, he heard the movement of horsemen beyond the walls. Had the innkeeper betrayed them?

The axe was already in his hands. "Get behind me."

He stared at the door, ready for anything.

A bark sounded outside the inn, the door flew open, and Faolán rushed inside, accompanied by Morwen. Soldiers of Munster lingered behind them in the doorway, along with the befuddled innkeeper, who still hadn't quite pieced their identities together yet.

Faolán nearly knocked him over as she leapt on him, licking his hands.

"It's all right, girl. I'm fine."

Morwen threw her arms around him, wrapping him in

a hug. "I'm so happy you're alive. And you also, Your Grace."

"How did you find us?" Ravenna asked.

Morwen released her hold on him and turned to the princess, offering a slight bow. "We set out from Cashel after you were taken, but the trail ran cold until Faolán appeared and led us to you."

Berengar glanced at Ravenna. "We must get you back to Cashel at once. Morwen can tend to my injuries on the road." He left the rest unsaid. They would have to leave their conversation unfinished, at least for now.

The princess agreed, and they followed Morwen outside the inn, where a great host waited for them. Berengar helped the princess onto a horse and squeezed her hand before mounting the steed beside her. They rode into the night, safe for the moment, but not yet out of danger.

CHAPTER SEVENTEEN

IN ALL HIS YEARS, he had never seen a city of such size so quiet. Deafening silence from inside Cashel's walls greeted their approach. A cry went out to open the gate at the sight of their banners. As they drew nearer, a sentry recognized the princess among the company. A trumpet sounded, and a triumphant roar carried through the streets as Ravenna entered the city. She waved at all those gathered near the gate. Even disheveled and missing a crown, she was the very image of a monarch, offering her subjects a weary smile.

More came running at the news of the princess' return, cheering and openly weeping. A few muttered disparaging remarks about the prospect of life under rule of the Tainted Princess, but most appeared relieved that the heir to the throne had survived unharmed. Word quickly spread that the Viking stronghold had fallen, and Berengar heard more than a few rumors of his hand in Gorr Stormsson's death as he passed by. He never thought he would be so glad to glimpse the castle again. He was fortunate the guards sent to retrieve them had an ample supply of food and drink, and the extent of the injuries he suffered were well within Morwen's capabilities to heal. Despite his protests, the magician all but forced him to take a potion to eliminate any lingering effects of Agatha's poison. A little rest, and he would be back to his old self again.

Ravenna noticed him watching her, and the two exchanged a fleeting glance, one of many such looks they'd shared over the previous days. Given the close proximity of their companions, it proved impossible for them to share more than two words in private, something Berengar was secretly grateful for. He still didn't know how he would answer her. No matter his feelings for her, things were more complicated than that. With both her parents dead, Ravenna was the sole heir to the throne. Her people needed her now more than ever. Then there were Berengar's obligations to Nora. He could not easily forsake his oaths and responsibilities to run away with the princess. At the same time, he'd been offered a chance to make a new start with someone he cared for, a possibility he'd never dared hope for.

Morwen caught him staring at the princess and an expression of annoyance flashed over her face. Berengar wondered if it was out of any lingering resentment toward the princess, considering their history, or if Morwen simply felt protective of him. Though he couldn't deny that he'd come to feel an unexpected fondness for the girl, he hoped she hadn't grown too attached to him. Soon he would be gone from Munster, and their temporary partnership would come to its inevitable end.

Upon entering the city, the company made for the castle with haste. Order had been restored to Cashel in their absence. There were relatively few visible reminders of the Danes' attack. The castle was unmarred by the flames, a sign the guards managed to extinguish the fires before they spread. The bodies of the fallen were gone, removed for burial, and all the damaged property had been cleared away. The Rock of Cashel endured, as it had for centuries, but the victory was bittersweet. Queen Alannah was dead. Even with Gorr Stormsson dealt with, his co-conspirator remained at large. Berengar wasn't sure if they were returning Princess Ravenna closer to danger or delivering her to safety.

Corrin waited for them outside the entrance to the castle. His face betrayed relief when he noticed the princess, and he ordered his men to help her from her horse. Ravenna, more than capable of dismounting on her own, waved them away. At Berengar's approach, the captain of the guard bowed so low it seemed as though he might tip over.

Corrin looked ashamed. "I beseech your forgiveness, Warden Berengar. I nearly led you to your death."

"There is nothing to forgive. You were not yourself."

"You saved me from the witch's curse. From this day forward, I am in your debt."

"I'll keep that in mind." Berengar noticed Seamus standing in the background. He and his companions had returned in the warden's absence. "Escort the princess inside, will you? I have business to deal with first." He waited until the procession left him behind before making his way to Seamus and his friends, who stood beside a wagon. "Well? Did you discover anything of note?"

Careful to keep his distance from Faolán, Seamus nodded to one of his companions, and the guard lifted the sheet covering the wagon's rear. "See for yourself."

Berengar inspected the wagon's contents. "Just as I

thought. You've done well." He marched to the castle and gestured for them to follow.

Despite the throne room's occupants, the chamber felt emptier without Alannah's presence. He arrived in time to see Princess Ravenna reunited with Ronan, who embraced her as a father might greet a long-lost daughter. Berengar lingered in the background as Ronan walked the princess to the dais, where her father's crown rested upon the throne.

"This belongs to you now." The thane handed it to her.

Ravenna took the crown and held it in her hands for a long moment before placing it on her head.

Ronan retreated and knelt at the dais. "Forgive me, Your Grace. I failed to protect your mother, as I failed your father before her." He stared at the ground, clearly pained by his words. "When the king died, I was released from my oath. I remained in my position at Queen Alannah's request, but now I am no longer fit to serve as thane of Munster."

"It is with a heavy heart I accept your resignation." Ravenna stepped from the dais and put her hand on his shoulder. "Rise without shame. You have done honorably by our kingdom, and you have been my true friend since I was a girl. I took my first steps at your side. When my brother died, it was you who comforted me. For that reason, I appoint you my personal adviser."

One by one, the *Rí Tuaithe* knelt before the princess and laid their iron crowns at Ravenna's feet to offer oaths of loyalty, followed in turn by the other lords of Munster. Berengar noticed that Desmond was again missing, as he had been during Queen Alannah's coronation. He spotted Morwen standing nearby and asked her what she knew of the matter.

"I heard he's in mourning. Word reached Cashel from

Cill Airne that his father has died. Desmond is the new Laird Tierney." She waited, likely expecting Ravenna to call on her to reaffirm her oath, but instead the princess beckoned Marcus O'Reilly forward.

"Your Grace." The old man stooped and kissed her hand.

"I have heard you told my mother of your intention to step aside."

O'Reilly nodded. "The weight of my years is upon me, Your Grace. I long to return to Cóbh to live out my days in peace."

"I'm sure you do," Berengar interrupted, and all eyes fell on him. "And I think we both know why."

"I beg your pardon?"

When the warden stepped forward, Seamus and his companions walked the length of the throne room behind him, carrying a heavy chest.

"I dispatched Seamus and his friends to your estate at Cóbh. Care to see what they found?"

The guards heaved the chest onto the floor, where it overturned at O'Reilly's feet, spilling gold coins across the floor.

"These are coins from the royal treasury!" Ronan exclaimed. "What is the meaning of this?"

"It seems Marcus here discovered the true nature of King Mór's arrangement with the Witches of the Golden Vale," Berengar said. "I'm surprised I didn't see it sooner. If anyone could have uncovered such a well-guarded secret, it would have been you."

Most of the court appeared taken aback, but Ravenna seemed to have pieced everything together. The princess' eyes narrowed in O'Reilly's direction. "It was you. You were the blackmailer."

"I would never—"

"Don't bother," Berengar said. "Your handwriting matches the alterations made in the Exchequer's records. You used your position to extort the king of Munster to enrich yourself and then tried to cover it up. With the investigation into his murder, you were afraid of being exposed, so you sent your servant to raid his chambers in a search for his journal. It's funny—the king's journal never mentioned you. If you hadn't told your man to spy on us, I might not have suspected your involvement."

The reason O'Reilly had tried so hard to convince him that Alannah and Ronan were engaged in an affair suddenly became clear. He was trying to deflect blame away from himself. O'Reilly probably planned to step down from the very moment he learned of the king's death. He wanted to be as far away from the castle as possible.

"This is an outrage," O'Reilly protested.

"I'm betting you tipped off the Danes about the ship-ment of gold as well, which probably means you helped them enter Cashel on the night of the queen's coronation. You were working with Stormsson all along, weren't you?"

"You treacherous snake." Ravenna's voice was full of wrath. "You killed them."

O'Reilly glanced around the room, looking for allies, but he had none. He bowed his head in defeat. "I admit I knew of the affair with the witches. I used that knowledge to extort King Mór, but I never conspired to murder him. You have to believe me! I would never have wanted him dead, or Queen Alannah for that matter. I cared for them."

"You have a funny way of showing it." Berengar loomed inches from O'Reilly. The old man swallowed and took a step back, but there was nowhere to flee to. He was caught like a rat in a trap. He turned instead to Princess

Ravenna. "I never helped Gorr Stormsson. I knew nothing of the stolen shipments."

Berengar frowned. O'Reilly was a talented liar, but there was something in the old man's desperate plea that gave him pause. While O'Reilly had confessed his culpability in the matter of the king's blackmail, that didn't necessarily mean he was the assassin, even if it provided ample motive for the crime. No, there was something else that concerned the warden, but before he could proceed, he needed to be certain.

Ronan reached for his sword. "Princess, allow me to bring you this traitor's head."

O'Reilly threw himself at the princess' feet. "Show mercy, Your Grace—I beg you."

"You shall not die." Ravenna's voice was full of venom. "You would have had me live out my days as a prisoner. It seems only right you should suffer the same fate. You will spend the rest of your wretched life locked within the dungeon, under the very halls you once walked. Captain Corrin, see to it this filth never sees the sunlight again."

For once, O'Reilly had nothing to say. The guards seized him and carried him from the throne room.

"What of Gorr Stormsson?" one of the *Rí Tuaithe* asked the princess. "He must be brought to justice for his part in the queen's death. We cannot allow the Danes to attack our city unanswered."

"Gorr Stormsson is dead." Ravenna's remarks were greeted by a stunned silence. "Warden Berengar defeated him in combat and overthrew his stronghold, yet the Viking threat remains." She looked again to Ronan. "That is why I entrust you with this additional responsibility. In your last act as thane, you will take half of our army to the coast to destroy their fleet. When they see their captain is dead, they will flee and never return."

Ronan bowed low. "It will be done, Your Grace."

Ravenna returned to the dais. "With the Witches of the Golden Vale, the crone of the Devil's Bit, and Gorr Stormsson dead, it will not be long before Munster will again be at peace. I will require your help to restore our land to greatness in the days to come."

"You'll need someone here to keep order while I'm gone," Ronan said. "If I'm to take half the army, our forces will be stretched thin. I advise you to appoint a new thane at once."

"I have a suggestion," Berengar interjected. "Why not Desmond of Cill Airne?"

"Desmond?" Ronan's surprise was evident.

Berengar nodded. "He has proven himself loyal many times. It was Desmond who helped me rescue Morwen from Innisfallen. He has experience running a large city, and he and the princess are childhood friends."

"Very well," Ravenna said. "I will summon him here at once."

"Actually, I was hoping to be the one to deliver the news."

The princess raised an eyebrow. "As you wish. Now, my lords, I take my leave of you to pay my respects to my mother."

The warden departed the castle once more outfitted in his armor and bearskin cloak. It felt good to have his weapons at his side again. After a lengthy walk, he came to Desmond's city dwelling, a lofty mansion built into the hillside to look out over Cashel. It was said to have been in Laird Tierney's family for generations. Berengar arrived at the residence with only Faolán for company, the princess' letter in hand. Well-dressed servants immediately ushered him inside. The chamberlain led him into a sunlit hall adorned with windows and gold tapestries, where Berengar waited until Desmond appeared.

"Word reached me of your return, Warden Berengar. I'm glad to see you here safely, my friend."

"It's been an eventful day."

"Indeed. I've heard the rumors of that nasty business with Marcus O'Reilly, although I can't say I'm surprised. I gather he was the man responsible for the king's murder?"

"Perhaps. But I didn't come here to talk about the king's death. I'm here at the princess' behest." Berengar handed Desmond the princess' message and watched as he digested its contents. "I believe congratulations are in order, Laird Tierney. Or should I say, Thane Tierney?"

Desmond smiled. "You honor me, Warden Berengar. I thought I had fallen out of favor with the princess when she rejected my proposal, but it says here you personally advised Ravenna on my appointment. This calls for a celebration." He summoned a servant, who produced a pitcher of wine.

"None for me."

"I take it you've heard of my father's passing, then."

"You were quite devoted to him, as I recall."

"He was ill for a long time. I am content his suffering has ended." Desmond took a goblet and raised it to his lips. "Now we must look to the future. Rest assured, I will not forget the role you played in my ascension. Tara will have a friend in Munster's thane whenever you require."

"I'm glad to hear it." They walked together down the hall. The guards Desmond brought with him from Cill Airne stared forward blindly, motionless at their posts. "There were those who spoke against your appointment. Some found your absence on the night of the queen's coronation suspicious."

"Utter nonsense." Desmond shook his head. "I knew Alannah from our time at Tuathal's Keep. I would never have harmed her."

"That's exactly what I said." Berengar laid a hand on Desmond's shoulder and lowered his voice, as if they were two old friends speaking about old times. "Of course, I did find it curious to discover that Gorr Stormsson had taken you prisoner some years ago."

Desmond's expression betrayed a sign of unease. "Where did you hear that?"

"Princess Ravenna told me on the eve of the coronation. It came as a surprise, since you denied any dealings with the Danes. Still, I was saddened to learn your father refused to pay the ransom. It must have been awful for you, a Viking prisoner for months."

The muscles around Desmond's jaw tightened. "It was unpleasant, yes, though I understood sacrifices must be made in the name of the realm."

Berengar removed his hand. "Of course, then I learned that you studied alchemy from the masters at Cill Airne in your youth, before your father forbade it. That's when it struck me—for someone skilled in such arts, arranging a poisoning would have been an easy matter."

Desmond came to a sudden stop. "What are you saying?"

"I suspect it was easy to poison your father. He was an old man to begin with. But why stop there, when your bloodline puts you within reach of the throne? The Demon's Whisper was likely more difficult to manage. Thankfully you had the Witches of the Golden Vale to lend a helping hand. I wonder if you hatched the plan before you were taken captive, or if it was in your mind from the start? Perhaps you and Stormsson planned to divide Munster between you. The Danes would rule to the east, and you to the west. That's why you weren't at the coronation, wasn't it? You smuggled the raiding party into the city to murder Alannah and abduct Ravenna."

"Have you shared this theory with anyone else?"

"No. I wanted to discuss it with you first."

Desmond relaxed, and the smile returned to his face. "I'm afraid it's true. You're cleverer than you look, Warden Berengar, but not as clever as you think. Guards!"

Desmond's guards drew their weapons and stepped forward. Faolán barked a warning, and when the warden glanced around the room, he found himself completely surrounded.

"I won't go down without a fight." Berengar reached for his axe.

Desmond laughed. "I believe you. With you out of my way and Ronan kind enough to leave the city with half the army, I only have to reach out my hand and take the castle for myself. Given my new powers as thane, it should be an easy task. Then I will be king of Munster. This is how it ends for you, my friend. It seems the famous warden is only a man after all. You were a fool to trust me."

"I didn't."

Desmond's look of triumph faded. At that moment, a host of castle guards stormed inside the hall, vastly outnumbering the opposing forces. Archers trained their arrows at the guards surrounding Berengar, who broke ranks around him to form a single unit.

"We heard his confession," Corrin said. "Just as you said."

"What is this?" Desmond demanded.

Berengar nodded and pointed his axe at Desmond. "Laird Tierney, for the high crime of regicide, I sentence you to die, in the name of the High Queen."

"Kill them!" Desmond shouted to his men.

The two sides regarded each other before Berengar issued a battle cry and charged at Desmond, and open conflict broke out within the confines of the hall. In such tight quarters, the fighting was close and bloody. Corrin's archers unleashed their arrows as the foot soldiers marched forward with their spears out. Though fewer in number, Desmond's guards stood their ground, even as their comrades dropped left and right. Berengar hacked at the enemies' shields while Faolán attacked their legs, until at last he broke through the enemy ranks and ran in pursuit of Desmond.

The clamor of battle echoed at his back as he sprinted into the adjoining chamber, a narrow hallway that ended in a balcony overlooking the city. Desmond appeared to have vanished from sight. The warden slowed his pace and advanced cautiously. Faolán growled, alerting him to the presence of a servant girl crouched low, shaking in fear. Berengar looked at her, and the girl's eyes shifted toward an open doorway a short distance away, from which Desmond leapt at him, wielding a sword.

"It's over." Berengar met the first strike with his axe. "Your forces are outmatched. You've lost. Give up."

"Never." Desmond's movements were swift and dexterous. Each attack was timed with near perfect precision. It was clear he had been well trained in the art of combat by the sword masters at Cill Airne.

The pair exchanged blows several times in rapid succession. Each time, Berengar countered Desmond's attack and forced him back, but the tight space limited his advantage in size. The duel took them the length of the hallway, and the fight spilled onto the balcony, where at last Berengar overpowered his foe, striking repeatedly with his axe until Desmond lost his footing and fell. The sword went flying over the side.

"Surrender now," Berengar said.

When Desmond grabbed a hidden dagger in his sleeve and lunged at Berengar, Faolán pounced on him and sank her teeth into his forearm. Desmond stared into the wolfhound's amber eyes, paralyzed by fear.

"I'm tempted to let her have you," Berengar said. "Though I suppose I should take you to the princess to give an account of your misdeeds and answer for your crimes. On your feet."

Desmond stood, Berengar's axe pointed at his chest. He opened his mouth as if to say something but stopped suddenly. He looked over his shoulder, and a strange expression came over his face.

"Don't try it." Berengar reached for him, but it was too late.

Desmond jumped from the balcony, falling to his death.

B erengar again faced the throne. The attention of every soul in the room was fixed upon the warden, from the lords of Munster to the guards at their posts. None uttered a word as he delivered his account to the princess. Starting with his initial summons from King Mór, Berengar recounted all the events that followed, detailing his investigation into Mór's death. He did not do so alone. In front of all those gathered in their midst, he acknowledged Morwen's assistance as she stood at his side. The magician was unusually reluctant to speak, which was easy enough to understand. As the king's secret daughter, she'd spent her entire life in the shadows. For once, it was her time to be seen for who she truly was.

As scribes transcribed his words, Berengar pieced together all that occurred. No one stood to gain more from the death of the king and his family than Desmond, who was fourth in line to the throne. Having poisoned his father slowly over time to gain power within Cill Airne, he conspired with Gorr Stormsson to assassinate King Mór. Desmond used Laird Tierney's wealth to finance the déisi and contract the Brotherhood of Thieves, and Stormsson recruited the Witches of the Golden Vale to their side. Though Marcus O'Reilly had indeed blackmailed the king using the knowledge of Mór's affair with the witches, he was never a part of the plot. While some details were still unclear—Berengar remained uncertain how Desmond managed to uncover the route of the gold shipments—for the most part, everything fit.

A small uproar ensued when he revealed Desmond's role in the plot, until Ravenna held up a hand to silence the court. The princess remained stoic throughout. While the scribes completed their transcriptions, he took a moment to study her when he was finished speaking, unable to forget the softness of her lips against his. The vulnerability he'd witnessed in private had been replaced by the hardened expression she showed to the world. It wasn't the first time she'd been betrayed by someone close to her.

The room's occupants followed his gaze, looking to their new monarch. Ravenna ordered word of Berengar's discoveries to be spread through the city. Copies of the scribes' transcriptions were to be sent to Tara, the four remaining kings and queens of Fál, and each of Munster's noble houses.

Ravenna addressed the court. "This has been a dark chapter in Munster's history. But now the darkness has passed. In my father's name, I swear to you our kingdom will emerge stronger and more united than ever before.

Now is the time to remember the fallen and honor the living."

Starting with Berengar, she thanked those who had stood by her side, including Ronan, who had already left Cashel with his soldiers, and Corrin, who confirmed the warden's account of Desmond's admission. Last of all, she beckoned to Morwen from the throne.

"Lady Morwen, step forward."

Morwen knelt before the dais. "Your Grace."

"We have an ugly history," Ravenna said quietly before raising her voice. She looked not at Morwen, but at the crowd. "Was Munster not complicit in the purges that followed the Shadow Wars? Did you not allow Leinster's witch hunters into our realm to hunt those whose only crime was being something other than human? After my father's death, how quickly the tolerant and accepting people of Munster began burning imaginary fairies and running goblins from their businesses.

"Yet before you stands a magician who rescued the kingdom from destruction. So I say to you now—from this day forth, magic and nonhuman creatures are to be brought under the protection of the crown. Anyone who harms someone on suspicion of magic will have such harm done to them." There was grumbling in some corners of the room, and the princess' eyes flashed with anger. "If you do not enforce this proclamation, your lands and titles are forfeit."

"Thank you, Your Grace," said Morwen.

Ravenna returned her attention to the throne. "Now, Lady Morwen, in recognition of your services, I release you from your oath."

Morwen's smile faded, giving way to disbelief. "What?"

"It was my mother's last wish. It is a reward well-earned for your great deeds."

Morwen leapt to her feet and approached the dais without a moment's hesitation. "I have no wish to leave the castle, Your Grace. I am happy with my position."

Ravenna lowered her voice, but Berengar was close enough to hear her words. "I fear there will be much resistance to my new edict, perhaps even a backlash against nonhumans. I cannot guarantee your safety, and I will not have your blood on my hands."

Morwen fell to her knees before the throne and kissed her half-sister's hand. "Please, don't send me from your side. Cashel is my home."

"Do not weep, Lady Morwen. I will make sure you are well provided for. For the first time, you are truly free to chart your own destiny."

Morwen looked as if she'd been struck. She stumbled from the throne, ashen faced. He knew her expression all too well. It was a lesson he'd learned a long time ago, the realization things would never again be as they once were.

That night, he enjoyed his first true sleep in days. At Ravenna's request, he remained in Cashel for Queen Alannah's funeral. Berengar took the time to settle his accounts in the city. His time with Ravenna was bittersweet, as both knew it was coming to an end. He saw little of the princess, who was occupied with her new responsibilities. He saw even less of Morwen, who seemed to have retreated from castle life.

At last he prepared to return to Tara, aware the High Queen would want to hear the story of Mór's death. When he came to say farewell to the princess, she asked him if he had given any thought to her offer, and he told him he still didn't have an answer for her. With Ravenna's coronation as queen not set to take place until after Ronan destroyed the Viking fleet, Berengar promised he would return at that time with an answer.

A familiar figure in blue robes waited for him at the castle's entrance.

"You didn't think I'd let you leave without saying good-bye, did you?" Morwen asked.

"I know you better than that."

A long look passed between them. Berengar was a man of few words, and he wasn't exactly a sentimental sort to begin with, but he was certain Morwen knew how he felt.

"Farewell, Morwen of Cashel." He would miss her, maybe more than he cared to admit, but that was the way of things. Better not to dwell on it.

"Wait," Morwen called after him outside the castle.

He stopped for her.

"Take me with you." She glanced over her shoulder, and her gaze fell on the tower. "There's nothing left for me here."

It was true some wardens traveled with companions, but Berengar had always walked alone.

"Life on the road is too dangerous for a girl," he said, quickly adding, "even one as brave as you."

Morwen folded her arms across her chest. "In case you've forgotten, I'm a magician. I held my own against those witches and treated you when you were shot with that poisoned arrow, thank you very much. Think how useful it would be to have a magician on hand. I guarantee I know more about monsters than you do."

"Is that a fact?"

"Please. You know I can help."

What frightened him the most was how much he wanted to tell her yes.

"No. My decision is final."

Her voice was almost so quiet he didn't hear it. "I thought you were my friend."

For a moment, he remembered carrying her across the wilderness as she slept, the words of a long-forgotten lullaby on his tongue. Then he walked away, leaving her standing behind, head bowed low.

CHAPTER EIGHTEEN

THE WARDEN SAT ALONE inside an inn at the border with Leinster, reading a map by candlelight. Faolán lay stretched out at his feet, basking in the warmth of the nearby fire. A meadair rested on the table beside the map. The drink was an expression of thanks from the innkeeper for breaking up a brawl between two rowdy patrons earlier that evening. The warden raised the meadair to his lips and swallowed a mouthful of honeyed mead. God help him, he was actually developing a taste for the stuff. Next he'd be singing with the bards or playing ficheall.

It had been an eventful day. It seemed the townspeople had no shortage of troubles that needed sorting out. In addition to stopping the fight, he'd helped the local constable capture an elusive bandit and tracked down a local girl supposedly abducted by a leprechaun. In the end, most of the problems the townspeople bothered him with amounted to little more than ordinary errands. As it turned out, the "bandit" was just an orphaned child stealing food to feed himself, the missing girl simply stole away to see her sweetheart, and the "leprechaun" was nothing more than a very dirty and hairy man who lived near the swamp. Still, after weeks corralled within the city, it felt good to be back in the countryside again.

It was time to return to Tara, hopefully for a long rest before he was needed again. He'd earned it. His stay in Munster proved longer than he ever expected it would be, but it was finally over. He had avenged his friend's death and brought his killers to justice. Munster was at peace, and yet a shadow of doubt remained. He couldn't escape the feeling that nagged at him since his departure from Cashel, which had only grown stronger with time—the feeling he'd left something unfinished.

Again and again he returned to his time in the capital, searching in vain for the missing piece. On the surface, everything fit perfectly—perhaps *too* perfectly. It was as if all the answers had been left for him to find, purposely leading him to the truth. Life was rarely so neat and tidy. There was something troubling about the way Desmond looked at him just before he threw himself to his death. There was something more he had to say, one last secret to be revealed.

Berengar put the map away, frustrated, and drained the last of the honeyed mead. Why was he so uneasy? Maybe he simply no longer knew how to be happy. After all, everything turned out all right in the end. He'd rescued the princess and saved the kingdom, just like in the fairy tales. Perhaps that was the problem. The world wasn't like the one found in the stories. Even the true fairy tales were much darker than the ones he learned as a lad. Life was rarely so simple.

But what was he missing? The contents of the letter the king received before his death were still a mystery, though as the message had come from Cill Airne, it was likely Desmond was its source. There was the theft of shipments of gold from the treasury, done with help from someone inside the castle—a feat Desmond couldn't have accomplished from Cill Airne, and one O'Reilly denied, despite his attempt to alter the Exchequer's books to conceal his blackmail of the king.

Most troubling were the allusions Agatha made to the possibility there was an additional magic user somewhere within Munster's borders. Though that could be easily dismissed as another of the witch's lies, Lissa made a similar claim. Agatha appeared surprised when Berengar accused her of controlling Mór's mind. Was it shock that he knew the truth, or was she surprised to learn Mór had been controlled in the first place? Morwen believed such a power was beyond a mere witch. The more Berengar thought about his final confrontation with Agatha, the more it bothered him. Something made the floor open up beneath the witch, and he was fairly certain it wasn't that one of her spells had gone wrong.

It's no use. Berengar left some coins for the innkeeper and rose from the table. *I should get some rest. There's a long ride ahead tomorrow.* He made his way through the crowded hall with ease; it was an advantage of his size that people always seemed to clear out of his path. He was just outside his room when a line from Mór's journal came back to him.

Something else has its claws in me…something evil and familiar.

At once Berengar knew what he'd overlooked.

He departed the inn and rode south. If the truth was as he feared, every man, woman, and child in Cashel was in mortal peril.

.   .   .

When he passed through the city gate, it was as if nothing had changed from the day he arrived at the capital. Even at a distance, Cashel was a sight to behold under summer's golden sun, and the effect was only magnified up close. Thousands walked its streets. There were men and women of all walks of life—not simply nobles, priests, and soldiers, but musicians, merchants, and commoners too, from across Fál and beyond its shores. More than a few muttered a word of thanks when he went by, though despite all he had done in service to the realm, there were those who met him with insults or averted their eyes in the face of his scars. A merciful number didn't recognize the warden or ignored him altogether.

With the defeat of Gorr Stormsson and the deaths of those who conspired to murder King Mór, life had more or less returned to normal. To the people of Cashel, it was simply another ordinary day in the bustling, prosperous city. Talk of the evil crone that haunted the Devil's Bit had given way to rumors of a werewolf ravaging the country-side near Beaufort. Peddlers offered amulets and medal-lions to ward against dark magic in the wake of the princess' edict. All were blissfully unaware of the danger at their doorstep. If the people knew what he did, there would be panic in the streets, but the hour was far too late to evacuate the city.

Berengar immediately set out to find Corrin, who was busy settling a dispute between two nobles in the marketplace.

"Hail, Warden Berengar," Corrin said, pleased to see him. "I thought you'd gone."

"Never mind that. I need your help."

"For the man who saved Munster? Anything."

"Don't be too sure of that. This will not be easy, for

anyone involved." Berengar scanned the marketplace. Never had he seen such a meager number of guards. "Where are all your men?"

"I'm afraid our numbers are depleted at the moment. Ronan has not yet returned from the coast, and the princess sent several hundred soldiers to Cill Airne to determine the degree to which Laird Tierney's brothers were involved in the plot against her father's life."

"And Morwen? Where is she?"

"She's gone too—left just yesterday morning. Said something about not being needed anymore."

"That will make this harder. Muster all the soldiers under your command. We've no time to waste."

Corrin's smile faded. "What's happened?"

When Berengar told him, the captain of the guard looked back at him in disbelief. "That's impossible."

"Trust me, I wish it was. Ready your men for battle, Captain."

Corrin just stood there. "What you're asking me to do…it's a betrayal of every oath I've sworn to uphold."

"If you refuse to help, every person in this city will die. They may die anyway. You swore to protect the people of Cashel, did you not?" Berengar took a step closer and stared at Corrin, his gaze hard and unyielding. "The time has come to choose sides. Whom will you stand beside?"

Corrin nodded slowly. "I will give the order."

"Good." Berengar swung himself back onto his horse.

"And where are you going?"

"To the castle." He spurred the horse forward and never looked back.

When he neared the top of the hill, it became clear the castle's defenses were abandoned. There were no sentries manning the walls or standing watch at the gate. Gone too were the advisers and monks who so frequently traipsed about the grounds. Berengar, who had faced more battles than he could count, felt the hair on the back of his neck stand on end as he passed through the courtyard and encountered not a single living soul.

His horse rebelled against him as he neared the end of the road, and Berengar dismounted to continue on foot. The wind howled in disapproval at his approach. Muted thunder rumbled in the background as clouds covered the sky, and though the sun still cast its light over the city below, the sky above the castle grew hazy. When they reached the castle's entrance, Faolán growled, her fur bristling at danger within. Still Berengar did not reach for his axe.

The air was colder inside. The torches and candles had all gone out, leaving shadows to creep freely along the walls. The only sound came from his boots against the floor. He took the familiar path he had followed so many times before, certain of his destination. Again he looked around for guards, servants, nobles—anyone. Everyone was gone. There was something unnerving about walking through such grand, lofty halls while devoid of human companionship that made him feel utterly alone, even in a city of thousands. It was too late to turn back now, even if he wanted to.

The doors to the throne room had been left open. Berengar steeled himself for what waited ahead. It was utterly quiet inside. Gray light entered through the rose window behind the throne, where the room's sole occupant lingered.

Ravenna's back was to him. "I knew you would come."

"It was you. It was always you."

She turned to face him, her father's crown atop her head. She still wore a dress of mourning black, but now a purple cloak hung from her shoulders, falling to the floor.

"You're a sorceress, aren't you?"

She didn't answer, but her expression said it all.

The remnants of the coatl egg lay beside the throne. The egg's scaled surface, which once pulsed with a steady red glow, had fallen lifeless and cold. A dagger had been discarded beside the egg.

"There's no stopping it now." There was blood on her palm where she'd cut it. "Now that it's been fed, the coatl will shed its skin and emerge at almost half its full size."

"It's why you sent the soldiers away. You knew the city would be vulnerable. You planned all this from the start. You murdered your father." He shook his head. "I should have seen it earlier."

Her dark eyes never left his. "My father deserved to die, so I killed him."

"Tell me why. You owe me that much."

"My father wanted a magic child so desperately," she began. "When Morwen was born, he gave her all the love and attention he denied me." She examined the cut on her hand, which had already begun to heal. "But the blood of Brian Boru runs through my veins as well. Only my powers didn't manifest until I was on the cusp of womanhood, and they weren't pleasant like my half-sister's middling abilities. No, my magic was too strong to control. I had terrible visions of future events, set my bed aflame, shattered a statue…"

"They thought you were cursed," Berengar said quietly.

The princess nodded. "I was too afraid to tell anyone what I was, but my powers only grew stronger. There was only one person I could turn to."

"Your brother, the prince."

"Aiden thought the crone might be able to remove my powers."

That's why they traveled to the Devil's Bit. It was never about slaying the crone at all. "Only she wasn't able to help you."

"No, though she did reveal the truth about my father and the Witches of the Golden Vale. The grim attacked us when we started the journey home. I tried to use my powers to protect us, but I knew so little of magic. Aiden was killed because of me. When I returned home, my father hardly cared that he'd lost a son. He was only concerned that I learned he had fathered a bastard with a witch—that he was sending innocent people to be slaughtered." Her face tightened with rage. "So the great King Mór shipped his own daughter away like a broodmare to be traded, all to avoid a scandal."

"What about your mother? Did she deserve to die?"

"My mother, who allowed my father to give me to a monster to be beaten and broken? My mother, who stood by each month as he honored his arrangement with the witches?" The princess laughed, a hollow, bitter sound. "She would have despised me if she ever suspected I could use magic."

"Your husband didn't die of illness, did he?" Berengar asked, though he already knew the answer.

Ravenna shook her head, the hint of a cold smile on her face. "No, he did not. I escaped and fled into the wild. I was near death until fate led me to someone who taught me how magic worked and how to wield it properly."

"Who taught you these things?"

She ignored the question. "When I returned, I made my husband suffer for the things he did to me, and then I came home to seek justice."

"I think you mean revenge."

Ravenna flashed her teeth. "You more than anyone should understand that sometimes they're one and the same. My father didn't deserve the crown, so I took it from him. Even then, I would have been content simply to bend him to my will, but when you arrived, I had to alter my plans. I couldn't risk the chance he would confide in Morwen when she returned from Innisfallen.

"I could have stopped my father's heart with a single word, but I wanted him to suffer. I wanted to be there in the room when he died, so that I could look into his eyes and remind him of the children he forsook. The use of the Demon's Whisper made sure his death wasn't traced back to me, as the path led instead to Desmond, who had the perfect motive to want the king dead. Having suffered at the hands of his own father, he made an ideal co-conspirator."

She had gone to great lengths to bring about her plan, and very nearly succeeded in it. Even from the beginning, there were so many moving parts. The déisi, the Brother-hood of Thieves, Gorr Stormsson and the Danes, the Witches of the Golden Vale, Laird O'Reilly, and Desmond —they were all pawns in her game, all meant to obscure her involvement. She probably planned the attempt on her life at the Feast of Remembrance and her abduction at the coronation to throw suspicion away from her. She was never in any real danger. With her powers, she could have escaped from the Danes at any time. It would have been easy for her to arrange for the shipments of gold to be stolen with the knowledge the blame would fall on Laird O'Reilly, who had been blackmailing the king. She killed Stormsson to keep him from talking and made Desmond jump to his death to do the same.

The floor rumbled beneath their feet, a sign the coatl was stirring in the bowels of the castle.

"You used me." He'd done her dirty work, cleansing Munster of everyone who wronged her, exposing Mór's affair, imprisoning O'Reilly, and killing the witches.

"You killed none who did not deserve death. Isn't that the duty of a warden—to bring justice?"

"And now you're going to kill thousands of innocent people." He gestured outside the doors of the throne room. "Do you call that justice?"

"You think *they* are innocent? Underneath the gold and splendor, this kingdom is rotten to its core. Those who rule it are evil and corrupt, and its people are ignorant and cruel. They would condemn someone to death simply because of the accident of their birth—because they were different. Women are sold into bondage like cattle, and you call that justice?" Ravenna shook her head and drew closer to him, ignoring Faolán's snarls. "If we want justice, we have to take it for ourselves."

Berengar could not forget the memory of the kiss they shared, when he'd seen her true face for the first time. Her rage—her pain—it was there, lurking just beneath the surface in each of their preceding encounters. No matter how he'd hardened his heart, she had torn away the wall he'd built around it, until now it was raw and exposed. He wanted to hate her for it, but he found he could not, because he understood her suffering in a way no one else could. He knew what that kind of anger did to a soul—he had the blood on his hands to prove it.

"Was it all a lie? Was any of it real? Did you bewitch me with a spell or give me some potion to make me love you?"

Her eyes flashed with terrible anger. "You dare ask me that?"

She shook her head and regained her composure before speaking again, and Berengar thought he had never seen someone look quite so sad.

She gazed upon him with a tenderness that surprised him. "They call you a monster. From the moment I laid eyes on you, I knew better. I might have loved you then, even from the start. When the world looked at me and saw only a cursed, defiled princess, you threw yourself in front of that arrow without hesitation. Despite everything you've endured—all you've suffered—your heart is true. Yes, there is anger, but also kindness, courage, and compassion. With you, I was no longer alone. You woke something inside me I never expected to feel for anyone. That night at the inn, I would have gone away with you."

The night of Alannah's coronation, when I fought Agatha, he realized, *Ravenna was protecting me.* Before that, she'd sent Ronan to come to his aid against the Danes at Knockaney.

"I know you feel the same. It doesn't take a sorceress to see it." The princess reached out her hand to him across the distance that separated them. "I accept you—your scars and your anger and your past—without condition or hesitation. We can rule Munster together, perhaps even all Fál."

Berengar shook his head. "It's not too late. You don't have to do this. These people don't deserve to die."

Her expression hardened. "What was it you told me? This is who I am. It's the life I choose."

Berengar unlimbered his axe. "I'm sorry. I can't let you do it."

Her laughter reverberated across the empty chamber. "You're going to stop me with that?" She dragged a finger across the air, and suddenly the axe was in her hands. Ravenna lifted the axe as if it weighed nothing, turning it over to examine it more closely. In response to her touch, the charms Morwen inscribed appeared as a series of symbols running down the haft. "For all her failings, Morwen is a passable enchantress. The rune of resistance is a nice touch. Father always saw to it she had the best."

Ravenna cast the axe across the room, and it landed at his feet. "I'm afraid it won't be enough to stop me."

Berengar bent down to retrieve the axe without taking his eyes off her. He'd barely managed to hold his own against the Witches of the Golden Vale, even with Morwen's help. If Ravenna was a sorceress, it made her one of the most powerful beings in all of Fál. He had never before faced such a threat. Yet for all her power, by her own admission, she'd only learned to control her abilities after her brother's death. Most practitioners of magic took years to fully reach the limits of their power, and Ravenna was still a young woman.

The floor rumbled again, and it took all his effort to retain his footing.

"Time is running out." The princess paced the floor. "It won't be long now."

Berengar lifted the axe and charged. Ravenna raised her hands, and the room grew dim as a wave of living shadows poured from her hands with such strength it sent the axe flying from his hands. Berengar ignored the axe and kept running. He moved to draw his sword, but the princess muttered a word under her breath, and suddenly he was immobilized, unable to move. When Ravenna reached out her hand to his face, Faolán positioned herself between Berengar and the sorceress.

"Let him go!" Morwen stood at the throne room's entrance, staff in hand. She raised her palm and trained it on Berengar. "Trí mo chumhacht a shocrú saor in aisce. By my power, be set free."

Berengar's fingers closed around the sword, and he wrenched it free, training the blade on Ravenna. The sorceress ignored him and looked only at Morwen, her face full of contempt.

"I see you learned from your battle with the witches, sister."

Morwen stopped at Berengar's side, and her gaze darted to the shattered coatl egg. "What have you done, Ravenna?"

"I thought perhaps you might sense the power I unleashed, but you should have known to stay away." Ravenna's eyes narrowed at the magician like a snake waiting to strike. "Do you know what it was like, watching as Father gave you all the love and compassion he held back from his own heirs? I hated you for years. Even then, I would have let you live, but now that I see you…I think I'm going to enjoy watching you die."

Berengar glanced at Morwen, who nodded in response to his unspoken question. They attacked in tandem, moving as one. Berengar flung himself toward Ravenna and brought his sword down to meet her. No sooner had she deflected his blade than Morwen thrust her staff at Ravenna to cast a spell. The sorceress spun around and countered the spell with a burst of shadow magic. Berengar swung his sword at her again, and again she deftly avoided him, causing him to nearly collide with Morwen.

Ravenna stopped his next attack dead in its tracks. "Ithe scrios sruthán." The sword shook violently in his hands and the metal burned as if fresh from the forge. Berengar tossed it across the room moments before it shattered into shards, which Ravenna then redirected at Morwen. Morwen barely managed to deflect them in time, and the shards reassembled into a sword at her feet. Faolán ran at the princess, distracting her long enough for Morwen to run her hand along the surface of her staff, and the red rune at the head glowed with red light.

"Dóiteán," Morwen shouted, the same spell she'd

attempted in their battle with the coven. This time she spoke the word with confidence. A column of flame shot out of the staff, trapping Ravenna within a flaming circle.

The princess clapped her hands together, her feral delight visible in the firelight. "I'm afraid you'll have to do better than that." She held out her hand to touch the fire, and the flames drained into her outstretched palm, forming a fireball. "My turn," Ravenna said, heaving the fireball at Morwen.

Berengar hurled himself into Morwen, pushing her aside as the fireball struck the place where she had stood, leaving a scorch mark on the floor.

"On your feet, Morwen," Ravenna said. "Did you truly imagine a magician could stand against a sorceress?"

When Morwen leapt to her feet, the sorceress knocked her back to the floor with another blast of shadow magic. As she attempted to rise, Ravenna sent her crashing into a pillar.

"Enough." Berengar snatched his axe from the ground and ran at the sorceress, but she picked him off the ground and sent him flying across the room with an invisible force. She did the same to Faolán just before the wolfhound could strike.

Ravenna's attention returned to Morwen, who reached across the floor to grasp her staff and pushed herself to her feet in defiance of the princess. She raised the staff to cast a spell, but Ravenna made a single downward slash with her fist, and the staff clattered to the floor.

"Pick it up," Ravenna hissed.

When Morwen attempted to retrieve her staff, her arm froze. Ravenna spread her fingers out like claws and lifted Morwen off the ground with magic. Morwen fought against her half-sister's hold, her feet dangling in the air as she gasped for breath. Berengar snatched his battleaxe from the floor and rushed toward Ravenna, who unleashed a stream of living shadows at him with her free hand. The warden used his axe as a shield, and the black magic struck the silver rune at full force. With Ravenna's attention divided between Berengar and Morwen, the rune was able to absorb most of the attack. Still, the force of it pushed him back on his heels, threatening to knock the axe from his grip. Berengar held onto the axe with all his might and struggled against the unrelenting stream of shadows, advancing little by little toward the sorceress. Ravenna glanced from one to the other, her frustration mounting as Berengar neared striking distance. At the last moment she released her hold on Morwen in order to hit Berengar at full force with a wave of shadow magic. Berengar met her outstretched hands with the flat of his axe, and the silver rune produced a twang as the spell rebounded on them both.

Ravenna's silver crown went rolling across the floor, and Berengar was sent sliding backward. Morwen helped him to his feet—her staff in hand once more—and he looked up in time to see Ravenna on the dais, her chest rising and falling with labored breaths. The princess recovered quickly, her face lined with hate as they stared at each other. Suddenly, the sound of footsteps echoed behind them, and Corrin marched into the throne room at the head of three units.

Ravenna eyed the captain of the guard. "Arrest these traitors, Corrin."

Corrin stopped at Berengar's side and stood fast. At his command, the soldiers thrust their spears forward and advanced slowly toward the throne as archers took aim at the princess.

"It's over," Berengar said. "You will never be queen of Munster."

Ravenna's lips drew back into a smile. "This was never about the throne of Munster. A dark time is coming, Warden of Fál. The High Queen and her wardens will fall, and the shadows will again hold dominion over Fál."

Morwen clutched her chest, her face a mask of pain as if sensing great evil. The earth trembled, and the ground began to shift under their feet. Stones fell from the walls, and the rose window shattered into a thousand pieces. The floor in front of the throne broke apart, and a monstrous serpent shot out of the hole between Ravenna and her enemies. The sorceress' smile widened as the coatl unfurled its wings and unleashed a deafening roar. It lunged at the soldiers nearest the throne, tearing through their ranks and snapping them up in its jaws. The monster's tail ripped free of the floor and swatted aside those who fled before it.

Morwen watched in horror as it laid waste to the throne room. "It will destroy everything."

Berengar reached for his bow. "Not if I have anything to say about it. Keep the princess occupied."

"I'll try my best."

The warden nocked an arrow and aimed it at the coatl. The other archers' arrows all bounced off the monster's scales, as ineffective as they might have been against a dragon. Berengar held the arrow steady even as pieces of the ceiling fell around him, waiting for the serpent to expose its underbelly before he released his hold on the string. The shot found its mark, and the arrow lodged itself in the coatl, producing a stream of green blood. The snake's head turned swiftly in Berengar's direction, and its diamond-shaped pupils fell on him. When it lashed its tail toward him, Berengar whistled and Faolán sank her teeth into its flesh. The coatl sent her flying into the wall with a flick of tail, and Berengar nocked and released another arrow. Enraged, the serpent's frenzied attack intensified, sweeping dozens of soldiers from their feet. Berengar took aim at its head, but the coatl's tail came crashing down toward him, forcing him to leap out of its path. He lost his grip on his bow, and the column of soldiers behind him was crushed.

He glanced over at Morwen, but the magician's luck was no better than his. She was barely holding her own against Ravenna, who seemed to be toying with her. Each new burst of shadow magic pushed her back farther and farther. When she pointed her staff at Ravenna in a final desperate attempt to counter her attacks, the sorceress uttered a spell that caused the entire throne room to tremble, and the staff shattered in Morwen's hands. Morwen was knocked to the ground, defenseless, as the remnants of her staff were swept away.

"Finish her, my pet," Ravenna ordered the coatl.

The serpent hissed in obedience and opened its jaws to devour her. Armed with no weapon, Berengar put himself between Morwen and the coatl. Just before its fangs closed around him, the amulet around Morwen's neck glowed, and a sphere of light detonated around them. The force of the explosion sent the coatl crashing against the wall, which collapsed on it, exposing the throne room to the outside.

"Morwen." Berengar reached for her as dust swirled through the chamber. She moaned, her eyes barely open. Blood ran down from her nose.

"A powerful enchantment," Ravenna said while the coatl shifted under the weight of the stones, slowly working to free itself. "A pity you can only invoke its magic at such a great cost."

Amid the rubble, Berengar spotted the flame rune where it had landed when Morwen's staff was destroyed. He lunged for it at the same moment the coatl broke free.

When the serpent opened its mouth and let out a hiss, the warden hurled the rune at its open mouth. As Ravenna's eyes widened in surprise, Morwen reached up from the ground and invoked the rune's magic.

"Dóiteán."

Just before disappearing inside the coatl's jaws, the rune glowed red. Morwen slumped back, and her eyes closed. Berengar found himself alone facing the coatl. With Morwen's staff destroyed, he wasn't certain if the magic would work. The sound of a terrible explosion filled the room as fire shot out of the serpent's mouth. The great creature shrieked and collapsed onto the floor, writhing in pain, its scales seared and blackened.

Berengar reached for his axe and turned toward Ravenna. The pair faced each other across the wreckage. No one else was left standing. They clashed at the heart of the throne room, exchanging blows that rattled the chamber. Her connection with the coatl had weakened Ravenna, and expending so much power had left the sorceress drained, yet her fury was such it took all his strength to withstand each of her attacks.

They wrestled over possession of the axe, and Ravenna turned the weapon back toward him, cutting into his armor. Just before it would have drawn blood, Berengar rammed his shoulder under her jaw and brought the axe around, but he stopped short of hitting her. Ravenna seized the opportunity to knock him to the ground with a blast of shadow magic. She held him there, pinned to the floor by magic, and stared down at him. Berengar peered into her dark eyes, waiting for her to deliver the killing blow, but at the last moment she hesitated. An arrow struck her in the back. Ravenna's brow arched upward and she toppled forward, revealing Morwen behind her, the warden's bow clutched in her hands.

Berengar caught Ravenna in his arms and lowered her to the floor. She was shivering, and there was blood everywhere, but he doubted the wound was fatal. He followed the princess' eyes to his axe.

"Finish it," she pleaded. "Kill me. I won't be a prisoner again."

He held the axe at her throat, but it wavered in his grasp.

"Are you not Berengar the Merciless? Do it."

He had killed hundreds over the years. What was one more? Ravenna was too dangerous to be allowed to live. If she escaped, she would only grow more powerful. He knew what was required. He'd done it so many times before, and yet, as he looked into her sad eyes, he glimpsed the suffering beneath her anger and found he could not bring himself to do it again. Despite her crimes, no matter how misguided her beliefs, there was still something of the girl she had been before cruelty and betrayal had twisted her into something monstrous. He understood, because deep down he knew it was true of himself, and he pitied her for it.

Maybe it's not too late—for either of us.

Berengar lowered the axe, and Ravenna's mouth opened in surprise.

"I'm sorry. For everything."

Ravenna stood, cradling her injury. For just a moment, Berengar found himself looking at the woman from the tavern, so vulnerable and alone.

"Go," he told her. "Leave Munster and never return."

She would live, but as an exile and a criminal. Her title and wealth would be stripped from her. She would never sit on the throne. If she remained in Fál, she would always be a fugitive. That would be punishment enough.

Ravenna stared at him for a long time. The coat slithered across the floor to her feet, its movements labored and weak. She rested a hand on its scaled surface, and the creature spread its wings.

"Farewell, Warden Berengar."

Then she climbed on its back and flew away.

CHAPTER NINETEEN

The days were growing shorter.

Berengar stood at Mór's tomb. A steady breeze swept over the warden, carrying the last of summer's warmth. Fall would descend across the land soon enough. He gazed upon his friend's likeness, unable to reconcile the memory of the young man who had plucked him from the banks of the River Shannon and stood at his side against Azeroth's hordes with the man who neglected his family and failed his kingdom. While it was possible the king's power made him think himself infallible—a trap more than one monarch had fallen prey to—Berengar suspected it simply became easier for Mór to justify his wrongs with each new sin he committed. He must have told himself his alliance with the witches was for the greater good, as were the tributes he sent them. Mór probably imagined he was acting in defense of the realm when he sent his daughter away, when he was actually just protecting himself.

To do evil in the name of good—wasn't that what Ravenna had done, mistaking justice for vengeance? Berengar was no better. He had done terrible things in the belief he was making Fál safer. He thought that because the world was cruel, it needed a cruel man to make it a better place, but what if he was wrong? What if the world needed someone willing to stand above the ugliness and pain and offer something more? He had sneered at Morwen for being naïve, but maybe he was the one who saw things the wrong way.

He remembered how weary he felt when he arrived at Cashel. He'd been on the road for so long, traveling from place to place without a moment's rest. He threw himself headfirst into battle after battle against overwhelming odds, yet no matter how many he killed, there was always a new evil waiting to emerge. Perhaps Ravenna was right when she said he hoped for death, but instead of extinguishing his spirit, his time in Cashel left him with a renewed sense of purpose. Maybe he could fight for a world that didn't take little girls and turn them into monsters.

He looked at the clouds and again his thoughts turned toward Ravenna. Was she out there somewhere staring at the same sky, thinking of him? He wondered what might have happened if he had gone away with her when she offered. Even with the knowledge of what she was, the feelings he had for her remained. As he had many times over the previous days, Berengar went back and forth on if he'd made the right decision by showing her mercy. For good or ill, a dangerous sorceress was now at large in Fál. For her sake, he hoped she found some semblance of peace.

Berengar turned away from the tomb. It was almost time to leave Cashel behind, but not yet.

"Come on, Faolán." The limp from the injuries she'd sustained during the fight was almost gone.

They passed Prince Aiden's grave on the way from the royal crypt. It was almost fitting that the grave lay some distance from his father. Alannah had been laid to rest beside the prince, reunited in death with the son she lost. The line of kings stretching back to Brian Boru was ended. It was a reminder that nothing lasted forever, not even in storied Munster.

He walked along the outer wall, which was manned by defenders once more. Nearly three weeks had passed since his return to Cashel. Though the castle itself remained standing, the throne room lay in ruins, exposed for all to see where its walls had crumbled and fallen away in the wake of the coatl's rampage. Munster's stonemasons had already begun the work of rebuilding the walls. In time, the castle would be restored to its full splendor, perhaps even better than before. The deeper scars weren't physical.

Turmoil had seized the capital following the conflict in the throne room. Some believed the warden staged a coup to take power, while others still welcomed the news that the Tainted Princess was forced to flee the kingdom. Berengar remained in the days that followed to restore order. The task was made easier when Ronan and his men returned from the coast after their victory over the Viking fleet, but it would be many years before life in Munster returned to the way it was before Mór's murder.

Berengar entered the castle for the last time and made his way past the guards to the council chamber, where Ronan and Corrin were poring over maps, discussing the instability throughout the realm resulting from the unoccupied throne. Based on his demonstration of loyalty, Corrin had been named the new thane of Munster. The warden lingered in the background for a time, listening as a group of mercenaries gave a report detailing their successes hunting monsters. At last Ronan looked up and noticed him, and Berengar approached.

"I take it you're leaving, then." Ronan looked as if he'd aged five years in the last week. He'd watched the love of his life die before his eyes, only to discover the closest thing he had to a daughter was responsible for her death.

"Aye. My work here is finished." He handed Ronan the proclamation he'd received from Tara that morning. "The High Queen has appointed you regent of Munster," he explained as Ronan unfurled the scroll, revealing Nora's seal. "Until such time as the lords of Munster are able to name a new monarch."

"Are you certain the people will not doubt my allegiance? I served Mór and his household all my life." Ronan's face betrayed considerable unease, which Berengar understood all too well. Though he served the throne with great distinction, he never wanted to be thane of Munster. Now, despite all he had lost, he was again being asked to sacrifice for the good of the realm.

"You're the only man for the job. There's no one else who has your experience seeing to Munster's affairs. Munster needs a protector, now more than ever."

"Then it is with great reluctance that I accept this solemn responsibility. Lady Morwen assures me it is unlikely Ravenna will attempt to enter my mind again. She claims the magic won't work properly over great distances."

"I doubt Ravenna will ever return to Munster." Berengar spoke from experience. "There are too many unpleasant memories for her here."

Ronan looked away. "We failed her. I failed her."

Berengar shook his head. "Don't blame yourself. That way lies madness. Ravenna's choices were her own. For what it's worth, I think you were the one person who was always there for her."

Ronan returned his attention to the map before him. "Are you sure you won't stay a little longer? Rumor has it that several lords who were loyal to Laird Tierney are talking openly of rebellion. It might be helpful to have a warden on hand."

"You will. I've had word from Tara on that account as well. Darragh is on his way. He should arrive within a fortnight. Between him and Corrin, you should manage all right. Darragh is better at peace than I am." He looked at Corrin. "Word has it you're looking for someone to replace you as captain of the guard."

"Aye. Haven't had much luck, sorry to say."

"If you're open to suggestions, I'd consider Seamus. He's young and headstrong, but loyal when it counts."

"Apologies, my thane," said a guard stationed at the entrance. "There's a messenger from Cill Airne asking to see you at once. He says it's urgent."

Berengar stepped away. "It's time for me to take my leave."

"Warden Berengar," Ronan said just before he crossed the threshold.

Berengar stopped.

"Munster owes you a debt it can never repay."

"Farewell. I wish you good fortune." He didn't look back.

Before departing the castle, he loaded up his belongings. He took little with him—Berengar was accustomed to traveling light. He set out from the royal stables with a new horse, one of Munster's finest, and made the descent into the city. Were he a sentimental man, he might have walked the city streets, or at least looked back at the castle one final time, but Berengar was not a man given to sentiment.

Morwen waited for him outside the city gate. She wore her gray traveling cloak. The magician held a mare by its lead rope, and Berengar noticed its saddlebags were weighed down with her belongings.

"Ronan offered to reinstate me," she said.

"He'd be a fool to do otherwise. I couldn't have defeated Ravenna without you. You helped bring justice to your father's killers and restore peace to Munster. Mór would be proud."

"I turned him down." She drew nearer. "Cashel was my home, but I think it's time for me to move on. There's a whole world out there waiting for me."

Berengar studied her carefully. It had been a long time since he allowed himself to care for someone. He walked alone for a reason. He thought friends were a weakness. Perhaps he was wrong about that too. Morwen hadn't just saved his life—she'd given him something to live for, as Nora had years ago.

"Please. I want to go with you."

"I promised your father I would keep you safe. I believed bringing you with me would only put you in harm's way, but now I see you're more than capable of finding danger on your own. So it seems the only thing to do is keep a closer eye on you."

Faolán barked loudly.

"I know." Berengar returned his gaze to Morwen. "Kneel."

The magician looked confused for a moment but dropped to one knee. Berengar released his hold on his horse and stood above her.

"Wardens are allowed to choose our own replacements. I didn't think I'd find someone worthy to follow in my footsteps, until now. I'll warn you—this life isn't an easy one. If you come with me, our road will be steeped in peril, with danger hidden in every corner. We will make enemies and face great hardships. Do you understand?"

She nodded.

"Morwen of Cashel, will you forswear all allegiances, save to Nora, High Queen of Fál?"

"I will."

"Do you give your life to her service, no matter the cost?"

"I do."

"Then rise, Morwen, servant of Fál." He handed her a golden brooch adorned with a silver fox—the High Queen's sigil. "Wear this on your cloak. Watch me and learn. One day you will be warden in my place."

"Thank you. I won't let you down."

"I know." Berengar returned to his horse and swung himself onto the saddle. Morwen hurried to her horse and caught up with him. "So, where are we going?"

"Why?"

"I'll need a new staff first, if you don't mind stopping along the way."

"Not at all." He chuckled softly. "Try to keep up."

The warden spurred his horse forward, and together they rode north.

THE CITY OF THIEVES

Chapter One

"We're lost." A crease formed across Morwen's brow as she pored over the map.

Berengar, sitting across her at a table near the fire, said nothing. The pair had spent the last two days holed up at the Forgotten Stop, an out-of-the-way tavern deep in the heart of rural Leinster. Outside, the last vestiges of summer faded, and soon the leaves had begun to turn.

Morwen held the map closer and studied it in the firelight, as if there was something she had missed. "I don't understand. According to the map, we should have reached the Wrenwood by now." She jabbed a speck on the map with her finger. "We passed The Mount of Guarding not three days ago and turned north at the River Nore, just like we were supposed to."

Faolán, a wolfhound nearly Morwen's size, nudged her head over the young woman's shoulder and sniffed the weathered parchment. As a rule, Faolán disliked people almost as much as Berengar, but in Morwen's case, she had

371

made an exception. For her part, Morwen had taken to spoiling Faolán whenever she thought Berengar wasn't looking, and in her presence the fierce hound became as docile as a pup.

Exasperated, Morwen returned the map to the table and let out a protracted sigh. "Useless." She cast a glance at a stack of books beside her. "If only there was some enchantment to…" She stopped suddenly and narrowed her gaze in Berengar's direction. "You're awfully quiet. Even for you."

"You're the one who said you wanted a life of adventure. You can't adjust to a life on the road until you learn how to properly read a map."

"I'm a magician, not a cartographer." Morwen waved a hand in the air dismissively and patted Faolán's head. "And don't think I'm letting you off that easy—I can tell you're hiding something."

Berengar tried to keep the amusement out of his voice. Usually, she was the one to tease him. "Is that so?" He raised his tankard to his lips, gulped down a mouthful of ale, and wiped his unruly red beard with his forearm.

They drew a number of glances from the hall's other occupants, and with good reason. Berengar and Morwen made for a pair of unusual traveling companions. Even seated, Berengar was easily recognizable as the tallest and largest man in the room. Unlike Morwen—who, at sixteen, was in the bloom of youth—he was well into his forties. Scars marred the right side of his face, and a patch covered his right eye. None would mistake him for anything other than a hardened warrior. In contrast, there was little to hint that Morwen—having discarded the blue robes she wore as Munster's court magician in favor of mundane traveling clothes—was about as far from an ordinary girl as one could get and still remain human. Anyone taking a look at the potions and spellbooks inside her satchel would quickly realize there was much more to her under the surface.

Morwen ran a hand through bushy brown hair and tucked a loose strand behind her ear. "You don't fool me. I know that look. You're waiting for something, aren't you?" She glanced around the room. "And you're not the only one. Everyone in here seems on edge."

The barmaid approached to refill Berengar's tankard. Preoccupied by this sight of his scars, she spilled a portion of ale, flushed a deep shade of red, and fled with a frightened yelp.

Berengar, who was accustomed to his appearance having such an effect, drank from the tankard without missing a beat. "I don't know what you mean." In truth, he had stayed at the Forgotten Stop some months back, and the proprietors were no less afraid of him now than they were then.

"In case you've forgotten, we're supposed to be looking for the Oakseers' Grotto so I can craft a new staff." Her previous magician's staff was destroyed weeks earlier in a fight against a dark sorceress and a winged serpent.

Berengar shrugged. "So we are. I knew this tavern was in the area and thought it would be a good place to rest while we searched for your grotto. I spent some time here before receiving King Mór's summons."

Morwen was in fact Mór's illegitimate daughter—the product of a union between the king and a particularly nasty witch—though Berengar felt no need to call attention to that fact with prying ears about. When Mór was murdered, Berengar and Morwen had worked together to identify the king's killer—Morwen's half-sister, the princess Ravenna. Berengar, who owed Mór a debt, agreed afterward to allow Morwen to accompany him on his travels.

Intrigued, Morwen leaned closer. "The affair with the ogre?"

"Aye. I had some unfinished business when I left."

"I knew it." She flashed a triumphant grin. "I thought we agreed to stay out of trouble until I replaced my staff."

Berengar kicked his feet up on the table and gave a grunt. "Don't forget who's in charge. You may be clever, but you still have a lot to learn." He gestured to her stack of books. "Those aren't going to be much use to you in a fight."

Morwen folded her arms across her chest. "I might no longer have access to my library at Cashel, but I still need to learn and practice my arts—which would be a great deal easier if I had my staff." Their ages and appearances weren't the only things that set them apart. An avowed pacifist, Morwen had mostly resisted his efforts to train her in the ways of combat. "And I don't recall you complaining about my fighting abilities when we took on that coatl."

Before Berengar could form a response, the door to the tavern opened, and a gentle wind brushed fallen leaves inside. A nondescript man in simple clothes entered and made his way to a lonely table. A hood concealed most of his face. The hall's other occupants paid the newcomer little heed, but Berengar watched him closely.

Finally. Morwen's suspicions were well-founded, as he had indeed chosen the tavern for a very specific reason. "Don't stare."

Morwen lowered her voice to a whisper. "Who is he?"

Berengar remained perfectly still, doing nothing to attract the stranger's attention. "A member of Leinster's Thieves Guild, I'd wager."

"The Thieves Guild?" Her astonishment soon faded, and she chuckled softly. "And here I thought we were trying to keep *out* trouble. What's a member of the Thieves Guild doing in a place like this?"

"Before I rode south to Munster to answer King Mór's summons, I spent the better part of spring hunting a group of mercenaries called the Black Hand. Someone had hired them to retrieve a thunder rune."

Morwen's eyes widened with alarm. As a magician—and someone who carried a variety of runes herself—she knew well the danger such a relic posed.

"I dealt with the Black Hand and recovered the rune, but it was stolen from me by hobgoblins before I could store it someplace safe. When I found them, the hobgoblins were starving and hunted to the point of extinction. The money the rune would fetch would allow them to start a new life somewhere else. I chose to let them keep it." He hesitated, and there was a hard edge to the words that followed. "I came across their corpses on the road to Munster, just north of the border. They'd been slaughtered, and the rune was gone."

"I see. It seems likely whoever was after the rune hasn't given up on acquiring it."

Berengar gave an almost imperceptible nod. "I asked around. The Thieves Guild uses this tavern to conduct business in the region at the end of each month. They trade in black market goods and dangerous wares. Whoever took the rune from the hobgoblins will come looking for a payoff, and when they do, I'll be ready."

Almost as if on cue, the tavern door opened again, and four men entered together. The companions were dressed in padded armor, and they wore bright red cloaks and swords sheathed at their sides.

Berengar recognized the sigil on their cloaks. "Lady Imogen's soldiers."

The soldiers laughed at some private joke and made a beeline for the bar. They were a long way from Castle Blackthorn, though not so far as to raise suspicion. Their presence in the tavern was far from unusual, especially if they were out on patrol.

Morwen shuddered, and her back straightened immediately. "They carry the rune. I can feel its power calling to me." Outside the tavern's walls, faint thunder murmured in agreement.

Armed with tankards and flagons brimming with ale and wine, the soldiers settled at the stranger's table. Berengar watched and listened.

"We've been waiting for you to show your face in here," the soldiers' leader said. "You Guild lot are secretive bunch, I'll give you that." He stared at the thief with a measure of suspicion. "You had better have our gold, Ryland."

Ryland laughed under his breath. "That depends on whether or not you really brought what you say you have."

The soldier's ruddy face broke out into a cruel grin. "Of course we did. Keenan, show Ryland what he came here to see." He nodded to one of his companions, who produced a closed pouch.

Ryland took a peek at what was inside. "My client will be pleased. Let's talk about your fee."

The ruddy-faced soldier raised his cup, and his companions clanked their tankards and cheered. "To new business ventures!" He slapped his thigh. "It was a stroke of luck finding the thing. The lads and I stopped for a bit of fun with some hobgoblins near the border, and we found it among their things—not that we wouldn't have killed the little monsters just for the sport of it."

At the mention of the hobgoblins, Berengar's hands

balled into fists. He pushed away from the table, and Faolán sprang to attention beside him.

Morwen winked at him with evident amusement. "Try not to dismember anyone. Those are Lady Imogen's soldiers, after all."

"I know." There was a reason he preferred to keep his head down while in Leinster. He wasn't exactly welcome within its borders. Besides, he needed the men alive to tell him who wanted the runestone so badly.

Patrons cleared out of his path on his way across the room. The tavern went quiet as Berengar approached the table where the soldiers gathered, and onlookers exchanged worried glances.

"What the devil do you want?" the soldiers' leader demanded with the characteristic arrogance of authority. "Can't you see we're busy, you ugly brute?" The others at the table laughed—all except Ryland, who studied Berengar's cloak and weapons with growing recognition. "Now clear out of here, or we'll teach you not to intrude on matters that don't concern you."

Berengar hit him in the face, and the soldier's teeth broke against his knuckles. He grabbed the man's head and slammed it hard against the table, and the soldier fell from his chair to the floor. The man's companions were out of their seats in the next instant.

"I don't know who you are, stranger, but you'll regret that," one said.

Berengar didn't flinch. "I want the stone—and the name of the person who paid you for it."

His knowledge of their affairs seemed to take them aback, if only for a moment. Berengar turned their surprise to his advantage. He snatched a tankard from the table and bashed it against the closest man's skull. When another went for his sword, Berengar seized his arm in a

377

viselike grip. Before the third soldier could intervene, Faolán pounced on him and pinned him underneath, her jaws inches from his throat. Berengar and his foe struggled over possession of the weapon until he slammed the man against the bar and forced his arm behind his back.

"Now talk," Berengar ordered. "Who are you working for?"

"Go to hell," the soldier shot back.

With a twist, Berengar snapped the man's arm out of socket, prompting a scream. "Try again."

The soldiers' leader rushed forward with an angry shout, wielding a dagger. Berengar took a step back and avoided the first jab. His leather armor bore the brunt of the next strike. Berengar grabbed the soldier's wrist, drove his forehead into the man's skull, and wrested away control of the dagger. With one thrust of the blade he anchored the man's wrist to the bar.

Faolán barked to warn him of danger, and Berengar caught a flash of movement out of the corner of his eye as a final assailant raised a sword behind him. Before Berengar could react, the sword toppled from the man's hand, and he slumped to the floor.

Morwen stood behind the fallen soldier, a wry smile on her face. In her hands was her satchel, stuffed to the brim with spellbooks. "I told you they'd be useful." She turned her attention to the soldiers, who were either unconscious or in considerable pain. "You left them all in one piece this time—more or less. Good work."

Berengar's gaze moved again to the table where the thief sat moments ago. "Blast it. He's gone."

"He must have taken the stone with him." Morwen was already sprinting toward the door. "He can't have gone far. Come on!"

To the visible relief of the others within the tavern,

Berengar followed her outside into the crisp fall air. Faolán sniffed out a set of fresh tracks left behind in the mud and bounded down the trail.

Morwen put two fingers into her mouth and whistled to Nessa, her horse. The mare came charging toward her, and in one fluid motion, Morwen swung herself onto the saddle and took hold of the reins. She glanced at Berengar over her shoulder and aimed a wink at him. "Do try and keep up." With that, she took off in pursuit of Ryland.

Berengar scowled and hurried to his horse. Despite her youth, Morwen was easily the better rider. Although the kingdom of Munster was most famous for its great wealth and vibrant culture, its people were also great horse masters. Morwen, whose father had spared no expense on all aspects of her education, was no exception. If anything, her sensitivity to magic gave her a greater connection to her mount.

Morwen had already disappeared down the path by the time Berengar put his foot in the stirrup. He kicked his horse in the sides and hurried after her.

"There you are," she called after him. "I thought I lost you. Come on, old man—he's getting away."

Berengar gritted his teeth and spurred his horse forward, but Morwen easily outpaced him before he could catch up to her. Faolán led them along a winding dirt road that ran northeast from the tavern, far removed from any vestiges of civilization. Trees sprouted up on either side of the road, and the brush, weeds, and thorns intruding on the path were overgrown from the frequent rainfall commonplace throughout Leinster. A signpost at a cross-roads was the sole sign of human presence in the area.

Morwen veered right at the crossroads and galloped after Faolán across a shallow brook, leaving Berengar to do his best to keep up with both. The path straightened, and in the distance the thief appeared, headed for a wooded area farther down the road.

"There it is," Morwen said. "The Wrenwood."

"I told you we were in the area."

According to Morwen, the Wrenwood was home to the Oak-Seers' Grotto, a grove sacred to Druids for centuries. The trees there possessed strong magical properties that made them ideal for fashioning a new staff. Berengar had strong misgivings about venturing anywhere touched by magic—and even more reasons to avoid Druids—but Morwen assured him the area was safe.

Ahead, Ryland drew nearer to the wood's entrance.

"We're losing him," Berengar said. "We can't let him slip away."

"Leave it to me." Morwen made a clicking noise with her tongue, and her horse picked up speed. The mare galloped past Faolán and quickly closed the distance with Ryland. "Give us the stone! You don't know how dangerous it is."

When Ryland ignored her request, Morwen pulled alongside him and leaned sideways in the saddle, grasping for the pouch containing the thunder rune. Ryland jerked the reins to the right, and Morwen came up empty. She caught up to him again, said something to her horse Berengar couldn't hear, and let go of the reins.

Berengar frowned. *What's she doing?*

Before he could stop her, Morwen jumped from the saddle and landed on the back of Ryland's horse. Ryland produced a hidden blade and stabbed at Morwen, who deftly avoided the knife while the thief's horse followed the road into the Wrenwood. Berengar spurred his horse forward, but he was too far behind to be of help. Before Ryland could thrust the knife at her again, Morwen reached over and touched the horse's coat with the flat of her palm. The stallion reared up, throwing Ryland onto the earth, though Morwen maintained her hold. He scrambled forward in the mud, only to find himself face to face with Faolán. He looked to his fallen knife, which lay just out of his reach, and the wolfhound bared her fangs.

Morwen dismounted and stood victoriously over the thief. "I wouldn't do that if I were you." She turned her gaze to Berengar. "Took you long enough."

Berengar suppressed a smile. "Showoff." He snapped his fingers, and Faolán backed away from Ryland. "Unless you want to be my hound's next meal, I'd suggest you start giving me some answers."

Ryland stared back at him with open defiance. "I'd sooner lose my tongue than reveal the details of a contract."

Berengar growled impatiently, kicked Ryland onto the flat of his back, and planted his boot on the man's chest. "That can be arranged. The last time I came across a Guild member who wouldn't talk, I took his hand."

Ryland's eyes flickered over to Morwen, who simply nodded.

"It's true. I was there. Callum, I think, was his name. Perhaps he was a friend of yours?"

At the mention of Callum, all the color drained from Ryland's face.

Berengar reached for his axe. "Let's see how well you thieve without fingers."

"He means it," Morwen said. "This one isn't a man you want to cross."

"Wait!" Ryland held up his hands in a show of surrender. "Take it!" He reached for the pouch containing the thunder rune and tossed it to Morwen.

She stiffened suddenly, and her eyes widened with dread. Berengar knew that look. She sensed danger.

"We're not alone."

Berengar searched the swaying trees for the source of Morwen's discomfort. Suddenly, an arrow streaked by and missed him by inches. A second arrow struck Ryland's horse, killing it almost instantly. *Black arrows.* "Goblins!"

Faolán barked loudly, and Berengar, Morwen, and Ryland took cover under a fallen tree.

"They must've followed us from the tavern," Morwen said to Ryland. "I'm guessing whoever hired you doesn't like loose ends. What'll it be, Berengar? We've got the rune. Maybe we should leave him to the goblins."

Three goblins approached on foot while others scurried through the trees above. Goblins came in a variety of shapes and sizes, but the three moving toward them were all slender and just shorter than the average human man. Their skin had a dark green hue, and their ears were sharply pointed.

"Have mercy." Ryland clutched at Morwen's cloak. "Get me away from those monsters and I'll tell you anything you want to know."

"Remember that. Morwen, meet me back at the cross-roads. You know what to do." Berengar stepped out to meet the goblins with his axe in hand. The goblins continued, undeterred by the sight of him. Although many goblins were capable of conversing in the human tongue—their native language was full of harsh, discordant sounds—the goblins did not extend the courtesy of surrender, and neither did he.

Berengar charged, his axe held high, and the goblins rushed to meet him. They pressed him on all sides, wielding clubs and rusted iron blades. They were fast and agile, but Berengar had been killing goblins for a long time, and he had become very good at it. He used his size to his advantage and overwhelmed them through sheer strength.

A single swing of his axe cleaved through a goblin's armor and opened the creature's chest wall. Berengar wrenched the axe free and beheaded the next goblin in his path in one fell swoop. The third goblin hissed and launched himself at Berengar, who tossed the creature aside as if he were weightless and stopped on his head until the goblin stopped kicking.

Another arrow sailed by his head. Faolán sprinted by him to the trees, and moments later the goblin archer shrieked and went silent. Berengar heard a whistle, and soon Morwen and Ryland were riding away on the back of Morwen's horse. His distraction had worked.

At the sight of Morwen escaping with their target, the remaining goblins ignored Berengar and went after her on horseback. Berengar called to Faolán and sprinted to his mount to give chase.

Though Morwen was clearly the superior rider, the goblins outnumbered her, forcing her to go deeper into the Wrenwood rather than heading for the crossroads. She led her horse off the path and jumped over a fallen log to keep out of range of the archers' arrows. Berengar followed behind, picking off goblins one by one.

He looked up from raking his axe along a horse's flank in time to witness an archer take aim at Morwen, who was too busy evading the others to notice. The goblin was beyond the reach of his axe, which left him with few options. Berengar swore and drove his mount directly at the other rider, resulting in a violent collision. The two horses crashed together, and Berengar was thrown from the saddle. He hit the ground hard, and the impact knocked the air out of his lungs.

Berengar pushed himself up and crawled away from the thrashing horses.

He looked around, searching for the archer. His axe lay

just out of reach. The goblin was on him in an instant. The creature's claws dug into his armor, and the goblin's jagged teeth strained toward his face.

As he pushed the goblin away, Berengar glimpsed another with its face hidden behind a helmet scurry up a tree ahead of Morwen. Before he could shout out a warning, the goblin tackled her off the horse, and Morwen, the creature, and Ryland were scattered across the dry leaves. Berengar heaved his attacker off him with an angry growl and bashed the creature's face until he felt bones cracking under his bloodstained fists. He released his hold on the goblin's mangled corpse, snatched his axe from the ground, and hurried toward Morwen and Ryland.

Morwen's characteristic confidence faded as the helmeted goblin bore down on her and clawed at the pouch bearing the thunder rune. Ryland attempted to flee, only to find himself surrounded by three mounted goblins. Berengar looked from one to the other. There wasn't time to save both.

He lowered his shoulder and charged the goblin atop Morwen. The creature rolled away unharmed, holding the pouch.

Berengar tightened his grip on the axe and stared down the goblin. "Let's finish this, vermin."

A hiss sounded nearby, and the goblin leapt onto a companion's horse. The remaining creatures followed suit, and soon the Wrenwood was quiet once more.

Berengar's gaze fell on Ryland, who lay in a pool of his own blood. Even as they hurried to the thief's side, he could tell it was too late. Multiple stab and covered Ryland's abdomen, and his face was white from blood loss.

"The pain…" Ryland trembled. "It hurts."

"A name," Berengar said. "Give me a name, and I'll ease your passing."

Morwen glared at him, reached into her satchel, and retrieved a bottle containing a murky scarlet liquid. She pried off the lid and held the bottle to Ryland's lips. "Drink this. It will help with the pain."

Ryland did as she said, and his trembling slowly subsided. "Thank you." With that, he breathed his last and fell still.

"Blast it." Berengar kicked a goblin's corpse to vent his anger. "They got away with the stone."

Morwen wore an impish grin. "No—they didn't." She opened her satchel to reveal the thunder rune gleaming inside. "Goblins are tricky, but so are magicians. I switched out the stone."

"Aye, but they don't know that. If the goblins think they have the stone, we can track them to whoever they're working for." He frowned. "Of course, we wouldn't have to if you hadn't gotten Ryland killed, and yourself nearly with him. Magician or not, if you ride with me, you'll need to learn how to defend yourself properly."

Morwen offered no retort, a sign she took his criticism to heart.

Berengar started toward his horse, which seem to have recovered enough for travel. "Can you track them with a spell?"

Morwen shrugged apologetically. "Without my staff…"

Berengar sighed. "All right. We'll stop by Oak-Seers' Grotto before resuming the goblins' trail. Where I grew up, the country was filled goblins. I don't need magic to track them, as long as the trail's still warm."

Morwen brightened immediately. "It won't take long to gather the wood. I can do most of the enchanting on the road." She led her horse by the reins and accompanied him along the trail with a renewed spring in her step. "The Oak-Seers' Grotto shouldn't be far."

Wind rustled through the trees, scattering multicolored leaves. "So, what *can* you do without your staff?"

The question was innocent, born out of ignorance and curiosity, but Morwen seem to take it as an insult. "Plenty! I can still sense magic and human emotions. For example, right now you're feeling angry and hungry."

Berengar snorted. "I'm always angry. And hungry."

Morwen quickened her pace, and her annoyance with him seems to fade, replaced by a palpable wave of excitement. "We're close. There is old magic in this place." She came to an abrupt halt, and her brow furrowed. "It can't be."

The Oakseers' Grotto was a ruin. The trees had been cleared away.

ACKNOWLEDGMENTS

The *Warden of Fál* series came about because I wanted to write a mystery.

I had just finished reading the first book in a friend's cozy mystery series, and I wondered what a mystery series might look like written by me. How could I bring anything different to the genre?

Around that time, I was at a book signing, and a local publisher told me how well fantasy was selling. I decided I would write a fantasy-mystery series, blending traditional mystery stories with a fantasy-world setting. Suddenly, it all clicked. I had previously written some unpublished fantasy novels set in the world of Fál.

Blood of Kings started out as the first book in the series, until *Wrath of Lords* (which began as a prequel) took its place. *Wrath of Lords* is a darker story than *Blood of Kings*. The Berengar we meet in *Wrath of Lords* is a broken man. No matter what he does, nothing ever seems to get better.

In *Wrath of Lords,* a dying Rose tells Berengar it's worth risking the pain to open his heart to the possibility of friendship. Then along comes Morwen in *Blood of Kings,* and everything changes. In contrast to the cynical, hardened Berengar, Morwen is youthful and optimistic. Unlike Berengar, who prefers to lead with his axe, Morwen is an avowed pacifist who truly believes she can make a difference. In short, she's the perfect companion and foil, and I can't wait to continue their adventures together.

There are a number of people who deserve my thanks for their hard work making this book a reality—first and foremost my parents, Robert and Pamela Romines. Then there's my team: Jeff Brown, my cover artist; Matt Forsyth, my character illustrator; Maxime Plasse, my map designer; Katie King, my copyeditor; and Margaret Dean, my proofreader. Thank you for helping bring the world of Fál to life. I would also like to thank my cousin, novelist Jacob Romines, for penning the Ballad of the Bloody Red Bear.

And finally, I'd like to thank you—the reader of this book. I used to drive myself crazy trying to find fantasy books that didn't require spending hours reading other books to know what was going on. I have tried to make each installment in this series relatively self-contained and standalone in nature, while still offering a broader story for returning readers.

And if you enjoyed *The Blood of Kings*, be sure to check out the next installment—*The City of Thieves*.

ABOUT THE AUTHOR

Kyle Alexander Romines is a teller of tales from the hills of Kentucky. He enjoys good reads, thunderstorms, and anything edible. His writing interests include fantasy, science fiction, horror, and westerns.

Kyle's lifelong love of books began with childhood bedtime stories and was fostered by his parents and teachers. He grew up reading *Calvin and Hobbes*, R.L. Stine's *Goosebumps* series, and *Harry Potter*. His current list of favorites includes Justin Cronin's *The Passage*, *Red Rising* by Pierce Brown, and *Bone* by Jeff Smith. The library is his friend.

Kyle is a graduate of the University of Louisville School of Medicine, from which he received his M.D.

He plans to continue writing as long as he has stories to tell.

You can contact Kyle at thekylealexander@hotmail.com. You can also subscribe to his author newsletter to receive email updates and a FREE electronic copy of his science fiction novella, The Chrononaut, at http://eepurl.com/bsvhYP.

Made in the USA
Middletown, DE
11 November 2020